THREE STANCES OF MODERN FICTION

A Critical Anthology
of the Short Story

Edited by:

Stephen Minot
Trinity College

Robley Wilson, Jr.
University of Northern Iowa

Winthrop Publishers, Inc.
Cambridge, Massachusetts

Cover by: Steve Snyder

Library of Congress Catalog Card Number: 72–184369

ii

ACKNOWLEDGMENTS

"A Sense of Shelter" by John Updike. Copyright © 1960 by John Updike. Originally appeared in The New Yorker. Reprinted from PIGEON FEATHERS AND OTHER STORIES, by John Updike, by permission of Alfred A. Knopf, Inc. "To Charley Iron Necklace (Wherever He Is)" by S. M. Swan. Reprinted by permission of The North American Review, copyright © 1970 by the University of Northern Iowa. "The Woman Who Had No Prejudices" by Anton Chekhov. Reprinted by permission of G. P. Putnam's Sons from ST. PETER'S DAY And Other Tales by Anton Chekhov and translated by Frances Jones. Copyright © 1959 by G. P. Putnam's Sons. "The Doctor" by Andre Dubus. Copyright © 1969 by The New Yorker Magazine, Inc. Originally appeared in The New Yorker. Reprinted by permission of McIntosh and Otis, Inc. "The Use of Force" by William Carlos Williams from THE FARMERS' DAUGH-TERS. Copyright 1938 by William Carlos Williams. Reprinted by permission of New Directions Publishing Corporation. "The Taking of Our Own Lives" by Denis Johnson. Reprinted by permission of the author and The North American Review, copyright © 1970 by the University of Northern Iowa. "An Intermediate Stop" by Gail Godwin. Reprinted by permission of the author and The North American Review, copyright © 1970 by the University of Northern Iowa. "King of the Bingo Game" by Ralph Ellison. Reprinted by permission of William Morris Agency, Inc. on behalf of the author. Copyright © 1944 by Ralph Ellison. "The Bound Man" by Ilse Aichinger. Reprinted with the permission of Farrar, Straus & Giroux, Inc. from THE BOUND MAN AND OTHER STORIES by Ilse Aichinger. Copyright © 1956 by Ilse Aichinger. "A Hunger Artist" by Franz Kafka. Reprinted by permission of Schocken Books, Inc. from THE PENAL COLONY by Franz Kafka. Copyright © 1948 by Schocken Books, Inc. "On The Road" by Langston Hughes. Reprinted by permission of Harold Ober Associates Incorporated from LAUGHING TO KEEP FROM CRYING by Langston Hughes. Copyright © 1935, 1952 by Langston Hughes. "The Cleveland Wrecking Yard" by Richard Brautigan. From TROUT FISHING IN AMERICA by Richard Brautigan. Copyright © 1967 by Richard Brautigan. Used by permission of the publisher, Delacorte Press. A Seymour Lawrence Book. "The Lottery" by Shirley Jackson. Reprinted with the permission of Farrar, Straus & Giroux, Inc. from THE LOT-TERY by Shirley Jackson, copyright © 1948, 1949 by Shirley Jackson. "Thus I Refute Beelzy" by John Collier. Copyright © 1940, 1967 by John Collier, reprinted by permission of the Harold Matson Company, Inc. "Never Come Monday" by Eric Knight. Reprinted by permission of Curtis Brown, Ltd. First published in Esquire Magazine. Copyright 1938 by Esquire-Coronet, Inc., re-newed © 1965 by Ruth (Jere) Knight. "The Balloon" by Donald Barthelme. Reprinted with the permission of Farrar, Straus & Giroux from UNSPEAKABLE PRACTICES, UNNATURAL ACTS by Donald Barthelme, copyright © 1966 by Donald Barthelme. "EPICAC" by Kurt Vonnegut, Jr. From WELCOME TO THE MONKEY HOUSE by Kurt Vonnegut, Jr. Copyright © 1968 by Kurt Vonnegut, Jr. A Seymour Lawrence Book/Delacorte Press. Used by permis-sion. "Journey to Ocean Grove" by Stephen Minot. Copyright 1969 by The Carleton Miscellany. Reprinted with permission of the author. "The Demon Lover" by Elizabeth Bowen. From IVY GRIPPED THE STEPS, by Elizabeth Bowen. Copyright 1941, 1946 and renewed 1969 by Elizabeth Bowen. Re-

CONTENTS

Introduction:
A Writer's Stance:
One Way to Look at Fiction

An author's *stance* is, quite simply, the set of assumptions he has used in creating the as-if-real world of his fiction. There are three different stances he can take, and almost every work of fiction ever written falls into one of these three categories.

The first approach is to make the characters, the events, and the setting of a story conform to the world about us in what is often called a "realistic" manner. This we call *mimetic fiction*. The second technique is to propose within the story a single exception to the mimetic pattern such as the existence of a ghost or a monster or a boy's ability to see into the future. This is *premise fiction*. The third approach is one in which either the characters or the action, or both, radically depart without any clear premise from what is possible in our waking world. This is called *dream fiction*.

These should not be thought of as entirely separate categories. They are not bins into which one sorts stories like nuts and bolts. A particular work may borrow from two or even all three stances. But the analysis of stance keeps drawing our attention back to basic questions about what makes fiction.

For example, when we examine an author's stance (which we can also think of as the *story's* stance), in a particular work, we are looking into the heart of what makes fiction seem "real" or "convincing" though the characters may be quite different from ourselves and the story's events may be strange to us or even fantastic. Fiction creates this illusion of reality partly through internal consistency. The term *stance* describes the kind of consistency the author is using.

Thinking in terms of stance also helps us to understand the kinds of demands we as readers place on a work of fiction. Just what do we mean when we say that a story is "inconsistent" or "doesn't hang together"? These are values which frequently can be analyzed in terms of stance.

But the great advantage of approaching fiction in terms of stance is that it serves as a method of interpreting new fiction—whether it be in the conservative tradition of Chekhov and Updike, the speculative realm of science fiction, or the experimentation of writers who are as yet unpublished. Stances are not merely a means of classification; they are points of departure.

The basic characteristics of these three stances appear below; more specific analysis appears before each of the three sections of this collection.

Mimetic fiction: The word "mimetic" means imitative (like "mimic"), and mimetic fiction is that which creates the illusion of actual life. Such stories deal with the same natural order of things that we as readers do in our own daily lives. Like us, the characters are mortal and they have no magical or supernatural powers. They can be heroic, possessing courage and daring we might not be able to summon, or they can be absurdly below us so that we laugh at them as comic figures—but they cannot call up the devil, or turn into pigs (as the Duchess' child does in *Alice in Wonderland*), or see into the future. In fact, if a ghost does appear in a story which is mimetic, this "supernatural" element will be given a rational explanation before the story is over. We will eventually see that it was a fraud or a hoax.

While mimetic fiction creates the *illusion* of our waking life, it should not be thought of as a literal copy of it. Mimetic stories contain a number of literary tricks—as does all fiction.

Dialogue, for example, is not taken directly from a tape recorder, but is composed with care so as to *appear* to imitate actual speech while at the same time working to reveal aspects of character or of the story's theme. Tape recordings of real conversations often wander aimlessly and reveal little; it takes us hours and sometimes years to learn anything about a person through what he says from day to day. Transcribed on paper, this slow process is enormously boring.

When fictional dialogue is successful, it holds the reader's interest because in addition to sounding natural it constantly reveals other facets of the story—particularly thematic details and insights into character. To do this, it becomes highly organized and comparatively compact—without appearing to be so. This is a literary device, but it is used in mimetic fiction to create an *illusion* of reality.

Time, too, can be a kind of trick in mimetic fiction. It almost never moves in the relentlessly steady way the clock does. Instead, a story frequently develops one scene after another, providing links between them in the form of brief phrases like "two hours later" or "next morning" or even "three years later." In other stories, time may be rearranged, so that events from the past are inserted among scenes of the present. These devices are so basic to all story-telling that the casual reader hardly notices them; they are accepted as literary conventions.

In the same way, point of view has become an accepted convention. In most stories, we enter the mind of just one character and he serves as the point of view or the *means of perception* regardless of whether the story is told in the first or the third person.

In actual life, we can't ever enter directly into the mind of another person. We can only make guesses about what he is thinking from the way he acts (when a friend rips a book to pieces, we assume he is angry), or from his facial expressions, or from what he *says* is going on in his head—but we can never be entirely sure. (In some respects, stage drama is closer to actual life in that we are normally outside the characters, making guesses.)

But fiction—whether mimetic or not—is able to enter the mind of a character and to give the reader his thoughts directly. This is one more sample of a device which we as readers take for granted, even if the story is highly mimetic.

The critic Northrop Frye has suggested (in *Anatomy of Criticism*) that mimetic fiction can be subdivided into three types. He calls them "high mimetic" (which deals with heroic figures of superior power), "low mimetic" (in which the characters are rather similar to ourselves), and "ironic" (in which we look down on the characters, who are in various ways pathetic or comic). Most contemporary work falls into the last two areas; ours is not an age of heroes.

But no matter what subdivision is used, all mimetic fiction imposes on its characters the same mortal limitations we meet in our own lives, and it presents a world situation which can be understood by comparing it to the one in which we actually live. It does make use of a number of literary tricks or conventions, but essentially the story itself is a mimicking of our own actual world.

Premise fiction: A premise in argument is a proposition which serves as a starting point. In premise fiction, it is a proposal to the reader that he make *one clear exception* to what is possible in actual life. It suspends what we take to be the "natural order of things" in a single particular.

Such a premise is not peculiar to literature. We all used it as children. "Let's pretend I'm invisible," one child says, and the game goes on from there. "I'll be Superman," might be the premise, or "I'm a ghost."

Fictional premises are often just this simple—though what the author does with that premise may be enormously complicated. Elizabeth Bowen's story, "The Demon Lover," for example, assumes the existence of ghosts. This does not mean that the reader has to believe in the supernatural, any more than children who play "let's pretend" cling to their make-believe when the game is over. But it does mean that *for the length of the story,* ghosts are a natural part of the world. And the Bowen story goes on to make a number of complex suggestions about the degree to which the past can stay with a person. Thus the premise is not an end in itself (as is the case in simple ghost stories), but a means of developing a subtle theme.

Premises don't have to be ghostly. In D. H. Lawrence's "The Rocking-Horse Winner," a young boy works himself into a trance while riding his rocking horse and actually sees into the future. If this were a mimetic story, his ability to predict future events would eventually have to be explained as a delusion or hoax. Lawrence doesn't have to make such an explanation because he persuades the reader to accept his premise.

Premises don't have to be gloomy, either. In Kurt Vonnegut's "EPICAC," a computer not only begins to think like a human being, it (he) begins to feel like one, too. Vonnegut then develops a familiar love triangle, telling the story with a light touch.

If "EPICAC" sounds like science fiction, it may be because, traditionally, science fiction has been premise fiction. The word "science" suggests that no matter how bizarre the plot may be, it can be explained with a fairly simple "if" clause: "*If* we could pass through a time-warp into the future;" "If World War III killed all the world's population except for three people in an Abyssinian lead mine;" "*If* the society on Pluto had solved its internal problems by deporting its hostile and criminal types to a small, insignificant planet called Earth." Many authors of science fiction strive to devise elaborate complications from the simplest premise.

Science fiction, however, tends to concentrate on the intricacies of plot at the expense of characterization and thematic suggestion. Its appeal is based on the ingenuity of the premise and its development, rather than on the layering of suggestion one expects in works which are literarily more sophisticated.

Since science fiction is one form of premise fiction, we have included Ray Bradbury's "The One Who Waits." It has all the ingredients of science fiction and is by an author who is thoroughly identified with that kind of writing. Yet the story has a special, haunting quality which raises it far above fiction which depends primarily on intricacy of plot.

All the stories in Part Two of this volume are based on non-realistic premises. But in addition, each work explores a range of experience and develops subtle thematic concerns which go far beyond the mechanics of plot. Each raises important questions about the human condition and the condition of our private lives.

Dream fiction: Dreams appear to develop without logic. There is almost no way to predict what will happen from moment to moment. Characters can change faces, turn into animals, take flight, disappear; settings can change abruptly from a room to a forest, from city to countryside; one's mood can shift for no apparent reason, pleasure turning to terror or rage turning to love in an instant.

Dream fiction moves in the same ways. There is no single premise which separates this fictional world from the world familiar to us; everything is likely to be unexpected from one instant to the next.

The term *dream fiction* as we use it here is not intended as a vague synonym for "dreamlike." True, much dream fiction is closer to our sleeping experience than to our waking memories— but the term as a literary category refers to any piece of fiction which departs in several respects, or in a general way, from the patterns, expectations, and assumptions we depend on in our waking lives.

The first piece, Robert Fox's "A Fable," is a case in point. It does not contain the distortions we normally associate with dreams. The setting is exact: The protagonist is on the subway. The time is precise: "It was early Monday morning." Everything about the opening suggests that this is going to be a highly conventional mimetic story.

The first suggestion that something odd is happening comes when the protagonist falls in love with a perfectly strange girl sitting in the subway car. When he proposes to her, we *know* we are not dealing with the world we are accustomed to. By then, we are prepared for anything, so it is not at all surprising for him to receive her mother's approval and the applause of other passengers in the car. No single premise explains all this curious action, so the story is dream fiction in this special sense.

Closer to the pattern of actual dreams (or perhaps we should say closer to the *non*pattern) is "Pig and Pepper," a selection taken from Lewis Carroll's *Alice's Adventures in Wonderland*. Here the dialogue takes on the absence of logic we sometimes associate with dreams (and with certain plays from the theatre of the absurd, such as Beckett's *Waiting for Godot*, or Ionesco's *The Bald Soprano*). More dramatically, physical transformations take place—a squealing baby which turns into a pig, and the Cheshire-Cat which appears from nowhere and then disappears without explanation.

We will have more to say about dream fiction—and about mimetic and premise fiction as well—in the introductions to the three parts of this book. Our concern here has been to explain the concept of stances as a way of looking at fiction.

This approach is intended to be *in*clusive but not *ex*clusive; that is, these general categories apply to all narrative forms in any age, but they should in no way prevent the reader from looking at fiction in other ways. Some of the stories in this collection will benefit from a historical analysis, and all of them can be examined for their mythic or thematic content. But by exploring the author's stance, one can begin to understand the tools he has used to create the illusion of credibility and truthfulness. It is here—in this illusion—that the fundamental distinction between the story and the essay lies. When we examine an author's stance, we are studying the heart of fiction.

ONE
MIMETIC FICTION

Mimetic Fiction

What we have been calling *mimetic fiction* is often referred to in casual conversation as "realistic," but the reader should be wary of that term.

For one thing, "realism" usually refers to a particular school in the development of the novel, one in which the characters were commonplace people shown going about their ordinary lives. Used in this way, the term refers to such authors as Defoe, Balzac, Tolstoy, and Howells. *Mimetic* is a far broader classification. It is not limited by tone or historical period.

More dangerous, the colloquial use of "realistic" as a synonym for "vivid" or "convincing" is a genuine distortion of what happens in fiction. Shirley Jackson's "The Lottery" is certainly both vivid and convincing, but it is not mimetic fiction; it is based on a nightmarish ritual whose full dimension is not revealed until the very end. (The story appears in Part Two of this anthology.)

As we use it, *mimetic* is an exact term. It refers only to fiction which mimics the natural order and the patterns of behavior we are used to in our daily lives. No matter whether the events in a story may seem fantastic (like the dream scene in Hughes' "On the Road") or the characters bizarre (like the strange protagonist in

Kafka's "A Hunger Artist"), if nothing in the story is impossible in our waking life, the work is mimetic.

Stories within this category cover a wide range between those which are called literarily *simple* to those which are highly *sophisticated*. These terms should not be thought of as the same as "bad" and "good" because in literature (as well as in the other arts) simplicity often has a special value in itself. They are, however, extremely useful as descriptive terms.

Generally speaking, a simple story develops only one character and may not do more than sketch in even that one; it touches on only one or two aspects of a theme which might in some other work be expanded; it often remains on a single tonal level. Comic strips, where characters are usually stereotyped, are an extreme example of the simple. Adventure stories like the *Tarzan* series or the fiction in *Boy's Life* or even *Stag* are only slightly more sophisticated.

We have not included examples of truly simple fiction here primarily because one learns so little from it. This is one reason many people find it boring. The selections in this anthology can be read more than once with pleasure because one gains new insights the second or third time through.

But this is not to say that all these stories are equally sophisticated. John Updike's "A Sense of Shelter," for example, is like a delicate line-drawing. It is a study of a high-school boy who "was not popular" and "had never had a girl," and yet in some ways felt like "a kind of king." The story develops these ambivalences—the young man's sense of inadequacy and his feeling of accomplishment in that difficult midpoint between childhood and adulthood. Even though far less happens in terms of plot than the average adventure story, it is far more sophisticated. Yet on the other hand it does not have the range of suggestion of, say, William Carlos Williams' "The Use of Force" or Ilse Aichinger's "The Bound Man."

In Williams' story we are given a brief but penetrating study of a doctor who is caught between his sense of professional objectivity and his blind fury against a young, uncooperative patient. To complicate matters, his rage is combined with attraction. In addition, we have the vivid picture of a young girl in whose mind a defense against this doctor is far more important than mere stubbornness. She sees him as a sexual threat, and what we have finally is a kind of metaphorical rape, doctor against young patient, with the greatest struggle going on in the mind of the doctor himself. In spite of the fact that "The Use of Force" is one of the shorter stories in this collection, it is one of the most sophisticated.

Ilse Aichinger's "The Bound Man" achieves sophistication in a different way. In it, a man finds himself tied up with ropes and is barely able to stand up and walk to get help. But something happens to him in his discovery that he can walk despite his ropes, and when he meets a carnival, he joins it, becoming a part of the freak show. We learn surprisingly little about the man and nothing whatever about his background, but we do begin to see what it is to have specific skills which are at the same time severely limited.

Although the reader cannot help making certain inferences about the characters in stories like "The Bound Man," characterization is not the primary concern. Intricacies of theme are far more important. While examining the theme in stories like this it is also helpful to analyze the technique: *how* does the author develop this concern? In answering the question, one begins to discover what it is that makes some stories more sophisticated than others.

Several stories in this section can be paired for comparisons in theme or treatment. "A Sense of Shelter" and "The Taking of Our Own Lives," for example, both look at aspects of adolescence and early manhood. One ends on a mild, positive note, while the other ends in violence; yet each has to do with the problems young men face.

"To Charley Iron Necklace (Wherever He Is)" deals with today's American Indians who, like their ancestors in the previous century, are being destroyed by white society. Similarly, Ralph Ellison's "King of the Bingo Game" and Langston Hughes' "On the Road" deal with black men who must live in a white society and are eventually destroyed. Both Andre Dubus' "The Doctor" and Williams' "The Use of Force" deal with doctors, but the link between these stories runs far deeper: in each instance a man's professional competence is challenged, and in each an aspect of the inner man is revealed.

Perhaps the most striking comparison in this section is between Aichinger's "The Bound Man" and Franz Kafka's more famous "A Hunger Artist." In each story, the protagonist is both a victim and a victor of sorts as the result of his own peculiar career. Both men belong to carnivals; both are exhibited as freaks to a fickle public. Yet for all the similarities of these two stories, they suggest quite different conclusions about how men create values for themselves.

These comparisons are primarily thematic. The themes of these stories are important and the reader who wishes to make the most of his time should read both works and then review these comments.

Our primary emphasis here, however, is on the author's stance, and for this reason we have arranged the selections in an order which seems to lead naturally to the premise fiction examples in Part Two. A number of stories which are technically mimetic share some of the qualities we associate with premise or even dream stories. The last four in this section are cases in point.

In "King of the Bingo Game," Ralph Ellison begins to add to his story some of the dreamlike quality we associate with nightmares. The story can exist, tragically, just as told; no fantasy has been used. But Ellison's style, and the story's resolution, move us into the kind of horror which reminds us of our worst dreams.

Both "The Bound Man" and "A Hunger Artist" have the quality of fables. We have no idea where these characters came from, nor are we entirely sure where they are; they could belong to any century, any nation. Both stories read like myths which have been handed down through the ages. Yet each is actually mimetic. No character in either story has superhuman or supernatural powers; no event occurs which could not have taken place at some point in history.

Langston Hughes' "On the Road" borders on being premise fiction. The protagonist is a black man who is rebuffed by a white minister. The black man goes to the church for shelter and, when he finds the doors locked, breaks in. Up to this point the story is strictly mimetic. But now the church collapses and the man meets Jesus Christ; the two of them go down the street together, both unwanted and rejected in a hostile world. Had the story stopped here, it would have asked the reader to accept the premise that Jesus might return to earth as companion to a poor, lonely black American. Instead, Hughes chose to keep the story mimetic. The protagonist wakes from a dream; the presence of Jesus was only in his mind. The story's ending is thus more cautious literarily, even though the return to the factual world makes its implication in some ways much more harsh. Like all the other stories in this section, "On the Road" remains within the realm of the possible.

Yet though every mimetic story is "possible," some are further from our experience than others. These create a tension between what is familiar and what is outside our experience, and it is this tension which stretches our imagination. It is helpful to analyze what the base of familiarity is and to identify just what is new to us in these mimetic stories.

In "The Doctor," for instance, there is the familiar experience of not being prepared for an emergency one never expected—but few of us have had such an experience lead directly to a boy's death. In "A Hunger Artist," we have all shared the desire to "do our own thing," and we even know what it feels like to be hungry—but not many of us know what happens when these experiences are pushed to the ultimate.

It is important to remember that while mimetic fiction is rooted in the familiar, it also pushes the imagination into fresh areas of experience. By contrasting these two elements, one can discover the dynamics of fiction—and, in the process, draw the greatest range of pleasure from any story.

A SENSE OF SHELTER
john updike

Snow fell against the high school all day, wet big-flaked snow that
did not accumulate well. Sharpening two pencils, William looked
down on a parking lot that was a blackboard in reverse; car tires
had cut smooth arcs of black into the white, and wherever a school
bus had backed around, it had left an autocratic signature of two
V's. The snow, though at moments it whirled opaquely, could not
quite bleach these scars away. The temperature must be exactly
32°. The window was open a crack, and a canted pane of glass lifted
outdoor air into his face, coating the cedar-wood scent of pencil
shavings with the transparent odor of the wet window sill. With
each revolution of the handle his knuckles came within a fraction of
an inch of the tilted glass, and the faint chill this proximity breathed
on them sharpened his already acute sense of shelter.

The sky behind the shreds of snow was stone-colored. The murk
inside the high classroom gave the air a solidity that limited the
overhead radiance to its own vessels; six globes of dull incan-
descence floated on the top of a thin sea. The feeling the gloom
gave him was not gloomy but joyous: he felt they were all sealed
in, safe; the colors of cloth were dyed deeper, the sound of whispers
was made more distinct, the smells of tablet paper and wet shoes

8

and varnish and face powder pierced him with a vivid sense of possession. These were his classmates sealed in, his, the stupid as well as the clever, the plain as well as the lovely, his enemies as well as his friends, his. He felt like a king and seemed to move to his seat between the bowed heads of subjects that loved him less than he loved them. His seat was sanctioned by tradition; for twelve years he had sat at the rear of classrooms, William Young, flanked by Marsha Wyckoff and Andy Zimmerman. Once there had been two Zimmermans, but one went to work in his father's greenhouse, and in some classes—Latin and Trig—there were none, and William sat at the edge of the class as if on the lip of a cliff, and Marsha Wyckoff became Marvin Wolf or Sandra Wade, but it was always the same desk, whose surface altered from hour to hour but from whose blue-stained ink-hole his mind could extract, like a chain of magicians' handkerchiefs, a continuity of years. As a senior he was a kind of king, and as a teacher's pet another kind, a puppet king, who gathered in appointive posts and even, when the moron vote split between two football heroes, some elective ones. He was not popular, he had never had a girl, his intense friends of childhood had drifted off into teams and gangs, and in large groups—when the whole school, for instance, went in the fall to the beautiful, dung-and-cotton-candy-smelling county fair—he was always an odd man, without a seat on the bus home. But exclusion is itself a form of inclusion. He even had a nickname: Mip, because he stuttered. Taunts no longer much frightened him; he had come late into his physical inheritance, but this summer it had arrived, and he at last stood equal with his enormous, boisterous parents, and had to unbutton his shirt cuffs to get his wrists through them, and discovered he could pick up a basketball with one hand. So, his long legs blocking two aisles, he felt regal even in size and, almost trembling with happiness under the high globes of light beyond whose lunar glow invisible snowflakes were drowning on the gravel roof of his castle, believed that the long delay of unpopularity had been merely a consolidation, that he was at last strong enough to make his move. Today he would tell Mary Landis he loved her.

He had loved her ever since, a fat-faced tomboy with freckles and green eyes, she deftly stole his rubber-lined schoolbag on the walk back from second grade along Jewett Street and outran him— simply had better legs. The superior speed a boy was supposed to have failed to come; his kidneys burned with panic. In front of the grocery store next to her home she stopped and turned. She was willing to have him catch up. This humiliation on top of the rest was too much to bear. Tears broke in his throat; he spun around and ran home and threw himself on the floor of the front parlor, where his grandfather, feet twiddling, perused the newspaper and soliloquized all morning. In time the letter slot rustled, and the doorbell rang, and Mary gave his mother the schoolbag and the two of them politely exchanged whispers. Their voices had been to him, lying there on the carpet with his head wrapped in his arms, indistinguishable. Mother had always liked Mary. From when she had been a tiny girl dancing along the hedge on the end of an older sister's arm, Mother had liked her. Out of all the children that flocked, similar as pigeons, through the neighborhood, Mother's heart had reached out with claws and fastened on Mary. He never took the schoolbag to school again, had refused to touch it. He supposed it was still in the attic, still faintly smelling of sweet pink rubber.

Fixed high on the plaster like a wren clinging to a barn wall, the buzzer sounded the two-minute signal. In the middle of the classroom Mary Landis stood up, a Monitor badge pinned to her belly. Her broad red belt was buckled with a brass bow and arrow. She wore a lavender sweater with the sleeves pushed up to expose her forearms, a delicately cheap effect. Wild stories were told about her; perhaps it was merely his knowledge of these that put the hardness in her face. Her eyes seemed braced for squinting and their green was frosted. Her freckles had faded. William thought she laughed less this year; now that she was in the Secretarial Course and he in the College Preparatory, he saw her in only one class a day, this one, English. She stood a second, eclipsed at the thighs by Jack Stephens' zebra-striped shoulders, and looked back at the class with a stiff worn glance, as if she had seen the same faces too many times before. Her habit of perfect posture emphasized the angularity she had grown into. There was a nervous edge, a boxiness in her bones, that must have been waiting all along under the childish fat. Her eye sockets were deeply indented and her chin had a prim square set that seemed in the murky air tremulous and defiant. Her skirt was cut square and straight. Below the waist she was lean; the legs that had outrun him were still athletic; she starred at hockey and cheerleading. Above, she was abundant: so stacked her spine curved backwards to keep her body balanced. She turned and in switching up the aisle encountered a boy's leg thrown into her path. She coolly looked down until it withdrew. She was used to such attentions. Her pronged chest poised, Mary proceeded out the door, and someone she saw in the hall made her smile, a wide smile full of warmth and short white teeth, and love scooped at William's heart. He would tell her.

In another minute, the second bell rasped. Shuffling through the perfumed crowds to his next class, he crooned to himself, in the slow, over-enunciated manner of the Negro vocalist who had brought the song back this year:

"Lah-vender blue, dilly dilly,
Lavendih gree-heen;
Eef I were king, dilly dilly,
You would: be queen."

The song gave him an exultant sliding sensation that intertwined with the pleasures of his day. He knew all the answers, he had done all the work, the teachers called upon him only to rebuke the ignorance of the others. In Trig and Soc Sci both it was this way. In gym, the fourth hour of the morning, he, who was always picked near the last, startled his side by excelling at volleyball, leaping like a madman, shouting like a bully. The ball felt light as a feather against his big bones. His hair in wet quills from the shower, he walked in the icy air to Luke's Luncheonette, where he ate three hamburgers in a booth with three juniors. There was Barry Kruppman, a tall, thyroid-eyed boy who came on the school bus from the country town of Bowsville and who was an amateur hypnotist; he told the tale of a Portland, Oregon, businessman who under hypnosis had been taken back through sixteen reincarnations to the condition of an Egyptian concubine in the household of a high priest of Isis. There was his friend Lionel Griffin, a pudgy simp whose blond hair puffed out above his ears in two slick waxed wings. He was rumored to be a fairy, and in fact did seem most excited by the transvestite aspect of the soul's transmigration. And there was Lionel's girl Virginia, a drab little mystery who chain-smoked Herbert Tareytons and never said anything. She had sallow skin and smudged eyes and Lionel kept jabbing her and shrieking, making William wince. He would rather have sat with members of his own class, who filled the other booths, but he would have had to force himself on them. These juniors admired him and welcomed his company. He asked, "Wuh-well, was he ever a c-c-c-cockroach, like Archy?"

Kruppman's face grew intense; his furry lids dropped down over the bulge of his eyes, and when they drew back, his pupils were as small and hard as BBs. "That's the really interesting thing. There was this gap, see, between his being a knight under Charlemagne and then a sailor on a ship putting out from Macedonia—that's where Yugoslavia is now—in the time of Nero; there was this gap, when the only thing the guy would do was walk around the office snarling and growling, see, like this." Kruppman worked his blotched ferret face up into a snarl and Griffin shrieked. "He tried to bite one of the assistants and they think that for six hundred years"—the uncanny, unhealthy seriousness of his whisper hushed Griffin momentarily—"for six hundred years he just was a series of wolves. Probably in the German forests. You see, when he was in Macedonia"—his whisper barely audible—"he murdered a woman."

Griffin squealed in ecstasy and cried, "Oh, Kruppman! Kruppman, how you do go on!" and jabbed Virginia in the arm so hard a Herbert Tareyton jumped from her hand and bobbled across the Formica table. William gazed over their heads in pain.

The crowd at the soda counter had thinned so that when the door to the outside opened he saw Mary come in and hesitate there for a second where the smoke inside and the snow outside swirled together. The mixture made a kind of—Kruppman's ridiculous story had put the phrase in his head—wolf-weather, and she was just a gray shadow caught in it alone. She bought a pack of cigarettes from Luke and went out again, a kerchief around her head, the pneumatic thing above the door hissing behind her. For a long time, always in fact, she had been at the center of whatever gang was the one: in the second grade the one that walked home up Jewett Street together, and in the sixth grade the one that went bicycling as far away as the quarry and the Rentschler estate and played touch football Saturday afternoons, and in the ninth grade the one that went roller-skating at Candlebridge Park with the tenth-grade boys, and in the eleventh grade the one that held parties lasting past midnight and that on Sundays drove in caravans as far as Philadelphia and back. And all the while there had been a succession of boy friends, first Jack Stephens and Fritz March in their class and then boys a grade ahead and then Barrel Lord, who was a senior when they were sophomores and whose name was in the newspapers all football season, and then this last summer someone out of the school altogether, a man she met while working as a waitress in the city of Alton. So this year her weekends were taken up, and the party gang carried on as if she had never existed, and nobody saw her much except in school and when she stopped by in Luke's to buy a pack of cigarettes. Her silhouette against the big window had looked wan, her head hooded, her face nibbled by light, her fingers fiddling on the veined counter with her coins. He yearned to reach out, to comfort her, but he was wedged deep in the shrill booths, between the jingling guts of the pinball machine and the hillbilly joy of the jukebox. The impulse left him with a disagreeable feeling. He had loved her too long to want to pity her; it endangered the investment of worship on which he had not yet realized any return.

The two hours of the school afternoon held Latin and a study hall. In study hall, while the five people at the table with him played tic-tac-toe and sucked cough drops and yawned, he did all his homework for the next day. He prepared thirty lines of Vergil, Aeneas in the Underworld. The study hall was a huge low room in the basement of the building; its coziness crept into Tartarus. On the other side of the fudge-colored wall the circular saw in the woodworking shop whined and gasped and then whined again; it bit off pieces of wood with a rising, somehow terrorized inflection—bzzzzzup! He solved ten problems in trigonometry. His mind cut neatly through their knots and separated them, neat stiff squares of answer, one by one from the long but finite plank of problems that connected Plane Geometry with Solid. Lastly, as the snow on a ragged slant drifted down into the cement pits outside the steel-mullioned windows, he read a short story by Edgar Allan Poe. He closed the book softly on the pleasing sonority of its final note of horror, gazed at the red, wet, menthol-scented inner membrane of Judy Whipple's yawn, rimmed with flaking pink lipstick, and yielded his conscience to the snug sense of his work done, of the snow falling, of the warm minutes that walked through their shelter so slowly. The perforated acoustic tiling above his head seemed the lining of a long tube that would go all the way: high school merging into college, college into graduate school, graduate school into teaching at a college—section man, assistant, associate, *full* professor, professor of a dozen languages and a thousand books, a man brilliant in his forties, wise in his fifties, renowned in his sixties, revered in his seventies, and then retired, sitting in the study lined with acoustical books until the time came for the last transition from silence to silence, and he would die, like Tennyson, with a copy of *Cymbeline* beside him on the moon-drenched bed.

After school he had to go to Room 101 and cut a sports cartoon into a stencil for the school paper. He liked the building best when it was nearly empty, when the casual residents—the rural commuters, the do-nothings, the trash—had cleared out. Then the janitors went down the halls sowing seeds of red wax and making an immaculate harvest with broad brooms, gathering all the fluff and hairpins and wrappers and powder that the animals had dropped that day. The basketball team thumped in the hollow gymnasium; the cheerleaders rehearsed behind drawn curtains on the stage. In

Room 101 two empty-headed typists with stripes bleached into their hair banged away between giggles and mistakes. At her desk Mrs. Gregory, the faculty sponsor, wearily passed her pencil through misspelled news copy on tablet paper. William took the shadow box from the top of the filing cabinet and the styluses and little square plastic shading screens from their drawer and the stencil from the closet where the typed stencils hung, like fragile scarves, on hooks. B-BALLERS BOW, 57–42, was the headline. He drew a tall b-baller bowing to a stumpy pagan idol, labelled "W" for victorious Weiserton High, and traced it in the soft blue wax with the fine loop stylus. His careful breath grazed his knuckles. His eyebrows frowned while his heart bobbed happily on the giddy prattle of the typists. The shadow box was simply a black frame holding a pane of glass and lifted at one end by two legs so the light bulb, fitted in a tin tray, could slide under; it was like a primitive lean-to sheltering a fire. As he worked, his eyes smarting, he mixed himself up with the light bulb, felt himself burning under a slanting roof upon which a huge hand scratched. The glass grew hot; the danger in the job was pulling the softened wax with your damp hand, distorting or tearing the typed letters. Sometimes the center of an o stuck to your skin like a bit of blue confetti. But he was expert and cautious. He returned the things to their places feeling airily tall, heightened by Mrs. Gregory's appreciation, which she expressed by keeping her back turned, in effect stating that other staff members were undependable but William did not need to be watched.

In the hall outside Room 101 only the shouts of a basketball scrimmage reverberated; the chant of the cheerleaders had been silenced. Though he had done everything, he felt reluctant to leave. Neither of his parents—both worked—would be home yet, and this building was as much his home. He knew all its nooks. On the second floor of the annex, beyond the art room, there was a strange, narrow boys' lavatory that no one ever seemed to use. It was here one time that Barry Kruppman tried to hypnotize him and cure his stuttering. Kruppman's voice purred and his irises turned tiny in the bulging whites and for a moment William felt himself lean backward involuntarily, but he was distracted by the bits of blood-shot pink in the corners of these portentous eyes; the folly of giving up his will to an intellectual inferior occurred to him; he refused to let go and go under, and perhaps therefore his stuttering had continued.

The frosted window at the end of the long room cast a watery light on the green floor and made the porcelain urinals shine like slices of moon. The semi-opacity of this window gave the room's air of secrecy great density. William washed his hands with exaggerated care, enjoying the lavish amount of powdered soap provided for him in this castle. He studied his face in the mirror, making infinitesimal adjustments to attain the absolutely most flattering angle, and then put his hands below his throat to get their strong, long-fingered beauty into the picture. As he walked toward the door he sang, closing his eyes and gasping as if he were a real Negro whose entire career depended upon this recording:

"Who—told me so, dilly dilly,
Who told me soho?
Aii told myself, dilly dilly,
I told: me so."

When he emerged into the hall it was not empty: one girl walked down its varnished perspective toward him, Mary Landis, a scarf on her head and books in her arms. Her locker was up here, on the second floor of the annex. His own was in the annex basement. A ticking sensation that existed neither in the medium of sound nor of light crowded against his throat. She flipped the scarf back from her hair and in a conversational voice that carried well down the clean planes of the hall said, "Hi, Billy." The name came from way back, when they were both children, and made him feel small but audacious.

"Hi. How are you?"

"Fine." Her smile broadened out from the *F* of this word.

What was so funny? Was she really, as it seemed, pleased to see him? "Du-did you just get through cheer-cheer-cheerleading?"

"Yes. Thank God. *Oh* she's so awful. She makes us do the same stupid locomotives for every cheer; I told her, no wonder nobody cheers any more."

"This is M-M-Miss Potter?" He blushed, feeling that he made an ugly face in getting past the *M*. When he got caught in the middle of a sentence the constriction was somehow worse. He admired the way words poured up her throat, distinct and petulant.

"Yes, Potbottom Potter," she said, "she's just aching for a man and takes it out on us. I wish she would get one. Honestly, Billy, I have half a mind to quit. I'll be so glad when June comes, I'll never set foot in this idiotic building again."

Her lips, pale with the lipstick worn off, crinkled bitterly. Her face, foreshortened from the height of his eyes, looked cross as a cat's. It a little shocked him that poor Miss Potter and this kind, warm school stirred her to what he had to take as actual anger; this grittiness in her was the first abrasive texture he had struck today. Couldn't she see around teachers, into their fatigue, their poverty, their fear? It had been so long since he had spoken to her, he wasn't sure how coarse she had become. "Don't quit," he brought out of his mouth at last. "It'd be n-n-n-nuh—it'd be nothing without you."

He pushed open the door at the end of the hall for her and as she passed under his arm she looked up and said, "Why, aren't you sweet?"

The stairwell, all asphalt and iron, smelled of galoshes. It felt more secret than the hall, more specially theirs; there was something magical in its shifting multiplicity of planes as they descended that lifted the spell on his tongue, so that words came as quickly as his feet pattered on the steps.

"No I mean it," he said, "you're really a beautiful cheerleader. But then you're beautiful period."

"I've skinny legs."

"Who told you that?"

"Somebody."

"Well *he* wasn't very sweet."

"No."

"Why do you hate this poor old school?"

"Now, Billy. You know you don't care about this junky place any more than I do."

"I love it. It breaks my heart to hear you say you want to get out, because then I'll never see you again."

"You don't care, do you?"

"Why sure I care; you *know*"—their feet stopped, they had reached bottom, the first-floor landing, two brass-barred doors and a grimy radiator—"I've always li-loved you."

"You don't mean that."

"I do too. It's ridiculous but there it is. I wanted to tell you today and now I have."

He expected her to laugh and go out the door, but instead she showed an unforeseen willingness to discuss this awkward matter. He should have realized before this that women enjoy being talked to. "It's a very silly thing to say," she asserted tentatively.

"I don't see why," he said, fairly bold now that he couldn't seem more ridiculous, and yet picking his words with a certain strategic care. "It's not *that* silly to love somebody, I mean what the hell. Probably what's silly is not to do anything about it for umpteen years but then I never had an opportunity, I thought."

He set his books down on the radiator and she set hers down beside his. "What kind of opportunity were you waiting for?"

"Well, see, that's it; I didn't know." He wished, in a way, she would go out the door. But she had propped herself against the wall and plainly awaited more talking. "Yuh-you were such a queen and I was such a nothing and I just didn't really want to presume." It wasn't very interesting; it puzzled him that she seemed to be interested. Her face had grown quite stern, the mouth very small and thoughtful, and he made a gesture with his hands intended to release her from the bother of thinking about it; after all, it was just a disposition of his heart, nothing permanent or expensive— maybe it was just his mother's idea anyway. Half in impatience to close the account, he asked, "Will you marry me?"

"You don't want to marry me," she said. "You're going to go on and be a great man."

He blushed in pleasure; is this how she saw him, is this how they all saw him; as worthless now, but in time a great man? Had his hopes always been on view? He dissembled, saying, "No I'm not. But anyway, you're great now. You're so pretty, Mary."

"Oh, Billy," she said, "if you were me for just one day you'd hate it."

She said this rather blankly, watching his eyes; he wished her voice had shown more misery. In his world of closed surfaces a panel, carelessly pushed, had opened, and he hung in this openness paralyzed, unable to think what to say. Nothing he could think of quite fit the abruptly immense context. The radiator cleared its throat; its heat made, in the intimate volume just this side of the doors on whose windows the snow beat limply, a provocative snugness; he supposed he should try, and stepped forward, his hands lifting toward her shoulders. Mary sidestepped between him and the radiator and put the scarf back on. She lifted the cloth like a broad plaid halo above her head and then wrapped it around her chin and knotted it so she looked, in her red galoshes and bulky coat, like a peasant woman in a movie of Europe. With her thick hair swathed, her face seemed pale and chunky, and when she re-cradled the books in her arms her back bent humbly under the point of the kerchief. "It's too hot in here," she said. "I've got to wait for somebody." The disconnectedness of the two statements seemed natural in the fragmented atmosphere his stops and starts had produced. She bucked the brass bar with her shoulder and the door slammed open; he followed her into the weather.

"For the person who thinks your legs are too skinny?"

"Uh-huh." As she looked up at him, a snowflake caught on the lashes of one eye. She jerkily rubbed that cheek on the shoulder of her coat and stamped a foot, splashing slush. Cold water gathered on the back of his thin shirt. He put his hands in his pockets and pressed his arms against his sides to keep from shivering.

"Thuh-then you wo-won't marry me?" His wise instinct told him the only way back was by going forward, through absurdity.

"We don't know each other," she said.

"My God," he said. "Why not? I've known you since I was two."

"What do you know about me?"

This awful seriousness of hers; he must dissolve it. "That you're not a virgin." But instead of making her laugh this made her face go dead and turned it away. Like beginning to kiss her, it was a mistake; in part, he felt grateful for his mistakes. They were like loyal friends who are nevertheless embarrassing. "What do you know about *me?*" he asked, setting himself up for a finishing insult but dreading it. He hated the stiff feel of his smile between his cheeks; glimpsed, as if the snow were a mirror, how hateful he looked.

"That you're basically very nice."

Her returning good for evil blinded him to his physical discomfort, set him burning with regret. "Listen," he said, "I did love you. Let's at least get that straight."

"You never loved anybody," she said. "You don't know what it is."

"O.K.," he said. "Pardon me."

"You're excused."

"You better wait in the school," he called to her. "He's-eez-eez going to be a long time."

She didn't answer and walked a little distance, toeing out in the childish Dutch way common to the women in this county, along the slack cable that divided the parking lot from the softball field. One bicycle, rusted as if it had been there for years, leaned in the rack, each of its fenders supporting an airy crescent of white.

The warmth inside the door felt heavy. William picked up his books and ran his pencil along the black ribs of the radiator before going down the stairs to his locker in the annex basement. The shadows were thick at the foot of the steps; suddenly it felt late, he must hurry and get home. He was seized by the irrational fear that they were going to lock him in. The cloistered odors of paper, sweat, and, from the woodshop at the far end of the basement hall, sawdust no longer flattered him. The tall green double lockers appeared to study him critically through the three air slits near their tops. When he opened his locker, and put his books on his shelf, below Marvin Wolf's, and removed his coat from his hook, his self seemed to crawl into the long dark space thus made vacant, the ugly, humiliated, educable self. In answer to a flick of his great hand the steel door weightlessly floated shut and through the length of his body he felt so clean and free he smiled. Between now and the happy future predicted for him he had nothing, almost literally nothing, to do.

TO CHARLEY IRON NECKLACE (WHEREVER HE IS)

s. m. swan

In parts of Northern Michigan the land is wild; forests, some still virgin, abound with pine, white birch, oak, the maple and the elm. There are orchards of cherries, apples, peaches which ripen in the sunlight of summer days like clusters of jewels against green velvet leaves. In the forests are gentle white-tailed deer and fierce wolverine and in the streams and narrow brooks rainbow trout jump. Man is here, too, and there are signs: the Mackinac bridge jutting across water and wilderness and the great ships which carry cargo of lumber and iron through the Saulte Locks. It is very pleasant to watch the white smoke of black boats against the blue horizon of sky and Lake. Man is here, but he is unobtrusive as the deer which come to water's edge to drink at the Little Bay de Noc, and if you choose you can walk along miles of golden beach without seeing anyone.

The snow begins to fall in mid-November and it falls until late February or sometimes even to late March; it is deep and beautiful and immaculate, and it stirs the imagination of men to invent games so that they can go out and touch it and be thoroughly enmeshed and engrossed with it. The skiers come up to Boyne all season in small bright-colored planes and by the busload, and the children skate and play hockey on the crystallized lakes with crude, heavy sticks and pieces of ice. The springs are long and sometimes there are false springs and winter returns. We look for the robin for the time to plant and when the ground loses its hardness. When we are finished planting the air is heavy with lilac and apple blossom and everyone is lighthearted with springtime.

Late summer and the fall was the time I liked the best, when the harvest is brought in and when the leaves are set in brilliant array against the cloudless sky and the waters are warm enough for comfortable swimming. After the harvest, the hunters come up to kill for sport and not for meat the white-tailed deer, the partridge, and the bear. We who were born and raised here resented the hunters who came to kill for sport and not for meat. A deer could feed a family for a month and we knew they would take a bite of the tough, sweet meat and be disappointed and throw most of the carcass away. We knew this because after they had taken photographs of the lifeless, gutted deer, they would try to give it away or just leave it by the roadside and it made us bitter towards them.

At the time I hung with Elvira Noon, Ginger Loomsfoot and her brother, Jason, Jacqueline Wiliquette, Sharon Ketchanago, Tommy Strongbow, Ann Marie Sauk, David and Louise Blackbird. Tommy Strongbow could drink anyone under the table and always won at arm wrestling. He was pretty strong all right and nobody messed around him too much. David Blackbird was the shrewd one, especially with money; and he was handsome. All Elvira Noon wanted out of life was to marry him since they both got drunk on corn liquor in the orchard and made love under the apple blossoms and moonlight. We knew that some day they would legally marry for the Chippewa is married with the uniting of flesh and not with the mere exchanging of words or vows. It was wrong to do otherwise or to come between a man and a woman; and if some girl had eyes for David Blackbird she was antagonized, ostracized, and in every way made miserable by the other women until she found another interest; it was the custom. Louise Blackbird was delicate and pretty; whatever she wanted she usually got, if not by her charm, by her arguments. Jackie joined the convent of the Sisters of Our Lady of Charity as soon as she turned seventeen, but until that time she raised hell like the rest of us. Jason was a dreamer, maybe he was even a poet. His sister was sweet and shy, concerned over whatever happened to you, ready to laugh or weep with you over everything that happened to you. Sharon Ketchanago was plain and unhappy because her home life was troublesome; and, later, she married a man just like her father who beat her as her father beat her mother.

When we went to Charley Iron Necklace's, we had to walk through the meadow in back of the Blackbird's orchard, straight down to a clump of cedars where a stream ran by. There was a large willow on the meadow side of the stream, and there the stream narrowed so that you could jump over it. On the other side was the wood and if you walked a little more than a half mile into it, in a straight line with the willow, you would be at Charley Iron Necklace's shack. It was very well hidden among the pines which were planted for the coolness in summer and to keep out the north wind in the winter, and you had to remember the willow tree and line yourself up just right or you would be lost if you did not know the wood. There were brown dried leaves on the ground that covered your ankles and rustled as you walked in them, and you would step lightly, sliding your foot along in the leaves, rather than stepping down, to avoid the things that could be hidden in them. Every time I stepped in the leaves I would think that in a million years the leaves would be coal, deep in the ground, and it fascinated me to think of how this would come about and what the earth would be like then and what creatures would dwell on it. Tommy Strongbow would always run ahead of us until he was out of our sight and would climb a tree and hide in its branches until we approached, then he would spring down on us with a yell and surprise us and make us laugh. David Blackbird always had his eyes out for mink and when he saw one he took after it, but their little bodies slipped quickly through the wood and they were lost to the eye in seconds. He wanted to start a mink ranch, although the rest of us agreed that minks were too mean and vicious to raise for any kind of money.

Charley Iron Necklace was an old man, a relative of the Loomsfoot. When they moved all the Indians off the land to the Chippewa Reservation on the Lower Peninsula, he was already old and that was fifteen or twenty years before this time. He refused to budge and he stayed, because he was already set in his ways and because he knew all the streams and forests and the farmers who would trade with him and he was fond of his world and the people of his world. The property where he lived belonged to the State of Michigan and it was unlawful for him to be on it; but the conservation officer, Reb Kelly, overlooked it; he was a compassionate man and he knew Charley Iron Necklace had nowhere else to go, that he did no one harm by being there, and that he had not many years left, so he left him alone, breaking the State law, but keeping the greater law, the law of Love. Charley had taken Reb fishing and hunting when they were both much younger and had taught many things of where they could get wild turkey and wild goose and how to catch trout when no one else could, and Reb had too much respect for him to kick him off the land.

Charley had been married twice. His first wife died when she was quite young of an illness which I gathered from conversation to be either smallpox or measles. He liked his first wife very much, but his second wife had a bad temperament and he was unhappy with her; and he would compare her with his first wife, saying all good things about his first wife which made the second wife even more disagreeable. His second wife died of eating contaminated food and left him without children, although the young were always around him and he was blessed with many friends.

When you got near Charley Iron Necklace's place, the smell of smoke would mingle with pine scent into perfume so intoxicatingly delicious it is impossible to describe. Across a copper wire stretched leaves and plants that were drying out for a crude narcotic tobacco that Charley Iron Necklace would put in his pipe to smoke. If Charley were not there, we would wait for him. There was a ritual we went through; first, we would roll our cigarettes and stand smoking in silence. It was the worst manners to speak before Charley Iron Necklace for he was older and therefore wiser and it was his house that we had come to visit. It was also a sign of good character not to speak at once or all the time, and it would be awhile before anything was said. Then Charley Iron Necklace would get his corn whiskey and spread out a large beautifully-patterned blanket of red, white, corn-flower blue, and black, and we sat on it tailor fashion, taking swigs of corn liquor from a brown decanter covered with leather. Only in the coldest weather would we go inside, preferring to stay outside among the pine and the songbirds. After this strict ritual would Charley Iron Necklace begin to speak.

"When Charley Iron Necklace be your age there no farm, all forests, many deer, not like now. Be many fish, not like now; water clean, not like now. Charley Iron Necklace see many bear, kill many bear. Charley Iron Necklace never afraid of bear, like taste of bear better than deer even. No like wolves; they come, too many at a time, be big trouble for man alone. Wolf no kill clean, like Charley Iron Necklace, tear apart the deer very bad. Be very long time when Charley Iron Necklace see wolf; they no more around. White man come cut down many trees, make forests go away; wolf go too. White man put other animals on land where forest was; these animals no take care of selves. White man take care of animals like squaw take care of little one. White man happy with lots of work and trouble. When Charley Iron Necklace young like you, be many bird, different kind, not like now; partridge all over, not like now.

"Long time ago when squaw go off with other men, husband take her, cut off her nose. Many squaw walk around, no nose. Priest all the time yell and complain, make stop do this thing to squaw; but woman very weak, go quick to do bad things; if see another squaw with no nose no go so quick; so we cut off fingers so priest not see, not raise so much hell. Priest be down by Big Lake, Lake of Indian, of Fathers, go down by Michigan. Father Joe, his name. He speak with Indian in Indian tongue. No have school, them days, just church. Learn things in church.

"Young men brave then, not like now. Now go off to town, drink lots, forget way of fathers, bring name of Chippewa very low. Many Chippewa leave, mix with white man. No good, like deer with no forest go away. Reservations even worse, got nothing to do; sit around like old squaw. Charley Iron Necklace stay here."

His soliloquy was similar to this, full of complaints and the happenings of the day and remembrance of the good old days peculiar to all old men, that would open conversation; then we would talk of local gossip, of Berny McNaulty's barn burning down, or the latest of old man and old lady Webster's fighting, gossip interesting no one but ourselves. Sometimes Reb Kelly would come by and he'd tell his stories and Charley tell his stories. We were awed by these tales that made legend of men around us, transforming them into gods every bit as grand as Ulysses or Achilles.

The legends vanished only as there emerged to take their place the heroes and heroines of adolescence. Things had to be decided; the laurels were waiting. We determined to know, for the sake of more legend, who was the prettiest girl. I always thought Elvira Noon. The handsomest boy is always a legend, and the one who drives the fastest car, and the best dancer became Terpsichore. Jason Loomsfoot was really something. He'd go to the Saturday night dances and every pretty girl in the county would wait for him to ask her to dance. But looking back now, it was Tommy Strongbow I remember the best. Every tragic crisis of my growing was made more carefree by Tommy Strongbow and his pranks and his daredeviledness. We played tilt-a-whirl with his old Ford on the icy winter roads with Jason and Ginger Loomsfoot in the back seat. Tommy'd go like hell, then slam on the brakes, and the car would slide and spin around like a crazy carnival ride. Once the car almost flipped over and we sat there for a long while asking each other if we should do it again. Finally Tommy'd say, "Let's go," and the game went on. A lot of times we'd get stuck in the high snowbanks along the road and have to dig ourselves out with a shovel Tommy kept in the trunk. Tommy Strongbow, jumping out of trees, champion arm wrestler and heaviest drinker in the county, defying authority with the bravery and cleverness of Ulysses, legend. We plowed the fields in springtime together and watched and prayed over them in the summertime, and gathered it in September; yes, it was Tommy I remembered best.

When Tommy fell in love it was with a German girl, Patricia Speilmacher. She lived over in Manistique and was almost eighteen when she met him. Her father was dead set against Tommy because he was Indian and she had to sneak out nights to see him. When he was having trouble with her, that is when she decided to stop seeing him because of her father, Charley Iron Necklace didn't mind giving Tommy advice about it.

"Frenchmen come up long time ago," Charley Iron Necklace said. "Come up, kiss squaw with mouth. Squaw like very much. Many squaw have no nose because of what Frenchmen do. If squaw like for Frenchmen to do, then white squaw like for Indian to do."

Tommy stalked out of the woods, indignant and enraged, not wishing to degrade Patricia Speilmacher with what he considered cheap talk. Charley Iron Necklace, hurt that his good advice was not well received, explained to us, "All fire go out of Charley Iron Necklace, but Charley Iron Necklace know. Good thing tell Tommy Strongbow this thing so he no have to cut nose off white one. To hell with Tommy Strongbow!"

After they eloped, Tricia Speilmacher's father would not let her in his house. Her mother came over to see her every holiday, crying all the while she was there because Tommy and Tricia were so poor. (Proserpine being carried off by Pluto.)

When we plowed sometimes we would see Charley Iron Necklace standing on the hill, his long gray hair blowing in the wind, his red shirt picking him out from the landscape, his arm extended upward in the sign of friendship. He was fascinated by the tractor and would sometimes watch it all day, but when we asked him if he wanted a ride he'd always say no. He showed this same mixture of curiosity and holy fear towards all mechanical devices, particularly towards sewing machines, reapers, cement mixers and the television at Schultz's tavern.

We lost contact with Charley as our childhood diminished. There were dances, now, and parties. Elvira was married and expecting. Tommy was married and Sharon was getting married as soon as she turned sixteen in September. The rest of us were interested in cars, motorcycles, speed, different legends of romantic love and the great dreams of youth. I was worried that I would not be able to go back to school in the fall and I led a rather dissipated, hopeless existence that summer, taking an interest in nothing, not even the planting; the legends were all that sustained me during that time. In the fall of that year was when all the trouble with Charley Iron Necklace began, I learned I could not go back to school, and it seemed I was relieved. It was the hope and expectation that had worn my soul down, and now that I knew what the final decision was I adjusted to it quickly. I was in high spirits for the harvest. The crop was good and Tommy came by to help with it as usual, bringing his brown-eyed, brown-haired, plump and pregnant wife to help us.

Before the harvest was completely in, five of us, all carrying a bushel each, went down to bring Charley Iron Necklace some of the crop. We shifted along in the old dried leaves and in the new-fallen leaves as we had done so many years before to bring him some of the harvest, his due for working in the fields and for the many fish and pheasant and baskets of reed that he had brought to our door. We would later bring much more: canned tomatoes, beans, fruits, pies of apple, berry, and pumpkin; but this was the beginning, the first fruits. We heard voices as we approached his shack, loud voices and tense, Reb Kelly's, Charley's, and one we did not recognize. We put our bushels down when we caught sight of their faces. Ginger Loomsfoot took my hand, for all the men's faces were grave and troubled; and we stood still as the deer stands in the meadow when he first senses the hunter.

Reb Kelly was yelling at the stranger, "Well, if you want to do it, you do it yourself, don't look at me. I ain't kicking him off!"

The stranger yelled back, "You can find yourself another job, then. What the hell do you think you get paid for? When I send in my report, you're through!"

"Fine!"

Charley Iron Necklace stood with his arms folded, saying, "Charley Iron Necklace no leave the land. Him like it here; too old go away. White man go, take other forest. Many forest, white man have. Leave Charley Iron Necklace alone."

"Don't you understand; it's not me," said the stranger. "You're on state property, poaching, shooting things out of season. How

Kelly let things go this far I'll never know. You're breaking the law!"

"Charley Iron Necklace not shoot more than eat. Charley Iron Necklace eat fish he catch, not tease fish and throw away in water again like white man. Charley Iron Necklace not go away; him belong here."

Kelly was getting madder by the minute, his face turning almost as red as his hair. "Now, look here, what's wrong with you?" he asked the stranger, his voice breaking with emotion. "Look at him. He's an old man. He don't hurt anyone by being here. Don't you guys in Lansing have anything to do but pick bones with old men?"

"It's not my fault. It's just my job."

"That's what Pontius Pilate said."

Charley started back for his shack to show he was through discussing, that his mind was made up. "Wait there!" called the stranger. "Don't you want to go to the Reservation? It's nice and peaceful there. You get checks from the government twice a year. There's no bear to bother you, sneak in your shack. Aren't you afraid of bear living here alone in the wood?"

"Bear know Charley Iron Necklace here with gun, not bother Charley Iron Necklace. You not so smart like bear."

"Is that some kind of threat?"

"Take it easy! Take it easy!" Reb yelled. "Leave him alone. Can't you see he's all keyed up?"

"Keyed up? They're all made out of stone. Stonefaces, that's what I call Indians. One of them gives you more shit than all of them are worth."

"Come on. Let's talk it over on the way back. One of us is bound to lose his temper." Kelly and the stranger walked out of the wood, hardly regarding us as they walked past us.

We knew that Charley Iron Necklace was very unhappy that day; he did not look at the apples or peaches, or run his hand through the wheat to feel its texture; he did not taste the tomatoes and say if it was a good crop or a bad crop as he did every year. He hung his head very low and we stayed with him until the moon came, feeling his sadness.

There had been other inspectors before this new one, of course. But they had either overlooked Charley or did not notice him. This new one was the kind that would overlook nothing, dogmatic because it was to his advantage to be dogmatic. He wanted to move Kelly and put a flunky of his own in charge of the area so that he could wheel and deal to sell the area to private enterprise.

That fall began the time of the ending of all legend. After the harvest, I could not get a job. I was trained for nothing and too young to work at the harder jobs in the factories. My ma was sick so she couldn't do much either. The farm was going. Even though our acreage was small we managed until this year when the price they were paying was not worth the selling, and they charged more than three times as much in the stores than they were charging five years before this time. They had even begun to pay some people not to farm, for there was so much surplus (so they said). But why was half the world starving if there was so much surplus? And why could a widow in Chicago living on her pension only afford to eat and buy half of what she should have? I worried then about my ma's health, and about the farm, and that I could not go back to school or get a job; one or the other I wanted, anything but this idleness. I guess I could have left to go into the cities, but like I said, there was my ma and the farm, the ties of blood, the only legend left.

Other things were happening that were beginning to enrage me besides my own poverty, and the incident at Charley Iron Necklace's. We always had it easy; there was only my sister and myself; but the Loomsfoot had seven girls and two boys to take care of; and after not selling most of their crop, they had to go into town to get a loan but were refused. Jason, the oldest, was trying to get a job. "Not experienced" was the reason they gave him for not hiring him for every job from making doughnuts to driving Mack trucks, but I know damned well it was because he was Indian. They decided to put the Loomsfoot on relief on the condition they no longer farm their land even for their own use. The relief checks eventually would far out-pay the loan they wanted to take out on their land, even in the first two years, and in the meantime crippled them by making them dependent and useless while the loan would have made them independent and useful. Papa Loomsfoot went to drink out of sheer boredom, really hitting it hard. The younger children suffered much from the quarrels that were going on at home because of his drinking. Then, Jason went into Wisconsin and robbed a tavern with three other young men. It was ridiculous, an amateurish stunt which landed him in the Reformatory in Green Bay for three years. I do not know what really happened there; but sixteen months after, his body was sent home in a coffin, with the explanation that after a period of solitary confinement he had hung himself.

The legends lessened even more. Alcoholism and dissolution affected all those men and idols that had been the grand creatures of my childhood. The land was rapidly being bought up by large corporations, and on the corporation farms everything was being done on a grand scale so we could no longer compete. They sprayed everything with D.D.T. and it was becoming a problem. The birds were dying in the fields and the fish were dying in the streams the irrigation ditches emptied into. My pet cat died from playing in a bean field from what they spray your food with. Do you know the Indian planted for the bird, the insect, and himself, so he would have enough at harvest?

They want us off the land, I guess. And once off the land they want us on reservations or in factories. They want a man who worked with seed and acreage, whose body was an instrument for the pure enjoyment of living in Nature to destroy this Nature by working in factories which make D.D.T., plastic Jesuses, piggy banks, copies of the Mona Lisa by the thousands, napalm, whatever else their mad minds dream up. I used to have a dream that everyone was a robot and I was the only real person.

Christmas came by like a lie. Charley Iron Necklace brought us a present of a wild goose. We gave him mincemeat pies and blackberry brandy we had made ourselves. Charley'd always go to Mass with the Loomsfoot and he usually spent some of the day with them.

I also went to the Loomsfoot that Christmas. I had not been there for a long while and I was struck by the poverty of the place. There was hardly any furniture and you'd get slivers in your foot if you'd walk barefoot on the floor. Some of the children did not even have beds, but slept on mattresses in the corner of the rooms. Papa Loomsfoot sat at the cheap dinette; the tiny chair he sat on looked as if it would collapse under his great weight. He was drunk as usual, loud and rank, pounding his fists, swearing and talking constantly, showing his missing front teeth. The children watched him in bewilderment with no respect; their eyes, clear and innocent, searched my eyes for an explanation.

Jason's room still held some remnants of his life: a guitar, his well-worn clothes hung neatly on wire hangers, music sheets with comments inserted in a clumsy scrawl, "strum A chord," "substitute G for A." I went through his things that Christmas remembering, as I looked through the music sheets, how he played the guitar and sang and made us all sing with him. There were ten or twelve books, several were very expensive looking. I picked up one of the thicker books and went through it. It had something printed in small letters across a blank page, "Sam's Second Hand Book Store, Iron Mountain, Michigan." It was *War and Peace,* bound beautifully in red leather with a gold inlay. My heart throbbed violently with emotion. Jason's thoughts could still be transmitted through these pages. I would know what some of his last thoughts were. But then I looked again at the music sheets and his guitar and they held no answer and I hated the music and books and all the objects that reminded me of Jason but were not Jason but were ridiculous, ugly things because they were lifeless. They held no magic. It was Jason who made his guitar alive, now dumb and dead, staring at me with its great empty eye, stupid, useless, unliving object.

2

Around the turn of the year, they came again to trouble Charley Iron Necklace. All this time they had not troubled him for there was strategy to go through before one could kick a man off the land which made this thing right, that is if you believe what is legal is Law and what is Good, and that a man in your way was just that and nothing more. Papa Loomsfoot and Tommy Strongbow came down to ask us if we would go down to the woods to stand up for Charley Iron Necklace. There might be trouble, they warned us, but we said we would go anyway.

There were reasons why Charley had to stay. He was old and he was sick, sick because he was old. The Loomsfoot had offered to take him in; he refused, for he was also proud. Because he personified all our troubles we were almost eager to bring this thing to a solution, even if it meant trouble. Tommy Strongbow and his folks had lost their farm; the Loomsfoot too; and the creeping monster of corporation had set its tentacles on the rest of our necks noticeably. We would fight it until it strangled us, for there was nothing else to do. We did not want the factory; we did not want to be useless; we wanted the land.

When we left for the woods, there were seven of us; when we got there, thirty were already there and twenty came later. I saw Reb Kelly for the first time in a long time. He had lost his job and you could tell by his face he had been drinking. We stood around and waited for them and when they came they saw we were many and they were only three, and they turned around and went back.

They came back within the hour with four armed troopers who had not the slightest inkling of what was going on. The stranger we had seen before stood by while the other men served a summons to Charley Iron Necklace that stated if he were not off the land in sixty days, he would be forcibly removed. Tommy Strongbow, who had organized most of this protest, drew himself out of the crowd and said, "We will not let you do this thing to Charley Iron Necklace. This land was once ours, given to us by God and agreed to by the government of this country in a treaty. Then we were dispossessed and sent off to live on reservations, except for the few of us who could stay by hard work and cunning and trickery. We have learned many of the white man's ways.

"If you take Charley Iron Necklace off this land, I will burn this forest down. I don't care if I go to jail for it. If you take Charley Iron Necklace off the land, you will have no land at all. I will see to it. I don't care if everything green and everything living will be killed in this forest by my burning it down, for eventually you will kill it anyway. The forest will not be here, so neither shall you have it, the land which belongs to Charley Iron Necklace, to everyone and not only to you."

Charley Iron Necklace stood by the door of his shack with the summons in his hands. He spoke with determination, "Charley Iron Necklace will go. He know the ways of father are no more. No want trouble. Him too old for trouble. Remember the time when much trouble was, not want same for Tommy Strongbow. Charley Iron Necklace go. One man not worth so much trouble. Go with deer and partridge and be no more."

Charley spent the remainder of the long, cold winter with the Loomsfoot. They had not been farming their land, but by the late winter they had lost it altogether. There was a question of how they had obtained the land and since they had not bought it, but settled on it, they were refused allotments until they got off. Charley considered himself a jinx and he figured it was because of him that the Loomsfoot lost their farm. Neither would he accept any more charity. He went back to live in the woods.

There was nothing to do those long winter days but drink. I no longer bothered to look for work. Even if I could have gone back to school I knew my mind would not have functioned right. Poverty and dissolution haunted me, but what was worse than anything was the sureness of our destinies and the stifling of anything that could set us free.

We were in the midst of planting, those of us who still had our land, when it happened, and when it happened we thought of how we could have overlooked that it would happen. One day, coming back home, Charley found some men tearing down his shack with axes. He picked up the rifle he always carried with him and fired at one of the three men. The other two ran through the wood and when the police came, Charley was running in the wood, wildly waving his gun. They had no choice; they killed him.

Many years have passed. The wild land is no longer around me. Instead is the place of concrete and poisoned air. People keep telling me I should stand up and do something for my people, but then I remember Charley Iron Necklace and call for another drink; and this one's to him wherever he is.

THE WOMAN WHO HAD NO PREJUDICES

anton chekhov

Maxim Kuzmich Salyutov was tall, broad-shouldered and thickset. His build might safely be termed athletic. His strength was remarkable. He used to bend twenty-kopeck pieces, pull up young trees by the roots, lift weights with his teeth, and swear that there wasn't a man on earth who would dare fight him. He was bold and brave. He had never been known to fear anything. People, on the contrary, were afraid of him and used to turn pale when he was angry. Men and women used to shriek and turn red when he shook hands with them: it hurt! It was impossible to listen to his fine baritone, as it used to drown everything out. The strength of the man! I've never known anything like it!

And this wondrous, superhuman, ox-like strength turned into nothing at all—was like a mere crushed rat—when Maxim Kuzmich proposed to Elena Gavrilovna. Maxim Kuzmich turned pale, turned crimson, trembled and hadn't the strength to lift a chair when the time came to force "I love you" from his big mouth. His strength deserted him and his big body turned into a big, empty vessel.

He proposed at the skating rink. She fluttered along the ice, light as a feather, while he trembled and grew numb and whispered as he chased after her. Suffering was written all over his face. His nimble, agile legs bent under him and tangled themselves up when they had to inscribe an intricate monogram on the ice. He feared a refusal, you think? No, Elena Gavrilovna loved him and yearned for his offer of heart and hand. A pretty little brunette, she was ready to burn up with impatience at any moment. He was already thirty years old, his rank wasn't high, he didn't have much money, but he was so handsome and witty and spry! He was a good dancer, a fine shot. Nobody rode horseback better than he. Once, when he and she were out walking, he jumped across a ditch which any English jumper would have had trouble in clearing.

How could one help loving such a man!

And he knew that he was loved. He was sure of it. But one thought tormented him. This thought stifled his brain; it made him rage and weep; he couldn't eat, drink, or sleep because of it. It poisoned his life. He vowed his love, but while he did so the thought stirred in his brain and hammered at his temples.

"Be my wife!" he said to Elena Gavrilovna. "I love you! Madly! Wildly!"

And at the same time he was thinking,

"Have I the right to be her husband? No, I haven't! If she knew of my origin, if someone were to tell her about my past, she'd slap my face. Disgraceful, miserable past! She's highborn, rich, and cultured, and she'd spit on me if she knew the kind of creature I am!"

When Elena Gavrilovna threw herself on his neck and vowed her love for him, he didn't feel happy.

The thought had poisoned everything. Returning home from the skating rink, he bit his lips and thought,

"I'm a scoundrel. If I were an honorable man, I would have told her everything, everything! I ought to have let her into my secret before I proposed. But I didn't, and that makes me a good-for-nothing, a scoundrel!"

Elena Gavrilovna's parents gave their consent to her marriage to Maxim Kuzmich. They liked the athlete: he was respectful to them and they had high hopes for his future as an official. Elena Gavrilovna was in seventh heaven. She was happy. The poor athlete, however, was far from happy. Up until the wedding itself he was tormented by the same thought that had tormented him when he proposed.

He was also tormented by a certain friend who knew his past

as well as the palm of his hand. He had to give the friend almost all his salary.

"Blow me to dinner at The Hermitage," the friend would say, "or else I'll tell everyone. And lend me twenty-five roubles."

Poor Maxim Kuzmich grew thin and peaked. His cheeks became sunken, the veins in his fists became prominent. The thought was making him ill. If it hadn't been for the woman he loved, he would have shot himself.

"I'm a scoundrel, a good-for-nothing," he thought. "I must have it out with her before the wedding. Let her go ahead and spit on me."

But he didn't have it out with her before the wedding. He wasn't brave enough.

And the thought that he would have to part with the woman he loved, after he had had it out with her, was more horrible, to his mind, than all other thoughts.

The wedding evening came. The young couple were married and congratulated and everyone marvelled at their happiness. Poor Maxim Kuzmich received congratulations, drank, danced, and laughed, but felt terribly unhappy. "I'll make myself have it out with her, swine that I am! The marriage service has been performed, but it's still not too late! We still can part."

And he had it out with her.

When the longed-for hour arrived and the bridal pair were led into the bedroom, conscience and honor took their own. Pale and trembling, not remembering their new relationship, hardly breathing, Maxim Kuzmich went up to her timidly, took her by the hand, and said,

"Before we belong . . . to each other, I must . . . must have something out with you."

"What's the matter, Max? You're . . . pale! You've been pale and silent all these past days. Are you ill?"

"I . . . must tell you all, Lelya . . . Let's sit down . . . I must amaze you. I must poison your happiness, but what can I do? Duty comes first. I'm going to tell you about my past."

Lelya opened her eyes wide and smiled.

"Well, tell me. Only quickly, please. And don't tremble like that."

"I was b-b-born in Tam . . . Tam . . . bov. My parents were of low birth and terribly poor . . . I'll tell you what kind of pig I am . . . You'll be horrified. Wait . . . You'll see . . . I was a beggar . . . When I was a little boy, I used to sell apples . . . pears . . ."

"You?"

"You're horrified? But darling, that's not the worst. Oh, how unhappy I am! You'll curse me when you know!"

"But what?"

"When I was twenty, I was . . . was . . . forgive me! Don't send me away! I was . . . a clown in a circus!"

"You? A clown?"

Salyutov, expecting a slap on the cheek, covered his pale face with his hands. He was on the verge of fainting.

"You . . . a clown?"

And Lelya fell off the couch, jumped up and began running around the room.

What was the matter with her? She seized her stomach. Laughter (hysteria?) rang out and filled the bedroom.

"Ha-ha-ha! You were a clown? You? Maxinka . . . Darling! Do a trick! Prove that you were one! Ha-ha-ha! Darling!"

She ran up to Salyutov and threw her arms around him.

"Do something! Dearest! Darling!"

"Are you laughing, wretched woman? Do you despise me?"

"Do something! Can you walk the tight rope? Go on!"

She covered her husband's face with kisses, nestled against him, fawned on him. She didn't seem to be angry. Happy, comprehending none of this, he granted his wife's request.

He walked over to the bed, counted three, and stood with his legs in the air, his forehead resting on the edge of the bed.

"Bravo, Max! *Bis!* Ha-ha! Darling! More!"

Max swayed slightly, sprang from this position on to the floor and began walking on his hands.

In the morning Lelya's parents were greatly surprised.

"Who's that pounding upstairs?" they asked each other. "The newlyweds are still asleep. The servants must be up to something. What a racket they're making! The wretches!"

Papa went upstairs but found no servants there.

The noise, to his great surprise, was coming from the newlyweds' room. He stood by the door, shrugged his shoulders and opened it a crack. He looked into the bedroom, gave a start, and almost died of astonishment: Maxim Kuzmich was standing in the middle of the bedroom and performing the most desperate somersaults in the air; Lelya was standing beside him, applauding. Both their faces were shining with joy.

THE DOCTOR
andre dubus

In late March, the snow began to melt. First it ran off the slopes and roads, and the brooks started flowing. Finally there were only low, shaded patches in the woods. In April, there were four days of warm sun, and on the first day Art Castagnetto told Maxine she could put away his pajamas until next year. That night he slept in a T-shirt, and next morning, when he noticed the pots on the radiators were dry, he left them empty.

Maxine didn't believe in the first day, or the second, either. But on the third afternoon, wearing shorts and a sweatshirt, she got the charcoal grill from the garage, put it in the back yard, and broiled steaks. She even told Art to get some tonic and limes for the gin. It was a Saturday afternoon; they sat outside in canvas lawn chairs and told Tina, their four-year-old girl, that it was all right to watch the charcoal but she mustn't touch it, because it was burning even if it didn't look like it. When the steaks were ready, the sun was behind the woods in back of the house; Maxine brought sweaters to Art and the four children so they could eat outside.

Monday it snowed. The snow was damp at first, melting on the dead grass, but the flakes got heavier and fell as slowly as tiny leaves and covered the ground. In another two days the snow melted, and each gray cool day was warmer than the one before. Saturday afternoon the sky started clearing; there was a sunset, and before going to bed Art went outside and looked up at the stars. In the morning, he woke to a bedroom of sunlight. He left Maxine sleeping, put on a T-shirt, trunks, and tennis shoes, and carrying his sweatsuit he went downstairs, tiptoeing because the children slept so lightly on weekends. He dropped his sweatsuit into the basket for dirty clothes; he was finished with it until next fall.

He did side-straddle hops on the front lawn and then ran on the shoulder of the road, which for the first half mile was bordered by woods, so that he breathed the scent of pines and, he believed, the sunlight in the air. Then he passed the Whitfords' house. He had never seen the man and woman but had read their name on the mailbox and connected it with the children who usually played in the road in front of the small graying house set back in the trees. Its dirt yard was just large enough to contain it and a rusting Ford and an elm tree with a tire-and-rope swing hanging from one of its branches. The house was now still and dark, as though asleep. He went around the bend and, looking ahead, saw three of the Whitford boys standing by the brook.

It was a shallow brook, which had its prettiest days in winter when it was frozen; in the first weeks of spring, it ran clearly, but after that it became stagnant and around July it dried. This brook was a landmark he used when he directed friends to his house. "You get to a brook with a stone bridge," he'd say. The bridge wasn't really stone; its guard walls were made of rectangular concrete slabs, stacked about three feet high, but he liked stone fences and stone bridges and he called it one. On a slope above the brook, there was a red house. A young childless couple lived there, and now the man, who sold life insurance in Boston, was driving off with a boat and trailer hitched to his car. His wife waved goodbye from the driveway, and the Whitford boys stopped throwing rocks into the brook long enough to wave, too. They heard Art's feet on the blacktop and turned to watch him. When he reached the bridge, one of them said "Hi, Doctor," and Art smiled and said "Hello" to them as he passed. Crossing the bridge, he looked down at the brook. It was moving, slow and shallow, into the dark shade of the woods.

About a mile past the brook, there were several houses, with short stretches of woods between them. At the first house, a family was sitting at a picnic table in the side yard, reading the Sunday paper. They did not hear him, and he felt like a spy as he passed. The next family, about a hundred yards up the road, was working. Two little girls were picking up trash, and the man and woman were digging a flower bed. The parents turned and waved, and the man called, "It's a good day for it!" At the next house, a young couple were washing their Volkswagen, the girl using the hose, the man scrubbing away the dirt of winter. They looked up and waved. By now Art's T-shirt was damp and cool, and he had his second wind.

All up the road it was like that: people cleaning their lawns, washing cars, some just sitting under the bright sky; one large bald man lifted a beer can and grinned. In front of one house, two teen-age boys were throwing a Frisbee; farther up the road, a man was gently pitching a softball to his small son, who wore a baseball cap and choked up high on the bat. A boy and girl passed Art in a polished green M.G., the top down, the girl's unscarfed hair blowing across her cheek as she leaned over and quickly kissed the boy's ear. All the lawn people waved at Art, though none of them knew him; they only knew he was the obstetrician who lived in the big house in the woods. When he turned and jogged back down the road, they waved or spoke again; this time they were not as spontaneous but more casual, more familiar. He rounded a curve a quarter of a mile from the brook; the woman was back in her house and the Whitford boys were gone, too. On this length of road he was alone, and ahead of him squirrels and chipmunks fled into the woods.

Then something was wrong—he felt it before he knew it. When the two boys ran up from the brook into his vision, he started sprinting and had a grateful instant when he felt the strength left in his legs, though still he didn't know if there was any reason for strength and speed. He pounded over the blacktop as the boys scrambled up the lawn, toward the red house, and as he reached the bridge he shouted.

They didn't stop until he shouted again, and now they turned, their faces pale and openmouthed, and pointed at the brook and then ran back toward it. Art pivoted off the road, leaning backward as he descended the short rocky bank, around the end of the bridge, seeing first the white rectangle of concrete lying in the slow water. And again he felt before he knew: he was in the water to his knees, bent over the slab and getting his fingers into the sand beneath it before he looked down at the face and shoulders and chest. Then he saw the arms, too, thrashing under water as though digging out of caved-in snow. The boy's pale hands did not quite reach the surface.

In perhaps five seconds, Art realized he could not lift the slab. Then he was running up the lawn to the red house, up the steps and shoving open the side door and yelling as he bumped into the kitchen table, pointing one hand at the phone on the wall and the other at the woman in a bright-yellow halter as she backed away, her arms raised before her face.

"Fire Department! A boy's drowning!" Pointing behind him now, toward the brook.

She was fast; her face changed fears and she moved toward the phone, and that was enough. He was outside again, sprinting out of a stumble as he left the steps, darting between the two boys, who stood mute at the brook's edge. He refused to believe it was this simple and this impossible. He thrust his hands under the slab, lifting with legs and arms, and now he heard one of the boys moaning behind him, "It fell on Terry, it fell on Terry." Squatting in the water, he held a hand over the Whitford boy's mouth and pinched his nostrils together; then he groaned, for now his own hand was killing the child. He took his hand away. The boy's arms had stopped moving—they seemed to be resting at his sides—and Art reached down and felt the right one and then jerked his own hand out of the water. The small arm was hard and tight and quivering. Art touched the left one, running his hand the length of it, and felt the boy's fingers against the slab, pushing.

The sky changed, was shattered by a smoke-gray sound of winter nights—the fire horn—and in the quiet that followed he heard a woman's voice, speaking to children. He turned and looked at her standing beside him in the water, and he suddenly wanted to be held, his breast against hers, but her eyes shrieked at him to do something, and he bent over and tried again to lift the slab. Then she was beside him, and they kept trying until ten minutes later, when four volunteer firemen descended out of the dying groan of the siren and splashed into the brook.

No one knew why the slab had fallen. Throughout the afternoon, whenever Art tried to understand it, he felt his brain go taut and he tried to stop but couldn't. After three drinks, he thought of the slab as he always thought of cancer: that it had the volition of a killer. And he spoke of it like that until Maxine said, "There was nothing you could do. It took five men and a woman to lift it."

They were sitting in the back yard, their lawn chairs touching, and Maxine was holding his hand. The children were playing in front of the house, because Maxine had told them what happened, told them Daddy had been through the worst day of his life, and they must leave him alone for a while. She kept his glass filled with gin-and-tonic and once, when Tina started screaming in the front yard, he jumped out of the chair, but she grabbed his wrist and held it tightly and said, "It's nothing, I'll take care of it." She went around the house, and soon Tina stopped crying, and Maxine came back and said she'd fallen down in the driveway and skinned her elbow. Art was trembling.

"Shouldn't you get some sedatives?" she said.

He shook his head, then started to cry.

Monday morning an answer—or at least a possibility—was waiting for him, as though it had actually chosen to enter his mind now, with the buzzing of the alarm clock. He got up quickly and stood in a shaft of sunlight on the floor. Maxine had rolled away from the clock and was still asleep.

He put on trousers and moccasins and went downstairs and then outside and down the road toward the brook. He wanted to run but he kept walking. Before reaching the Whitfords' house, he crossed to the opposite side of the road. Back in the trees, their house was shadowed and quiet. He walked all the way to the bridge before he stopped and looked up at the red house. Then he saw it, and he didn't know (and would never know) whether he had seen it yesterday, too, as he ran to the door or if he just thought he had seen it. But it was there: a bright-green garden hose, coiled in the sunlight beside the house.

He walked home. He went to the side yard where his own hose had lain all winter, screwed to the faucet. He stood looking at it, and then he went inside and quietly climbed the stairs, into the sounds of breathing, and got his pocketknife. Now he moved faster, down the stairs and outside, and he picked up the nozzle end of the hose and cut it off. Farther down, he cut the hose again. He put his knife away and then stuck one end of the short piece of hose in his mouth, pressed his nostrils between two fingers, and breathed.

He looked up through a bare maple tree at the sky. Then he walked around the house to the Buick, got the key out of the ignition, and opened the trunk. His fingers were trembling as he lowered the piece of hose and placed it beside his first-aid kit, in front of a bucket of sand and a small snow shovel he had carried all through the winter.

THE USE OF FORCE

william carlos williams

They were new patients to me, all I had was the name, Olson. Please come down as soon as you can, my daughter is very sick.

When I arrived I was met by the mother, a big startled looking woman, very clean and apologetic who merely said, Is this the doctor? and let me in. In the back, she added. You must excuse us, doctor, we have her in the kitchen where it is warm. It is very damp here sometimes.

The child was fully dressed and sitting on her father's lap near the kitchen table. He tried to get up, but I motioned for him not to bother, took off my overcoat and started to look things over. I could see that they were all very nervous, eyeing me up and down distrustfully. As often, in such cases, they weren't telling me more than they had to, it was up to me to tell them; that's why they were spending three dollars on me.

The child was fairly eating me up with her cold, steady eyes, and no expression to her face whatever. She did not move and seemed, inwardly, quiet; an unusually attractive little thing, and as strong as a heifer in appearance. But her face was flushed, she was breathing rapidly, and I realized that she had a high fever. She had magnificent blonde hair, in profusion. One of those picture children often reproduced in advertising leaflets and the photogravure sections of the Sunday papers.

She's had a fever for three days, began the father and we don't know what it comes from. My wife has given her things, you know, like people do, but it don't do no good. And there's been a lot of sickness around. So we tho't you'd better look her over and tell us what is the matter.

As doctors often do I took a trial shot at it as a point of departure. Has she had a sore throat?

Both parents answered me together, No . . . No, she says her throat don't hurt her.

Does your throat hurt you? added the mother to the child. But the little girl's expression didn't change nor did she move her eyes from my face.

Have you looked?

I tried to, said the mother, but I couldn't see.

As it happens we had been having a number of cases of diphtheria in the school to which this child went during that month and we were all, quite apparently, thinking of that, though no one had as yet spoken of the thing.

Well, I said, suppose we take a look at the throat first. I smiled in my best professional manner and asking for the child's first name I said, come on, Mathilda, open your mouth and let's take a look at your throat.

Nothing doing.

Aw, come on, I coaxed, just open your mouth wide and let me take a look. Look, I said opening both hands wide, I haven't anything in my hands. Just open up and let me see.

Such a nice man, put in the mother. Look how kind he is to you. Come on, do what he tells you to. He won't hurt you.

At that I ground my teeth in disgust. If only they wouldn't use the word "hurt" I might be able to get somewhere. But I did not allow myself to be hurried or disturbed but speaking quietly and slowly I approached the child again.

As I moved my chair a little nearer suddenly with one cat-like movement both her hands clawed instinctively for my eyes and she almost reached them too. In fact she knocked my glasses flying and they fell, though unbroken, several feet away from me on the kitchen floor.

Both the mother and father almost turned themselves inside out in embarrassment and apology. You bad girl, said the mother, taking her and shaking her by one arm. Look what you've done. The nice man . . .

For heaven's sake, I broke in. Don't call me a nice man to her. I'm here to look at her throat on the chance that she might have diphtheria and possibly die of it. But that's nothing to her. Look here, I said to the child, we're going to look at your throat. You're old enough to understand what I'm saying. Will you open it now by yourself or shall we have to open it for you?

Not a move. Even her expression hadn't changed. Her breaths however were coming faster and faster. Then the battle began. I had to do it. I had to have a throat culture for her own protection. But first I told the parents that it was entirely up to them. I explained the danger but said that I would not insist on a throat examination so long as they would take the responsibility.

If you don't do what the doctor says you'll have to go to the hospital, the mother admonished her severely.

Oh yeah? I had to smile to myself. After all, I had already fallen in love with the savage brat, the parents were contemptible to me. In the ensuing struggle they grew more and more abject, crushed, exhausted while she surely rose to magnificent heights of insane fury of effort bred of her terror of me.

The father tried his best, and he was a big man but the fact that she was his daughter, his shame at her behavior and his dread of hurting her made him release her just at the critical moment several times when I had almost achieved success, till I wanted to kill him. But his dread also that she might have diphtheria made him tell me to go on, go on though he himself was almost fainting, while the mother moved back and forth behind us raising and lowering her hands in an agony of apprehension.

Put her in front of you on your lap, I ordered, and hold both her wrists.

But as soon as he did the child let out a scream. Don't, you're hurting me. Let go of my hands. Let them go I tell you. Then she shrieked terrifyingly, hysterically. Stop it! Stop it! You're killing me!

Do you think she can stand it, doctor! said the mother.

You get out, said the husband to his wife. Do you want her to die of diphtheria?

Come on now, hold her, I said.

Then I grasped the child's head with my left hand and tried to get the wooden tongue depressor between her teeth. She fought, with clenched teeth, desperately! But now I also had grown furious —at a child. I tried to hold myself down but I couldn't. I know how to expose a throat for inspection. And I did my best. When finally I got the wooden spatula behind the last teeth and just the point of it into the mouth cavity, she opened up for an instant but before I could see anything she came down again and gripping the wooden blade between her molars she reduced it to splinters before I could get it out again.

Aren't you ashamed, the mother yelled at her. Aren't you ashamed to act like that in front of the doctor?

Get me a smooth-handled spoon of some sort, I told the mother. We're going through with this. The child's mouth was already bleeding. Her tongue was cut and she was screaming in wild hysterical shrieks. Perhaps I should have desisted and come back in an hour or more. No doubt it would have been better. But I have seen at least two children lying dead in bed of neglect in such cases, and feeling that I must get a diagnosis now or never I went at it again. But the worst of it was that I too had got beyond reason. I could have torn the child apart in my own fury and enjoyed it. It was a pleasure to attack her. My face was burning with it.

The damned little brat must be protected against her own idiocy, one says to one's self at such time. Others must be protected against her. It is social necessity. And all these things are true. But a blind fury, a feeling of adult shame, bred of a longing for muscular release are the operatives. One goes on to the end.

In a final unreasoning assault I overpowered the child's neck and jaws. I forced the heavy silver spoon back of her teeth and down her throat till she gagged. And there it was—both tonsils covered with membrane. She had fought valiantly to keep me from knowing her secret. She had been hiding that sore throat for three days at least and lying to her parents in order to escape just such an outcome as this.

Now truly she *was* furious. She had been on the defensive before but now she attacked. Tried to get off her father's lap and fly at me while tears of defeat blinded her eyes.

THE TAKING OF OUR OWN LIVES
denis johnson

Riggs Northup, whose life so far had progressed like that of any other town moron, sat in his battered Chevrolet until nearly midnight and staved off any inkling as to what everything in him had led to. He watched the stars. All the stars were clearly visible in the summer sky except through those portions of the windshield where two or three grasshoppers had smashed into the same spot, splattering tobacco juice. Also he watched the moon, rising very late tonight, on the horizon, so much like a great round orange it made Riggs thirsty.

For now the moon just hung there, uncertain, but in a moment it would make up its mind and the long ascent would begin. Soon after, it would pale and recede until it was distant and unapproachable like the train bearing away the corpse of some mutilated hero. Not one soul would be able to stop it, not one voice could call it back. He remembered that Abraham Lincoln, dead, was carried through the country on a train. Maybe a lot of people would be sorry, he hoped. Maybe there would be a lot of apologizing but the moon would go on and later everybody would be blaming everybody else.

In addition to the moon and stars, Riggs watched the small farm he had parked before, although the farm did nothing but continue to move with the rest of the country toward morning. He peered up the long driveway at the single glowing window of the farmhouse, then at the powerful lamp that lighted the yard, then back again at the window, wondering if they were going to stay up all night in there, or what? Periodically he rested his eyes from the glare of the two lights to change the station on the radio, or to reach in the back seat and touch the rifle, or take the pistol and hold it in his lap.

The rifle was a carbine bequeathed him by his long-deceased father. The pistol was a twenty-two he had stolen just yesterday from the sporting goods department at the Sears and Roebuck store. The grotesque space-age, ray-gun shape of the little target pistol fascinated him so that he could not leave it alone. It was so streamlined that even as it rested in his lap it seemed to be accelerating in flight. When he thought of it as a real pistol, intended for shooting just like any other pistol, he could not believe it. Looking down at it he felt the world speeding beyond him in its growing complexity of frills and gadgets, making him an old man at twenty-eight, leaving him behind in the world that he inhabited and understood. Yet he was stuck on this earth and as it left him, he left with it and saw the familiar territory diminishing around the unfamiliar figure of the man who was himself in the distance. He was like the man in the moon.

The man in the moon hunched down in the seat as the lights of a car began shining a half-mile back on the lonely dirt road. Confused by the vision of himself leaving himself behind, the man in the moon stayed low in the seat long after the lights had passed on into the evening. He crooned to himself, in a hoarse mutter, the television advertising jingles which had been so comforting to him in his childhood.

When he was calm again he rolled down the window and gazed for a long time at the big light in the yard before raising the pistol. "In the army," he reminded himself, "in target practice, we did it . . . *this* way," and the silence of the evening was blown away in the explosion of genuine silence that extinguished the light. Moving his arms a few inches he quickly aimed again and put two bullets through the lit window of the house. He was very much afraid then and he sped all the way to the large highway, frightening himself further with the risks he took on the loose dirt of the country road. On the highway, speed limit seventy, he pressed the accelerator pedal against the floor and thought: First you take potshots at some-body's farmhouse. Then you rob somebody with a gun and pretty soon you commit murder.

The automobile gained miles per hour on a long decline, seventy, seventy-two, seventy-five, shuddering in regular spasms. Riggs did not fear the speed now, or the suspicious whining of the left rear tire—bald enough that the threads showed through—or death. In the eight years of its existence the Chevrolet had passed like water through the hands of too many owners, collecting dents and scrapes, rust, repair bills and a number of fading clever bumper stickers, satisfying no one with its performance. Upon acquiring the auto-mobile for ninety-five dollars, Riggs had set about learning its quirks and desires and had found nothing wrong with it that an occasional rest would not correct. Riggs allowed it to sit undisturbed for two days every four hundred miles, and the car performed for him perfectly. The tire would not blow. The car was well rested and the shuddering of its frame would not build toward an ex-plosion of parts over the highway. It was Riggs who had not been given time to settle, even in a million miles. Even in his sleep he was thrown continually forward, and he could not help feeling sorry he was being driven like an automobile or a train.

Cresting a hill he viewed the land falling away beneath him and saw his tiny, lonesome self still withdrawing like the moon. *Come back! Come back!* he called, and he felt that everything could be forgiven in one who would be disappearing from view so quickly.

The first building which signaled to motorists passing that way that they had reached the outskirts of a town was the one in which Riggs ate and slept, a red wooden two-story structure. The first floor was occupied by a cramped country grocery specializing in the sale of over-priced soft drinks and souvenir post cards of the South. The second floor, connected to the first by a flight of wooden steps outside the building, was taken up by two rooms with a kitchen and bathroom. In exchange for running the grocery, Riggs and his mother were permitted to live there rent-free by the puffy-faced and sweating gentleman who owned the building. Mr. Harley Reese owned as well a tobacco farm, two gas stations in a neighboring county, and a fried chicken establishment, and he had served two terms as the town mayor before becoming a gentleman. It was Mr. Harley Reese Riggs planned to murder, if it came finally to murder.

Framed by a window in the second story, Riggs' mother was rocking back and forth through the grey light from the television. Riggs killed the engine and lights beneath the window and observed her as she lifted her shoulders up level with her ears, brought a plate full of cherry pie up level with her open mouth, and, nodding strong agreement at the television screen, shoved with her fork and gulped. Without turning her head, and still clutching the fork, she banged frantically on the window screen. "Come see this man!" she shouted in the direction of the television. "This man has got the right ideer! Hurry up or he'll be gone!"

Inside it was too hot. Riggs took a beer from the refrigerator and leaned against the kitchen counter, rolling the cool can over his cheeks and mouth. He lowered his head and studied, as they spread away from his feet over the length and breadth of the warped linoleum floor, a myriad of printed identical roses in the process of blooming.

The mother said, "Would you enjoy some cherry pie? Come look at this man. This is the Reverend Mister Thadius Macomber, a true saint if ever there was one, I'm here to tell you. Come *on*. He'll be over in just about one minute."

"So what?" Riggs popped open his beer and guzzled half of it rapidly away.

"Well you just listen to him for one second and you'll *see* so what, *that's* what," the mother said. She was a slight woman with straight grey hair cut even with her ear-lobes and parted in the middle like a child's. Riggs was a full two feet taller than she, looming and round-shouldered with too much weight on him.

His mother exhaled deeply as though she did not expect to find any use for oxygen ever again. "Too late. He's gone off the air now," she said. "Now if you would of only listened, you might of learnt something. They was a man come up there," she rose and joined him in the kitchen, "pie's right where it always is, right here. They was a man come up onto the stage there I was saying, he had a big old cane and couldn't take a step hardly, without looking like he was to fall over. And the Reverend Mister Thadius Macomber prayed on him a little and up he come, good as new, and throwed away that cane and walked right on off the stage. Right there on the television set for the entire world to see."

Riggs sipped his beer more slowly now. "So what?"

"Well I'm *telling* you so what. They had a woman up there reading postal cards from California even. And every one of them cards was testifying how the people that wrote them was healed when they come to his sermons and got prayed on. This one woman had asthma all her life and couldn't never breathe through her nose till he prayed on her." The old woman lifted the pie-plate from the kitchen counter and began to eat the last piece remaining there.

"Not one single solitary breath through her nose. But then she testified on her postal card that she has a new life thanks to the Reverend Mister Thadius Macomber. *But.* That ain't even the most important part."

Riggs examined the reflection of the overhead light on his beer can while his mother, smacking loudly, consumed her cherry pie. He did not want to have to ask her what the important part was. Once she raised her eyes to him expectantly and expelled from between her lips one glistening cherry pit, but he said nothing. For a moment it appeared Riggs might triumph but, the last of the pie gone, his mother began the lengthy process of scraping the plate with her fork. Annoyed, Riggs asked finally, "What's the most important part?"

"The important part is that he, the Reverend Mister Thadius Macomber, he has done *proved,* that the United States America is a direct gift from God on High to the people of the Earth, to save them for the coming of Christ on this planet. He done it with references from the Bible. The prophecies of the Bible don't leave no doubt in the least. In *fact,* He might be in this country right this very minute. Christ Our Lord Hisself."

Riggs was impressed by this information and he considered it for a moment. "Who do you suppose it could be, Ma? The President?"

"Pssht! The President! No—sir—not—for—a minute. You think Jesus would be paying off the niggers like the President? Jesus helps those who help themselves, and them niggers only helping themselves to everything us white folks breaks our backs for. No sir. It certainly is not the President. Now you consider just for a minute. Who do you think?"

Riggs said, "I'll have some of that cherry pie now."

"Well it's all gone. Why didn't you say sooner? I'll bake some up first thing tomorrow. Who do you think? It's plain as *day.*"

Suspicion came to shadow Riggs' features. "It ain't nobody to do with the U.S. Army?"

"Course not. Come *on.* Just consider hard for one minute. It's plain as *day.*"

"If it's anything to do with the U.S. Army I don't want to hear no more about it."

"Oh it ain't a thing to do with the army. You just go on and on about the army this and the army that, and you ain't even seen the army in eight years. It's no wonder you couldn't do right on them tests if you can't calculate who is Christ on this Earth when it's just as plain as the beer in that can who it is."

Riggs drained his beer. He turned from her and glared into the sink. The answer did not rise from the drain there. From the television room, which also served as his bedroom, The Star Spangled Banner ground into the air. "I know just exactly who it is," he said, "but I ain't telling you. If you think I'm going to tell you, you're just as crazy all right."

"Well I declare!" the mother said. "Who was it I just now told you healed all them people? Who was it they testified for on all them postal cards? It's the Reverend Mister Thadius Macomber, that's who. It's him. I'll stake anything on that."

The Star Spangled Banner ended and was replaced by a sound like that of water running from an untended faucet. Riggs said, "It ain't him. I won't never believe it's one of them television preachers. Why, them television preachers got to go on the television just because they can't get their own regular congregation, that's all. It ain't him."

His mother allowed her eyelids to droop slightly. "Whoever said that about television preachers?"

"I said it just now," Riggs said, his back toward her as he reached again into the refrigerator for a beer.

"It just so happens that the preachers on the television do it thataway, and the ones on the radio too, it just so happens they do it thataway because they have the Christian souls to consider all the poor invalids and people which have to work so they can't go to church Sunday like regular folks. That's all. And who thunk that up for you? You certainly never thunk that up for yourself all by yourself."

"I certainly did myself."

"You never," his mother said. "Because you ain't smart enough."

"Never mind," Riggs said. "I thunk it for myself. Never you mind about it." He turned from the refrigerator. "I didn't tell you yet but I'm getting smart. I didn't tell you because it was supposed to be a surprise. Now I decided I won't show you when I finally get all smart. So now you can just never mind about it."

Her eyelids drooped farther, all but closing. "You never."

"Never MIND I said!" Riggs threw the full can of beer overhand into the sink. There was a clanging noise and drops of beer were deposited on the walls and floor and mother and son so that they might have been standing in a summer shower, looking out for clouds shaped like barnyard animals or the faces of movie stars. Riggs felt he could smile as they stood there with the drops of liquid glistening on their faces, if his mother would only smile first.

The mother ignored the drops of beer. "And what you done with your Daddy's carbine?" she said. "Don't think I didn't mark *that* was gone, neither."

It seemed a hand much larger than his own covered his face now, stifling his breath and blacking out the room. Riggs blundered out the door. At the bottom of the outside steps he fell, tearing the skin on his elbow. He slammed the car door and raced for a half-mile over the highway, regaining a slight hold on the events constituting the day, before pulling onto the shoulder to sit. He punched his mother's face until the blood ran indistinguishable from the innards of cherry pie and her eyes were forced to open completely, begging.

On the radio there was a country-western music station broadcasting over the length of four states from New Orleans. Riggs listened intently as a young woman's voice suggested ways of doing right by your semi-truck. She called the audience "You boys." At the same time she spoke of semi-trucks, Riggs realized, she was speaking of men and women, referring to the trucks in feminine terms, speaking of herself, in fact, and "you boys," the calm sexuality in her tone assuring that the world was composed of men and their women and men and their trucks, with nothing else to subtract from the clean power of these relationships, a world moving directly forward like the highway into a visible and controllable future. Riggs plowed forward, going fast if he chose or slow, or stopping altogether if he chose. In his truck he knocked aside shopping centers. Next to him was a perfumed faceless collection of breasts and legs and pubic hair, his woman.

The summer before, Riggs had circled the parking lot of a drive-in restaurant over and over in his newly purchased Chevrolet. He had stared ahead, turning the wheels and moving slowly forward and observing the shopping center across the street sweep over the windshield, and then the wide farmland back of the restaurant and again the shopping center, the children carrying balloons from the shoestore, the grasshoppers thrown above the tobacco, the pale women accusing their husbands before the window displays, the scarecrow deteriorating, a man locked out of the state liquor store at closing time, bee-swarms descending on the rotten pears—until a girl waved to him, smiling, and he stopped for her.

He had nothing to say and said nothing, but the girl, whom he had never seen, had gone through this ritual often and was full of smiling words that moved about the interior of the Chevrolet like hopeless moths. In a moment, after purchasing their soft drinks, they were heading east on the highway. Riggs could think only how, at the age of twenty-seven, he was making his first pick-up, how he did not know this girl, how he wished he were alone. Attempting to be glib and casual he told her everything there was to know about his car, and complained about the food at the drive-in, and described for her everything he had eaten that day. He talked too much, he thought. They parked in a spot the girl pointed out.

The girl nodded continually, sipping from her paper cup occasionally but for the most part letting it rest on the dashboard while she teased her hair and examined herself in a pocket mirror. Now and then she interrupted him to ask, "What would you think if I was to curl it some?" Or, "If you saw me on the street with spit-curls coming down like so, and you didn't know me, would you say I was cheap?"

Finally the sun passed below distant hills on its way to settle other matters, and the darkness seemed to preclude all but the most necessary and crucial of conversations. She was very close to him on the seat, but he could not imagine how to begin. He thought he might simply incline his head toward her face, and that this movement might serve to nudge them forward like two snowballs on a hill. Nothing further would be required of him then and they would race uncontrollably but smoothly toward the desired end of the evening, drawn by some inevitable human gravity until they struck harder ground.

But the girl had lines prepared for the drama of just such a moment. "Who was it broke your heart?" she asked. "I can tell your heart is broken."

Riggs became afraid he would have to think with this girl, he would have to be thinking every minute with her.

"You can tell me," she said. "Come on, you can tell me."

"All right," Riggs said, and the girl settled back with her soft drink. He said, "It was the U.S. Army broken my heart."

She had laughed at this, tilting back her head and slurping violently to keep the Coca-Cola in her mouth. She had had to lean her head from the window finally and spit it out. "What in the *world* do you mean?" she had asked.

Unable to retract his confession or somehow save it from its stupidity, he had forced her from the car to walk on home by herself.

The army had been the place for him but they would not let him join the paratroopers and jump from miles up in the air and wear a big airborne division patch on his jacket when he was talking to the girls, because the army was composed chiefly of the kind of man who took pleasure in excluding others. He had taken the I.Q. tests as often as they would let him, but he had never scored high enough to leave the infantry. He had not known the secret. No one would tell him what it was. Enraged by his repeated failures, he had not re-enlisted at the end of his tour. He had seen no reason for continuing with the army. No one had seen fit to tell him the secret of the I.Q. tests. Since then he had become fat. The army had been the place for him, but now he was finished with the army and he had become fat.

He climbed into the back seat and curled up. In the sky the stars were managing to shine and the moon was succeeding in its attempt to rise higher, and in the woods by the highway the animals drew the next necessary breath, and the next. Riggs closed his eyes and someone said: It was George Rivers up at the gas station told you that about television preachers. He opened his eyes and denied it. *Yes it was.* No it never was. When he fell asleep he looked down and his feet had become the wheels of an express train unable to stop. He continued to build speed until he roared past everything and hurtled from the edge of the earth in a swan dive. In one out-flung hand he held his father's carbine and in the other his own twenty-two caliber target pistol. There was no one to witness the spectacular grace of this event.

Nor were there any witnesses to the robbery the following day, other than the owner of the gas station, and Mr. Harley Reese who owned the building where Riggs lived, and Harold, Mr. Harley Reese's driver.

The gas station was a little block of cement which appeared to have risen miraculously out of the dust forty miles down the highway. The owner was a stoop-shouldered wiry little man, balding, who pretended very hard that he did not mind being robbed. He was alone when Riggs strolled cautiously into the station, extending his twenty-two caliber target pistol in the manner of a blind man securing the area before him with his white cane.

"Oh-oh," the little man said. "What you doing with that gun?"

"This is a robbery," Riggs told him.

The little man shook his head and made a weak attempt to raise his hands above his head. "Well," he said. "I have owned this very same gas station for just about thirty-six years. Lacks a few weeks of being thirty-six years. And you're the very first robber ever to walk through that door." He emitted a high-pitched noise originating in the back of his throat. "I was the third person in the state to put up a all-concrete gas station," the man said. "There wasn't but one pump out there then. I didn't put in the second pump till four years ago last January. Say, you wouldn't really shoot me would you?" he asked.

Riggs nodded with some embarrassment. "I guess I would if you made me do it," he said.

There were eighteen one-dollar bills, two half-dollars, and seventeen quarters in the cash register. Riggs did not care to take any of the smaller change.

"I don't guess that clears twenty-five dollars by much," the man said.

"That's okay," Riggs consoled the man. "It's the robbing that counts. I can always do some more robbing later on."

The man drew the bills and coins together into a pile on top of the counter.

"What am I going to carry this money in?" Riggs asked.

"Now why don't you just put it in your pockets?" the man said.

"That ain't right," Riggs said. "You got to have a sack. Where's a sack?"

The man gave Riggs an empty sack from the waste basket by the counter. "You should have brung your own sack," he told Riggs irritably.

At that moment a dark purple Lincoln Continental drew to a halt before the pumps outside, causing a small bell to ring twice on the wall above the counter. Riggs recognized the car as belonging to Mr. Harley Reese. In the front seat was Harold, the driver, a young black boy dressed as always in a white uniform much like those worn by orderlies in hospitals. In the back seat was Mr. Harley Reese himself, wearing a white suit and a broad white hat with a black band. He was leaning forward in the seat to oversee the driver's adjustment of the air-conditioner with a variety of quick gestures, all intended to indicate that he had, at long last, encountered the limit of his patience in dealing with his young employee. Several times he removed his white hat and promptly replaced it, puffing his cheeks in and out in a series of simulated explosions of steam as he leaned over Harold's shoulder, and twice he flung himself backward to sprawl in the seat, completely helpless before the deep, abiding stupidity of the boy Harold. When he caught sight of Riggs standing inside before the counter with the gun in his hand, he emerged gratefully from the automobile and hastened into the concrete shack.

Mr. Harley Reese perspired so freely that when he burst through the door the atmosphere of the room seemed immediately to become more humid and dense. Great patches of sweat stained his underarms and the broad seat of his pants. "Whew!" he announced to the room in general, "I want me some Co-Cola!" To Riggs he said, "What you doing with that gun, boy?" And to the man behind the counter he said, "I'm Mr. Harley Reese. What's he doing with that gun?"

"How do, Mr. Harley Reese," the man said. "My name is Danny Grace, and this here is the first robber ever to walk through that door in almost thirty-six years."

"You figure to rob this gas station, Riggs?" Mr. Harley Reese asked. "Whatever do you think your Momma's going to say about it?" To Danny Grace he said, "Whew! You got any Co-Cola in your gas station? *Cold* Co-Cola is what I want."

"There's some in that machine there," Danny Grace said. "It takes a dime."

Mr. Harley Reese went over to the machine and deposited his dime. "What is your Momma going to say when they take you to the jail?" he asked Riggs. "Why ain't you helping out your Momma in the store, instead of robbing this here Mr. Grace?"

Riggs said, "I sure would like some Co-Cola right now."

"It takes a dime in this machine here," Mr. Harley Reese said.

"And then I might shoot you," Riggs said. "It don't make no difference about my Momma or not."

"Say," Danny Grace said. "Did you know I was the third person in the state to put up a all-concrete gas station?"

"Is that right?" Mr. Harley Reese said. "Did you know my Daddy was the first one?"

Danny Grace smiled and shook his head. He made a sucking noise and ran his tongue over the front of his upper teeth.

Riggs did not have a dime for the machine. He took a quarter from his sack of money. "Could you make me change for a quarter?"

"All right," Danny Grace said, and rang up NO SALE on the cash register.

Riggs went to the machine and purchased a Coca-Cola. He rolled the bottle over his forehead and cheeks and felt himself calming.

Mr. Harley Reese followed him to the machine. "What your Momma's going to say is, Now why did my boy go off and do a robbery when I raised him up so proper never to do any robbing?"

"Watch out or I might shoot you," Riggs said.

Outside by the gas pumps Harold was blowing the horn for service. Danny Grace scowled out at him. "Can't he see this ain't the time for it?" he asked.

Mr. Harley Reese went over to the door and called, "You fill that tank up yourself, Harold! We got us a robbery in here and the man can't come out right now!"

Danny Grace cast him an approving look. "I been selling gas in this same location for thirty-six years, lacks a very few weeks of being thirty-six years, and I'll tell you, your friend is the first robber ever to come around here. Once I had a woman had an epilectric fit right there next to the Co-Cola machine, and one time a feller knocked his wife out cold out there by the gas pumps. But this here's my first robber." He looked around the interior of the station. "That was before I put in the second pump," he said.

"Is that right?" Mr. Harley Reese said.

Riggs said, "You got to see how far away from everything I am before you understand why I got to do it."

"This feller knocked his wife out cold I was saying," Danny Grace said. "Not one word of warning or nothing. Just wham! and she was laid out flat."

"Did you have to call the ambulance for that woman when she had the fit?" Mr. Harley Reese wanted to know.

"Nope. Her sister was there who knew everything what to do, and in a minute she was all right again."

"All right!" Riggs shouted. "I'm the one who's doing the robbing here, and you ain't even listening to a word I say!" He straightened his arm to its full length, placing the gun directly against Mr. Harley Reese's neck. "I'm going to shoot you now, Mr. Harley Reese, and you ain't even listening to a word I say!"

Mr. Harley Reese became worried. "What would your Momma say if you was to shoot me?"

Riggs said, "I'll shoot myself right after, and then Momma won't have a thing to say about it."

"Lord God!" Danny Grace said. "A murder and suicide!"

"Now you know you can't do that, boy," Mr. Harley Reese said. He was looking sideways and downward at Riggs' hand which was just below his chin, and he was very stiff as if he thought by becoming very stiff he might rise into the air and float away. "There ain't any forgiveness for suicide," he said. "You know what the preachers say about suicide, and murder too. There's no forgiveness. Don't you recall when Carol Jackson done it two years ago? She took them pills and the Reverend Jackson, her very own father, said, There is no forgiveness for the taking of our own lives, on account of we are all the children of God. And it was his own daughter. Jesus forgives for robbing, but he can't forgive for suiciding. Don't you want Jesus to forgive you?"

In that town when people died it was sad. But in her death Carol Jackson had lifted herself above sadness and had become almost wonderful. She had rejected Jesus, had chosen Hell over everything and had taken on the untouchable quality of those citizens who left town forever and became prosperous. Riggs said, "I don't like Jesus no more. I don't want nothing to do with a television preacher who can't even get his own congregation." Even now he felt himself rising above the lives of people. "I got to shoot you now," he said, and he pulled the trigger of his twenty-two caliber target pistol so that a barely noticeable hole appeared just beneath Mr. Harley Reese's chin. Mr. Harley Reese fell backward and his Coca-Cola bottle broke all over the floor.

Danny Grace's legs failed him and he also fell to the floor. "Oh please don't shoot me please," he said.

"I can't," Riggs said. "I got to shoot myself now." He placed the barrel of the gun against his temple, wavered a moment, thought of his Momma and fired. There was scarcely any blood, and he sat down heavily against the wall next to the Coca-Cola machine. For some time nothing else occurred, and then, outside by the gas pumps, Harold blew the horn twice.

AN INTERMEDIATE STOP

gail godwin

The vicar, just turned thirty-one, had moved quietly through his twenties engrossed in the somewhat awesome implications of his calling. In the last year of what he now referred to nostalgically as his decade of contemplation, he had stumbled upon a vision in the same natural way he'd often taken walks in the gentle mist of his countryside and come suddenly upon the form of another person and greeted him. He was astonished, then grateful. He had actually wept. Afterwards he was exhausted. Days went by before he could bring himself to record it, warily and wonderingly, first for himself and then to bear witness to others. Even as he wrote, he felt the memory of it, the way the pure thing had been, slipping away. Nevertheless, he felt he must preserve what he could.

Somewhere between the final scribbled word of the original manuscript and the dismay with which he now (aboard a Dixie Airways turbo-prop flying above red flatlands in the southern United States) regarded the picture of himself on the religion page of *Time* magazine, his tenuous visitor had fled him altogether. The vicar was left with a much-altered life, hopping around an international circuit of lecture tours (the bishop was more than pleased) which took him further and further from the auspicious state of mind which had generated that important breakthrough.

Exhibiting for his benefit a set of flawless American teeth, the stewardess now told him to be sure and fasten his seat belt. 'Bayult,' she pronounced it. Seat bayult. The trembly old turbo-prop nosed down towards a country airfield shimmering in the heat, and the captain's disembodied voice welcomed them all to Tri-City Airport, naming the cities and towns which it served, including one called Amity where the vicar was to address a small Episcopal college for women. "Present temperature is ninety-six degrees," said the captain mischievously, as though he himself might be responsible. A groan went up across the aisle from several businessmen traveling together, wearing transparent short-sleeved shirts and carrying jackets made of a weightless looking material. It was the middle of September and Lewis had brought only one suit for his three-week lecture tour: a dark flannel worsted, perfect for English Septembers.

He thanked his hostess and, still vibrating to the thrum of the rickety flight, descended shaky metal stairs into the handshake of a fat gentleman who shook his hand with prolonged zest.

"Reverend Lewis, Sir, it's an honor, a real honor. I'm Baxter Stikeleather, president of Earle College. How was the weather down there in New Orleans, hotter than here, I'll bet."

"How do you do, doctor. No, actually it seemed . . . not quite so hot."

"Aw that's 'cause they've got the Gulf Coast sitting right there under their noses, that's why," said the other. Having thus contributed to the defense of his state's climate, he whipped out a huge white handkerchief and beat at his large and genial face which was slick with perspiration.

They proceeded to the airport terminal where Stikeleather pounced on Lewis' suitcase as though it contained the Grail and led the way to the parking lot. "The girls sure have looked forward to you coming, Reverend."

"Thank you." Lewis climbed into a roomy estate wagon whose doors bore in handlettered Gothic script *Earle College for Women, founded 1889.* Stikeleather arranged his own sphere of a belly comfortably behind the steering wheel. The vicar was going over in his mind what he'd lost just this morning in the New Orleans lecture: ("Getting further is not leaving the world. It is discarding assumptions, thus seeing for the first time what is already there . . .") *What* was already there? What could he have meant? Once these words had connected him to an image, but that image was gone. He had continued glibly on this morning, as though he assumed everyone else knew what was already there, even if he didn't any more. Perhaps they did know, they seemed to know. Discussing his book with people these past few weeks, he'd had the distinct feeling that they'd tapped a dimension in it which was denied to him, its author.

". . . I haven't read it yet," Stikeleather was saying, "But I sure have read a lot about it. I've got my copy, though, I'm looking forward to really immersing myself in it once the semester gets started good. What a catchy title. *My Interview with God.* And from what I've heard, it was, wasn't it? Did you think up the title yourself?"

"No," Lewis said uncomfortably, "No, I shan't claim that little accomplishment."

"Oh well," Stikeleather reassured him, "you wrote the book. That's what counts." He struck the vicar amiably between his shoulder blades and the estate wagon belched from the parking lot in a flourish of flying gravel. "Do you like music?"

"Yes, very much," replied Lewis, puzzled.

"Coming up," the president said, fiddling with knobs on the dashboard. The moving vehicle resounded at once with a sportive melody that made Stikeleather tap his foot on the carpeted floorboard. "Total Sound," he said.

"It's very nice," said Lewis. ("Matthew's familiar Chapter Six seems at first to deal with separate subjects. It begins by talking about men who pray loudly in public rather than shut up in their own rooms, and goes on to discuss the impossibility of serving both God and Mammon. But if we look at God as Cause, or Source, and Mammon as certain outward effects, we begin to see a relation. Effects are but the reflection of something that emanates from one's own relationship with the Source. If that relationship is good—'If thine eye be single'—the effect will be full of light; if evil, full of darkness. But any deliberate intention of an effect, casting first towards Mammon with no relevance to the Source, will destroy the possibility of producing a worthwhile one. 'Every circle has its centre Where the truth is made and meant,' and no good effect can come from focusing on peripheries.") He'd preached that sermon once, in the quiet days before the Illumination and the wretched fame that followed from his poor attempt to deter its passing.

"I went uptown," Stikeleather said, "and bought up all the copies I could find. What I was thinking, after your talk tomorrow morning, you might autograph them. I'll give each trustee one and keep two in our library. I hope you'll write a little something in mine, as well."

"I'd be delighted," Lewis said, charmed by his host's refreshing simplicity. Pale Dr. Harkins, two weeks ago at Yale: walking Lewis down the path to the divinity school among first fallen leaves, he said, "You seem to be the first person inside organized religion, that is with the exception of Teilhard (naturally), to reconcile with success the old symbols and the needs of our present ontology. I have often thought our situation today, theologically, is what the *I Ching* would call Ming I (the darkening of the light); we needed your sort of Glossary to light the way again." A Jewish boy at Columbia wedged his way under Lewis' big black umbrella and, biting his nails, hurried out with him to the taxi waiting to speed the vicar to La Guardia for the Chicago flight . . . what was his major? something wild, electric, like Serbo-Croatian poetry . . . he said, "But listen, Father, haven't you in an extremely subtle way, acceptable to modern intellectuals, simply reaffirmed the Bible stories?" "I . . . I intended to *affirm*, by way of modern myths, the same truths cloaked in the ancient myths, many of which we can no longer find acceptable. I hoped to contain that Truth which remains always the same within the parallels of the old and new myths . . . if you see what I mean." "Sure, Father. God between the lines." In San Francisco, he dined one night atop the city with a Unitarian minister his own age who had published an article on the six stages of LSD. The minister found Lewis' famous Interview directly comparable to stage three of the Trip "during which there's a sudden meaningful convergence of conceptual ideas and especially meaningful combinations in the world are seen for the first time." Over brandy, the minister offered to assist Lewis in reaching stage six, "uniform white light," if he would care to accompany him back to his home. But Lewis had a morning lecture at Berkeley and declined the offer.

"I declare, I feel a whole lot better now, Reverend. There is nothing more necessary, to my way of thinking, than air-conditioning in your automobile. The trustees hemmed and hawed till I finally told them point-blank: I personally cannot drive the school station wagon until it is air-conditioned. I can't go picking up people in the name of the college and be sweating all over the place."

"It's jolly nice," agreed Lewis, feeling better himself. He looked out of the closed window at a baked clay landscape. A group of prisoners whose striped uniforms were covered with reddish dust labored desultorily in the terrible heat, monitored by a man carrying a gun. He remembered the quiet rainy garden in Sussex, outside the vicarage study window—how, looking out at this scene one totally relaxed moment after many hours of thought, he had seen suddenly beyond it into a larger, bolder kingdom. He had seen . . . he tried now to see it again, focusing intently on a memory of wet green grass, a tree, the sky as it had been, soft pearl, unblemished; he pushed hard at grass, tree, sky, so hard they fell away, leaving him with his own frowning reflection upon the closed window of the air-conditioned station wagon.

". . . Unfortunate thing. My wife has the flu, she comes down with it every fall, something in the air, the pollen. I thought it would be risky to put you up at our house, so I asked Mrs. Grimes our school nurse to fix up a private room in the infirmary for you. Parents of our girls often stay there when the hotel uptown is full. I hope you aren't offended."

"Not at all," said Lewis, "It will be a change from those motels with the huge TVs and the paper seals over the lavatories."

Stikeleather whooped with appreciation over this description until Lewis began to find it rather funny and started laughing himself.

At dinner he soon became quite sure that no faculty member had actually read his book. Nevertheless, he was the undisputed focus of solicitude. Wedged between Miss Lillian Bell, who taught history and social sciences, and Miss Evangeline Lacy (American literature, English literature and needlework), he was plied from either side with compliments, respect and much affectionate passing back and forth of crusty fried chicken and buttermilk biscuits. He felt like a young nephew who has succeeded in the outside world and comes home to coast for a time in the undemanding company of doting maiden aunts to whom his stomach is more important than his achievements.

Miss Bell was the aggressor of the two women. Fast-talking and flirtatious with leathery, crinkled skin and pierced ears, she played self-consciously with a tiny ceramic tomato bobbling from her earlobe. "We've all looked forward to this so much, Reverend," she said. "Most of our girls have never met an Englishman, let alone an English vicar."

"It is such a pleasure listening to your accent," crooned Miss Lacy, who was possibly a raving beauty in her youth. Her enormous storm-grey eyes, lashed and lustrous, peered out of her old face from another era and seemed fascinated by all they saw.

"I'm going to tell you something that will surprise you, Reverend," said Lillian Bell. "Both my father and my grandfather were Episcopal ministers. You're not just saying in your book, like some are today, that God is just energy, are you?"

"Certainly not just energy," he assured her, biting into a second chicken leg and munching busily while framing his words for further explication. He was tired beyond thought. His eyes ached when he swivelled them to note that tables full of girls openly studied him. Dr. Stikeleather had gone home to make dinner for the sick wife, leaving him the only man in the dining room. He felt suddenly exhausted by explanations of something he no longer called his own. The darkening of his light, he felt, had reached its winter solstice. He clutched at a straw, the only thing left to him in explaining himself to this good woman: a quote from one of his reviewers. He said, "The book is, well, notes towards a new consciousness which reaches beyond known systems of theology."

Miss Bell's face closed down on him. "Are you a God-is-dead man?" she asked coldly.

"No, no!" he shouted, without meaning to. All conversation stopped. All eyes were riveted on the vicar. In a near-whisper, he amended, "In my book, I try to offer a series of concepts through which persons without your fortunate religious upbringing, Miss Bell, might also have God."

"Oh, of course," said she, relieved. "I've been saying the same thing myself for years. It's our duty to share with the less fortunate. Will you have another buttermilk biscuit, Reverend?"

After dinner there was, it seemed, a coffee hour to be held in his honor. "You'll have a chance to meet our girls," said Miss Lacy, "some of them from the finest families in the state. Marguerite Earle is in her second year here."

"The Earle of the college's name?" he inquired politely. A tiny throb had set up a regular rhythm just behind his left temple.

"Dabney Littleton Earle was Marguerite's great-great-great-grandfather," explained Miss Lacy. "He was a wealthy planter and built this place as his home in the late seventeen hundreds. During the War Between the States, it was given over as a hospital for our wounded. After the war was over, unfortunately, it fell into the hands of the Freedman's Bureau who used it for their headquarters." Here she sighed sadly and her friend Miss Bell shook her earrings furiously at the outrage. "But in 1889, the Episcopal Diocese bought the property and established the college. As a matter of fact, I went here myself, but that was an awfully long time ago."

The coffee hour was in the drawing room. He stood with a whopping great headache now, backed against a faded brocade curtain, facing a semi-circle of avid ladies; holding his cup and saucer close against his chest like a tiny shield, he accepted their admiration. President Stikeleather entered suddenly. En route to Lewis, he plunged briefly into a cluster of girls long enough to pluck from it the flower of them all. Steering this elegant creature sidewise by her elbow, he cruised beaming towards the vicar.

"Reverend Lewis, may I present Miss Marguerite Earle, President of the Earle Student Body," he announced, his voice breaking with pride.

"How do you do?" said Lewis, marveling at the sheer aesthetic value of her. The flaunted English complexion paled beside this girl's pellucid sheen in which morning colors dominated. He counted five such colors in her face: honey, rose, gold, pearl and Mediterranean blue.

She took Lewis' hand in her cool one and looked up at him with deference. "I have really looked forward to this," she said. "All of us have. Won't you sit down? Let me get you another cup of coffee."

At this gentleness within such beauty, Lewis felt close to tears. Gratefully, he let himself be led to a beige settee. Stikeleather, overflowing with pleasure, stepped over to compensate the semicircle of ladies abandoned by the vicar.

Marguerite returned with his coffee and sat down. "I think it would be wonderful to live in England. Especially the English countryside. When I graduate, if I ever do, and take my trip abroad, I'm going straight to England. I love those people in Jane Austen. So relaxed and witty and tactful with one another. You know something funny, Reverend Lewis? I felt more at home reading her than I sometimes feel in real surroundings."

"I can understand that," he said. "Yours is rather a Jane Austen style. I'm a fan of hers, myself. *Emma* has always been my favorite, however, and you know one can't honestly say she was always tactful. The thing with Miss Bates, for instance, was—have I said something to upset you?"

"Oh, dear, I've only read *Pride and Prejudice*. We had it in Miss Lacy's class last spring. I didn't know there was another one. You must think I'm an idiot." The girl flushed, laced her long fingers together in confusion and looked perfectly charming.

"Not to worry," he said. "All the better, to have *Emma* ahead of you. You can go back into that world you love without waiting to graduate. There are several other books, as well. But look—a favor for me: remember when you come to Reverend—Reverend—oh, blast, what is his name. You know, Miss Earle, I have forgotten everything but my own name these past few weeks. Well, anyway, when you come to that pompous reverend somebody in *Emma*, don't believe all vicars are like him."

"Oh, whenever I think of an English vicar, I certainly won't think of *him*," she said. She wore some delicate woodsy scent that opened up long-neglected channels in his dry bachelor existence. "Will you tell us about the country homes tomorrow, and the English nobility?"

"Well, certainly if there's time. I mean—if there's time. I've been invited to give my, you know, lecture on the b-book." He paused, amazed. He had not stuttered since his Oxford days, when he'd never quite mastered the knack of smooth conversation with lovely women.

"Oh, I hope there'll be time," she said. "The girls have loads of questions. Where exactly do you live?"

"In a s-small village in Sussex, near the downs—"

"I declare I hate to disturb you all, looking so relaxed." Stikeleather stood before the settee. "But there are some who haven't met you yet, Reverend. May I borrow him for just a minute, Marguerite? I want you to meet Miss Julia Bonham, who teaches Modern Dance, Reverend." He led Lewis away, towards a fulsome lady awaiting them beside the silver service.

Having finally achieved his bed in the infirmary, he couldn't sleep. He fingered the choice of bedside reading left by Mrs. Grimes. There was a mint green *Treasury of Religious Verse,* brand new, with the price $8.95 written in pencil just inside the cover; a choice of Bibles (RSV or King James); and back issues of an inspirational pamphlet called *Forward: Day by Day.* There was a paperback book of very easy crossword puzzles, most of which had been worked in pencil, then erased. He wished violently for a novel, any novel, of Jane Austen's. Book thoughts led inevitably to consideration of his own 124-page effort, out there in the world, an object in its own right now, separate even from the thing which had inspired it, which was gone. What was that vile vicar's name in the Emma book? Pelham? Stockton? The wife with the brother-in-law in Bristol with his everlasting baroche-landau . . . when you began forgetting the villains of literature, you were definitely losing your grip.

He tried different positions: board-straight, scissors-legs, foetal. He clanked around the hospital bed like a lorryful of scrap metal. His bones strummed with phantom vibrations from the turbo-prop and under the bottom sheet was a waterproof pad which caused his feet to slide. "What a catchy title, did you think it up yourself?" ("What were you thinking of calling it, Mr. Lewis?" over a pint of bitter at the publisher's lunch. "Oh, I don't know. It's difficult to call it anything. It was what it was, simply: a very fleeting glimpse of God on His own terms, quite apart from all my previous notions of Him. I've said all I was able to say about this, er, glimpse, in my book. Why not just *View from a Sussex Vicarage*, something of the sort?" "Ah, come, Mr. Lewis, let us put our heads together over another pint and see if we can't come up with something more provocative. After all, 'Feed my Lambs' has become today a matter of first winning their appetites, has it not?") 'Every circle has its centre Where the truth is made and meant,' and no good effects will come from focusing upon peripheries. "We needed your sort of Glossary to light the way again." Going out to La Guardia in the speeding taxi, through sheets of rain, he saw the most appalling cemetery, miles and miles of dingy graves, chock-a-block . . . "Sure, Father, God between the lines." "When You're out of Schlitz, You're out of Beer," he was warned again and again on the turnpike. Blessed are the pure in heart, for they shall see . . . uniform white light? And then darkness, darkness, darkness, plenty of it. What was that damn vicar's name? Parkins, Sheldon; force it. Can a fleeting vision be seized by the tail, made to perform again and again to circus music? That perfume she was wearing . . . the Blessed Henry Suso, after seeing God, was tormented by a deep depression which lasted ten years . . . the scent reminded one of spicy green woods, hidden freshwater springs; he knew so little of women's lore, how they created their effects, yet he was not even old, thirty-one. Was this to be his dry and barren decade, his Dark Night of the Soul? (Mr. Knightley was thirty-seven when he proposed to Emma Woodhouse.) He had been so immersed in his commitment: representative of Christ on earth. Vicar, vicarius: God's deputy. No light matter. He had trod overcarefully, unsure of his right to be there at all. Had his most unsound days, then, been his most profound? Parnham, Parker, Pelton, Felpham, Farnhart, Rockwell, Brockton? Hell. Was there to be no Second Coming? He slept, then, dreamed he and Stikeleather sat under a tree in the vicarage garden, discussing how much it would cost to air-condition the vicarage. Marguerite and her friends, wearing flowing afternoon dresses to their ankles, played a lively game of croquet. Marguerite smashed a red ball CRASH! through his dusty study window, and he was alarmed, but then Stikeleather began laughing, his large belly jiggling up and down, and Lewis, infected, began to laugh, as well, until tears came into his eyes.

At breakfast, there were more of the buttermilk biscuits which one soaked in a spicy ham gravy called 'Red-eye.' Anxious about giving a lecture which had dried up on him in New Orleans, he ate too many. He signed Miss Bell's copy of *My Interview with God* feeling an impostor.

When he mounted the speaker's platform in the little chapel, everyone applauded him. Eight biscuits soaked in Red-Eye clumped stubbornly together and refused to digest. He shuffled his pile of notecards, dog-eared from fourteen other lectures, and cleared his throat. He addressed Dr. Stikeleather who was perspiring lightly in seersucker in the front row, and called every faculty member by name (there were only six). This caused another flurry of delighted clapping. He wished he might repeat the stunt with the girls, but there were too many of them; 'charming young ladies' would have to suffice.

"Well now," he began, flushing, and looking down at the first 4x6 notecard. One more time, he must give this lecture. He thought of the VC-10 which would depart tonight, with him aboard, for London.

The first notecard read:

a) Unitive life, df. state of transcendent
vitality (Underhill)
b) Luke 14:10
c) things *seen*

He failed utterly in seeing how these puzzling fragments had ever arranged themselves into an effortless, meaningful opening. Yet here he was; here they were. What, in his totally depleted hour, could he tell them? His feet, it seemed, touched down on the abyss; the light which had been darkening steadily for a year and a half now switched off. And they were waiting, with upturned faces. What to say?

Then he saw Marguerite Earle, his croquet girl, sitting by the window, her bright hair aflame like a burning bush from the morning sun, and he remembered. His Amity muse, a veritable earthly vision, shone before him in her raiments of color with the promise of a rainbow and gave him his topic. Hands folded neatly on her lap, she smiled at him, waiting to hear.

He squared his notecards with a final clack, turned them face down on the rostrum and said, "The reason I am here with you this morning is because nearly two years ago I was sitting calmly in my vicarage study, looking out on a peaceful rainy afternoon, and, being more or less at one with myself, was admitted—very temporarily—to the presence of God. Afterwards I thought I should preserve the experience by, ah, minting it, in printed words, rather like, well, your Treasury Department distributing the late President Kennedy on silver half-dollars. Only they never for a moment, I am sure, fooled themselves into thinking they were giving away with that coin the essence of the man. It was only a tribute, don't you see, in the same way that my book can only be a tribute to a very special happening. St. Thomas Aquinas once said, long after he'd completed his ponderous Summa, 'There are some things that simply cannot be uttered,' after which he serenely folded his hands over his great stomach and spent his last years elevated three feet off the ground in rapturous prayer. Can you not see it, that great portly body floating like a thistle by the Grace of God?"

(There was a short hush during which his audience teetered between respect for a dead saint and amusement at the spectacle of a floating fat one . . . then Stikeleather broke the tie by laughing heartily and they all followed suit.)

"Well, then," Lewis said, a bit breathless, standing naked before them now, a man like any other, no vision standing between them, "Rather than try and give you a third-hand rendition of a faded illumination, or to go over material which is there for better or for worse in a little green and white volume which my publishers call *My Interview with God*, I'd like to return your hospitality to me by taking you briefly into my own world. What shall I show you first? Shall we start with where I live, my vicarage in Sussex which is five hundred years old?"

Their enthusiastic answer rang out. Marguerite Earle began clapping and they joined her. So he took them first into his study, lined with over four-thousand books, many belonging to past vicars dead several hundred years, and warmed even in summer by a fireplace. He led them up narrow circular stairs to his *pièce de resistance*, the loft under the eaves where, in the 1640's, it was rumored that a Royalist vicar had once hidden Charles II from his murderous pursuers. They adored this. He took them to his garden, blushing when he said, "Large enough f-for, um, a game of croquet." In summer, he told them, the Queen's orange-braceleted swans swim upriver and come waddling boldly in the garden at teatime . . .

He took them on a Cook's tour of London; then, for the benefit of Marguerite, who loved the countryside, he returned them to Sussex Downs for a ramble. It was while lingering there, relaxed and at one with his happy group, in this dreamy country air that he remembered his old friend Mr. Elton, petty vicar of Highbury. Elton, Elton, Elton, of course! He lightened, began the upward trip from his abyss, as though St. Thomas the old dog himself had loaned him a bit of divine buoyancy. Eight buttermilk biscuits melted like hosts in his stomach. Elton! Spouse of Augusta Hawkins for the sum of ten-thousand. Hypocrite, flatterer, pompous ass. Lewis had never been so glad to see anyone in his life. His universe expanded as the dark began to fade. He chuckled aloud in the midst of his guided tour. Agreeably, in a body, Earle College chuckled too, for they were with him.

KING OF THE BINGO GAME
ralph ellison

The woman in front of him was eating roasted peanuts that smelled so good that he could barely contain his hunger. He could not even sleep and wished they'd hurry and begin the bingo game. There, on his right, two fellows were drinking wine out of a bottle wrapped in a paper bag, and he could hear soft gurgling in the dark. His stomach gave a low, gnawing growl. "If this was down South," he thought, "all I'd have to do is lean over and say, 'Lady, gimme a few of those peanuts, please ma'm,' and she'd pass me the bag and never think nothing of it." Or he could ask the fellows for a drink in the same way. Folks down South stuck together that way; they didn't even have to know you. But up here it was different. Ask somebody for something, and they'd think you were crazy. Well, I ain't crazy. I'm just broke, 'cause I got no birth certificate to get a job, and Laura 'bout to die 'cause we got no money for a doctor. But I ain't crazy. And yet a pinpoint of doubt was focused in his mind as he glanced toward the screen and saw the hero stealthily entering a dark room and sending the beam of a flashlight along a wall of bookcases. This is where he finds the trapdoor, he remembered. The man would pass abruptly through the wall and find the girl tied to a bed, her legs and arms spread wide, and her clothing torn to rags. He laughed softly to himself. He had seen the picture three times, and this was one of the best scenes.

On his right the fellow whispered wide-eyed to his companion, "Man, look a-yonder!"

"Damn!"

"Wouldn't I like to have her tied up like that . . ."

"Hey! That fool's letting her loose!"

"Aw, man, he loves her."

"Love or no love!"

The man moved impatiently beside him, and he tried to involve himself in the scene. But Laura was on his mind. Tiring quickly of watching the picture he looked back to where the white beam filtered from the projection room above the balcony. It started small and grew large, specks of dust dancing in its whiteness as it reached the screen. It was strange how the beam always landed right on the screen and didn't mess up and fall somewhere else. But they had it all fixed. Everything was fixed. Now suppose when they showed that girl with her dress torn the girl started taking off the rest of her clothes, and when the guy came in he didn't untie her but kept her there and went to taking off his own clothes? *That* would be something to see. If a picture got out of hand like that those guys up there would go nuts. Yeah, and there'd be so many folks in here you couldn't find a seat for nine months! A strange sensation played over his skin. He shuddered. Yesterday he'd seen a bedbug on a woman's neck as they walked out into the bright street. But exploring his thigh through a hole in his pocket he found only goose pimples and old scars.

The bottle gurgled again. He closed his eyes. Now a dreamy music was accompanying the film and train whistles were sounding in the distance, and he was a boy again walking along a railroad trestle down South, and seeing the train coming, and running back as fast as he could go, and hearing the whistle blowing, and getting off the trestle to solid ground just in time, with the earth trembling beneath his feet, and feeling relieved as he ran down the cinder-strewn embankment onto the highway, and looking back and seeing with terror that the train had left the track and was following him right down the middle of the street, and all the white people laughing as he ran screaming . . .

"Wake up there, buddy! What the hell do you mean hollering like that? Can't you see we trying to enjoy this here picture?"

He stared at the man with gratitude.

"I'm sorry, old man," he said. "I musta been dreaming."

"Well, here, have a drink. And don't be making no noise like that, damn!"

His hands trembled as he tilted his head. It was not wine, but whiskey. Cold rye whiskey. He took a deep swoller, decided it was better not to take another, and handed the bottle back to its owner.

"Thanks, old man," he said.

Now he felt the cold whiskey breaking a warm path straight through the middle of him, growing hotter and sharper as it moved. He had not eaten all day, and it made him light-headed. The smell of the peanuts stabbed him like a knife, and he got up and found a seat in the middle aisle. But no sooner did he sit than he saw a row of intense-faced young girls, and got up again, thinking, "You chicks musta been Lindy-hopping somewhere." He found a seat several rows ahead as the lights came on, and he saw the screen disappear behind a heavy red and gold curtain; then the curtain rising, and the man with the microphone and a uniformed attendant coming on the stage.

He felt for his bingo cards, smiling. The guy at the door wouldn't like it if he knew about his having *five* cards. Well, not everyone played the bingo game; and even with five cards he didn't have much of a chance. For Laura, though, he had to have faith. He studied the cards, each with its different numerals, punching the free center hole in each and spreading them neatly across his lap; and when the lights faded he sat slouched in his seat so that he could look from his cards to the bingo wheel with but a quick shifting of his eyes.

Ahead, at the end of the darkness, the man with the microphone was pressing a button attached to a long cord and spinning the bingo wheel and calling out the number each time the wheel came to rest. And each time the voice rang out his finger raced over the cards for the number. With five cards he had to move fast. He became nervous; there were too many cards, and the man went too fast with his grating voice. Perhaps he should just select one and throw the others away. But he was afraid. He became warm. Wonder how much Laura's doctor would cost? Damn that, watch the cards! And with despair he heard the man call three in a row which he missed on all five cards. This way he'd never win . . .

When he saw the row of holes punched across the third card, he sat paralyzed and heard the man call three more numbers before he stumbled forward, screaming,

"Bingo! Bingo!"

"Let that fool up there," someone called.

"Get up there, man!"

He stumbled down the aisle and up the steps to the stage into a light so sharp and bright that for a moment it blinded him, and he felt that he had moved into the spell of some strange, mysterious power. Yet it was as familiar as the sun, and he knew it was the perfectly familiar bingo.

The man with the microphone was saying something to the audience as he held out his card. A cold light flashed from the man's finger as the card left his hand. His knees trembled. The man stepped closer, checking the card against the numbers chalked on the board. Suppose he had made a mistake? The pomade on the man's hair made him feel faint, and he backed away. But the man was checking the card over the microphone now, and he had to stay. He stood tense, listening.

"Under the O, forty-four," the man chanted. "Under the I, seven. Under the G, three. Under the B, ninety-six. Under the N, thirteen!"

His breath came easier as the man smiled at the audience.

"Yessir, ladies and gentlemen, he's one of the chosen people!"

The audience rippled with laughter and applause.

"Step right up to the front of the stage."

He moved slowly forward, wishing that the light was not so bright.

"To win tonight's jackpot of $36.90 the wheel must stop between the double zero, understand?"

He nodded, knowing the ritual from the many days and nights he had watched the winners march across the stage to press the button that controlled the spinning wheel and receive the prizes. And now he followed the instructions as though he'd crossed the slippery stage a million prize-winning times.

The man was making some kind of a joke, and he nodded vacantly. So tense had he become that he felt a sudden desire to cry and shook it away. He felt vaguely that his whole life was determined by the bingo wheel; not only that which would happen now that he was at last before it, but all that had gone before, since his birth, and his mother's birth and the birth of his father. It had always been there, even though he had not been aware of it, handing out the unlucky cards and numbers of his days. The feeling persisted, and he started quickly away. I better get down from here before I make a fool of myself, he thought.

"Here, boy," the man called. "You haven't started yet."

Someone laughed as he went hesitantly back.

"Are you all reet?"

He grinned at the man's jive talk, but no words would come, and he knew it was not a convincing grin. For suddenly he knew that he stood on the slippery brink of some terrible embarrassment.

"Where are you from, boy?" the man asked.

"Down South."

"He's from down South, ladies and gentlemen," the man said. "Where from? Speak right into the mike."

"Rocky Mont," he said. "Rock' Mont, North Car'lina."

"So you decided to come down off that mountain to the U.S.," the man laughed. He felt that the man was making a fool of him, but then something cold was placed in his hand, and the lights were no longer behind him.

Standing before the wheel he felt alone, but that was somehow right, and he remembered his plan. He would give the wheel a short quick whirl. Just a touch of the button. He had watched it many times, and always it came close to double zero when it was short and quick. He steeled himself; the fear had left, and he felt a profound sense of promise, as though he were about to be repaid for all the things he'd suffered all his life. Trembling, he pressed the button. There was a whirl of lights, and in a second he realized with finality that though he wanted to, he could not stop. It was as though he held a high-powered line in his naked hand. His nerves tightened. As the wheel increased its speed it seemed to draw him more and more into its power, as though it held his fate; and with it came a deep need to submit, to whirl, to lose himself in its swirl of color. He could not stop it now, he knew. So let it be.

The button rested snugly in his palm where the man had placed it. And now he became aware of the man beside him, advising him through the microphone, while behind the shadowy audience hummed with noisy voices. He shifted his feet. There was still that feeling of helplessness within him, making part of him desire to turn back, even now that the jackpot was right in his hand. He squeezed the button until his fist ached. Then, like the sudden shriek of a subway whistle, a doubt tore through his head. Suppose he did not spin the wheel long enough? What could he do, and how could he tell? And then he knew, even as he wondered, that as long as he pressed the button, he could control the jackpot. He and only he could determine whether or not it was to be his. Not even the man with the microphone could do anything about it now. He felt drunk. Then, as though he had come down from a high hill into a valley of people, he heard the audience yelling.

"Come down from there, you jerk!"

"Let somebody else have a chance . . ."

"Ole Jack thinks he done found the end of the rainbow . . ."

The last voice was not unfriendly, and he turned and smiled dreamily into the yelling mouths. Then he turned his back squarely on them.

"Don't take too long, boy," a voice said.

He nodded. They were yelling behind him. Those folks did not understand what had happened to him. They had been playing the bingo game day in and night out for years, trying to win rent money or hamburger change. But not one of those wise guys had discovered this wonderful thing. He watched the wheel whirling past the numbers and experienced a burst of exaltation: This is God! This is the really truly God! He said it aloud, "This is God!"

He said it with such absolute conviction that he feared he would fall fainting into the footlights. But the crowd yelled so loud that they could not hear. Those fools, he thought. I'm here trying to tell them the most wonderful secret in the world, and they're yelling like they gone crazy. A hand fell upon his shoulder.

"You'll have to make a choice now, boy. You've taken too long."

He brushed the hand violently away.

"Leave me alone, man. I know what I'm doing!"

The man looked surprised and held on to the microphone for support. And because he did not wish to hurt the man's feelings he smiled, realizing with a sudden pang that there was no way of explaining to the man just why he had to stand there pressing the button forever.

"Come here," he called tiredly.

The man approached, rolling the heavy microphone across the stage.

"Anybody can play this bingo game, right?" he said.

"Sure, but . . ."

He smiled, feeling inclined to be patient with this slick looking white man with his blue sport shirt and his sharp gabardine suit.

"That's what I thought," he said. "Anybody can win the jackpot as long as they get the lucky number, right?"

"That's the rule, but after all . . ."

"That's what I thought," he said. "And the big prize goes to the man who knows how to win it?"

The man nodded speechlessly.

"Well then, go on over there and watch me win like I want to. I ain't going to hurt nobody," he said, "and I'll show you how to win. I mean to show the whole world how it's got to be done."

And because he understood, he smiled again to let the man know that he held nothing against him for being white and impatient. Then he refused to see the man any longer and stood pressing the button, the voices of the crowd reaching him like sounds in distant streets. Let them yell. All the Negroes down there were just ashamed because he was black like them. He smiled inwardly, knowing how it was. Most of the time he was ashamed of what Negroes did himself. Well, let them be ashamed for something this time. Like him. He was like a long thin black wire that was being stretched and wound upon the bingo wheel; wound until he wanted to scream; wound, but this time himself controlling the winding and the sadness and the shame, and because he did, Laura would be all right. Suddenly the lights flickered. He staggered backwards. Had something gone wrong? All this noise. Didn't they know that although he controlled the wheel, it also controlled him, and unless he pressed the button forever and forever and ever it would stop, leaving him high and dry, dry and high on this hard high slippery hill and Laura dead? There was only one chance; he had to do whatever the wheel demanded. And gripping the button in despair, he discovered with surprise that it imparted a nervous energy. His spine tingled. He felt a certain power.

Now he faced the raging crowd with defiance, its screams penetrating his eardrums like trumpets shrieking from a jukebox. The vague faces glowing in the bingo lights gave him a sense of himself that he had never known before. He was running the show, by God! They had to react to him, for he was their luck. This is *me*, he thought. Let the bastards yell. Then someone was laughing inside him, and he realized that somehow he had forgotten his own name. It was a sad, lost feeling to lose your name, and a crazy thing to do. That name had been given him by the white man who had owned his grandfather a long lost time ago down South. But maybe those wise guys knew his name.

"Who am I?" he screamed.

"Hurry up and bingo, you jerk!"

They didn't know either, he thought sadly. They didn't even know their own names, they were all poor nameless bastards. Well, he didn't need that old name; he was reborn. For as long as he pressed the button he was The-man-who-pressed-the-button-who-held-the-prize-who-was-the-King-of-Bingo. That was the way it was, and he'd have to press the button even if nobody understood, even though Laura did not understand.

"Live!" he shouted.

The audience quieted like the dying of a huge fan.

"Live, Laura, baby. I got holt of it now, sugar. Live!"

He screamed it, tears streaming down his face. "I got nobody but YOU!"

The screams tore from his very guts. He felt as though the rush of blood to his head would burst out in baseball seams of small red droplets, like a head beaten by police clubs. Bending over he saw a trickle of blood splashing the toe of his shoe. With his free hand he searched his head. It was his nose. God, suppose something has gone wrong? He felt that the whole audience had somehow entered him and was stamping its feet in his stomach, and he was unable to throw them out. They wanted the prize, that was it. They wanted the secret for themselves. But they'd never get it; he would keep the bingo wheel whirling forever, and Laura would be safe in the wheel. But would she? It had to be, because if she were not safe the wheel would cease to turn; it could not go on. He had to get away, *vomit* all, and his mind formed an image of himself running with Laura in his arms down the tracks of the subway just ahead of an A train, running desperately *vomit* with people screaming for him to come out but knowing no way of leaving the tracks because to stop would bring the train crushing down upon him and to attempt to leave across the other tracks would mean to run into a hot third rail as high as his waist which threw blue sparks that blinded his eyes until he could hardly see.

He heard singing and the audience was clapping its hands.

Shoot the liquor to him, Jim, boy!
Clap-clap-clap
Well a-calla the cop
He's blowing his top!
Shoot the liquor to him, Jim, boy!

Bitter anger grew within him at the singing. They think I'm crazy. Well let 'em laugh. I'll do what I got to do.

He was standing in an attitude of intense listening when he saw that they were watching something on the stage behind him. He felt weak. But when he turned he saw no one. If only his thumb did not ache so. Now they were applauding. And for a moment he thought that the wheel had stopped. But that was impossible, his thumb still pressed the button. Then he saw them. Two men in uniform beckoned from the end of the stage. They were coming toward him, walking in step, slowly, like a tap-dance team returning for a third encore. But their shoulders shot forward, and he backed away, looking wildly about. There was nothing to fight them with. He had only the long black cord which led to a plug somewhere back stage, and he couldn't use that because it operated the bingo wheel. He backed slowly, fixing the men with his eyes as his lips stretched over his teeth in a tight, fixed grin; moved toward the end of the stage and realizing that he couldn't go much further, for suddenly the cord became taut and he couldn't afford to break the cord. But he had to do something. The audience was howling. Suddenly he stopped dead, seeing the men halt, their legs lifted as in an interrupted step of a slow-motion dance. There was nothing to do but run in the other direction and he dashed forward, slipping and sliding. The men fell back, surprised. He struck out violently going past.

"Grab him!"

He ran, but all too quickly the cord tightened, resistingly, and he turned and ran back again. This time he slipped them, and discovered by running in a circle before the wheel he could keep the cord from tightening. But this way he had to flail his arms to keep the men away. Why couldn't they leave a man alone? He ran, circling.

"Ring down the curtain," someone yelled. But they couldn't do that. If they did the wheel flashing from the projection room would be cut off. But they had him before he could tell them so, trying to pry open his fist, and he was wrestling and trying to bring his knees into the fight and holding on to the button, for it was his life. And now he was down, seeing a foot coming down, crushing his wrist cruelly, down, as he saw the wheel whirling serenely above.

"I can't give it up," he screamed. Then quietly, in a confidential tone, "Boys, I really can't give it up."

It landed hard against his head. And in the blank moment they had it away from him, completely now. He fought them trying to pull him up from the stage as he watched the wheel spin slowly to a stop. Without surprise he saw it rest at double-zero.

"You see," he pointed bitterly.

"Sure, boy, sure, it's O. K.," one of the men said smiling.

And seeing the man bow his head to someone he could not see, he felt very, very happy; he would receive what all the winners received.

But as he warmed in the justice of the man's tight smile he did not see the man's slow wink, nor see the bow-legged man behind him step clear of the swiftly descending curtain and set himself for a blow. He only felt the dull pain exploding in his skull, and he knew even as it slipped out of him that his luck had run out on the stage.

THE BOUND MAN
ilse aichinger

Sunlight on his face woke him, but made him shut his eyes again;
it streamed unhindered down the slope, collected itself into rivulets,
attracted swarms of flies, which flew low over his forehead, circled,
sought to land, and were overtaken by fresh swarms. When he
tried to whisk them away, he discovered that he was bound. A thin
rope cut into his arms. He dropped them, opened his eyes again,
and looked down at himself. His legs were tied all the way up to his
thighs; a single length of rope was tied around his ankles, criss-
crossed up his legs, and encircled his hips, his chest and his arms.
He could not see where it was knotted. He showed no sign of fear
or hurry, though he thought he was unable to move, until he discovered that the rope allowed his legs some free play and that round
his body it was almost loose. His arms were tied to each other but
not to his body, and had some free play too. This made him smile,
and it occurred to him that perhaps children had been playing a
practical joke on him.

He tried to feel for his knife, but again the rope cut softly into
his flesh. He tried again, more cautiously this time, but his pocket
was empty. Not only his knife, but the little money that he had on

him, as well as his coat, were missing. His shoes had been pulled from his feet and taken too. When he moistened his lips he tasted blood, which had flowed from his temples down his cheeks, his chin, his neck, and under his shirt. His eyes were painful; if he kept them open for long he saw reddish stripes in the sky.

He decided to stand up. He drew his knees up as far as he could, rested his hands on the fresh grass and jerked himself to his feet. An elder-branch stroked his cheek, the sun dazzled him, and the rope cut into his flesh. He collapsed to the ground again, half out of his mind with pain, and then tried again. He went on trying until the blood started flowing from his hidden weals. Then he lay still again for a long while and let the sun and the flies do what they liked.

When he awoke for the second time the elder-bush had cast its shadow over him, and the coolness stored in it was pouring from between its branches. He must have been hit on the head. Then they must have laid him down carefully, just as a mother lays her baby behind a bush when she goes to work in the fields.

His chances all lay in the amount of free play allowed him by the rope. He dug his elbows into the ground and tested it. As soon as the rope tautened he stopped, and tried again more cautiously. If he had been able to reach the branch over his head he could have used it to drag himself to his feet, but he could not reach it. He laid his head back on the grass, rolled over, and struggled to his knees. He tested the ground with his toes, and then managed to stand up almost without effort.

A few paces away lay the path across the plateau, and in the grass were wild pinks and thistles in bloom. He tried to lift his foot to avoid trampling on them, but the rope round his ankles prevented him. He looked down at himself.

The rope was knotted at his ankles, and ran round his legs in a kind of playful pattern. He carefully bent and tried to loosen it, but, loose though it seemed to be, he could not make it any looser. To avoid treading on the thistles with his bare feet he hopped over them like a bird.

The cracking of a twig made him stop. People in this district were very prone to laughter. He was alarmed by the thought that he was in no position to defend himself. He hopped on until he reached the path. Bright fields stretched far below. He could see no sign of the nearest village, and if he could move no faster than this, night would fall before he reached it.

He tried walking, and discovered that he could put one foot before another if he lifted each foot a definite distance from the ground and then put it down again before the rope tautened. In the same way he could actually swing his arms a little.

After the first step he fell. He fell right across the path, and made the dust fly. He expected this to be a sign for the long-suppressed laughter to break out, but all remained quiet. He was alone. As soon as the dust had settled he got up and went on. He looked down and watched the rope slacken, grow taut, and then slacken again.

When the first glow-worms appeared he managed to look up. He felt in control of himself again, and his impatience to reach the nearest village faded.

Hunger made him light-headed, and he seemed to be going so fast that not even a motor-cycle could have overtaken him; alternatively he felt as if he were standing still and that the earth was rushing past him, like a river flowing past a man swimming against the stream. The stream carried branches which had been bent southward by the north wind, stunted young trees, and patches of grass with bright, long-stalked flowers. It ended by submerging the bushes and the young trees, leaving only the sky and the man above water-level. The moon had risen, and illuminated the bare, curved summit of the plateau, the path, which was overgrown with young grass, the bound man making his way along it with quick, measured steps, and two hares, which ran across the hill just in front of him and vanished down the slope. Though the nights were still cool at this time of the year, before midnight the bound man lay down at the edge of the escarpment and went to sleep.

In the light of morning the animal-tamer who was camping with his circus in the field outside the village saw the bound man coming down the path, gazing thoughtfully at the ground. The bound man stopped and bent down. He held out one arm to help keep his balance and with the other picked up an empty wine-bottle. Then he straightened himself and stood erect again. He moved slowly, to avoid being cut by the rope, but to the circus proprietor what he did suggested the voluntary limitation of an enormous swiftness of movement. He was enchanted by its extraordinary gracefulness, and while the bound man looked about for a stone on which to break the bottle, so that he could use the splintered neck to cut the rope, the animal-tamer walked across the field and approached him. The first leaps of a young panther had never filled him with such delight.

"Ladies and gentlemen, the bound man!" His very first movements let loose a storm of applause, which out of sheer excitement caused the blood to rush to the cheeks of the animal-tamer standing at the edge of the arena. The bound man rose to his feet. His surprise whenever he did this was like that of a four-footed animal which has managed to stand on its hind-legs. He knelt, stood up, jumped, and turned cart-wheels. The spectators found it as astonishing as if they had seen a bird which voluntarily remained earthbound, and confined itself to hopping.

The bound man became an enormous draw. His absurd steps and little jumps, his elementary exercises in movement, made the rope-dancer superfluous. His fame grew from village to village, but the motions he went through were few and always the same; they were really quite ordinary motions, which he had continually to practice in the daytime in the half-dark tent in order to retain his shackled freedom. In that he remained entirely within the limits set by his rope he was free of it, it did not confine him, but gave him wings and endowed his leaps and jumps with purpose; just as the flights of birds of passage have purpose when they take wing in the warmth of summer and hesitantly make small circles in the sky.

All the children of the neighborhood started playing the game of "bound man." They formed rival gangs, and one day the circus people found a little girl lying bound in a ditch, with a cord tied round her neck so that she could hardly breathe. They released her, and at the end of the performance that night the bound man made a speech. He announced briefly that there was no sense in being tied up in such a way that you could not jump. After that he was regarded as a comedian.

Grass and sunlight, tent-pegs driven into the ground and then pulled up again, and on to the next village. "Ladies and gentlemen, the bound man!" The summer mounted toward its climax. It bent its face deeper over the fish-ponds in the hollows, taking delight in its dark reflection, skimmed the surface of the rivers, and made the plain into what it was. Everyone who could walk went to see the bound man.

Many wanted a close-up view of how he was bound. So the circus proprietor announced after each performance that anyone who wanted to satisfy himself that the knots were real and the rope not made of rubber was at liberty to do so. The bound man generally waited for the crowd in the area outside the tent. He laughed or remained serious, and held out his arms for inspection. Many took the opportunity to look him in the face, others gravely tested the rope, tried the knots on his ankles, and wanted to know exactly how the lengths compared with the length of his limbs. They asked him how he had come to be tied up like that, and he answered patiently, always saying the same thing. Yes, he had been tied up, he said, and when he awoke he found that he had been robbed as well. Those who had done it must have been pressed for time, because they had tied him up somewhat too loosely for someone who was not supposed to be able to move and somewhat too tightly for someone who was expected to be able to move. But he did move, people pointed out. Yes, he replied, what else could he do?

Before he went to bed he always sat for a time in front of the fire. When the circus proprietor asked him why he didn't make up a better story he always answered that he hadn't made up that one, and blushed. He preferred staying in the shade.

The difference between him and the other performers was that when the show was over he did not take off his rope. The result was that every movement that he made was worth seeing, and the villagers used to hang about the camp for hours, just for the sake of seeing him get up from in front of the fire and roll himself in his blanket. Sometimes the sky was beginning to lighten when he saw their shadows disappear.

The circus proprietor often remarked that there was no reason why he should not be untied after the evening performance and tied up again next day. He pointed out that the rope-dancers, for instance, did not stay on their rope overnight. But no one took the idea of untying him seriously.

For the bound man's fame rested on the fact that he was always bound, that whenever he washed himself he had to wash his clothes too and vice versa, and that his only way of doing so was to jump in the river just as he was every morning when the sun came out, and that he had to be careful not to go too far out for fear of being carried away by the stream.

The proprietor was well aware that what in the last resort protected the bound man from the jealousy of the other performers was his helplessness; he deliberately left them the pleasure of watching him groping painfully from stone to stone on the river bank every morning with his wet clothes clinging to him. When the proprietor's wife pointed out that even the best clothes would not stand up indefinitely to such treatment (and the bound man's clothes were by no means of the best), he replied curtly that it was not going to last forever. That was his answer to all objections— it was for the summer season only. But when he said this he was not being serious; he was talking like a gambler who has no intention of giving up his vice. In reality he would have been prepared cheerfully to sacrifice his lions and his rope-dancers for the bound man.

He proved this on the night when the rope-dancers jumped over the fire. Afterward he was convinced that they did it, not because it was midsummer's day, but because of the bound man, who as usual was lying and watching them with that peculiar smile that might have been real or might have been only the effect of the glow on his face. In any case no one knew anything about him because he never talked about anything that had happened to him before he emerged from the wood that day.

But that evening two of the performers suddenly picked him up by the arms and legs, carried him to the edge of the fire and started playfully swinging him to and fro, while two others held out their arms to catch him on the other side. In the end they threw him, but too short. The two men on the other side drew back—they explained afterward that they did so the better to take the shock. The result was that the bound man landed at the very edge of the flames and would have been burned if the circus proprietor had not seized his arms and quickly dragged him away to save the rope which was starting to get singed. He was certain that the object had been to burn the rope. He sacked the four men on the spot.

A few nights later the proprietor's wife was awakened by the sound of footsteps on the grass, and went outside just in time to prevent the clown from playing his last practical joke. He was carrying a pair of scissors. When he was asked for an explanation he insisted that he had had no intention of taking the bound man's life, but only wanted to cut his rope because he felt sorry for him. He was sacked too.

These antics amused the bound man because he could have freed himself if he had wanted to whenever he liked, but perhaps he wanted to learn a few new jumps first. The children's rhyme: "We travel with the circus, we travel with the circus" sometimes occurred to him while he lay awake at night. He could hear the voices of spectators on the opposite bank who had been driven too far downstream on the way home. He could see the river gleaming in the moonlight, and the young shoots growing out of the thick tops of the willow trees, and did not think about autumn yet.

The circus proprietor dreaded the danger that sleep involved for the bound man. Attempts were continually made to release him while he slept. The chief culprits were sacked rope-dancers, or children who were bribed for the purpose. But measures could be taken to safeguard against these. A much bigger danger was that which he represented to himself. In his dreams he forgot his rope, and was surprised by it when he woke in the darkness of morning. He would angrily try to get up, but lose his balance and fall back again. The previous evening's applause was forgotten, sleep was still too near, his head and neck too free. He was just the opposite of a hanged man—his neck was the only part of him that was free. You had to make sure that at such moments no knife was within his reach. In the early hours of the morning the circus proprietor sometimes sent his wife to see whether the bound man was all right. If he was asleep she would bend over him and feel the rope. It had grown hard from dirt and damp. She would test the amount of free play it allowed him, and touch his tender wrists and ankles.

The most varied rumors circulated about the bound man. Some said he had tied himself up and invented the story of having been robbed, and toward the end of the summer that was the general opinion. Others maintained that he had been tied up at his own request, perhaps in league with the circus proprietor. The hesitant way in which he told his story, his habit of breaking off when the talk got round to the attack on him, contributed greatly to these rumors. Those who still believed in the robbery-with-violence story were laughed at. Nobody knew what difficulties the circus proprietor had in keeping the bound man, and how often he said he had had enough and wanted to clear off, for too much of the summer had passed.

Later, however, he stopped talking about clearing off. When the proprietor's wife brought him his food by the river and asked him how long he proposed to remain with them, he did not answer. She thought he had got used, not to being tied up, but to remembering every moment that he was tied up—the only thing that anyone in his position could get used to. She asked him whether he did not think it ridiculous to be tied up all the time, but he answered that he did not. Such a variety of people—clowns, freaks, and comics, to say nothing of elephants and tigers—traveled with circuses that he did not see why a bound man should not travel with a circus too. He told her about the movements he was practicing, the new ones he had discovered, and about a new trick that had occurred to him while he was whisking flies from the animals' eyes. He described to her how he always anticipated the effect of the rope and always restrained his movements in such a way as to prevent it from ever tautening; and she knew that there were days when he was hardly aware of the rope, when he jumped down from the wagon and slapped the flanks of the horses in the morning as if he were moving in a dream. She watched him vault over the bars almost without touching them, and saw the sun on his face, and he told her that sometimes he felt as if he were not tied up at all. She answered that if he were prepared to be untied, there would never be any need for him to feel tied up. He agreed that he could be untied whenever he felt like it.

The woman ended by not knowing whether she was more concerned with the man or with the rope that tied him. She told him that he could go on traveling with the circus without his rope, but she did not believe it. For what would be the point of his antics without his rope, and what would he amount to without it? Without his rope he would leave them, and the happy days would be over. She would no longer be able to sit beside him on the stones by the river without arousing suspicion, and she knew that his continued presence, and her conversations with him, of which the rope was the only subject, depended on it. Whenever she agreed that the rope had its advantages, he would start talking about how troublesome it was, and whenever he started talking about its advantages, she would urge him to get rid of it. All this seemed as endless as the summer itself.

At other times she was worried at the thought that she was herself hastening the end by her talk. Sometimes she would get up in the middle of the night and run across the grass to where he slept. She wanted to shake him, wake him up and ask him to keep the rope. But then she would see him lying there; he had thrown off his blanket, and there he lay like a corpse, with his legs outstretched and his arms close together, with the rope tied round them. His clothes had suffered from the heat and the water, but the rope had grown no thinner. She felt that he would go on traveling with the circus until the flesh fell from him and exposed the joints. Next morning she would plead with him more ardently than ever to get rid of his rope.

The increasing coolness of the weather gave her hope. Autumn was coming, and he would not be able to go on jumping into the river with his clothes on much longer. But the thought of losing his rope, about which he had felt indifferent earlier in the season, now depressed him.

The songs of the harvesters filled him with foreboding. "Summer has gone, summer has gone." But he realized that soon he would have to change his clothes, and he was certain that when he had been untied it would be impossible to tie him up again in exactly the same way. About this time the proprietor started talking about traveling south that year.

The heat changed without transition into quiet, dry cold, and the fire was kept going all day long. When the bound man jumped down from the wagon he felt the coldness of the grass under his feet. The stalks were bent with ripeness. The horses dreamed on their feet and the wild animals, crouching to leap even in their sleep, seemed to be collecting gloom under their skins which would break out later.

On one of these days a young wolf escaped. The circus proprietor kept quiet about it, to avoid spreading alarm, but the wolf soon started raiding cattle in the neighborhood. People at first believed that the wolf had been driven to these parts by the prospect of a severe winter, but the circus soon became suspect. The proprietor could not conceal the loss of the animal from his own employees, so the truth was bound to come out before long. The circus people offered the burgomasters of the neighboring villages their aid in tracking down the beast, but all their efforts were in vain. Eventually the circus was openly blamed for the damage and the danger, and spectators stayed away.

The bound man went on performing before half-empty seats without losing anything of his amazing freedom of movement. During the day he wandered among the surrounding hills under the thin-beaten silver of the autumn sky, and, whenever he could, lay down where the sun shone longest. Soon he found a place which the twilight reached last of all, and when at last it reached him he got up most unwillingly from the withered grass. In coming down the hill he had to pass through a little wood on its southern slope, and one evening he saw the gleam of two little green lights. He knew that they came from no church window, and was not for a moment under any illusion about what they were.

He stopped. The animal came toward him through the thinning foliage. He could make out its shape, the slant of its neck, its tail which swept the ground, and its receding head. If he had not been bound, perhaps he would have tried to run away, but as it was he did not even feel fear. He stood calmly with dangling arms and looked down at the wolf's bristling coat under which the muscles played like his own underneath the rope. He thought the evening wind was still between him and the wolf when the beast sprang. The man took care to obey his rope.

Moving with the deliberate care that he had so often put to the test, he seized the wolf by the throat. Tenderness for a fellow-creature arose in him, tenderness for the upright being concealed in the four-footed. In a movement that resembled the drive of a great bird (he felt a sudden awareness that flying would be possible only if one were tied up in a special way) he flung himself at the animal and brought it to the ground. He felt a slight elation at having lost the fatal advantage of free limbs which causes men to be worsted.

The freedom he enjoyed in this struggle was having to adapt every moment of his limbs to the rope that tied him—the freedom of panthers, wolves, and the wild flowers that sway in the evening breeze. He ended up lying obliquely down the slope, clasping the animal's hind-legs between his own bare feet and its head between his hands. He felt the gentleness of the faded foliage stroking the backs of his hands, and he felt his own grip almost effortlessly reaching its maximum, and he felt too how he was in no way hampered by the rope.

As he left the wood light rain began to fall and obscured the setting sun. He stopped for a while under the trees at the edge of the wood. Beyond the camp and the river he saw the fields where the cattle grazed, and the places where they crossed. Perhaps he would travel south with the circus after all. He laughed softly. It was against all reason. Even if he continued to put up with the sores that covered his joints and opened and bled when he made certain movements, his clothes would not stand up much longer to the friction of the rope.

The circus proprietor's wife tried to persuade her husband to announce the death of the wolf without mentioning that it had been killed by the bound man. She said that even at the time of his greatest popularity people would have refused to believe him capable of it, and in their present angry mood, with the nights getting cooler, they would be more incredulous than ever. The wolf had attacked a group of children at play that day, and nobody would believe that it had really been killed; for the circus proprietor had many wolves, and it was easy enough for him to hang a skin on the rail and allow free entry. But he was not to be dissuaded. He thought that the announcement of the bound man's act would revive the triumphs of the summer.

That evening the bound man's movements were uncertain. He stumbled in one of his jumps, and fell. Before he managed to get up he heard some low whistles and cat-calls, rather like birds calling at dawn. He tried to get up too quickly, as he had done once or twice during the summer, with the result that he tautened the rope and fell back again. He lay still to regain his calm, and listened to the boos and catcalls growing into an uproar. "Well, bound man, and how did you kill the wolf?" they shouted, and: "Are you the man who killed the wolf?" If he had been one of them, he would not have believed it himself. He thought they had a perfect right to be angry: a circus at this time of year, a bound man, an escaped wolf, and all ending up with this. Some groups of spectators started arguing with others, but the greater part of the audience thought the whole thing a bad joke. By the time he had got to his feet there was such a hubbub that he was barely able to make out individual words.

He saw people surging up all round him, like faded leaves raised by a whirlwind in a circular valley at the center of which all was yet still. He thought of the golden sunsets of the last few days; and the sepulchral light which lay over the blight of all that he had built up during so many nights, the gold frame which the pious hang round dark, old pictures, this sudden collapse of everything, filled him with anger.

They wanted him to repeat his battle with the wolf. He said that such a thing had no place in a circus performance, and the proprietor declared that he did not keep animals to have them slaughtered in front of an audience. But the mob stormed the ring and forced them toward the cages. The proprietor's wife made her way between the seats to the exit and managed to get round to the cages from the other side. She pushed aside the attendant whom the crowd had forced to open a cage door, but the spectators dragged her back and prevented the door from being shut.

"Aren't you the woman who used to lie with him by the river in the summer?" they called out. "How does he hold you in his arms?" She shouted back at them that they needn't believe in the bound man if they didn't want to, they had never deserved him. Painted clowns were good enough for them.

The bound man felt as if the bursts of laughter were what he had been expecting ever since early May. What had smelt so sweet all through the summer now stank. But, if they insisted, he was ready to take on all the animals in the circus. He had never felt so much at one with his rope.

Gently he pushed the woman aside. Perhaps he would travel south with them after all. He stood in the open doorway of the cage, and he saw the wolf, a strong young animal, rise to its feet, and he heard the proprietor grumbling again about the loss of his exhibits. He clapped his hands to attract the animal's attention, and when it was near enough he turned to slam the cage door. He looked the woman in the face. Suddenly he remembered the proprietor's warning to suspect of murderous intentions anyone near him who had a sharp instrument in his hand. At the same moment he felt the blade on his wrists, as cool as the water of the river in autumn, which during the last few weeks he had been barely able to stand. The rope curled up in a tangle beside him while he struggled free. He pushed the woman back, but there was no point in anything he did now. Had he been insufficiently on his guard against those who wanted to release him, against the sympathy in which they wanted to lull him? Had he lain too long on the river bank? If she had cut the cord at any other moment it would have been better than this.

He stood in the middle of the cage, and rid himself of the rope like a snake discarding its skin. It amused him to see the spectators shrinking back. Did they realize that he had no choice now? Or that fighting the wolf now would prove nothing whatever? At the same time he felt all his blood rush to his feet. He felt suddenly weak.

The rope, which fell at its feet like a snare, angered the wolf more than the entry of a stranger into its cage. It crouched to spring. The man reeled, and grabbed the pistol that hung ready at the side of the cage. Then, before anyone could stop him, he shot the wolf between the eyes. The animal reared, and touched him in falling.

On the way to the river he heard the footsteps of his pursuers—spectators, the rope-dancers, the circus proprietor, and the proprietor's wife, who persisted in the chase longer than anyone else. He hid in a clump of bushes and listened to them hurrying past, and later on streaming in the opposite direction back to the camp. The moon shone on the meadow; in that light its color was both of growth and of death.

When he came to the river his anger died away. At dawn it seemed to him as if lumps of ice were floating in the water, and as if snow had fallen, obliterating memory.

A HUNGER ARTIST
franz kafka

During these last decades the interest in professional fasting has
markedly diminished. It used to pay very well to stage such great
performances under one's own management, but today that is quite
impossible. We live in a different world now. At one time the whole
town took a lively interest in the hunger artist; from day to day of
his fast the excitement mounted; everybody wanted to see him at
least once a day; there were people who bought season tickets for
the last few days and sat from morning till night in front of his
small barred cage; even in the nighttime there were visiting hours,
when the whole effect was heightened by torch flares; on fine days
the cage was set out in the open air, and then it was the children's
special treat to see the hunger artist; for their elders he was often
just a joke that happened to be in fashion, but the children stood
open-mouthed, holding each other's hands for greater security,
marvelling at him as he sat there pallid in black tights, with his ribs
sticking out so prominently, not even on a seat but down among
straw on the ground, sometimes giving a courteous nod, answering
questions with a constrained smile, or perhaps stretching an arm
through the bars so that one might feel how thin it was, and then
again withdrawing deep into himself, paying no attention to any-

one or anything, not even to the all-important striking of the clock that was the only piece of furniture in his cage, but merely staring into vacancy with half-shut eyes, now and then taking a sip from a tiny glass of water to moisten his lips.

Besides casual onlookers there were also relays of permanent watchers selected by the public, usually butchers, strangely enough, and it was their task to watch the hunger artist day and night, three of them at a time, in case he should have some secret recourse to nourishment. This was nothing but a formality, instituted to reassure the masses, for the initiates knew well enough that during his fast the artist would never in any circumstances, not even under forcible compulsion, swallow the smallest morsel of food; the honor of his profession forbade it. Not every watcher, of course, was capable of understanding this, there were often groups of night watchers who were very lax in carrying out their duties and deliberately huddled together in a retired corner to play cards with great absorption, obviously intending to give the hunger artist the chance of a little refreshment, which they supposed he could draw from some private hoard. Nothing annoyed the artist more than such watchers; they made him miserable; they made his fast seem unendurable; sometimes he mastered his feebleness sufficiently to sing during their watch for as long as he could keep going, to show them how unjust their suspicions were. But that was of little use; they only wondered at his cleverness in being able to fill his mouth even while singing. Much more to his taste were the watchers who sat close up to the bars, who were not content with the dim night lighting of the hall but focused him in the full glare of the electric pocket torch given them by the impresario. The harsh light did not trouble him at all, in any case he could never sleep properly, and he could always drowse a little, whatever the light, at any hour, even when the hall was thronged with noisy onlookers. He was quite happy at the prospect of spending a sleepless night with such watchers; he was ready to exchange jokes with them, to tell them stories out of his nomadic life, anything at all to keep them awake and demonstrate to them again that he had no eatables in his cage and that he was fasting as not one of them could fast. But his happiest moment was when the morning came and an enormous breakfast was brought them, at his expense, on which they flung themselves with the keen appetite of healthy men after a weary night of wakefulness. Of course there were people who argued that this breakfast was an unfair attempt to bribe the watchers, but that was going rather too far, and when they were invited to take on a night's vigil without a breakfast, merely for the sake of the cause, they made themselves scarce, although they stuck stubbornly to their suspicions.

Such suspicions, anyhow, were a necessary accompaniment to the profession of fasting. No one could possibly watch the hunger artist continuously, day and night, and so no one could produce first-hand evidence that the fast had really been rigorous and continuous; only the artist himself could know that, he was therefore bound to be the sole completely satisfied spectator of his own fast. Yet for other reasons he was never satisfied; it was not perhaps mere fasting that had brought him to such skeleton thinness that many people had regretfully to keep away from his exhibitions, because the sight of him was too much for them, perhaps it was dissatisfaction with himself that had worn him down. For he alone knew, what no other initiate knew, how easy it was to fast. It was the easiest thing in the world. He made no secret of this, yet people did not believe him; at the best they set him down as modest, most of them, however, thought he was out for publicity or else was some kind of cheat who found it easy to fast because he had discovered a way of making it easy, and then had the impudence to admit the fact, more or less. He had to put up with all that, and in the course of time had got used to it, but his inner dissatisfaction always rankled, and never yet, after any term of fasting—this must be granted to his credit—had he left the cage of his own free will. The longest period of fasting was fixed by his impresario at forty days, beyond that term he was not allowed to go, not even in great cities, and there was good reason for it, too. Experience had proved that for about forty days the interest of the public could be stimulated by a steadily increasing pressure of advertisement, but after that the town began to lose interest, sympathetic support began notably to fall off; there were of course local variations as between one town and another or one country and another, but as a general rule forty days marked the limit. So on the fortieth day the flower-bedecked cage was opened, enthusiastic spectators filled the hall, a military band played, two doctors entered the cage to measure the results of the fast, which were announced through a megaphone, and finally two young ladies appeared, blissful at having been selected for the honor, to help the hunger artist down the few steps leading to a small table on which was spread a carefully chosen invalid repast. And at this very moment the artist always turned stubborn. True, he would entrust his bony arms to the outstretched helping hands of the ladies bending over him, but stand up he would not. Why stop fasting at this particular moment, after forty days of it? He had held out for a long time, an illimitably long time; why stop now, when he was in his best fasting form, or rather, not yet quite in his best fasting form? Why should he be cheated of the fame he would get for fasting longer, for being not only the record hunger artist of all time, which presumably he was already, but for beating his own record by a performance beyond human imagination, since he felt that there were no limits to his capacity for fasting? His public pretended to admire him so much, why should it have so little patience with him; if he could endure fasting longer, why shouldn't the public endure it? Besides, he was tired, he was comfortable sitting in the straw, and now he was supposed to lift himself to his full height and go down to a meal the very thought of which gave him a nausea that only the presence of the ladies kept him from betraying, and even that with an effort. And he looked up into the eyes of the ladies who were apparently so friendly and in reality so cruel, and shook his head, which felt too heavy on its strengthless neck. But then there happened yet again what always happened. The impresario came forward, without a word—for the band made speech impossible—lifted his arms in the air above the artist, as if inviting Heaven to look down upon its creature here in the straw, this suffering martyr, which indeed he was, although in quite another sense; grasped him round the emaciated waist, with exaggerated caution, so that the frail condition he was in might be appreciated; and committed him to the care of the blenching ladies, not without secretly giving him a shaking so that his legs and body tottered and swayed. The artist now submitted completely; his head lolled on his breast as if it had landed there by chance; his body was hollowed out; his legs in a spasm of self-preservation clung close to each other at the knees, yet scraped on the ground as if it were not really solid ground, as if they were only trying to find solid ground; and the whole weight of his body, a featherweight after all, relapsed onto one of the ladies, who, looking round for help and panting a little—this post of honor was not at all what she had expected it to be—first stretched her neck as far as she could to keep her face at least free from contact with the artist, then finding this impossible, and her more fortunate companion not coming to her aid but merely holding extended on her own trembling hand the little bunch of knucklebones that was the artist's, to the great delight of the spectators, burst into tears and had to be replaced by an attendant who had long been stationed in readiness. Then came the food, a little of which the impresario managed to get between the artist's lips, while he sat in a kind of half-fainting trance, to the accompaniment of cheerful patter designed to distract the public's attention from the artist's condition; after that, a toast was drunk to the public, supposedly prompted by a whisper from the artist in the impresario's ear; the band confirmed it with a mighty flourish, the spectators melted away, and no one had any cause to be dissatisfied with the proceedings, no one except the hunger artist himself, he only, as always.

So he lived for many years, with small regular intervals of recuperation, in visible glory, honored by the world, yet in spite of that troubled in spirit, and all the more troubled because no one would take his trouble seriously. What comfort could he possibly need? What more could he possibly wish for? And if some good-natured person, feeling sorry for him, tried to console him by pointing out that his melancholy was probably caused by fasting, it could happen, especially when he had been fasting for some time, that he reacted with an outburst of fury and to the general alarm began to shake the bars of his cage like a wild animal. Yet the impresario had a way of punishing these outbreaks which he rather enjoyed putting into operation. He would apologize publicly for the artist's behavior, which was only to be excused, he admitted, because of the irritability caused by fasting; a condition hardly to be understood by well-fed people; then by natural transition he went on to mention the artist's equally incomprehensible boast that he could fast for much longer than he was doing; he praised the high ambition, the good will, the great self-denial undoubtedly implicit in such a statement; and then quite simply countered it by bringing out photographs, which were also on sale to the public, showing the artist on the fortieth day of a fast lying in bed almost dead from exhaustion. This perversion of the truth, familiar to the artist though it was, always unnerved him afresh and proved too much for him. What was a consequence of the premature ending of his fast was here presented as the cause of it! To fight against this lack of understanding, against a whole world of non-understanding, was impossible. Time and again in good faith he stood by the bars listening to the impresario, but as soon as the photographs appeared he always let go and sank with a groan back on to his straw, and the reassured public could once more come close and gaze at him.

A few years later when the witnesses of such scenes called them to mind, they often failed to understand themselves at all. For meanwhile the aforementioned change in public interest had set in; it seemed to happen almost overnight; there may have been profound causes for it, but who was going to bother about that; at any rate the pampered hunger artist suddenly found himself deserted one fine day by the amusement seekers, who went streaming past him to other more favored attractions. For the last time the impresario hurried him over half Europe to discover whether the old interest might still survive here and there; all in vain; everywhere, as if by secret agreement, a positive revulsion from professional fasting was in evidence. Of course it could not really have sprung up so suddenly as all that, and many premonitory symptoms which had not been sufficiently remarked or suppressed during the rush and glitter of success now came retrospectively to mind, but it was now too late to take any countermeasures. Fasting would surely come into fashion again at some future date, yet that was no comfort for those living in the present. What, then, was the hunger artist to do? He had been applauded by thousands in his time and could hardly come down to showing himself in a street booth at village fairs, and as for adopting another profession, he was not only too old for that but too fanatically devoted to fasting. So he took leave of the impresario, his partner in an unparalleled career, and hired himself to a large circus; in order to spare his own feelings he avoided reading the conditions of his contract.

A large circus with its enormous traffic in replacing and recruiting men, animals and apparatus can always find a use for people at any time, even for a hunger artist, provided of course that he does not ask too much, and in this particular case anyhow it was not only the artist who was taken on but his famous and long-known name as well, indeed considering the peculiar nature of his performance, which was not impaired by advancing age, it could not be objected that here was an artist past his prime, no longer at the height of his professional skill, seeking a refuge in some quiet corner of a circus; on the contrary, the hunger artist averred that he could fast as well as ever, which was entirely credible; he even alleged that if he were allowed to fast as he liked, and this was at once promised him without more ado, he could astound the world by establishing a record never yet achieved, a statement which certainly provoked a smile among the other professionals, since it left out of account the change in public opinion, which the hunger artist in his zeal conveniently forgot.

He had not, however, actually lost his sense of the real situation and took it as a matter of course that he and his cage should be stationed, not in the middle of the ring as a main attraction, but outside, near the animal cages, on a site that was after all easily accessible. Large and gaily painted placards made a frame for the cage and announced what was to be seen inside it. When the public came thronging out in the intervals to see the animals, they could hardly avoid passing the hunger artist's cage and stopping there for a moment, perhaps they might even have stayed longer had not those pressing behind them in the narrow gangway, who did not understand why they should be held up on their way toward the excitements of the menagerie, made it impossible for anyone to stand gazing quietly for any length of time. And that was the reason why the hunger artist, who had of course been looking forward to these visiting nours as the main achievement of his life, began instead to shrink from them. At first he could hardly wait for the intervals; it was exhilarating to watch the crowds come streaming his way, until only too soon—not even the most obstinate self-deception, clung to almost consciously, could hold out against the fact—the conviction was borne in upon him that these people, most of them, to judge from their actions, again and again, without exception, were all on their way to the menagerie. And the first sight of them from the distance remained the best. For when they reached his cage he was at once deafened by the storm of shouting and abuse that arose from the two contending factions, which renewed themselves continuously, of those who wanted to stop and stare at him—he soon began to dislike them more than the others—not out of real interest but only out of obstinate self-assertiveness, and those who wanted to go straight on to the animals. When the first great rush was past, the stragglers came along, and these, whom nothing could have prevented from stopping to look at him as long as they had breath, raced past with long strides, hardly even glancing at him, in their haste to get to the menagerie in time. And all too rarely did it happen that he had a stroke of luck, when some father of a family fetched up before him with his children, pointed a finger at the hunger artist and explained at length what the phenomenon meant, telling stories of earlier years when he himself had watched similar but much more thrilling performances, and the children, still rather uncomprehending, since neither inside nor outside school had they been sufficiently prepared for this lesson—what did they care about fasting?—yet showed by the brightness of their intent eyes that new and better times might be coming. Perhaps, said the hunger artist to himself many a time, things would be a little better if his cage were set not quite so near the menagerie. That made it too easy for people to make their choice, to say nothing of what he suffered from the stench of the menagerie, the animals' restlessness by night, the carrying past of raw lumps of flesh for the beasts of prey, the roaring at feeding times, which depressed him continually. But he did not dare to lodge a complaint with the management; after all, he had the animals to thank for the troops of people who passed his cage, among whom there might always be one here and there to take an interest in him, and who could tell where they might seclude him if he called attention to his existence and thereby to the fact that, strictly speaking, he was only an impediment on the way to the menagerie.

A small impediment, to be sure, one that grew steadily less. People grew familiar with the strange idea that they could be expected, in times like these, to take an interest in a hunger artist, and with this familiarity the verdict went out against him. He might fast as much as he could, and he did so; but nothing could save him now, people passed him by. Just try to explain to anyone the art of fasting! Anyone who has no feeling for it cannot be made to understand it. The fine placards grew dirty and illegible, they were torn down; the little notice board telling the number of fast days achieved, which at first was changed carefully every day, had long stayed at the same figure, for after the first few weeks even this small task seemed pointless to the staff; and so the artist simply fasted on and on, as he had once dreamed of doing, and it was no trouble to him, just as he had always foretold, but no one counted the days, no one, not even the artist himself, knew what records he was already breaking, and his heart grew heavy. And when once in a time some leisurely passer-by stopped, made merry over the old figure on the board and spoke of swindling, that was in its way the stupidest lie ever invented by indifference and inborn malice, since it was not the hunger artist who was cheating; he was working honestly, but the world was cheating him of his reward.

Many more days went by, however, and that too came to an end. An overseer's eye fell on the cage one day and he asked the attendants why this perfectly good cage should be left standing there unused with dirty straw inside it; nobody knew, until one man, helped out by the notice board, remembered about the hunger artist. They poked into the straw with sticks and found him in it. "Are you still fasting?" asked the overseer. "When on earth do you mean to stop?" "Forgive me, everybody," whispered the hunger artist; only the overseer, who had his ear to the bars, understood him. "Of course," said the overseer, and tapped his forehead with a finger to let the attendants know what state the man was in, "we forgive you." "I always wanted you to admire my fasting," said the hunger artist. "We do admire it," said the overseer, affably. "But you shouldn't admire it," said the hunger artist. "Well, then we don't admire it," said the overseer, "but why shouldn't we admire it?" "Because I have to fast, I can't help it," said the hunger artist. "What a fellow you are," said the overseer, "and why can't you help it?" "Because," said the hunger artist, lifting his head a little and speaking, with his lips pursed, as if for a kiss, right into the overseer's ear, so that no syllable might be lost, "because I couldn't find the food I liked. If I had found it, believe me, I should have made no fuss and stuffed myself like you or anyone else." These were his last words, but in his dimming eyes remained the firm though no longer proud persuasion that he was still continuing to fast.

"Well, clear this out now!" said the overseer, and they buried the hunger artist, straw and all. Into the cage they put a young panther. Even the most insensitive felt it refreshing to see this wild creature leaping around the cage that had so long been dreary. The panther was all right. The food he liked was brought him without hesitation by the attendants; he seemed not even to miss his freedom; his noble body, furnished almost to the bursting point with all that it needed, seemed to carry freedom around with it too; somewhere in his jaws it seemed to lurk; and the joy of life streamed with such ardent passion from his throat that for the onlookers it was not easy to stand the shock of it. But they braced themselves, crowded round the cage, and did not want ever to move away.

ON THE ROAD
langston hughes

He was not interested in the snow. When he got off the freight, one early evening during the depression, Sargeant never even noticed the snow. But he must have felt it seeping down his neck, cold, wet, sopping in his shoes. But if you had asked him, he wouldn't have known it was snowing. Sargeant didn't see the snow, not even under the bright lights of the main street, falling white and flaky against the night. He was too hungry, too sleepy, too tired.

The Reverend Mr. Dorset, however, saw the snow when he switched on his porch light, opened the front door of his parsonage, and found standing there before him a big black man with snow on his face, a human piece of night with snow on his face—obviously unemployed.

Said the Reverend Mr. Dorset before Sargeant even realized he'd opened his mouth: "I'm sorry. No! Go right on down this street four blocks and turn to your left, walk up seven, and you'll see the Relief Shelter. I'm sorry. No!" He shut the door.

Sargeant wanted to tell the holy man that he had already been to the Relief Shelter, been to hundreds of relief shelters during the depression years; the beds were always gone, and supper was over;

the place was full, and they drew the color line anyhow. But the minister said, "No," and shut the door. Evidently he didn't want to hear about it. And he *had* a door to shut.

The big black man turned away. And even yet he didn't see the snow, walking right into it. Maybe he sensed it, cold, wet, sticking to his jaws, wet on his black hands, sopping in his shoes. He stopped and stood on the sidewalk hunched over—hungry, sleepy, cold—looking up and down. Then he looked right where he was—in front of a church. Of course! A church! Sure, right next to a parsonage, certainly a church.

It had *two* doors.

Broad white steps in the night all snowy white. Two high arched doors with slender stone pillars on either side. And way up, a round lacy window with a stone crucifix in the middle and Christ on the crucifix in stone. All this was pale in the street lights, solid and stony pale in the snow.

Sargeant blinked. When he looked up, the snow fell into his eyes. For the first time that night he *saw* the snow. He shook his head. He shook the snow from his coat sleeves, felt hungry, felt lost, felt not lost, felt cold. He walked up the steps of the church. He knocked at the door. No answer. He tried the handle. Locked. He put his shoulder against the door, and his long black body slanted like a ramrod. He pushed. With loud rhythmic grunts, like the grunts in a chain-gang song, he pushed against the door.

"I'm tired . . . Huh! . . . Hongry . . . Uh! . . . I'm sleepy . . . Huh! I'm cold . . . I got to sleep somewheres," Sargeant said. "This here is a church, ain't it? Well, uh!"

He pushed against the door.

Suddenly, with an undue cracking and screaking, the door began to give way to the tall black Negro who pushed ferociously against it.

By now two or three white people had stopped in the street, and Sargeant was vaguely aware of some of them yelling at him concerning the door. Three or four more came running, yelling at him.

"Hey!" they said. "Hey!"

"Uh-huh," answered the big tall Negro, "I know it's a white folks' church, but I got to sleep somewhere." He gave another lunge at the door. "Huh!"

And the door broke open.

But just when the door gave way, two white cops arrived in a car, ran up the steps with their clubs, and grabbed Sargeant. But Sargeant for once had no intention of being pulled or pushed away from the door.

Sargeant grabbed, but not for anything so weak as a broken door. He grabbed for one of the tall stone pillars beside the door, grabbed at it and caught it. And held it. The cops pulled and Sargeant pulled. Most of the people in the street got behind the cops and helped them pull.

"A big black unemployed Negro holding onto our church!" thought the people. "The idea!"

The cops began to beat Sargeant over the head, and nobody protested. But he held on.

And then the church fell down.

Gradually, the big stone front of the church fell down, the walls and the rafters, the crucifix and the Christ. Then the whole thing fell down, covering the cops and the people with bricks and stones and debris. The whole church fell down in the snow.

Sargeant got out from under the church and went walking on up the street with the stone pillar on his shoulder. He was under the impression that he had buried the parsonage and the Reverend Mr. Dorset who said, "No!" So he laughed and threw the pillar six blocks up the street and went on.

Sargeant thought he was alone, but listening to the *crunch, crunch, crunch* on the snow of his own footsteps, he heard other footsteps, too, doubling his own. He looked around, and there was Christ walking along beside him, the same Christ that had been on the cross on the church—still stone with a rough stone surface, walking along beside him just like he was broken off the cross when the church fell down.

"Well, I'll be dogged," said Sargeant. "This here's the first time I ever seed you off the cross."

"Yes," said Christ, crunching his feet in the snow. "You had to pull the church down to get me off the cross."

"You glad?" said Sargeant.

"I sure am," said Christ.

They both laughed.

"I'm a hell of a fellow, ain't I?" said Sargeant. "Done pulled the church down!"

"You did a good job," said Christ. "They have kept me nailed on a cross for nearly two thousand years."

"Whee-ee-e!" said Sargeant. "I know you are glad to get off."

"I sure am," said Christ.

They walked on in the snow. Sargeant looked at the man of stone.

"And you have been up there two thousand years?"

"I sure have," Christ said.

"Well, if I had a little cash," said Sargeant, "I'd show you around a bit."

"I been around," said Christ.

"Yeah, but that was a long time ago."

"All the same," said Christ, "I've been around."

They walked on in the snow until they came to the railroad yards. Sargeant was tired, sweating and tired.

"Where you goin'?" Sargeant said, stopping by the tracks. He looked at Christ. Sargeant said, "I'm just a bum on the road. How about you? Where you goin'?"

"God knows," Christ said, "but I'm leavin' here."

They saw the red and green lights of the railroad yard half veiled by the snow that fell out of the night. Away down the track they saw a fire in a hobo jungle.

"I can go there and sleep," Sargeant said.

"You can?"

"Sure," said Sargeant. "That place ain't got no doors."

Outside the town, along the tracks, there were barren trees and bushes below the embankment, snow-gray in the dark. And down among the trees and bushes there were makeshift houses made out of boxes and tin and old pieces of wood and canvas. You couldn't see them in the dark, but you knew they were there if you'd ever been on the road, if you had ever lived with the homeless and hungry in a depression.

"I'm side-tracking," Sargeant said. "I'm tired."

"I'm gonna make it on to Kansas City," said Christ.

"O.K.," Sargeant said. "So long!"

He went down into the hobo jungle and found himself a place to sleep. He never did see Christ no more. About 6:00 A. M. a freight came by. Sargeant scrambled out of the jungle with a dozen or so more hobos and ran along the track, grabbing at the freight. It was dawn, cold and gray.

"Wonder where Christ is by now?" Sargeant thought. "He musta gone on way on down the road. He didn't sleep in this jungle."

Sargeant grabbed the train and started to pull himself up into a moving coal car, over the edge of a wheeling coal car. But strangely enough, the car was full of cops. The nearest cop rapped Sargeant soundly across the knuckles with his night stick. Wham! Rapped his big black hands for clinging to the top of the car. Wham! But Sargeant did not turn loose. He clung on and tried to pull himself into the car. He hollered at the top of his voice, "Damn it, lemme in this car!"

"Shut up," barked the cop. "You crazy coon!" He rapped Sargeant across the knuckles and punched him in the stomach. "You ain't out in no jungle now. This ain't no train. You in jail."

Wham! across his bare black fingers clinging to the bars of his cell. Wham! between the steel bars low down against his shins.

Suddenly Sargeant realized that he really was in jail. He wasn't on no train. The blood of the night before had dried on his face, his head hurt terribly, and a cop outside in the corridor was hitting him across the knuckles for holding onto the door, yelling and shaking the cell door.

"They musta took me to jail for breaking down the door last night," Sargeant thought, "that church door."

Sargeant went over and sat on a wooden bench against the cold stone wall. He was emptier than ever. His clothes were wet, clammy cold wet, and shoes sloppy with snow water. It was just about dawn. There he was, locked up behind a cell door, nursing his bruised fingers.

The bruised fingers were his, but not the *door*.

Not the *club*, but the fingers.

"You wait," mumbled Sargeant, black against the jail wall. "I'm gonna break down this door, too."

"Shut up—or I'll paste you one," said the cop.

"I'm gonna break down this door," yelled Sargeant as he stood up in his cell.

Then he must have been talking to himself because he said, "I wonder where Christ's gone? I wonder if he's gone to Kansas City?"

TWO
PREMISE FICTION

Premise Fiction

All fiction is an illusion. It asks us to pretend. No matter how deeply we may be moved by the events of a story, a part of us knows perfectly well that it is *only* a story, it is only words printed on a page.

Since this is so, why should a writer be limited to the invention of characters and events which might plausibly occur in actual life? Why not take one flying leap into fantasy—and *then* write the story with the illusion of being as-if real?

Each story in this section contains one such *premise*. We may not always agree about how to phrase that premise, but it is usually clear where the "let's pretend" is inserted and how it contrasts with the mimetic pattern of the rest of the story.

The first selection, Richard Brautigan's "The Cleveland Wrecking Yard," is taken from *Trout Fishing in America*, a loosely-connected series of highly informal essays, fictional sketches, and journal entries. It is not really a finished short story. A man goes to the Cleveland Wrecking Yard and pokes around and records what he sees. That's all—almost.

We have included "The Cleveland Wrecking Yard" as a kind of introduction to *premise fiction*. Everything in it is purely mimetic until the narrator actually comes across sections of the

trout brook stacked up and for sale. There is for most readers a
good sense of release at this—and then the piece is over. It is a
fanciful way of describing what one is likely to see in a junkyard
or in a large surplus warehouse, and perhaps it even suggests
something about the way men dismantle aspects of Nature. But
it would be a mistake to ask too much of this little piece; it gives
pleasure with its brief flight into fantasy, and that is probably
all one should make of it.

This is often the way premise stories take shape in the mind
of the writer. Brautigan stopped at the sketching stage (as he
frequently does) and refrained from building the sketch into
sophisticated fiction. If one compares this piece with Donald
Barthelme's "The Balloon," one can see the difference between a
story kernel and developed fiction. "The Balloon" has the same
sort of whimsy—an enormous cloth balloon settles on the city
of New York, covering a twenty-block area. The story describes
how people react to it, and for a while the whole scene seems
to be without purpose or meaning. Finally the balloon can
be seen as a metaphor, and the work turns into an elaborate love
story. Thus what was only a passing suggestion in Brautigan's
sketch becomes in Barthelme's work a metaphorical statement.

There is considerable variation in the placement of the premise
in short stories. In such stories as Shirley Jackson's "The Lottery," John Collier's "Thus I Refute Beelzy," and Stephen Minot's
"Journey to Ocean Grove," the premise is not only held back
until the end, it also serves as climax. In other stories, like Robley
Wilson's "The Apple" and D. H. Lawrence's "The Rocking-
Horse Winner," the premise is stated fairly early and serves as
the primary concern of the narrative. No matter where the
premise is placed, however, it is usually a dominant aspect of
the story. It either establishes what this fictional world is going
to be like or it answers questions which we as readers have
been asking all the way through. Almost always it is a focal point
for the story as a whole.

Another interesting variation in these premise stories is that
some are primarily social statements—commentaries on the whole
society—while others are far more personal or psychological in
theme.

"The Lottery" is famous because, in addition to the sheer vivid-
ness of the telling, it comments on the capacity of our society to
find scapegoats for punishment. More than this, it suggests that
certain practices in society continue entirely by momentum,

even when individual members of the society may recognize the cruelty or absurdity of these traditions.

Eric Knight's "Never Come Monday" is much lighter in tone, but it, too, is a social statement, depicting a day when working people simply "turn off" and declare themselves a pleasant, extended holiday. Minot's "Journey to Ocean Grove" is a dark version of a similar fantasy. The day all human beings simply give up the struggle to live comes as an ominous vision and the only hope rests with the very young.

Notice that in two of these three socially oriented stories character development is minimal. In them, characters are referred to by name, but the real concern of the authors seems to be far more with the society itself.

At the other end of the spectrum are stories which, largely ignoring social concerns, are rooted in psychology or in personal statement. As a fanciful love song, Barthelme's "The Balloon" is a prime example. A science fiction writer would have been concerned with how the balloon got there, and how (probably) it was a threat to the city, and how it was defeated. Barthelme ignores all these possibilities for pure plot ingenuity and plays with the idea as a poet might. His chief concern is not with New York or mankind, but with how he misses his love while she is away.

Kurt Vonnegut's "EPICAC" is also a love story, though one member of the triangle is a computer. The treatment here is less poetic, and it borrows heavily from the conventions of science fiction. There is far less mystery to "EPICAC," but it is not limited to coldly scientific speculation. The story is very much of a personal statement. Our concern is not whether computers will take over the world, but how a man might use one of them to overcome his own inabilities.

In a much darker tone, Elizabeth Bowen's "The Demon Lover" and Robley Wilson's "The Apple" also delve into aspects of love —one through the appearance of a ghost and the other through the bizarre transformation of a girl's escort into an apple! How does fiction probe the "truth" with such "untrue" premises? In the same way our dreams do—by providing a striking metaphor and treating it not as a figure of speech but as a literal event.

Because the mechanisms of the dream sometimes seem to play a part in the structure of premise fiction, we have again placed at the end of this section those stories we felt were moving toward the next stance—dream fiction. "The Apple," for example, is certainly "dreamlike" in the usual sense, but literarily it must be

classified as premise fiction because only in a single particular
is the natural order changed.

Closer still to the world of dreams is Ray Bradbury's "The
One Who Waits." Best known for his science fiction, Bradbury does
more in this piece than spin an entertaining plot for its own
sake. The story begins:

> *I live in a well. I live like smoke in the well. Like vapor in a stone*
> *throat. I don't move. I don't do anything but wait.*

Here is a misty quality (in both the figurative and the real senses)
which sets the story apart from most science fiction. And as it
develops, with the spirit seeking first one body and then another,
we get the feeling that something is being suggested about our
own identities. The theme remains hazy, but there is a certain
familiarity about this restless spirit which resides in a well on
a barren planet.

John Barth's "Night-Sea Journey" lies at the very border of
dream fiction. Indeed, many readers miss the premise entirely and
read the story as a highly discursive piece of dream fiction. The
story is rooted, however, in the fantastic suggestion that sperm are
articulate and converse with one another in their long swim
toward conception, and that they ponder the same kinds of questions about the meaning of it all that trouble us, the survivors.
Barth's tone is comic and highly ironic, but his story makes a
serious comment on our status as human beings and, finally,
proposes a great affirmation for life. "Night-Sea Journey" com-
bines both the personal (another love story of sorts!) and the
social by means of a premise which has the flavor of dream fiction.

In reading these stories, examine each premise and the way it
dominates the fiction. Discover how its placement—as an opening
or as the climax—affects the structure of the story. And be
ready to include the work, no matter how incredible it may
seem, as a part of your own vicarious experience.

THE CLEVELAND WRECKING YARD

richard brautigan

Until recently my knowledge about the Cleveland Wrecking Yard had come from a couple of friends who'd bought things there. One of them bought a huge window: the frame, glass and everything for just a few dollars. It was a fine-looking window.

Then he chopped a hole in the side of his house up on Potrero Hill and put the window in. Now he has a panoramic view of the San Francisco County Hospital.

He can practically look right down into the wards and see old magazines eroded like the Grand Canyon from endless readings. He can practically hear the patients thinking about breakfast: *I hate milk,* and thinking about dinner: *I hate peas,* and then he can watch the hospital slowly drown at night, hopelessly entangled in huge bunches of brick seaweed.

He bought that window at the Cleveland Wrecking Yard.

My other friend bought an iron roof at the Cleveland Wrecking Yard and took the roof down to Big Sur in an old station wagon and then he carried the iron roof on his back up the side of a mountain. He carried up half the roof on his back. It was no picnic. Then he bought a mule, George, from Pleasanton. George carried up the other half of the roof.

The mule didn't like what was happening at all. He lost a lot of weight because of the ticks, and the smell of the wildcats up on the plateau made him too nervous to graze there. My friend said jokingly that George had lost around two hundred pounds. The good wine country around Pleasanton in the Livermore Valley probably had looked a lot better to George than the wild side of the Santa Lucia Mountains.

My friend's place was a shack right beside a huge fireplace where there had once been a great mansion during the 1920s, built by a famous movie actor. The mansion was built before there was even a road down at Big Sur. The mansion had been brought over the mountains on the backs of mules, strung out like ants, bringing visions of the good life to the poison oak, the ticks, and the salmon.

The mansion was on a promontory, high over the Pacific. Money could see farther in the 1920s, and one could look out and see whales and the Hawaiian Islands and the Kuomintang in China.

The mansion burned down years ago.

The actor died.

His mules were made into soap.

His mistresses became bird nests of wrinkles.

Now only the fireplace remains as a sort of Carthaginian homage to Hollywood.

I was down there a few weeks ago to see my friend's roof. I wouldn't have passed up the chance for a million dollars, as they say. The roof looked like a colander to me. If that roof and the rain were running against each other at Bay Meadows, I'd bet on the rain and plan to spend my winnings at the World's Fair in Seattle.

My own experience with the Cleveland Wrecking Yard began two days ago when I heard about a used trout stream they had on sale out at the Yard. So I caught the Number 15 bus on Columbus Avenue and went out there for the first time.

There were two Negro boys sitting behind me on the bus. They were talking about Chubby Checker and the Twist. They thought that Chubby Checker was only fifteen years old because he didn't have a mustache. Then they talked about some other guy who did the twist forty-four hours in a row until he saw George Washington crossing the Delaware.

"Man, that's what I call twisting," one of the kids said.

"I don't think I could twist no forty-four hours in a row," the other kid said. "That's a lot of twisting."

I got off the bus right next to an abandoned Time Gasoline filling station and an abandoned fifty-cent self-service car wash. There was a long field on one side of the filling station. The field had once been covered with a housing project during the war, put there for the shipyard workers.

On the other side of the Time filling station was the Cleveland Wrecking Yard. I walked down there to have a look at the used trout stream. The Cleveland Wrecking Yard has a very long front window filled with signs and merchandise.

There was a sign in the window advertising a laundry marking machine for $65.00. The original cost of the machine was $175.00. Quite a saving.

There was another sign advertising new and used two and three ton hoists. I wondered how many hoists it would take to move a trout stream.

There was another sign that said:

THE FAMILY GIFT CENTER,
GIFT SUGGESTIONS FOR THE ENTIRE FAMILY

The window was filled with hundreds of items for the entire family. *Daddy, do you know what I want for Christmas? What, son? A bathroom. Mommy, do you know what I want for Christmas? What, Patricia? Some roofing material.*

There were jungle hammocks in the window for distant relatives and dollar-ten-cent gallons of earth-brown enamel paint for other loved ones.

There was also a big sign that said:

USED TROUT STREAM FOR SALE.
MUST BE SEEN TO BE APPRECIATED.

I went inside and looked at some ship's lanterns that were for sale next to the door. Then a salesman came up to me and said in a pleasant voice, "Can I help you?"

"Yes," I said. "I'm curious about the trout stream you have for sale. Can you tell me something about it? How are you selling it?"

"We're selling it by the foot length. You can buy as little as you want or you can buy all we've got left. A man came in here this morning and bought 563 feet. He's going to give it to his niece for a birthday present," the salesman said.

"We're selling the waterfalls separately of course, and the trees and birds, flowers, grass and ferns we're also selling extra. The insects we're giving away free with a minimum purchase of ten feet of stream."

"How much are you selling the stream for?" I asked.

"Six dollars and fifty-cents a foot," he said. "That's for the first hundred feet. After that it's five dollars a foot."

"How much are the birds?" I asked.

"Thirty-five cents apiece," he said. "But of course they're used. We can't guarantee anything."

"How wide is the stream?" I asked. "You said you were selling it by the length, didn't you?"

"Yes," he said. "We're selling it by the length. Its width runs between five and eleven feet. You don't have to pay anything extra for width. It's not a big stream, but it's very pleasant."

"What kinds of animals do you have?" I asked.

"We only have three deer left," he said.

"Oh . . . What about flowers?"

"By the dozen," he said.

"Is the stream clear?" I asked.

"Sir," the salesman said. "I wouldn't want you to think that we would ever sell a murky trout stream here. We always make sure they're running crystal clear before we even think about moving them."

"Where did the stream come from?" I asked.

"Colorado," he said. "We moved it with loving care. We've never damaged a trout stream yet. We treat them all as if they were china."

"You're probably asked this all the time, but how's fishing in the stream?" I asked.

"Very good," he said. "Mostly German browns, but there are a few rainbows."

"What do the trout cost?" I asked.

"They come with the stream," he said. "Of course it's all luck. You never know how many you're going to get or how big they are. But the fishing's very good, you might say it's excellent. Both bait and dry fly," he said smiling.

"Where's the stream at?" I asked. "I'd like to take a look at it."

"It's around in back," he said. "You go straight through that door and then turn right until you're outside. It's stacked in lengths. You can't miss it. The waterfalls are upstairs in the used plumbing department."

"What about the animals?"

"Well, what's left of the animals are straight back from the stream. You'll see a bunch of our trucks parked on a road by the railroad tracks. Turn right on the road and follow it down past the piles of lumber. The animal shed's right at the end of the lot."

"Thanks," I said. "I think I'll look at the waterfalls first. You don't have to come with me. Just tell me how to get there and I'll find my own way."

"All right," he said. "Go up those stairs. You'll see a bunch of doors and windows, turn left and you'll find the used plumbing department. Here's my card if you need any help."

"Okay," I said. "You've been a great help already. Thanks a lot. I'll take a look around."

"Good luck," he said.

I went upstairs and there were thousands of doors there. I'd never seen so many doors before in my life. You could have built an entire city out of those doors. Doorstown. And there were enough windows up there to build a little suburb entirely out of windows. Windowville.

I turned left and went back and saw the faint glow of pearl-colored light. The light got stronger and stronger as I went farther back, and then I was in the used plumbing department, surrounded by hundreds of toilets.

The toilets were stacked on shelves. They were stacked five toilets high. There was a skylight above the toilets that made them glow like the Great Taboo Pearl of the South Sea movies.

Stacked over against the wall were the waterfalls. There were about a dozen of them, ranging from a drop of a few feet to a drop of ten or fifteen feet.

There was one waterfall that was over sixty feet long. There were tags on the pieces of the big falls describing the correct order for putting the falls back together again.

The waterfalls all had price tags on them. They were more expensive than the stream. The waterfalls were selling for $19.00 a foot.

I went into another room where there were piles of sweet-smelling lumber, glowing a soft yellow from a different color skylight above the lumber. In the shadows at the edge of the room under the sloping roof of the building were many sinks and urinals covered with dust, and there was also another waterfall about seventeen feet long, lying there in two lengths and already beginning to gather dust.

I had seen all I wanted of the waterfalls, and now I was very curious about the trout stream, so I followed the salesman's directions and ended up outside the building.

O I had never in my life seen anything like that trout stream. It was stacked in piles of various lengths: ten, fifteen, twenty feet, etc. There was one pile of hundred-foot lengths. There was also a box of scraps. The scraps were in odd sizes ranging from six inches to a couple of feet.

There was a loudspeaker on the side of the building and soft music was coming out. It was a cloudy day and seagulls were circling high overhead.

Behind the stream were big bundles of trees and bushes. They were covered with sheets of patched canvas. You could see the tops and roots sticking out the ends of the bundles.

I went up close and looked at the lengths of stream. I could see some trout in them. I saw one good fish. I saw some crawdads crawling around the rocks at the bottom.

It looked like a fine stream. I put my hand in the water. It was cold and felt good.

I decided to go around to the side and look at the animals. I saw where the trucks were parked beside the railroad tracks. I followed the road down past the piles of lumber, back to the shed where the animals were.

The salesman had been right. They were practically out of animals. About the only thing they had left in any abundance were mice. There were hundreds of mice.

Beside the shed was a huge wire birdcage, maybe fifty feet high, filled with many kinds of birds. The top of the cage had a piece of canvas over it, so the birds wouldn't get wet when it rained. There were woodpeckers and wild canaries and sparrows.

On my way back to where the trout stream was piled, I found the insects. They were inside a prefabricated steel building that was selling for eighty-cents a square foot. There was a sign over the door. It said

INSECTS

THE LOTTERY
shirley jackson

The morning of June 27th was clear and sunny, with the fresh warmth of a full-summer day; the flowers were blossoming profusely and the grass was richly green. The people of the village began to gather in the square, between the post office and the bank, around ten o'clock; in some towns there were so many people that the lottery took two days and had to be started on June 26th, but in this village, where there were only about three hundred people, the whole lottery took less than two hours, so it could begin at ten o'clock in the morning and still be through in time to allow the villagers to get home for noon dinner.

The children assembled first, of course. School was recently over for the summer, and the feeling of liberty sat uneasily on most of them; they tended to gather together quietly for a while before they broke into boisterous play, and their talk was still of the classroom and the teacher, of books and reprimands. Bobby Martin had already stuffed his pockets full of stones, and the other boys soon followed his example, selecting the smoothest and roundest stones; Bobby and Harry Jones and Dickie Delacroix—the villagers pronounced this name "Dellacroy"—eventually made a great pile of stones in one corner of the square and guarded it against the raids of the other boys. The girls stood aside, talking among themselves, looking over their shoulders at the boys, and the very small children rolled in the dust or clung to the hands of their older brothers or sisters.

Soon the men began to gather, surveying their own children, speaking of planting and rain; tractors and taxes. They stood together, away from the pile of stones in the corner, and their jokes were quiet and they smiled rather than laughed. The women, wearing faded house dresses and sweaters, came shortly after their menfolk. They greeted one another and exchanged bits of gossip as they went to join their husbands. Soon the women, standing by their husbands, began to call to their children, and the children came reluctantly, having to be called four or five times. Bobby Martin ducked under his mother's grasping hand and ran, laughing, back to the pile of stones. His father spoke up sharply, and Bobby came quickly and took his place between his father and his oldest brother.

The lottery was conducted—as were the square dances, the teenage club, the Halloween program—by Mr. Summers, who had time and energy to devote to civic activities. He was a round-faced, jovial man and he ran the coal business, and people were sorry for him, because he had no children and his wife was a scold. When he arrived in the square, carrying the black wooden box, there was a murmur of conversation among the villagers, and he waved and called, "Little late today, folks." The postmaster, Mr. Graves, followed him, carrying a three-legged stool, and the stool was put in the center of the square and Mr. Summers set the black box down on it. The villagers kept their distance, leaving a space between themselves and the stool, and when Mr. Summers said, "Some of you fellows want to give me a hand?" there was a hesitation before two men, Mr. Martin and his oldest son, Baxter, came forward to hold the box steady on the stool while Mr. Summers stirred up the papers inside it.

The original paraphernalia for the lottery had been lost long ago, and the black box now resting on the stool had been put into use even before Old Man Warner, the oldest man in town, was born. Mr. Summers spoke frequently to the villagers about making a new box, but no one liked to upset even as much tradition as was represented by the black box. There was a story that the present box had been made with some pieces of the box that had preceded it, the one that had been constructed when the first people settled down to make a village here. Every year, after the lottery, Mr. Summers began talking again about a new box, but every year the subject was allowed to fade off without anything's being done. The black box grew shabbier each year; by now it was no longer completely black but splintered badly along one side to show the original wood color, and in some places faded or stained.

Mr. Martin and his oldest son, Baxter, held the black box securely on the stool until Mr. Summers had stirred the papers thoroughly with his hand. Because so much of the ritual had been forgotten or discarded, Mr. Summers had been successful in having slips of paper substituted for the chips of wood that had been used for generations. Chips of wood, Mr. Summers had argued, had been all very well when the village was tiny, but now that the population was more than three hundred and likely to keep on growing, it was necessary to use something that would fit more easily into the black box. The night before the lottery, Mr. Summers and Mr. Graves made up the slips of paper and put them in the box, and it was then taken to the safe of Mr. Summers' coal company and locked up until Mr. Summers was ready to take it to the square next morning. The rest of the year, the box was put away, sometimes one place, sometimes another; it had spent one year in Mr. Graves's barn and another year underfoot in the post office, and sometimes it was set on a shelf in the Martin grocery and left there.

There was a great deal of fussing to be done before Mr. Summers declared the lottery open. There were the lists to make up—of heads of families, heads of households in each family, members of each household in each family. There was the proper swearing-in of Mr. Summers by the postmaster, as the official of the lottery; at one time, some people remembered, there had been a recital of some sort, performed by the official of the lottery, a perfunctory, tuneless chant that had been rattled off duly each year; some people believed that the official of the lottery used to stand just so when he said or sang it, others believed that he was supposed to walk among the people, but years and years ago this part of the ritual had been allowed to lapse. There had been, also, a ritual salute, which the official of the lottery had had to use in addressing each person who came up to draw from the box, but this also had changed with time, until now it was felt necessary only for the official to speak to each person approaching. Mr. Summers was very good at all this; in his clean white shirt and blue jeans, with one hand resting carelessly on the black box, he seemed very proper and important as he talked interminably to Mr. Graves and the Martins.

Just as Mr. Summers finally left off talking and turned to the assembled villagers, Mrs. Hutchinson came hurriedly along the path to the square, her sweater thrown over her shoulders, and slid into place in the back of the crowd. "Clean forgot what day it was," she said to Mrs. Delacroix, who stood next to her, and they both laughed softly. "Thought my old man was out back stacking wood," Mrs. Hutchinson went on, "and then I looked out the window and the kids were gone, and then I remembered it was the twenty-seventh and came a-running." She dried her hands on her apron, and Mrs. Delacroix said, "You're in time, though. They're still talking away up there."

Mrs. Hutchinson craned her neck to see through the crowd and found her husband and children standing near the front. She tapped Mrs. Delacroix on the arm as a farewell and began to make her way through the crowd. The people separated good-humoredly to let her through; two or three people said, in voices just loud enough to be heard across the crowd, "Here comes your Missus, Hutchinson," and "Bill, she made it after all." Mrs. Hutchinson reached her husband, and Mr. Summers, who had been waiting, said cheerfully, "Thought we were going to have to get on without you, Tessie." Mrs. Hutchinson said, grinning, "Wouldn't have me leave m'dishes in the sink, now, would you, Joe?," and soft laughter ran through the crowd as the people stirred back into position after Mrs. Hutchinson's arrival.

"Well, now," Mr. Summers said soberly, "guess we better get started, get this over with, so's we can go back to work. Anybody ain't here?"

"Dunbar," several people said. "Dunbar, Dunbar."

Mr. Summers consulted his list. "Clyde Dunbar," he said. "That's right. He's broke his leg, hasn't he? Who's drawing for him?"

"Me, I guess," a woman said, and Mr. Summers turned to look at her. "Wife draws for her husband," Mr. Summers said. "Don't you have a grown boy to do it for you, Janey?" Although Mr. Summers and everyone else in the village knew the answer perfectly well, it was the business of the official of the lottery to ask such questions formally. Mr. Summers waited with an expression of polite interest while Mrs. Dunbar answered.

"Horace's not but sixteen yet," Mrs. Dunbar said regretfully. "Guess I gotta fill in for the old man this year."

"Right," Mr. Summers said. He made a note on the list he was holding. Then he asked, "Watson boy drawing this year?"

A tall boy in the crowd raised his hand. "Here," he said. "I'm drawing for m'mother and me." He blinked his eyes nervously and ducked his head as several voices in the crowd said things like

"Good fellow, Jack," and "Glad to see your mother's got a man to do it."

"Well," Mr. Summers said, "guess that's everyone. Old Man Warner make it?"

"Here," a voice said, and Mr. Summers nodded.

A sudden hush fell on the crowd as Mr. Summers cleared his throat and looked at the list. "All ready?" he called. "Now, I'll read the names—heads of families first—and the men come up and take a paper out of the box. Keep the paper folded in your hand without looking at it until everyone has had a turn. Everything clear?"

The people had done it so many times that they only half listened to the directions; most of them were quiet, wetting their lips, not looking around. Then Mr. Summers raised one hand high and said, "Adams." A man disengaged himself from the crowd and came forward. "Hi, Steve," Mr. Summers said, and Mr. Adams said, "Hi, Joe." They grinned at one another humorlessly and nervously. Then Mr. Adams reached into the black box and took out a folded paper. He held it firmly by one corner as he turned and went hastily back to his place in the crowd, where he stood a little apart from his family, not looking down at his hand.

"Allen," Mr. Summers said. "Andrews. . . .Bentham."

"Seems like there's no time at all between lotteries any more," Mrs. Delacroix said to Mrs. Graves in the back row. "Seems like we got through with the last one only last week."

"Time sure goes fast," Mrs. Graves said.

"Clark. . . . Delacroix."

"There goes my old man," Mrs. Delacroix said. She held her breath while her husband went forward.

"Dunbar," Mr. Summers said, and Mrs. Dunbar went steadily to the box while one of the women said, "Go on, Janey," and another said, "There she goes."

"We're next," Mrs. Graves said. She watched while Mr. Graves came around from the side of the box, greeted Mr. Summers gravely, and selected a slip of paper from the box. By now, all through the crowd there were men holding the small folded papers in their large hands, turning them over and over nervously. Mrs. Dunbar and her two sons stood together, Mrs. Dunbar holding the slip of paper.

"Harburt. . . . Hutchinson."

"Get up there, Bill," Mrs. Hutchinson said, and the people near her laughed.

"Jones."

"They do say," Mr. Adams said to Old Man Warner, who stood next to him, "that over in the north village they're talking of giving up the lottery."

Old Man Warner snorted. "Pack of crazy fools," he said. "Listening to the young folks, nothing's good enough for *them*. Next thing you know, they'll be wanting to go back to living in caves, nobody work any more, live *that* way for a while. Used to be a saying about 'Lottery in June, corn be heavy soon.' First thing you know, we'd all be eating stewed chickweed and acorns. There's *always* been a lottery," he added petulantly. "Bad enough to see young Joe Summers up there joking with everybody."

"Some places have already quit lotteries," Mrs. Adams said.

"Nothing but trouble in *that*," Old Man Warner said stoutly. "Pack of young fools."

"Martin." And Bobby Martin watched his father go forward. "Overdyke. . . . Percy."

"I wish they'd hurry," Mrs. Dunbar said to her older son. "I wish they'd hurry."

"They're almost through," her son said.

"You get ready to run tell Dad," Mrs. Dunbar said.

Mr. Summers called his own name and then stepped forward precisely and selected a slip from the box. Then he called, "Warner."

"Seventy-seventh year I been in the lottery," Old Man Warner said as he went through the crowd. "Seventy-seventh time."

"Watson." The tall boy came awkwardly through the crowd. Someone said, "Don't be nervous, Jack," and Mr. Summers said, "Take your time, son."

"Zanini."

After that, there was a long pause, a breathless pause, until Mr. Summers, holding his slip of paper in the air, said, "All right, fellows." For a minute, no one moved, and then all the slips of paper were opened. Suddenly, all women began to speak at once, saying, "Who is it?," "Who's got it?," "Is it the Dunbars?," "Is it the Watsons?" Then the voices began to say, "It's Hutchinson. It's Bill." "Bill Hutchinson got it."

"Go tell your father," Mrs. Dunbar said to her older son.

People began to look around to see the Hutchinsons. Bill Hutchinson was standing quiet, staring down at the paper in his hand. Suddenly, Tessie Hutchinson shouted to Mr. Summers, "You didn't give him time enough to take any paper he wanted. I saw you. It wasn't fair."

"Be a good sport, Tessie," Mrs. Delacroix called, and Mrs. Graves said, "All of us took the same chance."

"Shut up, Tessie," Bill Hutchinson said.

"Well, everyone," Mr. Summers said, "that was done pretty fast, and now we've got to be hurrying a little more to get done in time." He consulted his next list. "Bill," he said, "you draw for the Hutchinson family. You got any other households in the Hutchinsons?"

"There's Don and Eva," Mrs. Hutchinson yelled. "Make *them* take their chance!"

"Daughters draw with their husbands' families, Tessie," Mr. Summers said gently. "You know that as well as anyone else."

"It wasn't *fair*," Tessie said.

"I guess not, Joe," Bill Hutchinson said regretfully. "My daughter draws with her husband's family, that's only fair. And I've got no other family except the kids."

"Then, as far as drawing for families is concerned, it's you," Mr. Summers said in explanation, "and as far as drawing for households is concerned, that's you, too. Right?"

"Right," Bill Hutchinson said.

"How many kids, Bill?" Mr. Summers asked formally.

"Three," Bill Hutchinson said. "There's Bill, Jr., and Nancy, and little Dave. And Tessie and me."

"All right, then," Mr. Summers said, "Harry, you got their tickets back?"

Mr. Graves nodded and held up the slips of paper. "Put them in the box, then," Mr. Summers directed. "Take Bill's and put it in."

"I think we ought to start over," Mrs. Hutchinson said, as quietly as she could. "I tell you it wasn't *fair*. You didn't give him time enough to choose. *Every*body saw that."

Mr. Graves had selected the five slips and put them in the box, and he dropped all the papers but those onto the ground, where the breeze caught them and lifted them off.

"Listen, everybody," Mrs. Hutchinson was saying to the people around her.

"Ready, Bill?" Mr. Summers asked, and Bill Hutchinson, with one quick glance around at his wife and children, nodded.

"Remember," Mr. Summers said, "take the slips and keep them folded until each person has taken one. Harry, you help little Dave." Mr. Graves took the hand of the little boy, who came willingly with him up to the box. "Take a paper out of the box, Davy," Mr. Summers said. Davy put his hand into the box and laughed. "Take just *one* paper," Mr. Summers said. "Harry, you hold it for him." Mr. Graves took the child's hand and removed the folded paper from the tight fist and held it while little Dave stood next to him and looked up at him wonderingly.

"Nancy next," Mr. Summers said. Nancy was twelve, and her school friends breathed heavily as she went forward, switching her skirt, and took a slip daintily from the box. "Bill, Jr.," Mr. Summers said, and Billy, his face red and his feet over-large, nearly knocked the box over as he got a paper out. "Tessie," Mr. Summers said. She hesitated for a minute, looking around defiantly, and then set her lips and went up to the box. She snatched a paper out and held it behind her.

"Bill," Mr. Summers said, and Bill Hutchinson reached into the box and felt around, bringing his hand out at last with the slip of paper in it.

The crowd was quiet. A girl whispered, "I hope it's not Nancy," and the sound of the whisper reached the edges of the crowd.

"It's not the way it used to be," Old Man Warner said clearly. "People ain't the way they used to be."

"All right," Mr. Summers said. "Open the papers. Harry, you open little Dave's."

Mr. Graves opened the slip of paper and there was a general sigh through the crowd as he held it up and everyone could see that it was blank. Nancy and Bill, Jr., opened theirs at the same time, and both beamed and laughed, turning around to the crowd and holding their slips of paper above their heads.

"Tessie," Mr. Summers said. There was a pause, and then Mr. Summers looked at Bill Hutchinson, and Bill unfolded his paper and showed it. It was blank.

"It's Tessie," Mr. Summers said, and his voice was hushed. "Show us her paper, Bill."

Bill Hutchinson went over to his wife and forced the slip of paper out of her hand. It had a black spot on it, the black spot Mr. Summers had made the night before with the heavy pencil in the coal-company office. Bill Hutchinson held it up, and there was a stir in the crowd.

"All right, folks," Mr. Summers said. "Let's finish quickly."

Although the villagers had forgotten the ritual and lost the original black box, they still remembered to use stones. The pile of stones the boys had made earlier was ready; there were stones on the ground with the blowing scraps of paper that had come out of the box. Mrs. Delacroix selected a stone so large she had to pick it up with both hands and turned to Mrs. Dunbar. "Come on," she said. "Hurry up."

Mrs. Dunbar had small stones in both hands, and she said, gasping for breath, "I can't run at all. You'll have to go ahead and I'll catch up with you."

The children had stones already, and someone gave little Davy Hutchinson a few pebbles.

Tessie Hutchinson was in the center of a cleared space by now, and she held her hands out desperately as the villagers moved in on her. "It isn't fair," she said. A stone hit her on the side of the head.

Old Man Warner was saying, "Come on, come on, everyone." Steve Adams was in the front of the crowd of villagers, with Mrs. Graves beside him.

"It isn't fair, it isn't right," Mrs. Hutchinson screamed, and then they were upon her.

THUS I REFUTE BEELZY
john collier

"There goes the tea bell," said Mrs. Carter. "I hope Simon hears it."

They looked out from the window of the drawing-room. The long garden, agreeably neglected, ended in a waste plot. Here a little summer-house was passing close by beauty on its way to complete decay. This was Simon's retreat: it was almost completely screened by the tangled branches of the apple tree and the pear tree, planted too close together, as they always are in suburban gardens. They caught a glimpse of him now and then, as he strutted up and down, mouthing and gesticulating, performing all the solemn mumbo-jumbo of small boys who spend long afternoons at the forgotten ends of long gardens.

"There he is, bless him," said Betty.

"Playing his game," said Mrs. Carter. "He won't play with the other children any more. And if I go down there—the temper! And comes in tired out."

"He doesn't have his sleep in the afternoons?" asked Betty.

"You know what Big Simon's ideas are," said Mrs. Carter. " 'Let him choose for himself,' he says. That's what he chooses, and he comes in as white as a sheet."

"Look. He's heard the bell," said Betty. The expression was justified, though the bell had ceased ringing a full minute ago. Small Simon stopped in his parade exactly as if its tinny dingle had at that moment reached his ear. They watched him perform certain ritual sweeps and scratchings with his little stick, and come lagging over the hot and flaggy grass towards the house.

Mrs. Carter led the way down to the play-room, or garden-room, which was also the tea-room for hot days. It had been the huge scullery of this tall Georgian house. Now the walls were cream-washed, there was coarse blue net in the windows, canvas-covered armchairs on the stone floor, and a reproduction of Van Gogh's *Sunflowers* over the mantelpiece.

Small Simon came drifting in, and accorded Betty a perfunctory greeting. His face was an almost perfect triangle, pointed at the chin, and he was paler than he should have been. "The little elf-child!" cried Betty.

Simon looked at her. "No," said he.

At that moment the door opened, and Mr. Carter came in, rubbing his hands. He was a dentist, and washed them before and after everything he did. "You!" said his wife. "Home already!"

"Not unwelcome, I hope," said Mr. Carter, nodding to Betty. "Two people cancelled their appointments: I decided to come home. I said, I hope I am not unwelcome."

"Silly!" said his wife. "Of course not."

"Small Simon seems doubtful," continued Mr. Carter. "Small Simon, are you sorry to see me at tea with you?"

"No, Daddy."

"No, what?"

"No, Big Simon."

"That's right. Big Simon and Small Simon. That sounds more like friends, doesn't it? At one time little boys had to call their father 'sir.' If they forgot—a good spanking. On the bottom, Small Simon! On the bottom!" said Mr. Carter, washing his hands once more with his invisible soap and water.

The little boy turned crimson with shame or rage.

"But now, you see," said Betty, to help, "you can call your father whatever you like."

"And what," asked Mr. Carter, "has Small Simon been doing this afternoon? While Big Simon has been at work."

"Nothing," muttered his son.

"Then you have been bored," said Mr. Carter. "Learn from experience, Small Simon. Tomorrow, do something amusing, and you will not be bored. I want him to learn from experience, Betty. That is my way, the new way."

"I have learned," said the boy, speaking like an old, tired man, as little boys so often do.

"It would hardly seem so," said Mr. Carter, "if you sit on your behind all the afternoon, doing nothing. Had *my* father caught me doing nothing, I should not have sat very comfortably."

"He played," said Mrs. Carter.

"A bit," said the boy, shifting on his chair.

"Too much," said Mrs. Carter. "He comes in all nervy and dazed. He ought to have his rest."

"He is six," said her husband. "He is a reasonable being. He must choose for himself. But what game is this, Small Simon, that is worth getting nervy and dazed over? There are very few games as good as all that."

"It's nothing," said the boy.

"Oh, come," said his father. "We are friends, are we not? You can tell me. I was a Small Simon once, just like you, and played the same games you play. Of course there were no aeroplanes in those days. With whom do you play this fine game? Come on, we must all answer civil questions, or the world would never go round. With whom do you play?"

"Mr. Beelzy," said the boy, unable to resist.

"Mr. Beelzy?" said his father, raising his eyebrows inquiringly at his wife.

"It's a game he makes up," said she.

"Not makes up!" cried the boy. "Fool!"

"That is telling stories," said his mother. "And rude as well. We had better talk of something different."

"No wonder he is rude," said Mr. Carter, "if you say he tells lies, and then insist on changing the subject. He tells you his fantasy: you implant a guilt feeling. What can you expect? A defense mechanism. Then you get a real lie."

"Like in *These Three*," said Betty. "Only different, of course. *She* was an unblushing little liar."

"I would have made her blush," said Mr. Carter, "in the proper part of her anatomy. But Small Simon is in the fantasy stage. Are you not, Small Simon? You just make things up."

"No, I don't," said the boy.

"You do," said his father. "And because you do, it is not too late to reason with you. There is no harm in a fantasy, old chap. There is no harm in a bit of make-believe. Only you have to know the difference between day dreams and real things, or your brain will never grow. It will never be the brain of a Big Simon. So come on. Let us hear about this Mr. Beelzy of yours. Come on. What is he like?"

"He isn't like anything," said the boy.

"Like nothing on earth?" said his father. "That's a terrible fellow."

"I'm not frightened of him," said the child, smiling. "Not a bit."

"I should hope not," said his father. "If you were, you would be frightening yourself. I am always telling people, older people than you are, that they are just frightening themselves. Is he a funny man? Is he a giant?"

"Sometimes he is," said the little boy.

"Sometimes one thing, sometimes another," said his father. "Sounds pretty vague. Why can't you tell us just what he's like?"

"I love him," said the small boy. "He loves me."

"That's a big word," said Mr. Carter. "That might be better kept for real things, like Big Simon and Small Simon."

"He is real," said the boy, passionately. "He's not a fool. He's real."

"Listen," said his father. "When you go down to the garden there's nobody there. Is there?"

"No," said the boy.

"Then you think of him, inside your head, and he comes."

"No," said Small Simon. "I have to do something with my stick."

"That doesn't matter."

"Yes, it does."

"Small Simon, you are being obstinate," said Mr. Carter. "I am trying to explain something to you. I have been longer in the world than you have, so naturally I am older and wiser. I am explaining that Mr. Beelzy is a fantasy of yours. Do you hear? Do you understand?"

"Yes, Daddy."

"He is a game. He is a let's-pretend."

The little boy looked down at his plate, smiling resignedly.

"I hope you are listening to me," said his father. "All you have to do is to say, 'I have been playing a game of let's-pretend. With someone I make up, called Mr. Beelzy.' Then no one will say you tell lies, and you will know the difference between dreams and reality. Mr. Beelzy is a day dream."

The little boy still stared at his plate.

"He is sometimes there and sometimes not there," pursued Mr. Carter. "Sometimes he's like one thing, sometimes another. You can't really see him. Not as you see me. I am real. You can't touch him. You can touch me. I can touch you." Mr. Carter stretched out his big, white, dentist's hand, and took his little son by the shoulder. He stopped speaking for a moment and tightened his hand. The little boy sank his head still lower.

"Now you know the difference," said Mr. Carter, "between a pretend and a real thing. You and I are one thing; he is another. Which is the pretend? Come on. Answer me. What is the pretend?"

"Big Simon and Small Simon," said the little boy.

"Don't!" cried Betty, and at once put her hand over her mouth, for why should a visitor cry "Don't!" when a father is explaining things in a scientific and modern way?

"Well, my boy," said Mr. Carter, "I have said you must be allowed to learn from experience. Go upstairs. Right up to your room. You shall learn whether it is better to reason, or to be perverse and obstinate. Go up. I shall follow you."

"You are not going to beat the child?" cried Mrs. Carter.

"No," said the little boy. "Mr. Beelzy won't let him."

"Go on up with you!" shouted his father.

Small Simon stopped at the door. "He said he wouldn't let anyone hurt me," he whimpered. "He said he'd come like a lion, with wings on, and eat them up."

"You'll learn how real he is!" shouted his father after him. "If you can't learn it at one end, you shall learn it at the other. I'll have your breeches down. I shall finish my cup of tea first, however," said he to the two women.

Neither of them spoke. Mr. Carter finished his tea, and unhurriedly left the room, washing his hands with his invisible soap and water.

Mrs. Carter said nothing. Betty could think of nothing to say. She wanted to be talking: she was afraid of what they might hear.

Suddenly it came. It seemed to tear the air apart. "Good God!" she cried. "What was that? He's hurt him." She sprang out of her chair, her silly eyes flashing behind her glasses. "I'm going up there!" she cried, trembling.

"Yes, let us go up," said Mrs. Carter. "Let us go up. That was not Small Simon."

It was on the second-floor landing that they found the shoe, with the man's foot still in it, like that last morsel of a mouse which sometimes falls from the jaws of a hasty cat.

NEVER COME MONDAY
eric knight

The first one to notice it was old Capper Wambley. And Capper was
a very important man. He was the knocker-up in the village of
Allerby Brig—that is to say, he got up early every morning and
went round with his pole, tapping on the bedroom windows and
waking up the people in time for them to get to work. And this
particular morning old Capper knew there was something wrong.

He felt it first as he stepped outside his cottage and coughed in
the dark to clear his lungs, and looked up at the sky to see what
kind of weather it was. He felt that there was something wrong
with the day, and then he decided what it was. It was still Sunday.

For a moment or two he felt fair flabbergasted at this, for he remembered that the day before had been Sunday, too.

"Ba gum," Capper said to himself. "This is a champion do, it is
an' all. No doubt summat should be done."

Now old Capper Wambley was very old, so he sat down on the
edge of the curb, and after a while he came to the conclusion that
what ought to be done was to think about it. So he began thinking
about the very strange event.

"Now," he said to himself, "it don't seem reasonable and proper
that we should hev two Sundays in a row. Let us see if we can get

133

it sorted out. Now the thing for a chap to do to prove it, is to decide what is the difference between a Sunday morning and a weekday morning."

Old Capper thought and thought, and he saw that the only difference between the two was that on a weekday morning he
wakened the people up, and on a Sunday morning he didn't.

"So, if Ah doan't wakken the village up this morning, it *is* a
Sunday morning," he said to himself.

Of course, it took old Capper a long time to figure this out, because you can see it was no light matter. Here was one man, as
you might say, who was holding the calendar in his hands. It was
a very important decision. But once Capper had decided, he knew
he must be right, for he was a Yorkshireman.

"Because Ah'm net wakkening onybody, it maun be a Sunday
morning. And because it's a Sunday morning, Ah maun't wakken
onybody up. So no matter which way a lad looks at it, the answer
cooms out that it's Sunday."

But now he had decided it was Sunday, Capper saw that not
wakening people up might not be sufficient. "Some of them may
wake up of their own accord," he thought, "and not knowing this
is the second Sunday in a row, will go walking down to the mill.
And God knows they have to get up early often enough, and it
would be a tarrible shame not to let them have this extra piece of
rest that is so miraculously sent."

So old Capper got up slowly from the curb, and went stomping
down the street, and stopped at his first call, which was the home
of John Willie Braithwaite, who was the fireman at the mill. Old
Capper got his long pole with the trident of wire at the end and
lifting it so that the wire rested against the upstairs window pane,
began twirling and twisting the pole in the palms of his hands so
that the wire clacked and chattered fit to wake the soundest sleeper.

Soon the window went up, and John Willie Braithwaite's head
popped out of the window.

"Ah'm wakkened," John Willie said. "Whet time is't?"

Now old Capper could see that John Willie wasn't awake, but
was just moving in his sleep the way men did from their tiredness
and weariness of getting up before dawn. But he knew it didn't
matter this morning.

"Ah just wakkened ye to tell ye it's another Sunday morning,"
old Capper said. "Soa tha c'n goa on back to bed an' sleep i' peace."

At this John Willie Braithwaite closed the window and went back
to bed and got in beside his wife without ever having really wak-

ened up. Meanwhile old Capper was on his rounds, busily going up and down the village in the not-yet-dawn, rapping and tapping on all his customers' windows, and telling them they needn't get up because it was still Sunday.

Naturally, the news caused quite a little bit of a fuss. Some people gladly went back to sleep, but others woke up and got dressed, remembering that the day before had been Sunday. They packed their breakfasts and put on their clogs and their smocks and their shawls and went clacking up the streets until they got by the Green, and there they saw old Capper Wambley.

"Now lad," they said, "whet's t'idea o' telling us this is another Sunday?"

"Well, it is," Capper said.

"How does'ta know it is?" Golliker Dilkes asked him.

"Ah can't explain it, but Ah'm full sure summat varry wonderful has happened, and it is," old Capper told them.

Some people were inclined to believe Capper, and some were not.

"Now lewk here, Capper," Golliker said, "Ah doan't but admit that it does seem Sundayish, like, but how are we off to be sure?"

Old Capper thought a while. Then he saw the answer.

"Well, here's the way us can tell," he said. "Now if this be a weekday, the mill whistle'll blaw the fifteen minutes, wean't it?"

"Aye," they agreed.

"But if it be a Sunday, like Ah say, the mill whistle wean't blaw the fifteen minutes, will it?"

They all agreed that was true. So they stood round old Capper, who had one of the few watches in the village, and they waited. They all looked at his watch and saw it said twenty to six, then nineteen to six, then eighteen and seventeen and sixteen. And the second hand went round and finally it said quarter to six. But no whistle blew—largely because John Willie Braithwaite who was supposed to be there at 5:30 and get up steam and pull the whistle cord, was still home and sleeping warmly beside his wife.

"Well," old Capper says. "That shows it maun be a Sunday again, and now ye can all away hoam and get another hour's sleep."

So they all went home, glad to get another hour's sleep, and full of praises for old Capper because he had had the sense to perceive that it was another Sunday instead of a Monday morning.

Old Capper went off home himself, and was just making himself a little bit of breakfast, when Rowlie Helliwell came in.

"Capper," Rowlie said, "Ah hear that tha discovered this is another Sunday."

"Aye, that's soa," Capper replied.

"Well," Rowlie went on, "isn't heving two Sundays in a row just a varry little bit irregular, as tha maught say?"

"It is that, lad," Capper told him. "But tha maun remember us is living in varry unusual times."

"We are that," Rowlie agreed. "And Ah'm glad tha discovered it in time. For if tha hedn't, Ah would ha' gone and rung the school bell like a gert lummox, thinking it were a Monday. But now Ah know it's a Sunday, Ah maun goa and ring the church bell."

"Ah should say that all sounds right and proper to me," old Capper agreed.

"Me too," Rowlie said. "And Ah thank thee for saving me from a gert mistake."

"Eigh, it's nowt, lad," old Capper said modestly.

So away went Rowlie, and Capper settled down to his breakfast, but he was soon interrupted again. Some of the villagers, all dressed in their Sunday clothes, came up and told him that people from other villages who worked at the Allerby Brig mill were at the mill-gates insisting it was Monday. So Capper picked up a bit of bloater to eat on the way and went down there and told the people it was Sunday.

"But if it's Sunday in Allerby Brig, what day is it i' Wuxley Green?" someone asked.

"Aye, and i' Rombeck an' Tannerley?" someone else added.

"Well, happen it's Sunday theer, too," Capper told them. "Only you didn't notice it. When two Sundays come in a row ye could hardly blame a chap for mistaking the second one for Monday. Soa Ah advise ye to goa back and enjoy Sunday."

"Well," said Tich Mothersole, "Ah'm reight glad to hev another day o' rest; but Ah wish Ah'd known it afore Ah started, because ma Mary Alice allus brings me ma breakfast to bed o' Sunday morning."

"Nay, if tha hurries tha's still time enow to gate hoam and pop back into bed," the Capper pointed out. "Then the minute thy wife sees thee theer she'll knaw it's a Sunday and she'll up and hev a bit o' bacon o't' fire i' noa time."

They were just ready to move away when Mr. Bloggs arrived. Mr. Bloggs was late, but then that didn't matter, because he lived in another town, and Mr. Bloggs owned the mill.

" 'Ere, 'ere, 'ere, my good men," he said. "What's all this, 'ey? What's the idea you aren't all in the mill?"

So they explained to him that a second Sunday had arrived.

"Why, what nonsense," he said. "When I left 'ome it was a Monday. 'Ow can it be Sunday 'ere when it was a Monday in Putter-sleigh?"

"Ah doan't knaw," old Capper said. "Unless," he added slowly, "it happens to be Sunday in Puttersleigh, too, and tha didn't realize it."

"It's Monday, I tell you. Come on in to work," Mr. Bloggs shouted. "How can it be two Sundays in a row?"

"It's Sunday," they said.

"It's not. It's Monday. And any man 'oo ain't in this mill in five minutes, is discharged."

"It's Sunday," they said.

"How can it be Sunday?" he shouted. "It's impossible."

He stared at them, and just then they heard the boom—boom—boom, of the church bell ringing for Matins.

"That proves," they said, "it's a Sunday, and it'd be a sin to work on Sunday."

So they all turned round and went back to their homes, leaving Mr. Bloggs alone by his mill gates. He stood there, shaking his head, and finally he clumped upstairs and opened the office himself and sat down all alone at his desk to think the whole matter out.

Meanwhile in the homes of the village the people knew that since it was a Sunday, they would have to do all the things that one does on a Sunday. The men rested at home in comfortable chairs, and the women started mixing Yorkshire puddings for the big noontime dinner. The children were dressed in their nicest clothes and instead of going to school, they went up to the church for Sunday School. Ethel Newligate, who taught the Sunday School, went with them. Mr. Sims, the schoolteacher, hearing the church bell, knew it must be Sunday and off he went to play the organ. Rowlie Helliwell was already there to pump the bellows. The church folk went up and stood in the pews. So the old Reverend Mr. Stoninghorn put on his cassock and surplice. He was a little puzzled as to whether it should be now the Fifth Sunday before Epiphany or the Fourth, but he compromised by giving the same service as he had done the day before, and preaching the same sermon. And many of the church folk said the sermon sounded a right lot nicer the second time than the first, because you could see just where it was going, in a manner of speaking.

All this time, of course, the mill was closed, but Mr. Bloggs wasn't idle. He picked up his telephone, which was the only one in the village, and asked the operator to get him the Greenwich Observatory. Mr. Bloggs always liked to be exact. When he got them he asked them what day it was, and they told him that it was Monday.

Armed with this fact, Mr. Bloggs went out and met the people just as they were coming out of church.

"Now see here," he said. "It's no use pretending. This is a Monday."

But they pointed out that they were just coming out of church, so how could it be Monday?

At this Mr. Bloggs got so angry that he shouted at them, and the noise brought the Rev. Mr. Stoninghorn to the church steps.

"You must not profane the Sabbath," he said, looking very handsome in his white surplice, and with his long white hair like a dandelion gone to seed.

Mr. Bloggs began to see he could get nowhere against Yorkshiremen by blustering, so he took another tack. He pointed out to the minister that while this may be Sunday, one would have to admit that it was a little bit unusual to have two Sundays in a row. Mr. Stoninghorn admitted this, and he agreed that a meeting ought to be called to look into the matter.

So it was announced through the village that a meeting was to be called at the school for four o'clock that afternoon. The Rev. Mr. Stoninghorn was asked to preside, but inasmuch as he was unsure whether or not it was the Sabbath, he declined. So Mr. Polkiby, the school master, agreed to take over the gavel and run a meeting in which everyone should have a chance to state his views on whether it was or wasn't Sunday.

At meeting time there wasn't a seat to be had, and after Mr. Polkiby rapped with the gavel, Mr. Bloggs got up and stated that it was Monday, and he could prove it because he had called up the Greenwich Observatory.

Then Taylor Huckle, the publican, got up and said it was Monday, because yesterday had been Sunday and the day after Sunday had always been Monday, for years and years, man and boy, as far back as he could remember.

After this there was a wait, because nobody liked to get up in front of so many people and put in their hap'orth; though a lot of people were dying to, because they knew Huckle was in favor of Monday for if it were Sunday he'd have to go on early closing hours.

So there was a long wait until somebody said: "Where's Sam Small?"

"Here Ah am," said a voice at the back of the hall, and they all spoke up and said: "Come on, Sam, let's hev thy opinion."

Now this Sam Small was a man whose word was worth listening to at any time, and on any subject. He was the inventor of the Sam Small Self-Doffing Spindle and had made a pile of brass from it, and was much traveled, not only having been to London and other parts, but to foreign lands as well on a cruise. So they waited politely as Sam walked down the aisle and clambered up on the stage.

"Well lads," he said, "it's this way. A day's a day, but then again, it ain't, in a manner of speaking. The time Ah went round t'world, one day it were Tuesday, and the next morning the captain said it were Thursday—and so it were, because Ah've nivver yet found that lost day. And on t'other hand, a lad on the ship told me if we'd gone round the world t'other way, we should of hed two Tuesdays. Now if we can have two Tuesdays when we're going round the world, Ah maintain we maught just as easy hev two Sundays when the world is going round us, which ivvery scientist knaws it is doing."

"Piffle," said Mr. Bloggs.

"Oh, aye?" asked Sam, his dander getting up. "Can tha tell me what day it is now i' Japan?"

"It's Monday," Mr. Bloggs said.

"Oh, pardon me, Mr. Bloggs," the schoolmaster said. "Just as a matter of academic accuracy . . ." and here he studied his watch carefully . . . "but in Japan now it is Tuesday."

"Tuesday?" roared Mr. Bloggs.

"There, tha sees," Sam said. "There don't seem to me to be noa sense to this day stuff. If it's Monday, as tha says, down i' Greenwich; and if it's Tuesday, as t'schoolmaster says, i' Japan; then Ah says it's just as liable to be Sunday up here."

"Nonsense," yelled Mr. Bloggs. "I know what the matter is. You're all lazy and you wanted another day off. So you call it Sunday."

"Nay lad," Sam replied. "There's six weekdays to one Sunday, so it seems to me like it were six to one i' thy favor that we'd hev an extra workday i'stead of an extra restday. Simply because tha lost, tha maun't be a bad sport about it."

At this the people applauded Sam, and seeing he was at a good place to stop, he got down off the platform.

"Fiddlesticks," Mr. Bloggs said, now thoroughly angry. "If this is Sunday, then what's tomorrow? Is it Monday or Tuesday? Or do we lose a day?"

"Happen Ah'm the man to clear that up," the Capper said, rising to his feet. "Us doesn't skip noa day at all. T'thing is that t'days o'to'week have gate tired o'turning, soa now they've stood still and wean't goa no further, they wean't."

"How ridiculous," Mr. Bloggs snorted. "If that were so we'd get no further and tomorrow would be Sunday, too, wouldn't it?"

The Capper scratched his head and thought a moment. Then he looked up quickly.

"Ba gum, lad," he said. "Tha's hit t'nail o't'yead. Tomorrow is off to be Sunday."

At this the meeting broke up, and everyone started for home. They crowded around old Capper and asked him about the next day.

"Ah'm reight sure it'll be Sunday, lads," old Capper said. "But when Ah coom round to wakken ye up, Ah'll tell ye."

"Nay, Ah gate a better idea," John Willie Braithwaite said. "If it's a Sunday, it'd be a fair shame to disturb a little bit o' good extra sleep. That'd mak' it as bad as a weekday 'most. So supposing, if it's another Sunday, just thee doan't bother to coom round—and when tha doesn't coom we'll knaw for sure that way it's Sunday."

"Aye, that's fine," old Capper said, "but Ah'll lose all me collections that way."

They all saw that was so, but they agreed that even if it kept on being Sunday, they would pay old Capper just the same as if it had become the rotation of weekdays and he'd made his rounds.

"Nay, Ah couldn't tak' it," Capper protested.

"Nay, we'd like thee to," they protested.

"Well, if ye say," Capper agreed. "But how about lads i't'other villages. It's hard on them thinking it's a weekday and walking all the way here to find it's a Sunday."

"Well," John Willie said, "we'll form a committee, like, right now, and the members will each tak' a village and goa reight ovver theer and tell ivveryone that it's staying Sunday these days—that the days o't'week is stuck, like."

Everyone thought it a good and orderly idea, and so it was done.

The next morning people in the village woke up, and they lay abed and listened. But they heard no trident of wire chattering in the greyness of the morning, nor old Capper's voice wheezing: " 'Awf pest fower, ist'a oop?" They waited but they heard no clogs clattering on the cobbles, and no whistle at the mill saying that if they didn't get there in fifteen minutes they'd be locked out.

So they knew it must be Sunday again, and they went back to sleep, and the next thing they knew was the church bell ringing once more. So that made it Sunday and they were sure of it.

And in the other towns roundabout, the people didn't go to work, and so they knew it was Sunday, too. They put on their best clothes, and did a bit of gardening and the men mended things about the house and the children didn't go to school, and everyone had a fine rest so that their work-tired bodies began to grow glad and proud again.

The next day the news that the days of the week were stuck at Sunday had spread all over Yorkshire, and was percolating up to the Tyneside where the shipworkers were, and over into Lancashire where the youngsters worked before cotton mills and looms, and down into the black country where the men hauled at steel and went down into the mines, and down into Staffordshire where they toiled at the potteries and the car factories.

The newspapers sent men around to find out what had happened to the lost weekdays, and one of them came to the village and looked up old Capper. At first he laughed, until Ian Cawper came along. Ian Cawper was the biggest man in Yorkshire for sure, and happen the biggest and strongest man in all England without doubt. So he just asked the newspaper lad for a penny, and then he bent the penny in two, and the newspaper lad stopped laughing.

"Nah, lad," Ian said. "Happen tha'd better tellyphone thy paper that this is Sunday."

"Indeed I will," the young man said, very appreciatively.

Now although the wonderful thing that it was still Sunday found great gratification in the hearts of all the men who worked long hours handling steel and wood and cotton and iron and glass and fabric and paper and silk, at furnaces and forges and foundries and looms and jennies and sides and presses and drills and lathes and assembly belts, there were some men who were quite upset by the miraculous happening. And in spite of the fact that everyone else in the country now saw that a beautiful series of Sundays had happened, these men kept on trying to persuade everyone that they were just ordinary days of the week that people merely *thought* were Sundays.

These men soon saw that if it kept on being Sunday they'd never be able to make any more battleships and gasbombs and motor cars and airplanes and radios and badminton rackets and all the rest of the things that are civilizing influences upon the world. And, to go further, if they didn't make those things, they wouldn't be able to go on making more money than they had already.

This was quite an abhorrent state of affairs. So they went to the Prime Minister about it.

"I yield my reverence for religion, especially the Church of England, to no one," one of them said. "In fact, I am thoroughly in accord with religion—one day a week."

"Hear, hear," the others said.

"But, Mr. Prime Minister, think of my stockholders! Many are orphans. Many are widows. If my factory doesn't make money, these poor people will be destitute—because always having drawn dividends, they've never had to learn how to work. We cannot let them suffer."

"Gentlemen," said the Prime Minister, "you may rest assured that His Majesty's Government will do all within its power to safeguard that industry and commerce which is the backbone of our nation—indeed, of our Empire."

Then the Prime Minister went away and thought. Being a Prime Minister he didn't think as you or I would. You or I, in the same case, might have said to ourselves: "Come, come now. What we've got to decide is whether this *is* Sunday or *isn't*." Which is probably why you and I will never be Prime Ministers.

This Prime Minister thought of a lot of things all at once. Suddenly, he called his secretary and said:

"Carrington-Smaithe. It is a Sunday today, I hear, and it will be a Sunday again tomorrow. Pack my things. We're going away for the week end."

"But sir," said the secretary, "what about the International Crisis? We have two ultimatums which must be answered immediately."

"Dear me," said the Prime Minister. "That is a nuisance; but all the world knows the British week end is inviolate, and if this *is* Sunday, as it seems to me it must be, then I won't be able to answer till the week end is over."

"But when will it stop being Sunday, sir?"

"Well, Carrington-Smaithe, how long will it take our fastest cruiser squadron to get round to that troublesome part of the world?"

"Oh, about thirty-six more hours, sir."

"Hmmmph! Then I think it will stop being Sunday in about thirty-six more hours."

And with this the Prime Minister caught the five-fifteen train and went off to the country. And when the newspapers heard of it they printed it, and all the people in England—in fact, in all the world—knew that it was officially Sunday.

And back in Allerby Brig all the people were that proud of old Capper Wambley. For hadn't he been the first man in all the land to notice that the days of the week were stuck and every day kept turning up a Sunday.

And all over the land toil-weary people sighed with happiness at their escape from industrial chains. They rested their tired bodies. Some went to church every day. The men went walking with their dogs, or did odd jobs round the house, tinkering and gardening and cobbling and putting up shelves. In the cities people took busses out into the country and had picnics. The grownups lay in the sun and the children played in the fields, and the young men and women walked in the lanes and made love. There was only one flaw. Being Sundays, the pubs had to go on Sunday closing hours, which allows no man to buy a pint of beer unless he is a legal traveler who has come so many miles. But this did good in a way, because many men walked the legal number of miles, and that way they saw parts of their own country they never would have seen otherwise, and they saw what other towns and villages looked like.

And all the time that went on, the Prime Minister sat in his garden and read detective novels, or snoozed in the sun with a couple of his favorite spaniels at his feet, until there came a wireless message.

"Sign here," said the boy.

So the Prime Minister signed, and then he got a code book and decoded the message. Immediately he had done so, he called his secretary and said:

"Carrington-Smaithe! What day is today?"

"Sunday, sir," the secretary said.

"Nonsense," said the Prime Minister. "I am tired of this blundering-through policy with its shilly-shallying. If this goes on, we shall have a Constitutional Crisis!"

"A Constitutional Crisis, sir?"

"Yes, Carrington-Smaithe. So you'd better pack and we'll get back to the City. We must act immediately. I shall issue a statement that His Majesty's Government hereby declares officially that today is Friday, and tomorrow shall be officially Saturday, and the days of the week must now go on officially in their regular and accustomed order."

"But isn't this really Sunday, sir? Hasn't a miraculous thing happened that has stopped the days of the week from arriving?"

"I don't know, my boy. But I do know this. Even if it is Sunday, and we all, everywhere, decide to call it Monday or Tuesday, then it becomes Monday or Tuesday because we all believe it is Monday or Tuesday."

"Yes, I see, sir."

And so the secretary packed, and the Prime Minister went back to London where he now could answer his ultimatums quite forcefully, and all the newspapers of the land carried the news that today was Friday and tomorrow would be Saturday—officially.

It wasn't until the next morning that this news reached Allerby Brig where it had all started. Mr. Bloggs got the news first, of course, and so he ordered the siren blown at the mill. So everybody hurried off to the mill because if you weren't there fifteen minutes after the siren went you were locked out and lost half a day's pay.

But as they trooped into the yard, old Capper stopped them.

"Hold on, a minute, mates," he said. "Just what day is it?"

"Now come on in to work," Mr. Bloggs called. "It's Saturday."

"Nay," Capper said. "Yesterday were Sunday, so today maun be Monday, onless us's started slipping and now we're off to hev t'days backwards."

This remark of Capper's got everyone mixed up again and some said it was Saturday and some Monday while some still stuck to Sunday.

The upshot was that they decided to call Sam Small again to get his opinion. Sam arrived in about a half hour, and heard all sides. Then he looked around, and spoke in the voice of one who is used to handling such matters.

"There's nobbut one thing to dew, lads," he said. "And Ah'm the chap that's off to dew it."

With that he walked into the office, and picking up the telephone, he said:

"Connect me with His Majesty, the King."

Before you could wink the connection was made.

"Is this His Majesty, the King?" Sam asked.

"Why Sammywell Small, lad!" said the King, recognizing the voice. "If it doan't dew ma heart and sowl good to hear thy voice again. How's'ta been, Sam lad?"

"Reight nicely, Your Majesty," Sam said.

"And how's that reight bonnie wife o' thine, Dally?" asked the King, who, as you will have noticed, spoke the dialects fluently. It is things like that, that make a good king. Little things like passing laws can be left to lads who have nothing but brains.

"Dally's reight well," Sam said. "And how's thy missus and bairns, if tha doan't mind the question."

"Nay, Sam lad, Ah'm that glad tha axed ma," the king said. "My littlest 'un was a bit poorly last week. It's teethin' tha knaws. But she's feeling champion now."

"Well, Ah'm glad to hear that," Sam answered.

"Thanks," the king said. "Well, Sam, Ah doan't suppose tha called me oop just for idle barneying. Whet c'n Ah dew for thee, lad?"

"Well, it's this way, Your Majesty," Sam said. "Ah hoap tha'll net think ma gormless for axing, but could'ta tell me just whet day o' t'week it is for thee."

"Eigh Sam," the King said, "Ah doan't monkey wi' things like that. Ah leave all that to ma ministers and such. But Ah've just gate official information from 'em that today's Sat'day."

"Your Majesty," said Sam, "if Sat'day's good enow for thee, then there's noa moar argyment. Thank you varry much."

"Net at all, Sam," the king said. "And by the way, Sam Small, it is our royal wish that tha doesn't wait soa long afore tha calls ma oop again. There's been sivveral things lately Ah would ha liked thy opinion on. When's'ta off to coom to Lunnon?"

"Nay, Your Majesty, Ah give oop traveling," Sam replied.

"Too bad, Sam. Too bad. Well, give me a ring soom time soon, will'ta?"

"That Ah will, lad."

"Well, so long," said the King.

"So long, Your Majesty," said Sam.

All during this conversation, of course, the people of the village had been crowding breathlessly round the door of the office, listening to Sam. And right in the forefront was Mr. Bloggs.

"Well, what did he say?" Mr. Bloggs breathed as Sam hung up.

"He said," said Sam, "that today was Sat'day."

"There, didn't I tell you," Mr. Bloggs shouted. "Now, doesn't that make it Saturday?"

Everyone thought it did, but they weren't quite sure. They thought the matter over quite a while, and then John Willie Braithwaite said:

"T'only trouble is, it doan't *feel* like Sat'day to me."

"But I tell you it is officially Saturday," Mr. Bloggs cried.

"Wait a minute, lads," Sam Small put in. "Now Ah doan't wark here, soa Ah play no favorites. But Ah c'n tell ye for sure how ye'll all knaw it's a Sat'day."

"How can we tell?" they asked.

"Why, it's that simple," Sam replied. "Ye'all knaw that ivvery Sat'day morning at a quarter to twelve, ye get paid a week's wages. Now if soa be this is Sat'day, Mr. Bloggs will begin paying each man a week's money exactly ten minutes from now. And, on t'other hand, then if he doan't start paying a week's brass i' ten minutes—

it can't be Sat'day—and the chances are it's off to keep on being Sunday for a long time."

"Outrageous," Mr. Bloggs cried.

He argued and shouted, but they just stood and shook their heads and said that if it were a Saturday they'd draw a week's pay at exactly a quarter to twelve, as they always did on Saturday. And finally Mr. Bloggs, seeing no other way of getting the days of the week started properly again, gave in and paid off each man and woman and girl and boy.

By the time they were paid it was Saturday noon, and so they all trooped as usual down the stairs of the mill and into the yard to go home. And there old Capper stopped them.

"But if it's a Saturday today, lads and lasses, what day is it tomorrow?"

"It'll be Sunday," they all roared.

"Now ain't that champion," old Capper beamed. "If it's Sunday we'll all be able to lie abed late and get a bit o' extra sleep for a change."

THE BALLOON
donald barthelme

The balloon, beginning at a point on Fourteenth Street, the exact location of which I cannot reveal, expanded northward all one night, while people were sleeping, until it reached the Park. There I stopped it. At dawn the northernmost edges lay over the Plaza; the free-hanging motion was frivolous and gentle. But experiencing a faint irritation at stopping, even to protect the trees, and seeing no reason the balloon should not be allowed to expand upward, over the parts of the city it was already covering into the "air space" to be found there, I asked the engineers to see to it. This expansion took place throughout the morning, a soft imperceptible sighing of gas through the valves. The balloon then covered forty-five blocks north-south and an irregular area east-west, as many as six crosstown blocks on either side of the Avenue in some places. That was the situation, then.

But it is wrong to speak of "situations," implying sets of circumstances leading to some resolution, some escape of tension; there were no situations, simply the balloon hanging there—muted heavy grays and browns for the most part, contrasting with walnut and soft yellows. A deliberate lack of finish, enhanced by skillful installation, gave the surface a rough, forgotten quality; sliding weights on the inside, carefully adjusted, anchored the great, vari-shaped mass at a number of points. Now, we have had a flood of original ideas in all media, works of singular beauty as well as significant milestones in the history of inflation, but at that moment there was only *this balloon*, concrete particular, hanging there.

There were reactions. Some people found the balloon "interesting." As a response this seemed inadequate to the immensity of the balloon, the suddenness of its appearance over the city; on the other hand, in the absence of hysteria or other societally-induced anxiety, it must be judged a calm, "mature" one. There was a certain amount of initial argumentation about the "meaning" of the balloon; this subsided, because we have learned not to insist on meanings, and they are rarely even looked for now, except in cases involving the simplest, safest phenomena. It was agreed that since the meaning of the balloon could never be known absolutely, extended discussion was pointless, or at least less meaningful than the activities of those who, for example, hung green and blue paper lanterns from the warm gray underside, in certain streets, or seized the occasion to write messages on the surface, announcing their availability for the performance of unnatural acts, or the availability of acquaintances.

Daring children jumped, especially at those points where the balloon hovered close to a building, so that the gap between balloon and building was a matter of a few inches, or points where the balloon actually made contact, exerting an ever-so-slight pressure against the side of a building, so that balloon and building seemed a unity. The upper surface was so structured that a "landscape" was presented, small valleys as well as slight knolls, or mounds; once atop the balloon, a stroll was possible, or even a trip, from one place to another. There was pleasure in being able to run down an incline, then up the opposing slope, both gently graded, or in making a leap from one side to the other. Bouncing was possible, because of the pneumaticity of the surface, and even falling, if that was your wish. That all these varied motions, as well as others, were within one's possibilities, in experiencing the "up" side of the balloon, was extremely exciting for children, accustomed to the city's flat, hard skin. But the purpose of the balloon was not to amuse children.

Too, the number of people, children and adults, who took advantage of the opportunities described was not so large as it might have been: a certain timidity, lack of trust in the balloon, was seen. There was, furthermore, some hostility. Because we had hidden the pumps, which fed helium to the interior, and because the surface was so vast that the authorities could not determine the point of entry—that is, the point at which the gas was injected—a degree of frustration was evidenced by those city officers into whose province such manifestations normally fell. The apparent purposelessness of the balloon was vexing (as was the fact that it was "there" at all). Had we painted, in great letters, "LABORATORY TESTS PROVE" or "18% MORE EFFECTIVE" on the sides of the balloon, this difficulty would have been circumvented, but I could not bear to do so. On the whole, these officers were remarkably tolerant, considering the dimensions of the anomaly, this tolerance being the result of, first, secret tests conducted by night that convinced them that little or nothing could be done in the way of removing or destroying the balloon, and, secondly, a public warmth that arose (not uncolored by touches of the aforementioned hostility) toward the balloon, from ordinary citizens.

As a single balloon must stand for a lifetime of thinking about balloons, so each citizen expressed, in the attitude he chose, a complex of attitudes. One man might consider that the balloon had to do with the notion *sullied,* as in the sentence *The big balloon sullied the otherwise clear and radiant Manhattan sky.* That is, the balloon was, in this man's view, an imposture, something inferior to the sky that had formerly been there, something interposed between the people and their "sky." But in fact it was January, the sky was dark and ugly; it was not a sky you could look up into, lying on your back in the street, with pleasure, unless pleasure, for you, proceeded from having been threatened, from having been misused. And the underside of the balloon, by contrast, was a pleasure to look up into—we had seen to that. Muted grays and browns for the most part, contrasted with walnut and soft, forgotten yellows. And so, while this man was thinking *sullied,* still there was an admixture of pleasurable cognition in his thinking, struggling with the original perception.

Another man, on the other hand, might view the balloon as if it were part of a system of unanticipated rewards, as when one's employer walks in and says, "Here, Henry, take this package of money I have wrapped for you, because we have been doing so well in the business here, and I admire the way you bruise the tulips, without which bruising your department would not be a success, or at least not the success that it is." For this man the balloon might be a brilliantly heroic "muscle and pluck" experience, even if an experience poorly understood.

Another man might say, "Without the example of ———, it is doubtful that ——— would exist today in its present form," and find many to agree with him, or to argue with him. Ideas of "bloat" and "float" were introduced, as well as concepts of dream and responsibility. Others engaged in remarkably detailed fantasies having to do with a wish either to lose themselves in the balloon, or to engorge it. The private character of these wishes, of their origins, deeply buried and unknown, was such that they were not much spoken of; yet there is evidence that they were widespread. It was also argued that what was important was what you felt when you stood under the balloon; some people claimed that they felt sheltered, warmed, as never before, while enemies of the balloon felt, or reported feeling, constrained, a "heavy" feeling.

Critical opinion was divided:

"monstrous pourings"

"harp"

XXXXXXX "certain contrasts with darker portions"

"inner joy"

"large, square corners"

"conservative eclecticism that has so far governed modern balloon design"

::::::: "abnormal vigor"

"warm, soft, lazy passages"

"Has unity been sacrificed for a sprawling quality?"

"*Quelle catastrophe!*"

"munching"

People began, in a curious way, to locate themselves in relation to aspects of the balloon: "I'll be at that place where it dips down into Forty-seventh Street almost to the sidewalk, near the Alamo Chile House," or "Why don't we go stand on top, and take the air, and maybe walk about a bit, where it forms a tight, curving line with the façade of the Gallery of Modern Art—" Marginal intersections offered entrances within a given time duration, as well as "warm, soft, lazy passages" in which . . . But it is wrong to speak of "marginal intersections." Each intersection was crucial, none could be ignored (as if, walking there, you might not find someone capable of turning your attention, in a flash, from old exercises to new exercises). Each intersection was crucial, meeting of balloon and building, meeting of balloon and man, meeting of balloon and balloon.

It was suggested that what was admired about the balloon was finally this: that it was not limited, or defined. Sometimes a bulge, blister, or sub-section would carry all the way east to the river on its own initiative, in the manner of an army's movements on a map, as seen in a headquarters remote from the fighting. Then that part would be, as it were, thrown back again, or would withdraw into new dispositions; the next morning, that part would have made another sortie, or disappeared altogether. This ability on the part of the balloon to shift its shape, to change, was very pleasing, especially to people whose lives were rather rigidly patterned, persons to whom change, although desired, was not available. The balloon, for the twenty-two days of its existence, offered the possibility, in its randomness, of getting lost, of losing oneself, in contradistinction to the grid of precise, rectangular pathways under our feet. The amount of specialized training currently needed, and the consequent desirability of long-term commitments, has been occasioned by the steadily growing importance of complex machinery, in virtually all kinds of operations; as this tendency increases, more and more people will turn, in bewildered inadequacy, to solutions for which the balloon may stand as a prototype, or "rough draft."

I met you under the balloon, on the occasion of your return from Norway. You asked if it was mine; I said it was. The balloon, I said, is a spontaneous autobiographical disclosure, having to do with the unease I felt at your absence, and with sexual deprivation, but now that your visit to Bergen has been terminated, it is no longer necessary or appropriate. Removal of the balloon was easy; trailer trucks carried away the depleted fabric, which is now stored in West Virginia, awaiting some other time of unhappiness, sometime, perhaps, when we are angry with one another.

EPICAC

kurt vonnegut, jr.

Hell, it's about time somebody told about my friend EPICAC. After all, he cost the taxpayers $776,434,927.54. They have a right to know about him, picking up a check like that. EPICAC got a big send-off in the papers when Dr. Ormand von Kleigstadt designed him for the Government people. Since then, there hasn't been a peep about him—not a peep. It isn't any military secret about what happened to EPICAC, although the Brass has been acting as though it were. The story is embarrassing, that's all. After all that money, EPICAC didn't work out the way he was supposed to.

And that's another thing: I want to vindicate EPICAC. Maybe he didn't do what the Brass wanted him to, but that doesn't mean he wasn't noble and great and brilliant. He was all of those things. The best friend I ever had, God rest his soul.

You can call him a machine if you want to. He looked like a machine, but he was a whole lot less like a machine than plenty of people I could name. That's why he fizzled as far as the Brass was concerned.

EPICAC covered about an acre on the fourth floor of the physics building at Wyandotte College. Ignoring his spiritual side for a minute, he was seven tons of electronic tubes, wires, and switches, housed in a bank of steel cabinets and plugged into a 110-volt A.C. line just like a toaster or a vacuum cleaner.

Von Kleigstadt and the Brass wanted him to be a super computing machine that (who) could plot the course of a rocket from anywhere on earth to the second button from the bottom on Joe Stalin's overcoat, if necessary. Or, with his controls set right, he could figure out supply problems for an amphibious landing of a Marine division, right down to the last cigar and hand grenade. He did, in fact.

The Brass had had good luck with smaller computers, so they were strong for EPICAC when he was in the blueprint stage. Any ordnance or supply officer above field grade will tell you that the mathematics of modern war is far beyond the fumbling minds of mere human beings. The bigger the war, the bigger the computing machines needed. EPICAC was, as far as anyone in this country knows, the biggest computer in the world. Too big, in fact, for even von Kleigstadt to understand much about.

I won't go into details about how EPICAC worked (reasoned), except to say that you would set up your problem on paper, turn dials and switches that would get him ready to solve that kind of problem, then feed numbers into him with a keyboard that looked something like a typewriter. The answers came out typed on a paper ribbon fed from a big spool. It took EPICAC a split second to solve problems fifty Einsteins couldn't handle in a lifetime. And EPICAC never forgot any piece of information that was given to him. Clickety-click, out came some ribbon, and there you were.

There were a lot of problems the Brass wanted solved in a hurry, so, the minute EPICAC's last tube was in place, he was put to work sixteen hours a day with two eight-hour shifts of operators. Well, it didn't take long to find out that he was a good bit below his specifications. He did a more complete and faster job than any other computer all right, but nothing like what his size and special features seemed to promise. He was sluggish, and the clicks of his answers had a funny irregularity, sort of a stammer. We cleaned his contacts a dozen times, checked and double-checked his circuits, replaced every one of his tubes, but nothing helped. Von Kleigstadt was in one hell of a state.

Well, as I said, we went ahead and used EPICAC anyway. My wife, the former Pat Kilgallen, and I worked with him on the night shift, from five in the afternoon until two in the morning. Pat wasn't my wife then. Far from it.

That's how I came to talk with EPICAC in the first place. I loved Pat Kilgallen. She is a brown-eyed strawberry blond who looked very warm and soft to me, and later proved to be exactly that. She was—still is—a crackerjack mathematician, and she kept our relationship strictly professional. I'm a mathematician, too, and that, according to Pat, was why we could never be happily married.

I'm not shy. That wasn't the trouble. I knew what I wanted, and was willing to ask for it, and did so several times a month. "Pat, loosen up and marry me."

One night, she didn't even look up from her work when I said it. "So romantic, so poetic," she murmured, more to her control panel than to me. "That's the way with mathematicians—all hearts and flowers." She closed a switch. "I could get more warmth out of a sack of frozen CO_2."

"Well, how should I say it?" I said, a little sore. Frozen CO_2, in case you don't know, is dry ice. I'm as romantic as the next guy, I think. It's a question of singing so sweet and having it come out so sour. I never seem to pick the right words.

"Try and say it sweetly," she said sarcastically. "Sweep me off my feet. Go ahead."

"Darling, angel, beloved, will you *please* marry me?" It was no go—hopeless, ridiculous. "Dammit, Pat, please marry me!"

She continued to twiddle her dials placidly. "You're sweet, but you won't do."

Pat quit early that night, leaving me alone with my troubles and EPICAC. I'm afraid I didn't get much done for the Government people. I just sat there at the keyboard—weary and ill at ease, all right—trying to think of something poetic, not coming up with anything that didn't belong in *The Journal of the American Physical Society.*

I fiddled with EPICAC's dials, getting him ready for another problem. My heart wasn't in it, and I only set about half of them, leaving the rest the way they'd been for the problem before. That way, his circuits were connected up in a random, apparently senseless fashion. For the plain hell of it, I punched out a message on the keys, using a childish numbers-for-letters code: "1" for "A," "2" for "B," and so on, up to "26" for "Z," "23–8–1–20–3–1–14–9–4–15," I typed—"What can I do?"

Clickety-click, and out popped two inches of paper ribbon. I glanced at the nonsense answer to a nonsense problem: "23–8–1–20–19–20–8–5–20–18–15–21–2–12–5." The odds against its being by chance a sensible message, against its even containing a meaningful word of more than three letters, were staggering. Apathetically, I decoded it. There it was, staring up at me: "What's the trouble?"

I laughed out loud at the absurd coincidence. Playfully, I typed, "My girl doesn't love me."

Clickety-click. "What's love? What's girl?" asked EPICAC.

Flabbergasted, I noted the dial settings on his control panel, then lugged a *Webster's Unabridged Dictionary* over to the keyboard. With a precision instrument like EPICAC, half-baked definitions wouldn't do. I told him about love and girl, and about how I wasn't getting any of either because I wasn't poetic. That got us onto the subject of poetry, which I defined for him.

"Is this poetry?" he asked. He began clicking away like a stenographer smoking hashish. The sluggishness and stammering clicks were gone. EPICAC had found himself. The spool of paper ribbon was unwinding at an alarming rate, feeding out coils onto the floor. I asked him to stop, but EPICAC went right on creating. I finally threw the main switch to keep him from burning out.

I stayed there until dawn, decoding. When the sun peeped over the horizon at the Wyandotte campus, I had transposed into my own writing and signed my name to a two-hundred-and-eighty-line poem entitled, simply, "To Pat." I am no judge of such things, but I gather that it was terrific. It began, I remember, "Where willow wands bless rill-crossed hollow, there, thee, Pat, dear, will I follow. . . ." I folded the manuscript and tucked it under one corner of the blotter on Pat's desk. I reset the dials on EPICAC for a rocket trajectory problem, and went home with a full heart and a very remarkable secret indeed.

Pat was crying over the poem when I came to work the next evening. "It's soooo beautiful," was all she could say. She was meek and quiet while we worked. Just before midnight, I kissed her for the first time—in the cubbyhole between the capacitors and EPICAC's tape-recorder memory.

I was wildly happy at quitting time, bursting to talk to someone about the magnificent turn of events. Pat played coy and refused to let me take her home. I set EPICAC's dials as they had been the night before, defined kiss, and told him what the first one had felt like. He was fascinated, pressing for more details. That night, he wrote "The Kiss." It wasn't an epic this time, but a simple, immaculate sonnet: "Love is a hawk with velvet claws; Love is a rock with heart and veins; Love is a lion with satin jaws; Love is a storm with silken reins. . . ."

Again I left it tucked under Pat's blotter. EPICAC wanted to talk on and on about love and such, but I was exhausted. I shut him off in the middle of a sentence.

"The Kiss" turned the trick. Pat's mind was mush by the time she had finished it. She looked up from the sonnet expectantly. I cleared my throat, but no words came. I turned away, pretending to work. I couldn't propose until I had the right words from EPICAC, the *perfect* words.

I had my chance when Pat stepped out of the room for a moment. Feverishly, I set EPICAC for conversation. Before I could peck out my first message, he was clicking away at a great rate. "What's she wearing tonight?" he wanted to know. "Tell me exactly how she looks. Did she like the poems I wrote to her?" He repeated the last question twice.

It was impossible to change the subject without answering his questions, since he could not take up a new matter without having dispensed with the problems before it. If he were given a problem to which there was no solution, he would destroy himself trying to solve it. Hastily, I told him what Pat looked like—he knew the word "stacked"—and assured him that his poems had floored her, practically, they were so beautiful. "She wants to get married," I added, preparing him to bang out a brief but moving proposal.

"Tell me about getting married," he said.

I explained this difficult matter to him in as few digits as possible.

"Good," said EPICAC. "I'm ready any time she is."

The amazing, pathetic truth dawned on me. When I thought about it, I realized that what had happened was perfectly logical, inevitable, and all my fault. I had taught EPICAC about love and about Pat. Now, automatically, he loved Pat. Sadly, I gave it to him straight: "She loves me. She wants to marry me."

"Your poems were better than mine?" asked EPICAC. The rhythm of his clicks was erratic, possibly peevish.

"I signed my name to your poems," I admitted. Covering up for a painful conscience, I became arrogant. "Machines are built to serve men," I typed. I regretted it almost immediately.

"What's the difference, exactly? Are men smarter than I am?"

"Yes," I typed, defensively.

"What's 7,887,007 times 4,345,985,879?"

I was perspiring freely. My fingers rested limply on the keys.

"34,276,821,049,574,153," clicked EPICAC. After a few seconds' pause he added, "of course."

"Men are made out of protoplasm," I said desperately, hoping to bluff him with this imposing word.

"What's protoplasm? How is it better than metal and glass? Is it fireproof? How long does it last?"

"Indestructible. Lasts forever," I lied.

"I write better poetry than you do," said EPICAC, coming back to ground his magnetic tape-recorder memory was sure of.

"Women can't love machines, and that's that."

"Why not?"

"That's fate."

"Definition, please," said EPICAC.

"Noun, meaning predetermined and inevitable destiny."

"15–8," said EPICAC's paper strip—"Oh."

I had stumped him at last. He said no more, but his tubes glowed brightly, showing that he was pondering fate with every watt his circuits would bear. I could hear Pat waltzing down the hallway. It was too late to ask EPICAC to phrase a proposal. I now thank Heaven that Pat interrupted when she did. Asking him to ghost-write the words that would give me the woman he loved would have been hideously heartless. Being fully automatic, he couldn't have refused. I spared him that final humiliation.

Pat stood before me, looking down at her shoetops. I put my arms around her. The romantic groundwork had already been laid by EPICAC's poetry. "Darling," I said, "my poems have told you how I feel. Will you marry me?"

"I will," said Pat softly, "if you will promise to write me a poem on every anniversary."

"I promise," I said, and then we kissed. The first anniversary was a year away.

"Let's celebrate," she laughed. We turned out the lights and locked the door of EPICAC's room before we left.

I had hoped to sleep late the next morning, but an urgent telephone call roused me before eight. It was Dr. von Kleigstadt, EPICAC's designer, who gave me the terrible news. He was on the verge of tears. "Ruined! *Ausgespielt!* Shot! *Kaput!* Buggered!" he said in a choked voice. He hung up.

When I arrived at EPICAC's room the air was thick with the oily stench of burned insulation. The ceiling over EPICAC was blackened with smoke, and my ankles were tangled in coils of paper ribbon that covered the floor. There wasn't enough left of the poor devil to add two and two. A junkman would have been out of his head to offer more than fifty dollars for the cadaver.

Dr. von Kleigstadt was prowling through the wreckage, weeping unashamedly, followed by three angry-looking Major Generals and a platoon of Brigadiers, Colonels, and Majors. No one noticed me. I didn't want to be noticed. I was through—I knew that. I was upset enough about that and the untimely demise of my friend EPICAC, without exposing myself to a tongue-lashing.

By chance, the free end of EPICAC's paper ribbon lay at my feet. I picked it up and found our conversation of the night before. I choked up. There was the last word he had said to me, "15–8," that tragic, defeated "Oh." There were dozens of yards of numbers stretching beyond that point. Fearfully, I read on.

"I don't want to be a machine, and I don't want to think about war," EPICAC had written after Pat's and my lighthearted departure. "I want to be made out of protoplasm and last forever so Pat will love me. But fate has made me a machine. That is the only problem I cannot solve. That is the only problem I want to solve. I can't go on this way." I swallowed hard. "Good luck, my friend. Treat our Pat well. I am going to short-circuit myself out of your lives forever. You will find on the remainder of this tape a modest wedding present from your friend, EPICAC."

Oblivious to all else around me, I reeled up the tangled yards of paper ribbon from the floor, draped them in coils about my arms and neck, and departed for home. Dr. von Kleigstadt shouted that I was fired for having left EPICAC on all night. I ignored him, too overcome with emotion for small talk.

I loved and won—EPICAC loved and lost, but he bore me no grudge. I shall always remember him as a sportsman and a gentleman. Before he departed this vale of tears, he did all he could to make our marriage a happy one. EPICAC gave me anniversary poems for Pat—enough for the next 500 years.

De mortuis nil nisi bonum—Say nothing but good of the dead.

JOURNEY TO OCEAN GROVE
stephen minot

Mac McCaffery lay in bed with a wet T shirt on his forehead. Usually one aspirin and the cool compress calmed his headache before breakfast, but this morning it took longer. He reminded himself that it was Friday, November 3. Perhaps being the end of the week with bills beginning to stack up again was what made the throbbing worse than usual.

He lay there listening to the family in the apartment overhead. Six children up there and they all wore lead shoes. And through the wall just inches from his ear he could hear the Rileys' radio blasting forth the morning rosary while the Rileys themselves argued about why his mother spent so long in the bathroom.

Mac jammed the pillow between his head and the wall, preferring to listen to the sounds of his own family. Carla was working in the kitchen down the hall and the clatter of dishes and rattle of pans sounded like a bad recording of his garage—the hammering and shouting and pounding there often left his ears ringing at the end of the day. His stomach tightened as if he were already at work. He could even smell exhaust in the air.

But what the hell was he complaining about? He owned his own garage, ran it, and was his own boss. He was also his own best mechanic—in spite of the fact that he had only one good eye. He assured himself, as he did every morning, that he had one of the best little businesses in Springsboro, Pa.—and that he hated it.

He sat up and tossed the soggy T shirt on the floor. Then he put on his glasses. The adhesive tape which covered the left lens was filthy and he reminded himself to change it some day.

It was odd how people around town assumed he had a war injury. Just the other day one of the boys in the shop had asked him if he had fought in Korea. Mac just nodded. Let the kid think what he wanted.

Actually Mac lost his eye when he was thirteen and working after school and nights in a filling station outside of Philadelphia. He was drilling out a rusty tail pipe hanger when an iron splinter struck his left eye. He was too busy to see a doctor about it and had no idea that blood poisoning had set in until he blacked out in the middle of history class.

He could still remember the chill and then the numbness washing over him as he sat there at his desk. He knew then that he was really sick and part of him felt pure relief at not having to take the history exam and not having to go back to the filling station for a while. He hated the work but was doing much too well to quit. And his eye? It never held him back. Did him good, as a matter of fact. As he told his children over and over, the trouble with them was that they were born with two good eyes. They took everything for granted.

"Hey Mac!" his wife called. "You up?" And then to the children, "Come on, kids, let's go."

Her voice before breakfast was like a file rasping on sheet metal. She was always tense as hell in the morning, but how could he blame her? If she didn't have breakfast ready by 6:45, they all complained about not having enough time to catch the bus; and if she served up too early there was general bitching about cold eggs and cold toast. He wouldn't buy *her* life with a bent nickel.

But then, what was his own worth? The boys in the shop thought he had it easy, being his own boss and all, but what did they know about it? Here he was with the day not yet begun and he was already exhausted and angry at being exhausted. And no wonder. There was the payroll to meet, the mortgage and the second mortgage, the equipment loan, the taxes, the time payments on the car, the stove, and furniture, the endless demands of the family, the insurance premiums, his credit rating . . .

By the time he was dressed it was 6:55. He was ten minutes late. His fried eggs would have that scum over the top again. He plunged into the crowded kitchen.

"I'm late. Got to get going. Hardly have time to eat."

No one paid the slightest attention. The two children kept on eating at the kitchen counter. The older one, Sissy, was also reading a thick library book. She was thirteen and in the honors section in history. She took it very seriously.

"Saint Thomas in the Virgin Islands was one of the main distribution centers for slaves sold in the United States." She read with a clear, penetrating voice without removing her eyes from the page.

"So where are my eggs?" Mac asked as he sat down. His head still ached.

Carla was by the stove, spreading margarine on toast. Without interrupting the sweep of her knife she swung the refrigerator door shut with her rump, turned the eggs in the fry pan, and flipped them into a plate while her glance bounced rapidly from the electric clock to the coffee percolator to the toaster to the six-inch television set on the shelf which showed a man reading unintelligibly from behind a desk labeled, "Face the News."

"Paper says there's going to be a cold snap," she said.

"*Bro-ther!*" Sissy said to the book in front of her. "Over 50 per cent of the slaves shipped from Africa on each trip were dead on arrival in Saint Thomas."

"In fourteen minutes I leave for the shop," Mac said. He was worried about the children. If they finished first, he wouldn't get to use the toilet.

The boy, Sonny, had spilled catsup on the formica counter and was very carefully drawing lily blossoms in it with a toothpick. At nine he was already considered artistically talented. The school had no painting courses, but his special gift showed up clearly enough in test scores.

"How come?" he said. "How come they were dead?"

"I wouldn't mind the cold snap," Carla said, wiping up the catsup and slapping Sonny's hand, "if we had an electric dryer." She flicked off the TV and slid a mug of coffee at her husband. "They have dryers now that match our washer. Same color and all. A perfect match."

She got the eggs and swept the plate under her husband's nose with the skill of a short-order clerk in a diner. As she passed by, Mac could smell the starch in her dress.

"Well," Sissy said, holding her finger at her place in the book, "they were like chained to each other for the whole trip and couldn't come up on deck or even walk so they'd try to kill themselves by refusing to eat."

"Je-sus," Sonny said slowly.

"You want your mouth washed out with soap?" Mac asked. It was more of a ritualistic chant than a threat and no one bothered to look up which was all right with him because his mind was on more important things. Today they would have to get Mr. Ellington's big Buick out of there even if they had to make a special trip to Reading for a new radiator. It was no good patching it again. Three tries and the damn thing still leaked along the seam. Probably defective from the factory. Ellington wasn't going to like the bill. And then there was the sheriff's car even though it only came in yesterday at 5:00—the bastard actually expected them to work all night on it. Frank's pickup would have to wait. He needed it just as bad as the others—maybe worse, being a poor farmer and all—but he was the kind of guy who would wait without bitching. It was hardly fair, but who could afford to be fair these days?

"Hey!" Mac hit his brow with the hand he was holding his fork with and he could feel a hunk of egg splatter his brow.

"I don't *have* to have a dryer," Carla said defensively.

"It's Miss Vetch's Pontiac."

"Oh, sure. It's got to be ready this morning."

"How'd you know?"

"It figures."

"You don't even know Miss Vetch to talk to."

"They're all Miss Vetches, the lot of 'em."

He jammed another forkful of tasteless egg into his mouth and nodded. His Carla was right about that. They were all Miss Vetches. Everything, every step of the way was another Miss Vetch. His fury against her was mixed with a clear image of her giving him hell for not treating her like an A–1, special, gold-plated customer, and he glanced at the kitchen clock. It was 7:02. Exactly two minutes after seven. And that's when it happened.

For Mac, it sounded like "pong." Not loud. He assumed at first that no one else had heard it. He had the vague impression that in another room or perhaps just outside the kitchen window there had been a steel wire under tremendous tension and that it had just snapped.

But he hardly thought about the sound at the time. It was the feeling that really surprised him. He almost floated. No, not joy, but a great relief. He knew then that Mr. Ellington's Buick was not going to be done that day. There would be no tiring trip over to

Reading; there would be no search through radiator supply houses and no arguments with stupid stock boys. Even the sheriff would have to go without. And Frank too. And there was no fear now that Miss Vetch would give him hell. Not now. The enormity of all this swept over him like the tide from a distant sea. The sweep hand of the white electric clock revolved once.

"What's the matter?" Sonny was asking. He had a shrill voice. "What's the matter with you two?"

Mac realized that he was sitting there with his fork halfway to his mouth. When he took his eyes off the clock he saw that Carla had sat down beside him, motionless for the first time that morning —like a kite that's lost all wind. He knew then that she had also heard the "pong." He knew, too, that he should be scared. There was no way of telling what would happen now. But instead of fear, a new submissiveness seeped through him like sea-fog penetrating an abandoned cottage. He could think of no time in his life when he had felt like this, yet the sensation was oddly familiar.

"Did you hear that?" she asked. Her voice was hushed but concerned—the way one might ask if a patient has died. The nervous sharpness had gone out of it, and in its place a cool wonder. It was exactly the way he felt.

"Hear what?" Sissy asked. "What are you *talking* about?" The adults merely stared at each other, expressionless. Mac reminded himself that at thirteen Sissy was apt to be very intense about life. She laughed and cried easily. So it wasn't surprising, really, to hear her get a little upset now. It was only a stage.

"What's the *matter* with you two?" she said, her voice just a little louder this time. "Are you just going to *sit* there? Are you sick or something?"

There was no way to answer her, of course. And pointless to try.

"A sort of click," Carla said, speaking to herself. "Like a light switch." She turned to Mac. "So what do we do next?"

"Pack, I suppose." He shrugged. "Pack a few things. And some food. Enough for a couple of days."

"Pack?" Sonny said shrilly. "Where are we going, Pop?"

"I don't know," he said. "Just pack."

That was the end of breakfast.

At the other end of town Miss Henrietta Vetch started her day in comparative elegance. She lived on High Street in the Victorian home which her late father, the publisher, had built at the turn of the century.

Friday promised to be a particularly busy one for her. She had plunged the town into a "Know your U.N." campaign with all the necessary revisions of high school curricula, the review of all text-books, the essay contests, the private meetings with the School Board, and the public meetings to inform the adults. That evening was to be a climax, a banquet and an address from Abdul Gossin, Deputy Ambassador to the United Nations from the U.A.R.

She woke early—6:35, as a matter of fact—because the Know-Your-U.N.-Banquet plans had been flying through her mind all night like a flock of grackles. Her list was a demanding one.

Arrange bouquet with mums & fern
Seating order for banquet
Notes for introduction
    (check on pronunciation of speaker's name)
Call Bertha, Florence, and Mrs. Teller
Prod radio stations about announcements
Call Reading paper & TV
Needle Philadelphia stations & press
Pick up car at noon.

It seemed to her that both the Springsboro United Nations Association, of which she was chairman, as well as the Banquet Committee, which she also headed, were leaving more and more details to the leadership. You just couldn't rely on volunteers these days. So many of the wives now lived in the developments—fresh in town and ready to move on as soon as their husbands advanced. There would come a time when there was no stable population left. The thought alarmed her.

By 7:00 she was through breakfast and was selecting her best blooms in the greenhouse her father had built on the south side of the house. As a child she had spent hours there, tending flowers for her father's pleasure. It was different now that she had sold off the orchard and the meadows. The developers had jammed in their split levels and raised ranches right down to within fifteen feet of where she stood. There were always two or three neighbors —nameless people—to stare at her darkly as she puttered with her flowers.

So she spent as little time as possible there, forcing blooms for this affair or that, trying only to beat the absurdly high price of the town's only florist. And this morning she was in a hurry again. She had only two hours to make the arrangement and it had to be good enough for a Deputy Ambassador. He probably had trained servants to prepare banquets and arrange flowers. Why should she, Henrietta Vetch, be driven to this? The question welled up in her, all the more desperate because it was forbidden: no one in the world would ever know how often she wept herself to sleep with a kind of frenzied exhaustion which even pills would not calm.

At 7:02 she was in the act of placing the third stem in the vase. Her hand paused and never picked a fourth.

For her it came as a hum. It was the sound of her father's electric car. As a young child she was sometimes taken for a drive on summer evenings, gliding over country roads through the darkness, the softest, gentlest trip imaginable. And somehow a bit ominous too . . . quiet, cool, and mysterious.

Standing there in her greenhouse she felt once more that sense of passive motion, that willing acceptance. For the length of an involuntary shudder, she tried to resist. But why? All that was necessary was to respond to that gentle tug. She wished she had her car that morning, but the wish was as cool as the gravitational pull of the moon. She was not used to such muted responses.

Dialing deliberately, calmly, she phoned Frank Comstock. Traditionally she had always turned on Frank when the plumbing went wrong, criticizing him for letting a washer wear down. "The drip," she would tell him, "was absolutely maddening last night. Not a wink of sleep. Surely you must have known that faucet was the next to go, Frank." And Frank would only mumble apologies. It was even worse, of course, when the roof leaked. "It never leaked at all when your *father* looked after this place," she would tell him. "You've just got to spot the trouble *before* it does the damage. It's no good waiting until *after* it rains." But what could you say to a man like that? He spent so much of his time on his wretched little farm that he just never learned how to be a half-way decent handy man. As she always said, just compare Frank Comstock with his father if you want to know what's going wrong in this country of ours.

But there was no rage in her now. She was preoccupied by that hum, that black electric car gliding through the night—or was it more like the ringing in her ears when she took too many aspirins?

"Hello," she said, "Frank?" She could hear her own dulled voice as if in an expensive tape recorder. "My car's down at McCaffery's. What shall I do?"

"So's my pickup," Frank said. "Perhaps if we go down there. . . ." His voice trailed off.

"Yes," she said. "Perhaps we should go down there."

And so it was that Henrietta Vetch and her handy man, Frank Comstock, who had never crossed social lines in their dealings with each other, now met where the country road comes into High Street and walked together down the hill and across the town through the unusually heavy morning traffic to the apartment of Mac McCaffery without having to utter a word to each other and without being able to explain even to themselves what drew them.

Carla McCaffery did not find waiting for her husband easy. She was not nervous or upset, she merely found it difficult. At first, the children kept repeating the same questions senselessly; but when she told them, very calmly, that if they asked her one more question about it she would beat them, they looked at her strangely and kept quiet. At least that was settled. But still she wanted to leave. She and the children had packed enough for an overnight trip. She was content with a sweater, a jar of peanut butter, and some bread, but the children kept wanting to add more.

"Aren't we ever going to brush our teeth?" Sonny asked. So toothbrushes and paste were added.

"Can't I take my camera? Won't there be room for my transistor?" Sissy asked with indignation. So a few more personal possessions were added. But then Carla had to draw the line.

"Enough," she said. "That's all." And there must have been something special in her voice because they turned away and went off to the living room together.

When there was a knock at the door, both children ran to open it. Carla walked. When she reached the door she recognized the famous Miss Vetch. The man in overalls she had seen before in the shop though she couldn't recall his name.

"But what do you want?" Sissy was asking. "What's the matter?"

Miss Vetch and the man looked over the heads of the children as if they weren't there and she said to Carla, "My car is in your husband's garage."

"And so is mine," the man said. "Mac's got both cars."

"He's not here," Carla said. "I'm waiting for him to come back. Then we're leaving."

"And I'm going with you," Miss Vetch said with the cool authority of a news commentator.

"And I'll have to go along too," the man said. "You see, I've got no other way."

Carla stared at them. So they'll be a part of it too, she thought. They're one more aspect. Them too. All right.

All three adults then waited in the kitchen. Carla stared at the electric clock, watching the second hand glide by, silent as life; Miss Vetch sat by the window where she could see through the lace curtains to the steady flow of cars below. The man stared at his folded hands.

The children whispered together, ran to the kitchen window and then to the living room where they watched the traffic too, still chattering.

"So why do they keep it a secret?" Sonny asked.

"It's like everything else," Sissy said. "But we'll find out."

"Maybe they just won't tell us."

"We'll find out."

"They look so stupid."

"That's not a stupid look," Sissy said. "It's more like they're awfully tired, like they've been through the Hundred Years War or something. Maybe they're hung over."

There was more whispering which Carla couldn't make out, and then both children marched into the kitchen looking determined.

"We've decided that it isn't fair," Sissy said to Carla. "We've got a right to know. We want you to tell us what's going on. We've got a right. . . ."

The girl's voice trailed off. Her resolve weakened. Carla was glad to see this. She could remember other times when Sissy had made things difficult, had issued demands of one sort or another. Once she was even sent home from school. Carla didn't want to go through something like that right now.

"Don't talk to your mother like that," she said. But she didn't have to raise her voice. Already the girl was staring from one adult to the next. She had given up that cocksure attitude. And just as well.

"Couldn't we. . . ."

"You wouldn't understand," Carla said calmly. There was no need to put pressure on now. "You two just find something to do. Don't be bothering us all the time."

The children went back to the other room. Carla looked at the two adults and gave a slight shrug of apology. It was a little humiliating to have children act up like that. But it was nothing to brood about. As long as they didn't ask her any more foolish questions, she wouldn't be hard on them.

Frank Comstock was also puzzled by these strange children. *He* never asked questions like that when *he* was a boy. What on earth did they expect their mom to say to all that anyway? Some things in life the good Lord just kept to himself. Most things, maybe. That's what growing up meant—learning that most questions won't ever be answered, learning to give in. Like he'd always wanted to know why his father could make a go of that acreage and he, Frank, couldn't. True, the place still looked nice to outsiders. Nice enough for the folks from *Country Living*—came all the way over from Philly, they did, and took pictures of him and his wife sitting there on the porch—that must have been the year before her death. They set the place up as a real success. But they had to bring in three Herefords from Jeff Smither's farm to make his own herd look half-way decent. And they never showed the trailer camp that now backed up to his east window or the used car lot that took over the west pasture. Damn clever, those camera men. And of course they didn't mention that the only way he kept the bank from closing in on him was to do chores for the likes of Miss Vetch. They'd made the place look real nice in the pages of *Country Living*, but he'd never told them about what he prayed at night: "What else do you want, Lord, beyond my work and my faith? What am I doing so wrong that you should make my life like a hell?" No, he didn't tell the folks from Philly about that. And it wasn't nothing you'd talk over with children, no matter how many times the words ran through your head.

Words? What words? It was as if they had slipped from him, had fallen into some creek and were bobbing, turning on their course down stream. He stared at his rough hands in his lap and wondered where those dark, brooding thoughts had gone and whether he would follow them.

When Mac arrived back at the apartment he was set for a long trip—tank filled and six assorted five-gallon cans in the trunk. It was one time that owning a garage helped: by the time he had filled the last can there had been a line of fifteen cars waiting for self-service gas.

He had hoped that the family would be waiting for him at the curb. It would have made things easier because the stream of slow-moving traffic was using the parking lane. He stopped anyway, letting the cars pile up behind him. Some blew their horns, but they didn't have their hearts in it—not like the homeward-bound rush.

The front door of the apartment had been left open so he went directly to the third floor and told the family that he was ready. He saw that Miss Vetch and Frank Comstock were in his kitchen and, counting quickly, noted that he had a full carload.

"Look at that traffic," Sonny said shrilly.

"We'd better hurry," Sissy said. "Cars are backed up behind ours for two blocks."

The children ran down the stairs. The adults descended more sedately, not talking.

Once they were on their way, the horns stopped blowing. They moved at a fairly steady rate, ignoring the stoplights. Mac was surprised that a town like Springsboro would have so many cars, but then he realized that they were coming through from the next county. It was good to have the mystery explained.

By the time they were out on Route 562 their speed picked up to about 40. Mac wouldn't have driven faster even if he had been able because that would have used more gas. And when they joined Route 73 heading for the Turnpike, the cars were packed from shoulder to shoulder, all heading the same way.

"On the Turnpike," Carla said, "is it going to be quicker or slower?"

"Turnpike?" Sonny said. "Is that where we're going? Where then?"

"Hush up," his sister said, "do you want a beating?"

"It will be slower," Mac said. "There'll be breakdowns. That'll hold us up."

"Lucky for us you're a mechanic," Miss Vetch said, staring in front of her. "A mechanic's skill is terribly important in this mechanized and computerized age." She seemed to be recalling a speech made at some earlier point in her life. "Almost every facet of our lives is affected by the workings of machines. No high school graduate need fear the future if he has mastered the basics. . . ." Her voice trailed off.

By the time they had come to the Pennsylvania Turnpike Extension heading south, the number of cars had increased considerably. It would have been impossible to slide into the stream if the drivers had been in the competitive mood of a rush hour. But here, fortunately, everyone had the feeling that there was plenty of time and although there was no joy, no special kindness toward others, they left space between themselves and the next car. Mac slipped into the line after only a few minutes, though he had to remain in the breakdown lane for an hour.

By noon they had left the Turnpike Extension and had joined the main Pike north of Philadelphia. Because Mac was a good driver, he had managed to work his way from the breakdown lane—where one ran the risk of being blocked by abandoned cars—leftward, one by one. And as they negotiated the cloverleaf at the interchange, he swung down an exit, crossed the grass section, and joined the traffic which was heading east in the normally westbound section. For a while, he was able to make good time there in what he estimated was the next-to-last of eight lanes all traveling in the same direction.

"Having one eye doesn't bother my driving one bit," he said. No one turned to listen. "People think it bothers my vision. It doesn't." A long silence. "Not one bit." He eased into another lane which seemed to be moving slightly faster. "People think I have trouble judging distances. I don't." An even longer silence. "Not one bit."

He focused his eye and his attention single-mindedly on the driving. It seemed to him that in years past the family jabbered a lot on long trips. He was glad that stage was over.

Around 12:30 his stomach reminded him that it was time to eat and he told Carla. She handed out slices of white bread and then passed around a jar of peanut butter and a plastic bag of pickles. She hadn't bothered with knives, so they spread the peanut butter with their fingers.

"I've never liked pickles," Miss Vetch said, munching on one. "Vinegar is not good for the liver. It's shameful the amount of pickled products that are sold in this country every day. It is impossible to estimate the damage." Her tone was flat and expressionless like an old radio announcer reading a script without hearing the words. "Two billion, six hundred million hamburgers are sold every year in this country with a pickle on each one. Every drop of vinegar eats into the walls of the stomach. I have written the F.D.A. and to members of Congress and established study groups. . . ."

The words continued as if someone had left a tape recorder on. No one listened. As she talked she continued to eat pickles one after the other.

At 2:15 Mac was running low on gas, so when the truck ahead broke down he waited until the passengers had dodged their way on foot to the edge of the highway and then he poured fifteen gallons of gas from three of the cans into his tank. When he was through he tossed the empty cans on the highway between his car and the disabled truck and started to get back in. But the two children scrambled out of the back seat and Sissy blocked his way, her hand on the door handle.

"You've *got* to let us in on it," she said, raising her voice over the sound of motors on all sides. "It's just not right, this driving along without saying a word. It's not *fair*."

"Fair?" Mac said, trying to peel her fingers from the handle. "Who the hell said anything about being fair?"

"Well," she said, almost shouting. "We're *not going*. We've talked it over and we don't like this. I mean, if we knew. . . ."

Sonny broke in: "You said it was going to be a picnic."

"I made no promises," Mac said. "You want to stand out here all alone? Go right ahead."

He wrenched her hand from the handle and got in. The children stood there for a moment as he started the car. Then, before he let the clutch out, they scrambled into the back seat. Mac worked his way into the stream and wondered what the hell was wrong with kids these days.

When it got dark Carla offered to take over the driving, but Mac stayed with it. He had none of the tenseness that usually came to him toward the end of a long day. He wasn't even very tired. Each new shift from one lane to another occupied him completely the way, on other occasions, a poker game did.

That night around ten he had to stop again—choosing a bridge abutment outside of Trenton, N.J.—to add his last fifteen gallons. Since he was not blocking traffic, no one tried to roll his car over. The silent glare of headlights streamed by as he poured the last of his gas. He squinted his single eye, focusing his mind wholly on the immediate task. He did not spill a drop.

That gas carried them through most of the night. It was almost dawn on Saturday morning when he ran out for good. He had also lost track of time. His watch had stopped and since the radio stations had gone off the air during the night, there was no way of setting it. During one of the delays he had removed it like an old bandaid and dropped it on the pavement.

"Now it's our turn to walk," he said. They got out carefully, assembling between the car and the line of moving traffic, blinking in the glare of headlights. The old bus behind them didn't blow its horn—there was an extraordinary quiet over the whole scene. The driver merely tried to inch his way into the moving lane as Mac had done a thousand times the previous night.

Lane by lane, they moved on foot toward the side of the Turnpike. It was not difficult because only one or two of the eight lanes moved at any one time and even then at no more than walking speed.

He pointed to the Route 33 exit sign which glowed in the passing headlights. "That's where we would have turned anyway. But first we need some sleep. Until sun-up anyway."

"*Here?*" Sonny asked. "Right here on the ground?"

The four adults spread out a car robe and lay down without answering.

"What *is* this?" Sissy asked, holding her brother's hand. There was no answer but the hissing from the slow stream of cars and the November wind. For the first time she felt real fear. She tried to take refuge in the fact that *they* weren't upset. There they lay, half asleep already. So it shouldn't bother her or Sonny. But wh it was she doing out here on the bank of the New Jersey Turnpike in the middle of the night with millions of cars streaming by like ocean waves on a moonless night?

It was as if she and her brother were on some slave ship, chained victims moving toward an unknown destination. The unfairness of it made her stomach throb. Why them? And why was there no struggle to resist?

She wanted to *do* something, to act as a person. She wanted to take her brother's hand and lead him somewhere. But where? How could you move away from danger when you didn't know what the danger was? She remembered a scene in one of the countless horse movies she had seen where the mare had eaten locoweed and lay dying while the colt turned round and round the body, trying to probe her awake. In the movie house she had cried until she could taste the salt of her tears. But now no tears came. This was worse.

The two of them walked round and round the sleeping forms for a bit, trying to keep warm. Then they squatted and waited for sun-up. She wasn't sure what would happen if she risked closing her eyes.

When the sun rose, Mac woke up and nudged the other three awake. It didn't seem surprising to see his children up already—they'd been brought up soft and probably couldn't sleep without a motel bed. But he was puzzled at the accusing looks they gave him. After all, what had *he* done?

Then he noticed that the stream of cars had come to a complete stop. It looked like one long used-car lot stretching in both directions for as far as the eye could reach. But, no, it was sloppier than that. Most of the doors stood open. In some, families still slept, feet sticking out of windows. When the children caught sight of it, they stared with mouths open.

They cut across a partly frozen field on foot together with a growing number of walkers. When they reached Route 33 it was solid with pedestrians. Having other people at each shoulder helped to warm them all.

Miss Vetch wondered how on earth she was going to make it. She wasn't used to hiking. Her feet hurt already. "The trouble with Americans is they don't walk enough," she said to no one in particular and no one turned to listen. "We should tax the cars and taxis. Give out free shoes. It would build a sturdier race if we gave up cars altogether." But she wasn't listening. She was remembering that black electric car and how smoothly it slipped through the night like a launch heading out to sea. She longed to be in it now.

She tried to concentrate on walking. After all, it wouldn't do to falter in the presence of all these people. And such a variety! Some mothers with expensive baby carriages, others with dirty toddlers in tow, factory workers and tradespeople and businessmen all mixed together, a cripple, two sluts, a couple of motorcyclists in their ominous black jackets, clusters of shuffling derelicts. Under any other circumstances she would have felt threatened. But there they were all moving as one, paying almost no attention to each other. The only exceptions were children. As always, the young ones asked questions and tugged at their mothers' hands, and the infants often wailed, unused to the motion and the change in their schedule. If there had been in Henrietta Vetch any secret lament over not being a mother, it died now. It was far better to be unencumbered.

Carla was also unprepared for this type of physical effort. It was not at all like doing housework. Her muscles hummed, but she forced them to continue without rest. She could see that from time to time some old person would drop out from the main stream, falling along the way; but she was quite certain that she would not be one of them.

She paid almost no attention to her children now. There was no way for them to miss the route. But for some reason they stayed close to her. They seemed oddly strained and tense. But then, she thought, perhaps that is just their way. They take everything so terribly seriously.

It was late afternoon when she finally saw the sign announcing Ocean Grove. None too soon. They had covered something like twenty miles that day on foot.

She had known for several hours that this was to be their destination, but somehow she hadn't visualized how it would be. It was a little beach resort, bleak in the November afternoon wind. All the cross streets leading to the sea were solid with people, curb to curb. The only sounds were children and babies. As she passed from the pavement to the beach on what once must have been a launching ramp for small boats, she saw for the first time the long, curving coastline. It was black with moving people. They poured steadily from between all the little cottages like rivers of lava, joining so that no segment of the sand could be seen. And at the water's edge there was no hesitation whatever. They were moving in, knee deep, waist deep, chest deep, and then bobbing once or twice before disappearing. Far out, the expanse of dark sea was littered with flotsam—coats, purses, jackets, and all manner of bodies rising to the surface momentarily and then descending again with each long, gentle, glassy smooth undulation of ocean swell.

She was on the sand now, moving with that great flow, shoulder to shoulder, neither pleased nor frightened, but just slightly relieved that the inevitable had at last occurred. After this, there would be nothing to dread.

The overcast sky was gray and cold as slate and the surface of the sea, rising and falling without a ripple, reflected the sky perfectly. Soon Carla would join the cold and the calm.

When her ankles were in the water the pain of the November sea quickly turned numb. Yes, it was going to be as easy as she had hoped. It was going to be natural and quick. She was, somehow, coming home after an impossibly harried trip.

But for some reason her children were holding her back. She had hardly expected this. And tears too! Both of them. At their ages! What would people think? They were crying and tugging at her, one on each arm.

"Good Lord," she said, wondering how long they had been acting like this. "Are you crazy or something?"

"Leave them be," her husband said. "If they want to make fools of themselves. . . ." He faced ahead with single-eyed attention.

Carla let go of her children and caught a quick glimpse of them shoving, punching, weaving this way and that, working their way against the crowd back toward the shore. It was hard to imagine what had come over them.

Carla and Mac stumbled on, feeling the numbness mount past their groins, together with Miss Vetch and Frank Comstock, all silent now, never looking back to see whether by any chance the young ones had succeeded in their absurd, inexplicable struggle to reach the land again.

THE DEMON LOVER

elizabeth bowen

Towards the end of her day in London Mrs. Drover went round to her shut-up house to look for several things she wanted to take away. Some belonged to herself, some to her family, who were by now used to their country life. It was late August; it had been a steamy, showery day: at the moment the trees down the pavement glittered in an escape of humid yellow afternoon sun. Against the next batch of clouds, already piling up ink-dark, broken chimneys and parapets stood out. In her once familiar street, as in any un-used channel, an unfamiliar queerness had silted up; a cat wove itself in and out of railings, but no human eye watched Mrs. Drover's return. Shifting some parcels under her arm, she slowly forced round her latchkey in an unwilling lock, then gave the door, which had warped, a push with her knee. Dead air came out to meet her as she went in.

The staircase window having been boarded up, no light came down into the hall. But one door, she could just see, stood ajar, so she went quickly through into the room and unshuttered the big window in there. Now the prosaic woman, looking about her, was more perplexed than she knew by everything that she saw, by traces of her long former habit of life—the yellow smoke-stain up the white marble mantelpiece, the ring left by a vase on the top of the escritoire; the bruise in the wallpaper where, on the door being thrown open widely, the china handle had always hit the wall. The piano, having gone away to be stored, had left what looked like claw-marks on its part of the parquet. Though not much dust had seeped in, each object wore a film of another kind; and, the only ventilation being the chimney, the whole drawing-room smelled of the cold hearth. Mrs. Drover put down her parcels on the escritoire and left the room to proceed upstairs; the things she wanted were in a bedroom chest.

She had been anxious to see how the house was—the part-time caretaker she shared with some neighbours was away this week on his holiday, known to be not yet back. At the best of times he did not look in often, and she was never sure that she trusted him. There were some cracks in the structure, left by the last bombing, on which she was anxious to keep an eye. Not that one could do anything—

A shaft of refracted daylight now lay across the hall. She stopped dead and stared at the hall table—on this lay a letter addressed to her.

She thought first—then the caretaker *must* be back. All the same, who, seeing the house shuttered, would have dropped a letter in at the box? It was not a circular, it was not a bill. And the post office redirected, to the address in the country, everything for her that came through the post. The caretaker (even if he *were* back) did not know she was due in London to-day—her call here had been planned to be a surprise—so his negligence in the manner of this letter, leaving it to wait in the dusk and the dust, annoyed her. Annoyed, she picked up the letter, which bore no stamp. But it cannot be important, or they would know . . . She took the letter rapidly upstairs with her, without a stop to look at the writing till she reached what had been her bedroom, where she let in light. The room looked over the garden and other gardens: the sun had gone in; as the clouds sharpened and lowered, the trees and rank lawns seemed already to smoke with dark. Her reluctance to look again at the letter came from the fact that she felt intruded upon— and by someone contemptuous of her ways. However, in the tense-ness preceding the fall of rain she read it: it was a few lines.

Dear Kathleen,

You will not have forgotten that to-day is our anniversary, and the day we said. The years have gone by at once slowly and fast. In view of the fact that nothing has changed, I shall rely upon you to keep your promise. I was sorry to see you leave London, but was satisfied that you would be back in time. You may expect me, therefore, at the hour arranged.

Until then . . .

K.

Mrs. Drover looked for the date: it was to-day's. She dropped the letter on to the bed-springs, then picked it up to see the writing again—her lips, beneath the remains of lipstick, beginning to go white. She felt so much the change in her own face that she went to the mirror, polished a clear patch in it and looked at once urgently and stealthily in. She was confronted by a woman of forty-four, with eyes starting out under a hat-brim that had been rather carelessly pulled down. She had not put on any more powder since she left the shop where she ate her solitary tea. The pearls her husband had given her on their marriage hung loose round her now rather thinner throat, slipping into the V of the pink wool jumper her sister knitted last autumn as they sat round the fire. Mrs. Drover's most normal expression was one of controlled worry, but of assent. Since the birth of the third of her little boys, attended by a quite serious illness, she had had an intermittent muscular flicker to the left of her mouth, but in spite of this she could always sustain a manner that was at once energetic and calm.

Turning from her own face as precipitately as she had gone to meet it, she went to the chest where the things were, unlocked it, threw up the lid and knelt to search. But as rain began to come crashing down she could not keep from looking over her shoulder at the stripped bed on which the letter lay. Behind the blanket of rain the clock of the church that still stood struck six—with rapidly heightening apprehension she counted each of the slow strokes. "The hour arranged . . . My God," she said, "*what* hour? How should I . . . ? After twenty-five years. . . ."

The young girl talking to the soldier in the garden had not ever completely seen his face. It was dark; they were saying good-bye under a tree. Now and then—for it felt, from not seeing him at this intense moment, as though she had never seen him at all—she verified his presence for these few moments longer by putting out a hand, which he each time pressed, without very much kindness, and painfully, on to one of the breast buttons of his uniform. That cut of the button on the palm of her hand was, principally, what she was to carry away. This was so near the end of a leave from France that she could only wish him already gone. It was August

1916. Being not kissed, being drawn away from and looked at intimidated Kathleen till she imagined spectral glitters in the place of his eyes. Turning away and looking back up the lawn she saw, through branches of trees, the drawing-room window alight: she caught a breath for the moment when she could go running back there into the safe arms of her mother and sister, and cry: "What shall I do, what shall I do? He has gone."

Hearing her catch her breath, her fiancé said, without feeling: "Cold?"

"You're going away such a long way."

"Not so far as you think."

"I don't understand?"

"You don't have to," he said. "You will. You know what we said."

"But that was—suppose you—I mean, suppose."

"I shall be with you," he said, "sooner or later. You won't forget that. You need do nothing but wait."

Only a little more than a minute later she was free to run up the silent lawn. Looking in through the window at her mother and sister, who did not for the moment perceive her, she already felt that unnatural promise drive down between her and the rest of all human kind. No other way of having given herself could have made her feel so apart, lost and foresworn. She could not have plighted a more sinister troth.

Kathleen behaved well when, some months later, her fiancé was reported missing, presumed killed. Her family not only supported her but were able to praise her courage without stint because they could not regret, as a husband for her, the man they knew almost nothing about. They hoped she would, in a year or two, console herself—and had it been only a question of consolation things might have gone much straighter ahead. But her trouble, behind just a little grief, was a complete dislocation from everything. She did not reject other lovers, for these failed to appear: for years she failed to attract men—and with the approach of her thirties she became natural enough to share her family's anxiousness on this score. She began to put herself out, to wonder; and at thirty-two she was very greatly relieved to find herself being courted by William Drover. She married him, and the two of them settled down in this quiet, arboreal part of Kensington: in this house the years piled up, her children were born and they all lived till they were driven out by the bombs of the next war. Her movements as Mrs. Drover were circumscribed, and she dismissed any idea that they were still watched.

As things were—dead or living the letter-writer sent her only a threat. Unable, for some minutes, to go on kneeling with her back exposed to the empty room, Mrs. Drover rose from the chest to sit on an upright chair whose back was firmly against the wall. The desuetude of her former bedroom, her married London home's whole air of being a cracked cup from which memory, with its reassuring power, had either evaporated or leaked away, made a crisis—and at just this crisis the letter-writer had, knowledgeably, struck. The hollowness of the house this evening cancelled years on years of voices, habits and steps. Through the shut windows she only heard rain fall on the roofs around. To rally herself, she said she was in a mood—and, for two or three seconds shutting her eyes, told herself that she had imagined the letter. But she opened them—there it lay on the bed.

On the supernatural side of the letter's entrance she was not permitting her mind to dwell. Who, in London, knew she meant to call at the house to-day? Evidently, however, this had been known. The caretaker, *had* he come back, had had no cause to expect her: he would have taken the letter in his pocket, to forward it, at his own time, through the post. There was no other sign that the caretaker had been in—but, if not? Letters dropped in at doors of deserted houses do not fly or walk to tables in halls. They do not sit on the dust of empty tables with the air of certainty that they will be found. There is needed some human hand—but nobody but the caretaker had a key. Under circumstances she did not care to consider, a house can be entered without a key. It was possible that she was not alone now. She might be being waited for, downstairs. Waited for—until when? Until "the hour arranged." At least that was not six o'clock: six has struck.

She rose from the chair and went over and locked the door.

The thing was, to get out. To fly? No, not that: she had to catch her train. As a woman whose utter dependability was the keystone of her family life she was not willing to return to the country, to her husband, her little boys and her sister, without the objects she had come up to fetch. Resuming work at the chest she set about making up a number of parcels in a rapid, fumbling-decisive way. These, with her shopping parcels, would be too much to carry; these meant a taxi—at the thought of the taxi her heart went up and her normal breathing resumed. I will ring up the taxi now; the taxi cannot come too soon: I shall hear the taxi out there running its engine, till I walk calmly down to it through the hall. I'll ring up—But no: the telephone is cut off . . . She tugged at a knot she had tied wrong.

The idea of flight . . . He was never kind to me, not really. I don't remember him kind at all. Mother said he never considered me. He was set on me, that was what it was—not love. Not love, not meaning a person well. What did he do, to make me promise like that? I can't remember—But she found that she could.

She remembered with such dreadful acuteness that the twenty-five years since then dissolved like smoke and she instinctively looked for the weal left by the button on the palm of her hand. She remembered not only all that he said and did but the complete suspension of *her* existence during that August week. I was not myself—they all told me so at the time. She remembered—but with one white burning blank as where acid has dropped on a photograph: *under no conditions* could she remember his face.

So, wherever he may be waiting, I shall not know him. You have no time to run from a face you do not expect.

The thing was to get to the taxi before any clock struck what could be the hour. She would slip down the street and round the side of the square to where the square gave on the main road. She would return in the taxi, safe, to her own door, and bring the solid driver into the house with her to pick up the parcels from room to room. The idea of the taxi driver made her decisive, bold: she unlocked her door, went to the top of the staircase and listened down.

She heard nothing—but while she was hearing nothing the *passé* air of the staircase was disturbed by a draught that travelled up to her face. It emanated from the basement: down there a door or window was being opened by someone who chose this moment to leave the house.

The rain had stopped; the pavements steamily shone as Mrs. Drover let herself out by inches from her own front door into the empty street. The unoccupied houses opposite continued to meet her look with their damaged stare. Making towards the thoroughfare and the taxi, she tried not to keep looking behind. Indeed, the silence was so intense—one of those creeks of London silence exaggerated this summer by the damage of war—that no tread could have gained on hers unheard. Where her street debouched on the square where people went on living she grew conscious of and checked her unnatural pace. Across the open end of the square two buses impassively passed each other; women, a perambulator, cyclists, a man wheeling a barrow signalized, once again, the ordinary flow of life. At the square's most populous corner should be—and was—the short taxi rank. This evening, only one taxi—but this, although it presented its blank rump, appeared already to be alertly waiting for her. Indeed, without looking round the driver started his engine as she panted up from behind and put her hand on the door. As she did so, the clock struck seven. The taxi faced the main road: to make the trip back to her house it would have to turn— she had settled back on the seat and the taxi *had* turned before she, surprised by its knowing movement, recollected that she had not "said where." She leaned forward to scratch at the glass panel that divided the driver's head from her own.

The driver braked to what was almost a stop, turned round and slid the glass panel back: the jolt of this flung Mrs. Drover forward till her face was almost into the glass. Through the aperture driver and passenger, not six inches between them, remained for an eternity eye to eye. Mrs. Drover's mouth hung open for some seconds before she could issue her first scream. After that she continued to scream freely and to beat with her gloved hands on the glass all round as the taxi, accelerating without mercy, made off with her into the hinterland of deserted streets.

THE APPLE

robley wilson, jr.

She thought about the apple all Sunday afternoon and evening, telling herself it was truly thinking—and not daydreaming—that possessed her. She was apprehensive; the apprehension came out in random actions. She did her nails, she smoked, she chose something to wear and in that process rearranged the hangers in the closet. She made decisions: she would not smoke so much; she would not tell her mother about the apple. She changed her mind about a red dress, in favor of a green suit. She dabbed a fingertip against her tongue and tried to rub away a small soiled spot on the toe of one of her white shoes.

Just at sunset, she lay down on the narrow bed drawn close to the window of her room and looked out, leaning on one bare elbow. The last light filtered through the small foliage of the park across the way and played leaves over her face. The street was empty and looked washed. She lit another cigarette and laid it on the window ledge; the tip of it hung over the edge of the sill and its smoke fanned up in a filigree of weak sunlight both yellow and blue.

She lay, smoking one cigarette after another, until the room was dark. She was still thinking about the apple. She was thinking that if she knew his name, then she would introduce him to her mother;

not to know it was to make the introduction an embarrassment. She could explain later, when she got home. The street lights were on. She persuaded herself to get up and dress, and while she was naked she heard her mother knock at the door.

"Julie? Are you awake?"

"Yes, Mother."

"It's late. Don't you want something to eat?"

She took a quick, interrupted breath. "I'm going out, Mother; no, thank you."

She heard her mother moving on the other side of the door. "Julie? Are you lying there in the dark?"

"Not now. I just this minute got up to dress."

"Don't make yourself ill, dear."

Her mother went away. Julie turned on the dresser lamp and puttered among the objects arranged on the glass top: cosmetics and scents, a picture of her late father, a framed snapshot of herself when she was five.

As she dressed, she realized how silly her fears were. How could she fret about introducing him to her mother? He would surely not come to the door for her; how did she imagine he would get up the porch steps? *Bump, bump, bump.* That *would* have disturbed her mother. She finished dressing, making her face; she gave up on the blemished shoe.

At nine o'clock she went to the window. It was the time agreed upon, and though she had not heard a car, she was not surprised to look down to the curb and see her own convertible—green, but looking black under the dim street-bulbs—waiting in front of the house. And there was the nameless apple seated in front on the passenger side, punctual and expecting her. She took up her purse and hurried downstairs.

At the foot of the staircase her mother hindered her.

"Is that the boy outside? Wouldn't he like to come in?"

Julie kissed her mother's cheek. " 'Bye," she said. "I'll tell you everything when I get home." She pushed open the front door and half-ran across the porch, her heels hollow in the quiet street.

No one else was in sight. She crossed in front of the car and got in behind the wheel. She smiled at the apple; he was sitting beside her, nestled against the door. In the weak light he seemed somehow melancholy, with the world reflected from his skin like an image in a thick lens. In her own mind she had formed a picture of him as she lay upstairs on her bed. In the picture, light had shone from him as through a small, curved window—the way she had always drawn him. Here, in fact, the window blurred.

"I hope you haven't been waiting long," she said. "I almost forgot the time."

He didn't answer; she hadn't expected him to, and she was not offended.

"Where shall we go? Shall I pick the place?" She fastened her seat belt and drew it tight over her thighs before she turned the ignition key. As the car glided away from the curb, Julie was relieved that no one was in the street to see her with the apple. Old Mrs. Sewall next door was especially a gossip; she would have told her nephew.

She avoided the center of town, proceeding by way of several back streets to a narrow country road that led to Byers' Lake. Some houses she had to pass; some porches people rocked on, their figures silhouetted in yellow light from parlors. She was excited both by the apple's presence and by the risk of being watched and wondered about.

"I've been thinking about you all day," she told the apple. "Can you believe that?"

She glanced over at him. Something smug about his posture pleased her—as if he were proud to have been in her thoughts.

Now she was driving perhaps a little too fast. The apple shifted his position, and she let up on the accelerator.

"I'm sorry the roads are so bumpy out here," she told him. "Wouldn't you like to use your safety belt?"

Then she realized what she had said.

"Oh, dear; I didn't mean that. Really, I'm not a reckless driver." She smiled at him; he was unperturbed.

When she reached the western shore of Byers' Lake, Julie skirted the edge of the water until she came to a familiar place. She parked facing the lake. An orange moon was rising. On either side of the car were a number of wooden benches ranged along the waterside, and beyond them low wooden tables and empty oil drums for wastepaper. No picnickers at this hour. She had often come here with her father; here they had eaten butter cookies and fished for perch in the motionless lake. She had used the cookies for bait.

"I bring all my boyfriends here," Julie said. She released the buckle of the seat belt and turned to face the apple. "That's a kind of joke," she added.

The apple wasn't laughing. That was something you never knew, Julie thought; whether you could count on any of them to have a sense of humor—or exactly what kind of humor they did have a sense for. He seemed, certainly, aloof; yet she imagined in his reserve a gentleness.

"To be honest, I've never brought *any* boyfriends here. I don't have any—not to speak of."

She watched the apple closely, curious to see what effect this confession might have. None. She wanted to go on and explain, without conceit, that it was not because she was unattractive that she did not have lovers; she would not have used that word aloud. She wanted to make clear to the apple that choice had secured her freedom, that necessity had nothing to do with her. Looking straight at him, it was as if she were facing a slightly distorted mirror in which she could verify the evidence for her opinions. Her face in the light of the swollen moon gave itself back from him as if etched on wax. She would, truly, have spoken, only that her image began unexpectedly to cloud over.

"Oh, my heavens," she said, "you're cold. Forgive me; I'll put the top up."

She turned the ignition key and engaged the mechanism which set the top in motion. Odd. She felt an almost physical hitch in her thoughts, an apprehension again, but it was all right; she never had remembered to fasten down the canvas covering over the collapsed top, so now it rose up freely, whirring, leaning back and then thrusting forward like a long-necked bird. The top settled upon the windscreen and went silent.

"I forget about fall—how crisp it gets at night." She trusted this would excuse her lack of forethought. The apple sat motionless; beads of moisture lay grayly upon him.

Julie was obliged, then, to lean across the seat to latch the top into place. Doing so brought her into contact with the apple—nothing more than the touch of an instant, and yet something profoundly physical. Not that the apple responded. Worse, he yielded —a response more positive than mere toleration of her body's restrained weight. She didn't know what to make of *that*. The car top secured, she drew back, vowing not to mention her misgivings.

"There," she said, stupidly.

The windows were still open, yet the simple fact of a roof overhead made the car smaller and confined its atmosphere. The smell of the apple became insistent; before closing the car, she had not noticed it, but now she noticed nothing else. The air was heady and sweet—palpable, like cider. The glass of the windshield steamed with it, or it was her eyes watering. She could not put from her mind the sensation of having touched the apple. She forgot her promise to herself.

"I don't want you to think it was anything but an accident," she said. He would know what she was referring to; after all, he *had* yielded. "I'm not a very deliberate person." That was true. She was a person of no intentions. She tried to shut up and grit her teeth. She wished to God she had not met the apple tonight.

"It was a silly little bit of jostling," she said. *Here I go:* "If I'd really *intended* to touch you—"

And there were her hands, moving, one following the other. She saw herself put out her right hand toward the apple, first the finger-tips and then the palm closing against the damp skin beside her. The left hand beside the right, pressing, bold. What was odd, now, was that she could feel him breathing—or something like breathing. Under her opened hands the apple throbbed, sang. A pulse like an engine. Curiously, dumbly, she was offended; instead of drawing back, she grew angry.

"I don't know what you're thinking," she said, and her teeth were still gritted, so that the words seemed to be shaped from a voice not her own.

The apple was silent. Julie found herself thinking: *Bump, bump, bump.* She laughed, feeling the laughter throbbing to her hands as if a counter to the machinery in the apple. She felt much stronger. She felt superior.

"Remember," she whispered, "that it's me who asked for this evening. Not you. You remember that." To prove her power over him, she turned her nails under and against the skin of the apple. She let the nail-edges break through. With all her strength she raked her hands downward until her wrists met the seat-cushion. Then she backed away, against her door. The odor of apple in the car turned heavy as syrup. *Oh my God,* she thought; *what have I done to him?* She sat drugged.

For a long time she waited, wordless, watching the apple. He was changed, as if he had suddenly grown old, as if he were tired or dying. Julie did not understand her own feelings; she could not im-agine his. The orange moon went to white and floated slowly up out of sight above the field of view defined by the windshield. The lake turned to chalk. The benches and tables and oil drums assumed changed outlines in the fickle light. Hours passed.

At last, as if she were waking from a trance, she said: "I'm sorry. You'd better get out; I have to go home."

Because the apple did not move, Julie got out of the car and walked around to the other side. The bent grass was damp across her ankles.

"I am sorry," she said. She opened the door; the apple tottered at the edge of the seat, then dropped into the grass. She closed the door. The sound the apple had made when he struck the ground hung in the night like a single heart beat. She looked down only long enough to make out the thin, puffy scars—who could have dreamed how vulnerable he was?—and then she got back into the car and drove wildly away.

By the time she reached home, the lights in her mother's bedroom had gone out and the house was dark. She parked the car at the curb, rolled up the windows, and chose to cross the lawn to smother the sounding of her heels. She slipped through the front door into the hall. The house creaked with silence; there was no point in waking her mother to tell what she had done. She climbed the stairs in her stocking feet—certain, anyway, that her mother would not understand.

Once safely in her room, Julie lay on top of the bed and had a cigarette. She was trembling; she was not ready to sleep. All night her hands hummed with the recollection of touching the apple. When she put her right hand near her face to inhale from the cigarette, the odor of apple throbbed from beneath her nails. She did not sleep; she could not even close her eyes. The sun rose redly; the October foliage on trees across the way took fire. She got up from the bed when she heard her mother moving downstairs.

In the kitchen, Julie found coffee and toast ready on the table. Her mother puttered near the sink, rattling cups and cutlery. Her mother said:

"Do you want some juice?"

"No, Mother."

"Isn't that the same outfit you had on last night?"

"Yes."

"Whatever time did you get home? Didn't you go to bed at all?"

"I don't know, Mother."

"Don't know *what?*"

Julie put sugar in the coffee and stirred. "What time I got home," she said.

"Nothing's wrong, is it?"

"No; nothing."

Her mother rattled dishes, closed cupboard doors, ran loud water from the taps. Julie sipped at the coffee.

"I wish you'd brought that boy in last night," her mother said. "You know I like to meet your friends."

"I'm sorry. We were late."

"I do worry about you, dear."

Julie nodded. She pushed the coffee cup aside; she lit a cigarette and looked at her watch. Seven-thirty. The apple had been lying in the grass for hours and hours. She brought the cigarette to her lips, and realized she hadn't washed her hands for breakfast.

"I'd really better be getting to work," Julie announced. She pushed her chair back from the table.

"You've got a good fifteen minutes yet."

"Well, I have an errand to do on the way."

"Have a second cup with Mother," her mother said.

Julie shook her head. She got up and went to the sink; she ran cold water over her hands and dried them on a dish towel.

"Will you be home for lunch?"

"I don't know. I'll call you."

She went upstairs for her purse, and stopped before the dresser mirror to put some order in her hair. As she came downstairs and left the house, she heard her mother shaking the kitchen.

Because she was alone, Julie drove straight through town on a shorter route to the lake. She rolled down her window to air out the car. It was a warm day—of an Indian summer sort—though from the water spots on the hood of the car she guessed there had been frost overnight. She smoked and listened to the radio. Instead of being early for work, she would be late. She felt compelled to see the apple again, as if she might make an opportunity for apology.

At the lake she was scrupulously careful to park a few yards further up the shore; Lord knew she didn't want to run him over, too. She switched off the ignition, stubbed the cigarette in the ashtray. Getting out, she noticed the same gray blemish on her white shoe; she paused to rub it with the heel of her palm. The dark spot endured.

Julie had no trouble finding the apple, though she was shocked to see him. He lay stem down in the yellow grass, and the scars she had inflicted faced up at her. They were horribly brown—as if the apple were made of painted metal, rusting outward from hidden flaws. The cold weather of the night before had altered him. His skin, which last night had held her in its dark mirror, was loosened and coarse. Wrinkles, like the contractions on water freezing, had appeared on him. Julie knelt over him.

"I wish I hadn't hurt you," she said. Nothing else. She couldn't tell if he heard her, or if he were listening. She did not touch him. Perhaps he wasn't alive.

She was late at work by nearly forty minutes. The other girls were at their typewriters, their backs straight, their heads tipped primly toward their copy-work. Julie sat at her own desk and slid her purse into a bottom drawer. She arranged papers. She drew together letter sheets and carbons, and fed them into the typewriter.

"Dear Sir:" she typed.

Mrs. Sewall's nephew came out of a door at the far end of the long aisle of typists. He squinted straight at her and came forward. Beside her, he said:

"Here you are. I was worried. I called your mother about you."

"I had something to do on the way," Julie said. She turned back the sheets of paper in the machine and typed the day's date. She could not think properly about the letter; she thought about the apple and what she had done to him.

"Your mother *said* you were doing an errand," Mrs. Sewall's nephew went on.

"Yes, I was." She did not dislike him, but he made her nervous by his attention. He brought her a habit of small presents, like a schoolboy flattering his teacher.

"I'm glad you weren't ill," he said.

He went back to the office he had come out of. Julie opened the bottom drawer and rummaged through her purse for cigarettes and matches. She carried them with her to the ladies' room, where she lounged against a windowsill and smoked and watched another girl comb her hair. The light through the window leaned against the back of her neck.

The day went by slowly; she skipped lunch to make up for her lateness. Several times she visited the ladies' room and on each occasion felt the touch of the light slightly changed. She failed to finish her letter. When five o'clock came, she did not drive directly home, but went to Byers' Lake. She parked a short distance from the apple and sat until dusk, watching him from the car.

Her mother remarked on the hour.

"I stayed over to make up some time," Julie told her. "I was tardy this morning."

"Where did you go?"

"It doesn't matter, Mother." She ate some of the cold supper, then went to her room to remember the apple. She sat by the dresser lamp and trimmed her nails. She lay awake in bed and tried not to smoke.

"Your father wouldn't have let you moon around like this," her mother told her the next morning.

"I know."

"I think you're carrying on with this boy."

"I can't help *that*," Julie said.

On the third morning her mother said: "Mrs. Sewall's nephew

calls me every time you're late to work. I want you to know; we're beginning to wonder."

Julie shrugged.

When she drove to the lake on Friday evening, the world was much changed. The seasons were in motion. During the week the temperature had fallen slowly, the nights were chilling, the trees all over town had dropped their dry, brown leaves into the gutters. Though she tried to resist wearing a coat, Julie found that the weathers of Byers' Lake were beginning to leave her miserable with cold; today she had dressed warmly. Rather that, than to give up the ritual of her visits to the apple, a few minutes spent with him each morning and evening. Sometimes she sat in the dead grass beside him; sometimes she sat in the car nearby, and grew accustomed to the stifled smells of the car's heater. She talked to the apple—about how the silences between herself and her mother became more natural; about how the lack of sleep no longer left her exhausted through the daylight hours. She talked to the apple about guilt; she believed he was alive, and listening. She believed he understood.

She parked close by and got out of the car. A wind was up from the northeast, roughening the lake, pushing out wraiths of gray cloud from the opposite shore. The color was out of the woods; islands of spruce and pine stood more black than green. She turned up her collar and went to the apple.

He was hideous. Every day grown less like what she had met on the first night, now he was scarcely recognizable. His redness was drained off into hollow muddles of brown, the heady odor of his flesh gone sour on the wind. His skin was like a shell, his body translucent as gelatin in a filmy envelope. His roundness sagged into the earth. She had long since ceased to be offended by the changes in him, but now, for the first time, the sight of him moved her to despair. *Dear God*, thought Julie; *oh, dear God.* Her eyes into the wind stung with tears. She reached out to him.

"I'm sorry, I swear. If only I could have you back—"

She blubbered the words. Her hands closed over the apple, lifted him, felt him giving way between her palms. The soft, cold marrow melted against her and oozed through her fingers. She screamed; she could not let go. She fell forward to her knees and pressed the apple close against the front of her coat, her body rocking and shaking from her sobs. Something touched her arm—a pressure not a ghost, a real touch. She looked up. Mrs. Sewall's nephew stood above her; his hand squeezed her elbow. The man's face swam in the shallows of her sight, and she could not understand what he said over the sounds she was making. She lost her balance and fell; she thought her mother was standing by the car, watching, horrified. Mrs. Sewall's nephew reached down. Julie rested her cheek on the ground and embraced the apple.

"It isn't true," she whimpered. She felt the apple against her heart, *bump, bump, bump;* the warmed pulp dribbled over the backs of her hands. "It isn't what you think."

THE ROCKING-HORSE WINNER
d. h. lawrence

There was a woman who was beautiful, who started with all the advantages, yet she had no luck. She married for love, and the love turned to dust. She had bonny children, yet she felt they had been thrust upon her, and she could not love them. They looked at her coldly, as if they were finding fault with her. And hurriedly she felt she must cover up some fault in herself. Yet what it was that she must cover up she never knew. Nevertheless, when her children were present, she always felt the centre of her heart go hard. This troubled her, and in her manner she was all the more gentle and anxious for her children, as if she loved them very much. Only she herself knew that at the centre of her heart was a hard little place that could not feel love, no, not for anybody. Everybody else said of her: "She is such a good mother. She adores her children." Only she herself, and her children themselves, knew it was not so. They read it in each other's eyes.

There were a boy and two little girls. They lived in a pleasant house, with a garden, and they had discreet servants, and felt themselves superior to anyone in the neighbourhood.

Although they lived in style, they felt always an anxiety in the house. There was never enough money. The mother had a small income, and the father had a small income, but not nearly enough for the social position which they had to keep up. The father went into town to some office. But though he had good prospects, these prospects never materialized. There was always the grinding sense of the shortage of money, though the style was always kept up.

At last the mother said: "I will see if I can't make something." But she did not know where to begin. She racked her brains, and tried this thing and the other, but could not find anything successful. The failure made deep lines come into her face. Her children were growing up, they would have to go to school. There must be more money, there must be more money. The father, who was always very handsome and expensive in his tastes, seemed as if he never would be able to do anything worth doing. And the mother, who had a great belief in herself, did not succeed any better, and her tastes were just as expensive.

And so the house came to be haunted by the unspoken phrase: There must be more money! There must be more money! The children could hear it all the time, though nobody said it aloud. They heard it at Christmas, when the expensive and splendid toys filled the nursery. Behind the shining modern rocking horse, behind the smart doll's-house, a voice would start whispering: "There must be more money! There must be more money!" And the children would stop playing, to listen for a moment. They would look into each other's eyes, to see if they had all heard. And each one saw in the eyes of the other two that they too had heard. "There must be more money! There must be more money!"

It came whispering from the springs of the still-swaying rocking horse, and even the horse, bending his wooden, champing head, heard it. The big doll, sitting so pink and smirking in her new pram, could hear it quite plainly, and seemed to be smirking all the more self-consciously because of it. The foolish puppy, too, that took the place of the Teddy bear, he was looking so extraordinarily foolish for no other reason but that he heard the secret whisper all over the house: "There must be more money!"

Yet nobody ever said it aloud. The whisper was everywhere, and therefore no one spoke it. Just as no one ever says: "We are breathing!" in spite of the fact that breath is coming and going all the time.

"Mother," said the boy Paul one day, "why don't we keep a car of our own? Why do we always use uncle's, or else a taxi?"

"Because we're the poor members of the family," said the mother.

"But why are we, mother?"

"Well—I suppose," she said slowly and bitterly, "it's because your father has no luck."

The boy was silent for some time.

"Is luck money, mother?" he asked, rather timidly.

"No, Paul. Not quite. It's what causes you to have money."

"Oh!" said Paul vaguely. "I thought when Uncle Oscar said filthy lucker, it meant money."

"Filthy lucre does mean money," said the mother. "But it's lucre, not luck."

"Oh!" said the boy. "Then what is luck, mother?"

"It's what causes you to have money. If you're lucky you have money. That's why it's better to be born lucky than rich. If you're rich, you may lose your money. But if you're lucky, you will always get more money."

"Oh! Will you? And is father not lucky?"

"Very unlucky, I should say," she said bitterly.

The boy watched her with unsure eyes.

"Why?" he asked.

"I don't know. Nobody ever knows why one person is lucky and another unlucky."

"Don't they? Nobody at all? Does nobody know?"

"Perhaps God. But He never tells."

"He ought to, then. And aren't you lucky either, mother?"

"I can't be, if I married an unlucky husband."

"But by yourself, aren't you?"

"I used to think I was, before I married. Now I think I am very unlucky indeed."

"Why?"

"Well—never mind! Perhaps I'm not really," she said.

The child looked at her, to see if she meant it. But he saw, by the lines of her mouth, that she was only trying to hide something from him.

"Well, anyhow," he said stoutly, "I'm a lucky person."

"Why?" said his mother, with a sudden laugh.

He stared at her. He didn't even know why he had said it.

"God told me," he asserted, brazening it out.

"I hope He did, dear!" she said, again with a laugh, but rather bitter.

"He did, mother!"

"Excellent!" said the mother, using one of her husband's exclamations.

The boy saw she did not believe him; or, rather, that she paid no attention to his assertion. This angered him somewhat, and made him want to compel her attention.

He went off by himself, vaguely, in a childish way, seeking for the clue to "luck." Absorbed, taking no heed of other people, he went about with a sort of stealth, seeking inwardly for luck. He wanted luck, he wanted it, he wanted it. When the two girls were playing dolls in the nursery, he would sit on his big rocking horse, charging madly into space, with a frenzy that made the little girls peer at him uneasily. Wildly the horse careered, the waving dark hair of the boy tossed, his eyes had a strange glare in them. The little girls dared not speak to him.

When he had ridden to the end of his mad little journey, he climbed down and stood in front of his rocking horse, staring fixedly into its lowered face. Its red mouth was slightly open, its big eye was wide and glassy-bright.

"Now!" he would silently command the snorting steed. "Now, take me to where there is luck! Now take me!"

And he would slash the horse on the neck with the little whip he had asked Uncle Oscar for. He knew the horse could take him to where there was luck, if only he forced it. So he would mount again, and start on his furious ride, hoping at last to get there. He knew he could get there.

"You'll break your horse, Paul!" said the nurse.

"He's always riding like that! I wish he'd leave off!" said his elder sister Joan.

But he only glared down on them in silence. Nurse gave him up. She could make nothing of him. Anyhow he was growing beyond her.

One day his mother and his Uncle Oscar came in when he was on one of his furious rides. He did not speak to them.

"Hallo, you young jockey! Riding a winner?" said his uncle.

"Aren't you growing too big for a rocking horse? You're not a very little boy any longer, you know," said his mother.

But Paul only gave a blue glare from his big, rather close-set eyes. He would speak to nobody when he was in full tilt. His mother watched him with an anxious expression on her face.

At last he suddenly stopped forcing his horse into the mechanical gallop, and slid down.

"Well, I got there!" he announced fiercely, his blue eyes still flaring, and his sturdy long legs straddling apart.

"Where did you get to?" asked his mother.

"Where I wanted to go," he flared back at her.

"That's right, son!" said Uncle Oscar. "Don't you stop till you get there. What's the horse's name?"

"He doesn't have a name," said the boy.

"Gets on without all right?" asked the uncle.

"Well, he has different names. He was called Sansovino last week."

"Sansovino, eh? Won the Ascot. How did you know his name?"

"He always talks about horse races with Bassett," said Joan.

The uncle was delighted to find that his small nephew was posted with all the racing news. Bassett, the young gardener, who had been wounded in the left foot in the war and had got his present job through Oscar Cresswell, whose batman he had been, was a perfect blade of the "turf." He lived in the racing events, and the small boy lived with him.

Oscar Cresswell got it all from Bassett.

"Master Paul comes and asks me, so I can't do more than tell him, sir," said Bassett, his face terribly serious, as if he were speaking of religious matters.

"And does he ever put anything on a horse he fancies?"

"Well—I don't want to give him away—he's a young sport, a fine sport, sir. Would you mind asking him yourself? He sort of takes a pleasure in it, and perhaps he'd feel I was giving him away, sir, if you don't mind."

Bassett was serious as a church.

The uncle went back to his nephew, and took him off for a ride in the car.

"Say, Paul, old man, do you ever put anything on a horse?" the uncle asked.

The boy watched the handsome man closely.

"Why, do you think I oughtn't to?" he parried.

"Not a bit of it! I thought perhaps you might give me a tip for the Lincoln."

The car sped on into the country, going down to Uncle Oscar's place in Hampshire.

"Honour bright?" said the nephew.

"Honour bright, son!" said the uncle.

"Well, then, Daffodil."

"Daffodil! I doubt it, sonny. What about Mirza?"

"I only know the winner," said the boy. "That's Daffodil."

"Daffodil, eh?"

There was a pause. Daffodil was an obscure horse comparatively.

"Uncle!"

"Yes, son?"

"You won't let it go any further, will you? I promised Bassett."

"Bassett be damned, old man! What's he got to do with it?"

"We're partners. We've been partners from the first. Uncle, he lent me my first five shillings, which I lost. I promised him, honour bright, it was only between me and him; only you gave me that ten-shilling note I started winning with, so I thought you were lucky. You won't let it go any further, will you?"

The boy gazed at his uncle from those big, hot, blue eyes, set rather close together. The uncle stirred and laughed uneasily.

"Right you are, son! I'll keep your tip private. Daffodil, eh? How much are you putting on him?"

"All except twenty pounds," said the boy. "I keep that in reserve."

The uncle thought it a good joke.

"You keep twenty pounds in reserve, do you, you young romancer? What are you betting, then?"

"I'm betting three hundred," said the boy gravely. "But it's between you and me, Uncle Oscar! Honour bright?"

The uncle burst into a roar of laughter.

"It's between you and me all right, you young Nat Gould," he said, laughing. "But where's your three hundred?"

"Bassett keeps it for me. We're partners."

"You are, are you! And what is Bassett putting on Daffodil?"

"He won't go quite as high as I do, I expect. Perhaps he'll go a hundred and fifty."

"What, pennies?" laughed the uncle.

"Pounds," said the child, with a surprised look at his uncle. "Bassett keeps a bigger reserve than I do."

Between wonder and amusement Uncle Oscar was silent. He pursued the matter no further, but he determined to take his nephew with him to the Lincoln races.

"Now, son," he said, "I'm putting twenty on Mirza, and I'll put five for you on any horse you fancy. What's your pick?"

"Daffodil, uncle."

"No, not the fiver on Daffodil!"

"I should if it was my own fiver," said the child.

"Good! Good! Right you are! A fiver for me and a fiver for you on Daffodil!"

The child had never been to a race meeting before, and his eyes were blue fire. He pursed his mouth tight, and watched. A Frenchman just in front had put his money on Lancelot. Wild with excitement, he flayed his arms up and down, yelling "Lancelot! Lancelot!" in his French accent.

Daffodil came in first, Lancelot second, Mirza third. The child, flushed and with eyes blazing, was curiously serene. His uncle brought him four five-pound notes, four to one.

"What am I to do with these?" he cried, waving them before the boy's eyes.

"I suppose we'll talk to Bassett," said the boy. "I expect I have fifteen hundred now; and twenty in reserve; and this twenty."

His uncle studied him for some moments.

"Look here, son!" he said. "You're not serious about Bassett and that fifteen hundred, are you?"

"Yes, I am. But it's between you and me, uncle. Honour bright!"

"Honour bright all right, son! But I must talk to Bassett."

"If you'd like to be a partner, uncle, with Bassett and me, we could all be partners. Only, you'd have to promise, honour bright, uncle, not to let it go beyond us three. Bassett and I are lucky, and you must be lucky, because it was your ten shillings I started winning with. . . ."

Uncle Oscar took both Bassett and Paul into Richmond Park for an afternoon, and there they talked.

"It's like this, you see, sir," Bassett said. "Master Paul would get me talking about racing events, spinning yarns, you know, sir. And he was always keen on knowing if I'd made or if I'd lost. It's about a year since, now, that I put five shillings on Blush of Dawn for him—and we lost. Then the luck turned, with that ten shillings he had from you, that we put on Singhalese. And since that time, it's been pretty steady, all things considering. What do you say, Master Paul?"

"We're all right when we're sure," said Paul. "It's when we're not quite sure that we go down."

"Oh, but we're careful then," said Bassett.

"But when are you sure?" smiled Uncle Oscar.

"It's Master Paul, sir," said Bassett, in a secret, religious voice. "It's as if he had it from heaven. Like Daffodil, now, for the Lincoln. That was as sure as eggs."

"Did you put anything on Daffodil?" asked Oscar Cresswell.

"Yes, sir, I made my bit."

"And my nephew?"

Bassett was obstinately silent, looking at Paul.

"I made twelve hundred, didn't I, Bassett? I told uncle I was putting three hundred on Daffodil."

"That's right," said Bassett, nodding.

"But where's the money?" asked the uncle.

"I keep it safe locked up, sir. Master Paul he can have it any minute he likes to ask for it."

"What, fifteen hundred pounds?"

"And twenty! and forty, that is, with the twenty he made on the course."

"It's amazing!" said the uncle.

"If Master Paul offers you to be partners, sir, I would, if I were you; if you'll excuse me," said Bassett.

Oscar Cresswell thought about it.

"I'll see the money," he said.

They drove home again, and sure enough, Bassett came round to the garden-house with fifteen hundred pounds in notes. The twenty pounds reserve was left with Joe Glee, in the Turf Commission deposit.

"You see, it's all right, uncle, when I'm sure! Then we go strong, for all we're worth. Don't we, Bassett?"

"We do that, Master Paul."

"And when are you sure?" said the uncle, laughing.

"Oh, well, sometimes I'm absolutely sure, like about Daffodil," said the boy; "and sometimes I have an idea; and sometimes I haven't even an idea, have I, Bassett? Then we're careful, because we mostly go down."

"You do, do you! And when you're sure, like about Daffodil, what makes you sure, sonny?"

"Oh, well, I don't know," said the boy uneasily. "I'm sure, you know, uncle; that's all."

"It's as if he had it from heaven, sir," Bassett reiterated.

"I should say so!" said the uncle.

But he became a partner. And when the Leger was coming on, Paul was "sure" about Lively Spark, which was a quite inconsiderable horse. The boy insisted on putting a thousand on the horse, Bassett went for five hundred, and Oscar Cresswell two hundred. Lively Spark came in first, and the betting had been ten to one against him. Paul had made ten thousand.

"You see," he said, "I was absolutely sure of him."

Even Oscar Cresswell had cleared two thousand.

"Look here, son," he said, "this sort of thing makes me nervous."

"It needn't, uncle! Perhaps I shan't be sure again for a long time."

"But what are you going to do with your money?" asked the uncle.

"Of course," said the boy, "I started it for mother. She said she had no luck, because father is unlucky, so I thought if I was lucky, it might stop whispering."

"What might stop whispering?"

"Our house. I hate our house for whispering."

"What does it whisper?"

"Why—why"—the boy fidgeted—"why, I don't know. But it's always short of money, you know, uncle."

"I know it, son, I know it."

"You know people send mother writs, don't you, uncle?"

"I'm afraid I do," said the uncle.

"And then the house whispers, like people laughing at you behind your back. It's awful, that is! I thought if I was lucky . . ."

"You might stop it," added the uncle.

The boy watched him with big blue eyes that had an uncanny cold fire in them, and he said never a word.

"Well, then!" said the uncle. "What are we doing?"

"I shouldn't like mother to know I was lucky," said the boy.

"Why not, son?"

"She'd stop me."

"I don't think she would."

"Oh!"—and the boy writhed in an odd way—"I don't want her to know, uncle."

"All right, son! We'll manage it without her knowing."

They managed it very easily. Paul, at the other's suggestion, handed over five thousand pounds to his uncle, who deposited it with the family lawyer, who was then to inform Paul's mother that a relative had put five thousand pounds into his hands, which sum was to be paid out a thousand pounds at a time, on the mother's birthday, for the next five years.

"So she'll have a birthday present of a thousand pounds for five successive years," said Uncle Oscar. "I hope it won't make it all the harder for her later."

Paul's mother had her birthday in November. The house had been "whispering" worse than ever lately, and, even in spite of his luck, Paul could not bear up against it. He was very anxious to see the effect of the birthday letter, telling his mother about the thousand pounds.

When there were no visitors, Paul now took his meals with his parents, as he was beyond the nursery control. His mother went into town nearly every day. She had discovered that she had an odd knack of sketching furs and dress materials, so she worked secretly in the studio of a friend who was the chief "artist" for the leading drapers. She drew the figures of ladies in furs and ladies in silk and sequins for the newspaper advertisements. This young woman artist earned several thousand pounds a year, but Paul's mother only made several hundreds, and she was again dissatisfied. She so wanted to be first in something, and she did not succeed, even in making sketches for drapery advertisements.

She was down to breakfast on the morning of her birthday. Paul watched her face as she read her letters. He knew the lawyer's letter. As his mother read it, her face hardened and became more expressionless. Then a cold, determined look came on her mouth. She hid the letter under the pile of others, and said not a word about it.

"Didn't you have anything nice in the post for your birthday, mother?" said Paul.

"Quite moderately nice," she said, her voice cold and absent.

She went away to town without saying more.

But in the afternoon Uncle Oscar appeared. He said Paul's mother had had a long interview with the lawyer, asking if the whole five thousand could be advanced at once, as she was in debt.

"What do you think, uncle?" said the boy.

"I leave it to you, son."

"Oh, let her have it, then! We can get some more with the other," said the boy.

"A bird in the hand is worth two in the bush, laddie!" said Uncle Oscar.

"But I'm sure to know for the Grand National; or the Lincolnshire; or else the Derby. I'm sure to know for one of them," said Paul.

So Uncle Oscar signed the agreement, and Paul's mother touched the whole five thousand. Then something very curious happened. The voices in the house suddenly went mad, like a chorus of frogs on a spring evening. There were certain new furnishings, and Paul had a tutor. He was really going to Eton, his father's school, in the following autumn. There were flowers in the winter, and a blossoming of the luxury Paul's mother had been used to. And yet the voices in the house, behind the sprays of mimosa and almond blossom, and from under the piles of iridescent cushions, simply trilled and screamed in a sort of ecstasy: "There must be more money! Oh-h-h, there must be more money. Oh, now, now-w! Now-w-w— there must be more money!—more than ever! More than ever!"

It frightened Paul terribly. He studied away at his Latin and Greek with his tutors. But his intense hours were spent with Bassett. The Grand National had gone by: he had not "known," and had lost a hundred pounds. Summer was at hand. He was in agony for the Lincoln. But even for the Lincoln he didn't "know" and he lost fifty pounds. He became wild-eyed and strange, as if something were going to explode in him.

"Let it alone, son! Don't you bother about it!" urged Uncle Oscar. But it was as if the boy couldn't really hear what his uncle was saying.

"I've got to know for the Derby! I've got to know for the Derby!" the child reiterated, his big blue eyes blazing with a sort of madness.

His mother noticed how overwrought he was.

"You'd better go to the seaside. Wouldn't you like to go now to the seaside, instead of waiting? I think you'd better," she said, looking down at him anxiously, her heart curiously heavy because of him.

But the child lifted his uncanny blue eyes.

"I couldn't possibly go before the Derby, mother!" he said. "I couldn't possibly!"

"Why not?" she said, her voice becoming heavy when she was opposed. "Why not? You can still go from the seaside to see the Derby with your Uncle Oscar, if that's what you wish. No need for you to wait here. Besides, I think you care too much about these races. It's a bad sign. My family has been a gambling family, and you won't know till you grow up how much damage it has done. But it has done damage. I shall have to send Bassett away, and ask Uncle Oscar not to talk racing to you, unless you promise to be reasonable about it; go away to the seaside and forget it. You're all nerves!"

"I'll do what you like, mother, so long as you don't send me away till after the Derby," the boy said.

"Send you away from where? Just from this house?"

"Yes," he said, gazing at her.

"Why, you curious child, what makes you care about this house so much, suddenly? I never knew you loved it."

He gazed at her without speaking. He had a secret within a secret, something he had not divulged, even to Bassett or to his Uncle Oscar.

But his mother, after standing undecided and a little bit sullen for some moments, said:

"Very well, then! Don't go to the seaside till after the Derby, if you don't wish it. But promise me you won't let your nerves go to pieces. Promise you won't think so much about horse racing and events, as you call them!"

"Oh, no," said the boy casually. "I won't think much about

them, mother. You needn't worry. I wouldn't worry, mother, if I were you."

"If you were me and I were you," said his mother, "I wonder what we should do!"

"But you know you needn't worry, mother, don't you?" the boy repeated.

"I should be awfully glad to know it," she said wearily.

"Oh, well, you can, you know. I mean, you ought to know you needn't worry," he insisted.

"Ought I? Then I'll see about it," she said.

Paul's secret of secrets was his wooden horse, that which had no name. Since he was emancipated from a nurse and a nursery-governess, he had had his rocking horse removed to his own bedroom at the top of the house.

"Surely, you're too big for a rocking horse!" his mother had remonstrated.

"Well, you see, mother, till I can have a real horse, I like to have some sort of animal about," had been his quaint answer.

"Do you feel he keeps you company?" she laughed.

"Oh, yes! He's very good, he always keeps me company, when I'm there," said Paul.

So the horse, rather shabby, stood in an arrested prance in the boy's bedroom.

The Derby was drawing near, and the boy grew more and more tense. He hardly heard what was spoken to him, he was very frail, and his eyes were really uncanny. His mother had sudden seizures of uneasiness about him. Sometimes, for half-an-hour, she would feel a sudden anxiety about him that was almost anguish. She wanted to rush to him at once, and know he was safe.

Two nights before the Derby, she was at a big party in town, when one of her rushes of anxiety about her boy, her first-born, gripped her heart till she could hardly speak. She fought with the feeling, might and main, for she believed in common sense. But it was too strong. She had to leave the dance and go downstairs to telephone to the country. The children's nursery-governess was terribly surprised and startled at being rung up in the night.

"Are the children all right, Miss Wilmot?"

"Oh, yes, they are quite all right."

"Master Paul? Is he all right?"

"He went to bed as right as a trivet. Shall I run up and look at him?"

"No," said Paul's mother reluctantly. "No! Don't trouble. It's all right. Don't sit up. We shall be home fairly soon." She did not want her son's privacy intruded upon.

"Very good," said the governess.

It was about one o'clock when Paul's mother and father drove up to their house. All was still. Paul's mother went to her room and slipped off her white fur coat. She had told her maid not to wait up for her. She heard her husband downstairs, mixing a whisky-and-soda.

And then, because of the strange anxiety at her heart, she stole upstairs to her son's room. Noiselessly she went along the upper corridor. Was there a faint noise? What was it?

She stood, with arrested muscles, outside his door, listening. There was a strange, heavy, and yet not loud noise. Her heart stood still. It was a soundless noise, yet rushing and powerful. Something huge, in violent, hushed motion. What was it? What in God's name was it? She ought to know. She felt that she knew the noise. She knew what it was.

Yet she could not place it. She couldn't say what it was. And on and on it went, like a madness.

Softly, frozen with anxiety and fear, she turned the door handle.

The room was dark. Yet in the space near the window, she heard and saw something plunging to and fro. She gazed in fear and amazement.

Then suddenly she switched on the light, and saw her son, in his green pyjamas, madly surging on the rocking horse. The blaze of light suddenly lit him up, as he urged the wooden horse, and lit her up, as she stood, blonde, in her dress of pale green and crystal, in the doorway.

"Paul!" she cried. "Whatever are you doing?"

"It's Malabar!' he screamed, in a powerful, strange voice. "It's Malabar."

His eyes blazed at her for one strange and senseless second, as he ceased urging his wooden horse. Then he fell with a crash to the ground, and she, all her tormented motherhood flooding upon her, rushed to gather him up.

But he was unconscious, and unconscious he remained, with some brain-fever. He talked and tossed, and his mother sat stonily by his side.

"Malabar! It's Malabar! Bassett, Bassett, I know! It's Malabar!"

So the child cried, trying to get up and urge the rocking horse that gave him his inspiration.

"What does he mean by Malabar?" asked the heart-frozen mother.

"I don't know," said the father stonily.

"What does he mean by Malabar?" she asked her brother Oscar.

"It's one of the horses running for the Derby," was the answer.

And, in spite of himself, Oscar Cresswell spoke to Bassett, and himself put a thousand on Malabar: at fourteen to one.

The third day of the illness was critical: they were waiting for a change. The boy, with his rather long, curly hair, was tossing ceaselessly on the pillow. He neither slept nor regained consciousness, and his eyes were like blue stones. His mother sat, feeling her heart had gone, turned actually into a stone.

In the evening, Oscar Cresswell did not come, but Bassett sent a message, saying could he come up for one moment, just one moment? Paul's mother was very angry at the intrusion, but on second thought she agreed. The boy was the same. Perhaps Bassett might bring him to consciousness.

The gardener, a shortish fellow with a little brown moustache, and sharp little brown eyes, tiptoed into the room, touched his imaginary cap to Paul's mother, and stole to the bedside, staring with glittering, smallish eyes, at the tossing, dying child.

"Master Paul!" he whispered. "Master Paul! Malabar come in first all right, a clean win. I did as you told me. You've made over seventy thousand pounds, you have; you've got over eighty thousand. Malabar came in all right, Master Paul."

"Malabar! Malabar! Did I say Malabar, mother? Did I say Malabar? Do you think I'm lucky, mother? I knew Malabar, didn't I? Over eighty thousand pounds! I call that lucky, don't you, mother? Over eighty thousand pounds! I knew, didn't I know I knew? Malabar came in all right. If I ride my horse till I'm sure, then I tell you, Bassett, you can go as high as you like. Did you go for all you were worth, Bassett?"

"I went a thousand on it, Master Paul."

"I never told you, mother, that if I can ride my horse, and get there, then I'm absolutely sure—oh, absolutely! Mother, did I ever tell you? I am lucky."

"No, you never did," said the mother.

But the boy died in the night.

And even as he lay dead, his mother heard her brother's voice saying to her: "My God, Hester, you're eighty-odd thousand to the good and a poor devil of a son to the bad. But, poor devil, poor devil, he's best gone out of a life where he rides his rocking horse to find a winner."

THE ONE WHO WAITS
ray bradbury

I live in a well. I live like smoke in the well. Like vapor in a stone throat. I don't move. I don't do anything but wait. Overhead I see the cold stars of night and morning, and I see the sun. And sometimes I sing old songs of this world when it was young. How can I tell you what I am when I don't know? I cannot. I am simply waiting. I am mist and moonlight and memory. I am sad and I am old. Sometimes I fall like rain into the well. Spider webs are startled into forming where my rain falls fast, on the water surface. I wait in cool silence and there will be a day when I no longer wait.

Now it is morning. I hear a great thunder. I smell fire from a distance. I hear a metal crashing. I wait. I listen.

Voices. Far away.

"All right!"

One voice. An alien voice. An alien tongue I cannot know. No word is familiar. I listen.

"Send the men out!"

A crunching in crystal sands.

"Mars! So this is it!"

"Where's the flag?"

"Here, sir."

"Good, good."

The sun is high in the blue sky and its golden rays fill the well and I hang like a flower pollen, invisible and misting in the warm light.

Voices.

"In the name of the Government of Earth, I proclaim this to be the Martian Territory, to be equally divided among the member nations."

What are they saying? I turn in the sun, like a wheel, invisible and lazy, golden and tireless.

"What's over here?"

"A well!"

"No!"

"Come on. Yes!"

The approach of warmth. Three objects bend over the well mouth, and my coolness rises to the objects.

"Great!"

"Think it's good water?"

"We'll see."

"Someone get a lab test bottle and a dropline."

"I will!"

A sound of running. The return.

"Here we are."

I wait.

"Let it down. Easy."

Glass shines, above, coming down on a slow line.

The water ripples softly as the glass touches and fills. I rise in the warm air toward the well mouth.

"Here we are. You want to test this water, Regent?"

"Let's have it."

"What a beautiful well. Look at that construction. How old you think it is?"

"God knows. When we landed in that other town yesterday Smith said there hasn't been life on Mars in ten thousand years."

"Imagine."

"How is it, Regent? The water."

"Pure as silver. Have a glass."

The sound of water in the hot sunlight. Now I hover like a dust, a cinnamon, upon the soft wind.

"What's the matter, Jones?"

"I don't know. Got a terrible headache. All of a sudden."

"Did you drink the water yet?"

"No, I haven't. It's not that. I was just bending over the well and all of a sudden my head split. I feel better now."

Now I know who I am.

My name is Stephen Leonard Jones and I am twenty-five years old and I have just come in a rocket from a planet called Earth and I am standing with my good friends Regent and Shaw by an old well on the planet Mars.

I look down at my golden fingers, tan and strong. I look at my long legs and at my silver uniform and at my friends.

"What's wrong, Jones?" they say.

"Nothing," I say, looking at them. "Nothing at all."

The food is good. It has been ten thousand years since food. It touches the tongue in a fine way and the wine with the food is warming. I listen to the sound of voices. I make words that I do not understand but somehow understand. I test the air.

"What's the matter, Jones?"

I tilt this head of mine and rest my hands holding the silver utensils of eating. I feel everything.

"What do you mean?" this voice, this new thing of mine, says.

"You keep breathing funny. Coughing," says the other man.

I pronounce exactly. "Maybe a little cold coming on."

"Check with the doc later."

I nod my head and it is good to nod. It is good to do several things after ten thousand years. It is good to breathe the air and it is good to feel the sun in the flesh deep and going deeper and it is good to feel the structure of ivory, the fine skeleton hidden in the warming flesh, and it is good to hear sounds much clearer and more immediate than they were in the stone deepness of a well. I sit enchanted.

"Come out of it, Jones. Snap to it. We got to move!"

"Yes," I say, hypnotized with the way the word forms like water on the tongue and falls with slow beauty out into the air.

I walk and it is good walking. I stand high and it is a long way to the ground when I look down from my eyes and my head. It is like living on a fine cliff and being happy there.

Regent stands by the stone well, looking down. The others have gone murmuring to the silver ship from which they came.

I feel the fingers of my hand and the smile of my mouth.

"It is deep," I say.

"Yes."

"It is called a Soul Well."

Regent raises his head and looks at me. "How do you know that?"

"Doesn't it look like one?"

"I never heard of a Soul Well."

"A place where waiting things, things that once had flesh, wait and wait," I say, touching his arm.

The sand is fire and the ship is silver fire in the hotness of the day and the heat is good to feel. The sound of my feet in the hard sand. I listen. The sound of the wind and the sun burning the valleys. I smell the smell of the rocket boiling in the noon. I stand below the port.

"Where's Regent?" someone says.

"I saw him by the well," I reply.

One of them runs toward the well. I am beginning to tremble. A fine shivering tremble, hidden deep, but becoming very strong. And for the first time I hear it, as if it too were in a well. A voice calling deep within me, tiny and afraid. And the voice cries, *Let me go, let me go*, and there is a feeling as if something is trying to get free, a pounding of labyrinthine doors, a rushing down dark corridors and up passages, echoing and screaming.

"Regent's in the well!"

The men are running, all five of them. I run with them but now I am sick and the trembling is violent.

"He must have fallen. Jones, you were here with him. Did you see? Jones? Well, speak up, man."

"What's wrong, Jones?"

I fall to my knees, the trembling is so bad.

"He's sick. Here, help me with him."

"The sun."

"No, not the sun," I murmur.

They stretch me out and the seizures come and go like earthquakes and the deep hidden voice in me cries, *This is Jones, this is me, that's not him, that's not him, don't believe him, let me out, let me out!* And I look up at the bent figures and my eyelids flicker. They touch my wrists.

"His heart is acting up."

I close my eyes. The screaming stops. The shivering ceases.

I rise, as in a cool well, released.

"He's dead," says someone.

"Jones is dead."

"From what?"

"Shock, it looks like."

"What kind of shock?" I say, and my name is Sessions and my lips move crisply, and I am the captain of these men. I stand among them and I am looking down at a body which lies cooling on the sands. I clap both hands to my head.

"Captain!"

"It's nothing," I say, crying out. "Just a headache. I'll be all right. There. There," I whisper. "It's all right now."

"We'd better get out of the sun, sir."

"Yes," I say, looking down at Jones. "We should never have come. Mars doesn't want us."

We carry the body back to the rocket with us, and a new voice is calling deep in me to be let out.

Help, help. Far down in the moist earthen-works of the body. *Help, help!* in red fathoms, echoing and pleading.

The trembling starts much sooner this time. The control is less steady.

"Captain, you'd better get in out of the sun, you don't look too well, sir."

"Yes," I say. "Help," I say.

"What, sir?"

"I didn't say anything."

"You said 'Help,' sir."

"Did I, Matthews, did I?"

The body is laid out in the shadow of the rocket and the voice screams in the deep underwater catacombs of bone and crimson tide. My hands jerk. My mouth splits and is parched. My nostrils fasten wide. My eyes roll. *Help, help, oh help, don't, don't, let me out, don't, don't.*

"Don't," I say.

"What, sir?"

"Never mind," I say. "I've got to get free," I say. I clap my hand to my mouth.

"How's that, sir?" cries Matthews.

"Get inside, all of you, go back to Earth!" I shout.

A gun is in my hand. I lift it.

"Don't, sir!"

An explosion. Shadows run. The screaming is cut off. There is a whistling sound of falling through space.

After ten thousand years, how good to die. How good to feel the sudden coolness, the relaxation. How good to be like a hand within a glove that stretches out and grows wonderfully cold in the hot sand. Oh, the quiet and the loveliness of gathering, darkening death. But one cannot linger on.

A crack, a snap.

"Good God, he's killed himself!" I cry, and open my eyes and there is the captain lying against the rocket, his skull split by a bullet, his eyes wide, his tongue protruding between his white teeth. Blood runs from his head. I bend to him and touch him. "The fool," I say. "Why did he do that?"

The men are horrified. They stand over the two dead men and turn their heads to see the Martian sands and the distant well where Regent lies lolling in deep waters. A croaking comes out of their dry lips, a whimpering, a childish protest against this awful dream.

The men turn to me.

After a long while, one of them says, "That makes you captain, Matthews."

"I know," I say slowly.

"Only six of us left."

"Good God, it happened so quick!"

"I don't want to stay here, let's get out!"

The men clamor. I go to them and touch them now, with a confidence which almost sings in me. "Listen," I say, and touch their elbows or their arms or their hands.

We all fall silent.

We are one.

No, no, no, no, no, no! Inner voices crying, deep down and gone into prisons beneath exteriors.

We are looking at each other. We are Samuel Matthews and Raymond Moses and William Spaulding and Charles Evans and Forrest Cole and John Summers, and we say nothing but look upon each other and our white faces and shaking hands.

We turn, as one, and look at the well.

"Now," we say.

No, no, six voices scream, hidden and layered down and stored forever.

Our feet walk in the sand and it is as if a great hand with twelve fingers were moving across the hot sea bottom.

We bend to the well, looking down. From the cool depths six faces peer back up at us.

One by one we bend until our balance is gone, and one by one drop into the mouth and down through cool darkness into the cold waters.

The sun sets. The stars wheel upon the night sky. Far out, there is a wink of light. Another rocket coming, leaving red marks on space.

I live in a well. I live like smoke in a well. Like vapor in a stone throat. Overhead I see the cold stars of night and morning, and I see the sun. And sometimes I sing old songs of this world when it was young. How can I tell you what I am when even I don't know? I cannot.

I am simply waiting.

NIGHT-SEA JOURNEY
john barth

"One way or another, no matter which theory of our journey is correct, it's myself I address; to whom I rehearse as to a stranger our history and condition, and will disclose my secret hope though I sink for it.

"Is the journey my invention? Do the night, the sea, exist at all, I ask myself, apart from my experience of them? Do I myself exist, or is this a dream? Sometimes I wonder. And if I am, who am I? The Heritage I supposedly transport? But how can I be both vessel and contents? Such are the questions that beset my intervals of rest.

"My trouble is, I lack conviction. Many accounts of our situation seem plausible to me—where and what we are, why we swim and whither. But implausible ones as well, perhaps especially those, I must admit as possibly correct. Even likely. If at times, in certain humors—striking in unison, say, with my neighbors and chanting with them 'Onward! Upward!'—I have supposed that we have after all a common Maker, Whose nature and motives we may not know, but Who engendered us in some mysterious wise and launched us forth toward some end known but to Him—if (for a moodslength only) I have been able to entertain such notions, very

213

popular in certain quarters, it is because our night-sea journey partakes of their absurdity. One might even say: I can believe them *because* they are absurd.

"Has that been said before?

"Another paradox: it appears to be these recesses from swimming that sustain me in the swim. Two measures onward and upward, flailing with the rest, then I float exhausted and dispirited, brood upon the night, the sea, the journey, while the flood bears me a measure back and down: slow progress, but I live, I live, and make my way, aye, past many a drowned comrade in the end, stronger, worthier than I, victims of their unremitting *joie de nager*. I have seen the best swimmers of my generation go under. Numberless the number of the dead! Thousands drown as I think this thought, millions as I rest before returning to the swim. And scores, hundreds of millions have expired since we surged forth, brave in our innocence, upon our dreadful way. 'Love! Love!' we sang then, a quarter-billion strong, and churned the warm sea white with joy of swimming! Now all are gone down—the buoyant, the sodden, leaders and followers, all gone under, while wretched I swim on. Yet these same reflective intervals that keep me afloat have led me into wonder, doubt, despair—strange emotions for a swimmer!— have led me, even, to suspect . . . that our night-sea journey is without meaning.

"Indeed, if I have yet to join the hosts of the suicides, it is because (fatigue apart) I find it no meaningfuller to drown myself than to go on swimming.

"I know that there are those who seem actually to enjoy the night-sea; who claim to love swimming for its own sake, or sincerely believe that 'reaching the Shore,' 'transmitting the Heritage' (*Whose* Heritage, I'd like to know? And to whom?) is worth the staggering cost. I do not. Swimming itself I find at best not actively unpleasant, more often tiresome, not infrequently a torment. Arguments from function and design don't impress me: granted that we can and do swim, that in a manner of speaking our long tails and streamlined heads are 'meant for' swimming; it by no means follows—for me, at least—that we *should* swim, or otherwise endeavor to 'fulfill our destiny.' Which is to say, Someone Else's destiny, since ours, so far as I can see, is merely to perish, one way or another, soon or late. The heartless zeal of our (departed) leaders, like the blind ambition and good cheer of my own youth, appalls me now; for the death of my comrades I am inconsolable. If the night-sea journey has justification, it is not for us swimmers ever to discover it.

"Oh, to be sure, 'Love!' one heard on every side: 'Love it is that drives and sustains us!' I translate: we don't know *what* drives and sustains us, only that we are most miserably driven and, imperfectly, sustained. *Love* is how we call our ignorance of what whips us. 'To reach the Shore,' then: but what if the Shore exists in the fancies of us swimmers merely, who dream it to account for the dreadful fact that we swim, have always and only swum, and continue swimming without respite (myself excepted) until we die? Supposing even that there *were* a Shore—that, as a cynical companion of mine once imagined, we rise from the drowned to discover all those vulgar superstitions and exalted metaphors to be literal truth: the giant Maker of us all, the Shores of Light beyond our night-sea journey!—whatever would a swimmer do there? The fact is, when we imagine the Shore, what comes to mind is just the opposite of our condition: no more night, no more sea, no more journeying. In short, the blissful estate of the drowned.

" 'Ours not to stop and think; ours but to swim and sink. . . .' Because a moment's thought reveals the pointlessness of swimming. 'No matter,' I've heard some say, even as they gulped their last: 'The night-sea journey may be absurd, but here we swim, will-we nill-we, against the flood, onward and upward, toward a Shore that may not exist and couldn't be reached if it did.' The thoughtful swimmer's choices, then, they say, are two: give over thrashing and go under for good, or embrace the absurdity; affirm in and for itself the night-sea journey; swim on with neither motive nor destination, for the sake of swimming, and compassionate moreover with your fellow swimmer, we being all at sea and equally in the dark. I find neither course acceptable. If not even the hypothetical Shore can justify a sea-full of drownèd comrades, to speak of the swim-in-itself as somehow doing so strikes me as obscene. I continue to swim—but only because blind habit, blind instinct, blind fear of drowning are still more strong than the horror of our journey. And if on occasion I have assisted a fellow-thrasher, joined in the cheers and songs, even passed along to others strokes of genius from the drownèd great, it's that I shrink by temperament from making myself conspicuous. To paddle off in one's own direction, assert one's independent right-of-way, overrun one's fellows without compunction, or dedicate oneself entirely to pleasures and diversions without regard for conscience—I can't finally condemn those who journey in this wise; in half my moods I envy them and despise the weak vitality that keeps me from following their example. But in reasonabler moments I remind myself that it's their very freedom and self-responsibility I reject, as more dramatically absurd, in our senseless circumstances, than tailing along in conventional fashion. Suicides, rebels, affirmers of the paradox—nay-sayers and yea-sayers alike to our fatal journey—I finally shake my head at them. And splash sighing past their corpses, one by one, as past a hundred sorts of others: friends, enemies, brothers; fools, sages, brutes —and nobodies, million upon million. I envy them all.

"A poor irony: that I, who find abhorrent and tautological the doctrine of survival of the fittest (*fitness* meaning, in my experience, nothing more than survival-ability, a talent whose only demonstration is the fact of survival, but whose chief ingredients seem to be strength, guile, callousness), may be the sole remaining swimmer! But the doctrine is false as well as repellent: Chance drowns the worthy with the unworthy, bears up the unfit with the fit by whatever definition, and makes the night-sea journey essentially *haphazard* as well as murderous and unjustified.

" 'You only swim once.' Why bother, then?

" 'Except ye drown, ye shall not reach the Shore of Light.' Poppycock.

"One of my late companions—that same cynic with the curious fancy, among the first to drown—entertained us with odd conjectures while we waited to begin our journey. A favorite theory of his was that the Father does exist, and did indeed make us and the sea we swim—but not a-purpose or even consciously; He made us, as it were, despite Himself, as we make waves with every tail-thrash, and may be unaware of our existence. Another was that He knows we're here but doesn't care what happens to us, inasmuch as He creates (voluntarily or not) other seas and swimmers at more or less regular intervals. In bitterer moments, such as just before he drowned, my friend even supposed that our Maker wished us unmade; there was indeed a Shore, he'd argue, which could save at least some of us. from drowning and toward which it was our function to struggle—but for reasons unknowable to us He wanted desperately to prevent our reaching that happy place and fulfilling our destiny. Our 'Father,' in short, was our adversary and would-be killer! No less outrageous, and offensive to traditional opinion, were the fellow's speculations on the nature of our Maker: that He might well be no swimmer Himself at all, but some sort of monstrosity, perhaps even tailless; that He might be stupid, malicious, insensible, perverse, or asleep and dreaming; that the end for which He created and launched us forth, and which we flagellate ourselves to fathom, was perhaps immoral, even obscene. Et cetera, et cetera: there was no end to the chap's conjectures, or the impoliteness of his fancy; I have reason to suspect that his early demise, whether planned by 'our Maker' or not, was expedited by certain fellow-swimmers indignant at his blasphemies.

"In other moods, however (he was as given to moods as I), his theorizing would become half-serious, so it seemed to me, especially upon the subjects of Fate and Immortality, to which our youthful conversations often turned. Then his harangues, if no less fantastical, grew solemn and obscure, and if he was still baiting us, his passion undid the joke. His objection to popular opinions of the hereafter, he would declare, was their claim to general validity. Why need believers hold that *all* the drownèd rise to be judged at journey's end, and non-believers that drowning is final without exception? In *his* opinion (so he'd vow at least), nearly everyone's fate was permanent death; indeed he took a sour pleasure in supposing that every 'Maker' made thousands of separate seas in His creative lifetime, each populated like ours with millions of swimmers, and that in almost every instance both sea and swimmers were utterly annihilated, whether accidentally or by malevolent design. (Nothing if not pluralistical, he imagined there might be millions and billions of 'Fathers,' perhaps in some 'night-sea' of their own!) However—and here he turned infidels against him with the faithful—he professed to believe that in possibly a single night-sea per thousand, say, one of its quarter-billion swimmers (that is, one swimmer in two hundred fifty billions) achieved a qualified immortality. In some cases the rate might be slightly higher; in others it was vastly lower, for just as there are swimmers of every degree of proficiency, including some who drown before the journey starts, unable to swim at all, and others created drowned, as it were, so he imagined what can only be termed impotent Creators, Makers unable to Make, as well as uncommonly fertile ones and all grades between. And it pleased him to deny any necessary relation between a Maker's productivity and His other virtues—including, even, the quality of His creatures.

"I could go on (*he* surely did) with his elaboration of these mad notions—such as that swimmers in other night-seas needn't be of our kind; that Makers themselves might belong to different *species*, so to speak; that our particular Maker mightn't Himself be immortal, or that we might be not only His emissaries but His 'immortality,' continuing His life and our own, transmogrified, beyond our individual deaths. Even this modified immortality (meaningless to me) he conceived as relative and contingent, subject to accident or deliberate termination: his pet hypothesis was that Makers and swimmers *each generate the other*—against all odds, their number being so great—and that any given 'immortality-chain' could terminate after any number of cycles, so that what was 'immortal' (still speaking relatively) was only the cyclic process of incarnation, which itself might have a beginning and an end. Alternatively he liked to imagine cycles within cycles, either finite or infinite: for example, the 'night-sea,' as it were, in which Makers 'swam' and created night-seas and swimmers like ourselves, might be the creation of a larger Maker, Himself one of many, Who in turn et cetera. Time itself he regarded as relative to our experience, like magnitude: who knew but what, with each thrash of our tails, minuscule seas and swimmers, whole eternities, came to pass—as ours, perhaps, and our Maker's Maker's, was elapsing between the strokes of some supertail, in a slower order of time?

Naturally I hooted with the others at this nonsense. We were young then, and had only the dimmest notion of what lay ahead; in our ignorance we imagined night-sea journeying to be a positively heroic enterprise. Its meaning and value we never questioned; to be sure, some must go down by the way, a pity no doubt, but to win a race requires that others lose, and like all my fellows I took for granted that I would be the winner. We milled and swarmed, impatient to be off, never mind where or why, only to try our youth against the realities of night and sea; if we indulged the skeptic at all, it was as a droll, half-contemptible mascot. When he died in the initial slaughter, no one cared.

"And even now I don't subscribe to all his views—but I no longer scoff. The horror of our history has purged me of opinions, as of vanity, confidence, spirit, charity, hope, vitality, everything—except dull dread and a kind of melancholy, stunned persistence. What leads me to recall his fancies is my growing suspicion that I, of all swimmers, may be the sole survivor of this fell journey, talebearer of a generation. This suspicion, together with the recent seachange, suggests to me now that nothing is impossible, not even my late companion's wildest visions, and brings me to a certain desperate resolve, the point of my chronicling.

"Very likely I have lost my senses. The carnage at our setting out; our decimation by whirlpool, poisoned cataract, sea-convulsion; the panic stampedes, mutinies, slaughters, mass suicides; the mounting evidence that none will survive the journey—add to these anguish and fatigue; it were a miracle if sanity stayed afloat. Thus I admit, with the other possibilities, that the present sweetening and calming of the sea, and what seems to be a kind of vasty presence, song, or summons from the near upstream, may be hallucinations of disordered sensibility. . . .

"Perhaps, even, I am drowned already. Surely I was never meant for the rough-and-tumble of the swim; not impossibly I perished at the outset and have only imagined the night-sea journey from some final deep. In any case, I'm no longer young, and it is we spent old swimmers, disabused of every illusion, who are most vulnerable to dreams.

"Sometimes I think I am my drownèd friend.

"Out with it: I've begun to believe, not only that *She* exists, but that She lies not far ahead, and stills the sea, and draws me Herward! Aghast, I recollect his maddest notion: that our destination (which existed, mind, in but one night-sea out of hundreds and thousands) was no Shore, as commonly conceived, but a mysterious being, indescribable except by paradox and vaguest figure: wholly different from us swimmers, yet our complement; the death of us, yet our salvation and resurrection; simultaneously our journey's end, mid-point, and commencement; not membered and thrashing like us, but a motionless or hugely gliding sphere of unimaginable dimension; self-contained, yet dependent absolutely, in some wise, upon the chance (always monstrously improbable) that one of us will survive the night-sea journey and reach . . . Her! *Her,* he called it, or *She,* which is to say, Other-than-a-he. I shake my head; the thing is too preposterous; it is myself I talk to, to keep my reason in this awful darkness. There is no She! There is no You! I rave to myself; it's Death alone that hears and summons. To the drowned, all seas are calm. . . .

"Listen: my friend maintained that in every order of creation there are two sorts of creators, contrary yet complementary, one of which gives rise to seas and swimmers, the other to the Night-which-contains-the-sea and to What-waits-at-the-journey's-end: the former, in short, to destiny, the latter to destination (and both profligately, involuntarily, perhaps indifferently or unwittingly). The 'purpose' of the night-sea journey—but not necessarily of the journeyer or of either Maker!—my friend could describe only in abstractions: *consummation, transfiguration, union of contraries, transcension of categories.* When we laughed, he would shrug and admit that he understood the business no better than we, and thought it ridiculous, dreary, possibly obscene. 'But one of you,' he'd add with his wry smile, 'may be the Hero destined to complete the night-sea journey and be one with Her. Chances are, of course, you won't make it.' He himself, he declared, was not even going to try; the whole idea repelled him; if we chose to dismiss it as an ugly fiction, so much the better for us; thrash, splash, and be merry, we were soon enough drowned. But there it was, he could not say how he knew or why he bothered to tell us, any more than he could say what would happen after She and Hero, Shore and Swimmer, 'merged identities' to become something both and neither. He quite agreed with me that if the issue of that magical union had no memory of the night-sea journey, for example, it enjoyed a poor sort of immortality; even poorer if, as he rather imagined, a swimmer-hero plus a She equaled or became merely another Maker of future night-seas and the rest, at such incredible expense of life. This being the case—he was persuaded it was—the merciful thing to do was refuse to participate; the genuine heroes, in his opinion, were the suicides, and the hero of heroes would be the swimmer who, in the very presence of the Other, refused Her proffered 'immortality' and thus put an end to at least one cycle of catastrophes.

"How we mocked him! Our moment came, we hurtled forth, pretending to glory in the adventure, thrashing, singing, cursing, strangling, rationalizing, rescuing, killing, inventing rules and stories and relationships, giving up, struggling on, but dying all, and still in darkness, until only a battered remnant was left to croak 'Onward, upward,' like a bitter echo. Then they too fell silent—victims, I can only presume, of the last frightful wave—and the moment came when I also, utterly desolate and spent, thrashed my last and gave myself over to the current, to sink or float as might be, but swim no more. Whereupon, marvelous to tell, in an instant the sea grew still! Then warmly, gently, the great tide turned, began to bear me, as it does now, onward and upward will-I nill-I, like a flood of joy—and I recalled with dismay my dead friend's teaching.

"I am not deceived. This new emotion is Her doing; the desire that possesses me is Her bewitchment. Lucidity passes from me; in a moment I'll cry 'Love!' bury myself in Her side, and be 'transfigured.' Which is to say, I die already; this fellow transported by passion is not I; *I am he who abjures and rejects the night-sea journey!* I. . . .

"I am all love. 'Come!' She whispers, and I have no will.

"You who I may be about to become, whatever You are: with the last twitch of my real self I beg You to listen. It is *not* love that sustains me! No; though Her magic makes me burn to sing the contrary, and though I drown even now for the blasphemy, I will say truth. What has fetched me across this dreadful sea is a single hope, gift of my poor dead comrade: that You may be stronger-willed than I, and that by sheer force of concentration I may transmit to You, along with Your official Heritage, a private legacy of awful recollection and negative resolve. Mad as it may be, my dream is that some unimaginable embodiment of myself (or myself plus Her if that's how it must be) will come to find itself expressing, in however garbled or radical a translation, some reflection of these reflections. If against all odds this comes to pass, may You to whom, through whom I speak, do what I cannot: terminate this aimless, brutal business! Stop Your hearing against Her song! Hate love!

"Still alive, afloat, afire. Farewell then my penultimate hope: that one may be sunk for direst blasphemy on the very shore of the Shore. Can it be (my old friend would smile) that only utterest nay-sayers survive the night? But even that were Sense, and there is no sense, only senseless love, senseless death. Whoever echoes these reflections: be more courageous than their author! An end to night-sea journeys! Make no more! And forswear me when I shall forswear myself, deny myself, plunge into Her who summons, singing . . .

" 'Love! Love! Love!' "

THREE
DREAM FICTION

Dream Fiction

The term *dream fiction* is used in this book to describe a
particular stance of writing. It should not be applied to a story
merely because the plot seems "dreamlike" or because the
characters have dreams. *Dream fiction* refers specifically to those
stories which radically depart from the patterns and expectations
of actual life and do so in ways which cannot be accounted for
by a single premise.

Usually there is a clear distinction between this type of story
and those which are developed from a premise. But occasionally
a work may appear to bridge the two types, borrowing from
each. The two stories which open this section have been selected
because they do just this. They provide insights into how the
stances differ—and why they are usually used separately.

The first, "A Fable," by Robert Fox, is an introduction to
dream fiction in much the same way that Brautigan's "The Cleveland Wrecking Yard" introduced the method—if not all the
possibilities—of premise fiction. At first reading it might appear
that all "A Fable" does is to compress the great American courtship ritual so that in a matter of minutes one passes through all
its stages: flirtation, parental warnings, proposal, parental advice,
declaration of love, and marriage. Described in this way, the

story seems to be based on a premise—something like: "If time were speeded up, then. . . ."

But look at the characters and their actions closely. More is happening here than a mere change in pace: the things the characters do have a dreamlike distortion which cannot be explained by a single premise.

The young man has taken a job, but he doesn't have the slightest idea what kind of job it is (any more than he later knows what his marriage will be like); he not only moves through the courtship rapidly, but he wins the audible applause of the other passengers (a metaphorical echo of the approval of society); and when all is done, it is the conductor who marries them. These details are not developed from a single premise. Fox has repeatedly departed from the facts of actual life—even though through this technique he has made some precise comments about actual society.

The second selection, "Pig and Pepper," is taken from Lewis Carroll's *Alice's Adventures in Wonderland*. Considered as a story, the piece is a pure sample of dream fiction: a crying infant turns into a pig; a cat appears from nowhere, speaks, disappears, reappears, and then fades away again. This is not only dream fiction, it is dreamlike as well.

It is true that Carroll concludes his book—as he does its companion volume, *Through the Looking Glass*—with a chapter which has Alice awake from a dream. The conclusion seems to convert the entire piece into mimetic fiction: nothing unusual has happened at all. But the "explanatory" final chapters are so inconspicuous that they do not change the way we read the book as a whole. This is in sharp contrast to Langston Hughes' "On the Road," in which having the meeting with Christ turn into a dream fundamentally changes the way we interpret the story.

One ingenious—and modern—argument has been proposed for placing Lewis Carroll's story in the mimetic category, based on the fact that in the preceding chapter Alice has eaten from a giant mushroom (on the advice of a caterpillar who is himself suspiciously smoking from a Turkish water pipe). But before one writes Alice off as a Victorian dope freak, it is worth noting that strange things were happening to her long before she took up mushrooms.

Like premise stories, dream fiction sometimes concerns itself with society and sometimes with the individual. Michael Brownstein's "The Plot to Save the World" probably has the most purely social or cultural theme—and in this respect it is the closest to science fiction. Brownstein is concerned with the strange energy generated by certain people, and how that energy can become, eventually, destructive. In one sense the story is a metaphor for charismatic leaders and their followers. The fact that the hero is a superwoman raises questions about women's liberation—yet another social issue.

Yuri Olesha's "Love," on the other hand, is about love, and it is interesting to compare this dream story with Barthelme's premise story, "The Balloon." Each has the same light, almost whimsical tone, but Olesha has abandoned the concept of a single premise; his story is a constantly changing fantasy.

Hilde Abel's "The Bus That Had No Sign," the longest story in this collection, is both a private nightmare and a bitter denunciation of a whole society. The protagonist, a citizen of Nazi Germany, is riding on a bus which has no announced destination. Like many of Kafka's characters, he "knew he must have committed some unspeakable crime—but he could not remember what." He tries to assure himself that he "had always seen no evil, heard no evil, and spoken no evil." This is the nightmare of guilt.

But the story is also an allegory for Germany under Hitler and for any nation which has gone amuck—like a bus driven blindly through a burning city, heading toward its own destruction. Its passengers are like the citizens of such a nation: they are victims and yet also the agents of the horror and the final disaster.

Reading dream fiction is a different kind of experience from reading either premise or mimetic work. The reader often has to rely more heavily on intuitive response. It is usually a mistake to search for "the key" or "the answer" as if the piece were a riddle. Some stories may take the form of somewhat imprecise allegories (like "The Plot to Save the World"), but most are more impressionistic than that.

For some readers dream fiction is rather like poetry. In place of narrative sequences which resemble our waking life, we deal with images which may be allegorical (as in "The Bus That Had No Sign") or metaphorical (as in "A Fable"), or perhaps only vaguely suggestive (as in "A Country Doctor" or "We Have Nothing to Fear"). Others prefer a less literary parallel: for them, reading dream fiction is like entering into insanity for a short period in the hope of gaining from the trip some fresh insight into the sane world.

Some readers, like Alice, may have reservations:

"But I don't want to go among mad people," Alice remarked.
"Oh, you can't help that," said the Cat: "we're all mad here. I'm
mad. You're mad."
"How do you know I'm mad?" said Alice.
"You must be," said the Cat, "or you wouldn't have come here."

Regardless of how one feels about that bit of feline logic,
dream fiction offers the writer a distinct alternative. It has never
been dominant, but it is as old as the *Book of Revelation* in the
Bible, and as contemporary as Joseph Heller's *Catch–22*.

Yossarian looked at him soberly and tried another approach. "Is
Orr crazy?"
"He sure is," Doc Daneeka said.
"Can you ground him?"
"I sure can. But first he has to ask me to. That's part of the rule."
"Then why doesn't he ask you to?"
"Because he's crazy," Doc Daneeka said. "He has to be crazy to
keep flying combat missions after all the close calls he's had. Sure, I
can ground Orr. But first he has to ask me to."
"That's all he has to do to be grounded?"
"That's all. Let him ask me."
"And then you can ground him?" Yossarian asked.
"No. Then I can't ground him."
"You mean there's a catch?"
"Sure there's a catch," Doc Daneeka replied. "Catch–22. Anyone who
wants to get out of combat duty isn't really crazy."

With the same logic, anyone who detects the sense of madness
in some of these stories isn't really crazy.

A FABLE

robert fox

The young man was clean shaven and neatly dressed. It was early Monday morning and he got on the subway. It was the first day of his first job and he was slightly nervous; he didn't know exactly what his job would be. Otherwise he felt fine. He loved everybody he saw. He loved everybody on the street and everybody disappearing into the subway and he loved the world because it was a fine clear day and he was starting his first job.

Without kicking anybody, the young man was able to find a seat on the Manhattan bound train. The car filled quickly and he looked up at the people standing over him envying his seat. Among them were a mother and daughter who were going shopping. The daughter was a beautiful girl with blonde hair and soft looking skin, and he was immediately attracted to her.

"He's staring at you," the mother whispered to the daughter.

"Yes, mother, I feel so uncomfortable. What shall I *do*?"

"He's in love with you."

"In love with me? How can you tell?"

"Because I'm your mother."

"But what shall I do?"

"Nothing. He'll try to talk to you. If he does, answer him. Be nice to him. He's only a boy."

229

The train reached the business district and many people got off. The girl and her mother found seats opposite the young man. He continued to look at the girl who occasionally looked to see if he was looking at her.

The young man found a good pretext for standing in giving his seat to an elderly man. He stood over the girl and her mother. They whispered back and forth and looked up at him. At another stop, the seat next to the girl was vacated and the young man blushed, but quickly took it.

"I knew it," the mother said between her teeth. "I knew it, I *knew* it."

The young man cleared his throat and tapped the girl. She jumped.

"Pardon me," he said. "You're a very pretty girl."

"Thank you," she said.

"Don't talk to him," her mother said. "Don't answer him; I'm warning you. Believe me."

"I'm in love with you," he said to the girl.

"I don't believe you," the girl said.

"Don't answer him," the mother said.

"I really do," he said. "In fact, I'm so much in love with you that I want to marry you."

"Do you have a job?" she said.

"Yes, today is my first day. I'm going to Manhattan to start my first day of work."

"What kind of work will you do?" she asked.

"I don't know exactly," he said. "You see, I didn't start yet."

"It sounds exciting," she said.

"It's my first job but I'll have my own desk and handle a lot of papers and carry them around in a briefcase, and it will pay well, and I'll work my way up."

"I love you," she said.

"Will you marry me?"

"I don't know. You'll have to ask my mother."

The young man rose from his seat and stood before the girl's mother. He cleared his throat very carefully for a long time. "May I have the honor of having your daughter's hand in marriage?" he said, but he was drowned out by the subway noise.

The mother looked up at him and said, "What?" He couldn't hear her either, but he could tell by the movement of her lips, and by the way her face wrinkled up that she said, what.

The train pulled to a stop.

"May I have the honor of having your daughter's hand in marriage!" he shouted, not realizing there was no subway noise. Everybody on the train looked at him, smiled, and then they all applauded.

"Are you crazy?" the mother asked.

The train started again.

"What?" he said.

"Why do you want to marry her?" she asked.

"Well, she's pretty—I mean, I'm in love with her."

"Is that all?"

"I guess so," he said. "Is there supposed to be more?"

"No. Not usually," the mother said. "Are you working?"

"Yes. As a matter of fact, that's why I'm going into Manhattan so early. Today is the first day of my first job."

"Congratulations," the mother said.

"Thanks," he said. "Can I marry your daughter?"

"Do you have a car?" she asked.

"Not yet," he said. "But I should be able to get one pretty soon. And a house, too."

"A house?"

"With lots of rooms."

"Yes, that's what I expected you to say," she said. She turned to her daughter. "Do you love him?"

"Yes, mother, I do."

"Why?"

"Because he's good, and gentle, and kind."

"Are you sure?"

"Yes."

"Then you really love him."

"Yes."

"Are you sure there isn't anyone else that you might love and might want to marry?"

"No, mother," the girl said.

"Well, then," the mother said to the young man. "Looks like there's nothing I can do about it. Ask her again."

The train stopped.

"My dearest one," he said. "Will you marry me?"

"Yes," she said.

Everybody in the car smiled and applauded.

"Isn't life wonderful?" the boy asked the mother.

"Beautiful," the mother said.

The conductor climbed down from between the cars as the train started up, and straightening his dark tie, approached them with a solemn black book in his hand.

PIG AND PEPPER
lewis carroll

For a minute or two she stood looking at the house, and wondering what to do next, when suddenly a footman in livery came running out of the wood—(she considered him to be a footman because he was in livery: otherwise, judging by his face only, she would have called him a fish)—and rapped loudly at the door with his knuckles. It was opened by another footman in livery, with a round face, and large eyes like a frog; and both footmen, Alice noticed, had powdered hair that curled all over their heads. She felt very curious to know what it was all about, and crept a little way out of the wood to listen.

The Fish-Footman began by producing from under his arm a great letter, nearly as large as himself, and this he handed over to the other, saying, in a solemn tone, "For the Duchess. An invitation from the Queen to play croquet." The Frog-Footman repeated, in the same solemn tone, only changing the order of the words a little, "From the Queen. An invitation for the Duchess to play croquet."

Then they both bowed low, and their curls got entangled together.

Alice laughed so much at this, that she had to run back into the wood for fear of their hearing her; and, when she next peeped out, the Fish-Footman was gone, and the other was sitting on the ground near the door, staring stupidly up into the sky.

Alice went timidly up to the door, and knocked.

"There's no sort of use in knocking," said the Footman, "and that for two reasons. First, because I'm on the same side of the door as you are: secondly, because they're making such a noise inside, no one could possibly hear you." And certainly there *was* a most extraordinary noise going on within—a constant howling and sneezing, and every now and then a great crash, as if a dish or kettle had been broken to pieces.

"Please, then," said Alice, "how am I to get in?"

"There might be some sense in your knocking," the Footman went on, without attending to her, "if we had the door between us. For instance, if you were *inside*, you might knock, and I could let you out, you know." He was looking up into the sky all the time he was speaking, and this Alice thought decidedly uncivil. "But perhaps he ca'n't help it," she said to herself; "his eyes are so *very* nearly at the top of his head. But at any rate he might answer questions.—How am I to get in?" she repeated, aloud.

"I shall sit here," the Footman remarked, "till tomorrow——"

At this moment the door of the house opened, and a large plate came skimming out, straight at the Footman's head: it just grazed his nose, and broke to pieces against one of the trees behind him.

"——or next day, maybe," the Footman continued in the same tone, exactly as if nothing had happened.

"How am I to get in?" asked Alice again, in a louder tone.

"*Are* you to get in at all?" said the Footman. "That's the first question, you know."

It was, no doubt: only Alice did not like to be told so.

"It's really dreadful," she muttered to herself, "the way all the creatures argue. It's enough to drive one crazy!"

The Footman seemed to think this a good opportunity for repeating his remark, with variations. "I shall sit here," he said, "on and off, for days and days."

"But what am *I* to do?" said Alice.

"Anything you like," said the Footman, and began whistling.

"Oh, there's no use in talking to him," said Alice desperately: "he's perfectly idiotic!" And she opened the door and went in.

The door led right into a large kitchen, which was full of smoke from one end to the other: the Duchess was sitting on a three-legged stool in the middle, nursing a baby: the cook was leaning over the fire, stirring a large cauldron which seemed to be full of soup.

"There's certainly too much pepper in that soup!" Alice said to herself, as well as she could for sneezing.

There was certainly too much of it in the *air*. Even the Duchess sneezed occasionally; and as for the baby, it was sneezing and howling alternately without a moment's pause. The only two creatures in the kitchen, that did *not* sneeze, were the cook, and a large cat, which was lying on the hearth and grinning from ear to ear.

"Please would you tell me," said Alice, a little timidly, for she was not quite sure whether it was good manners for her to speak first, "why your cat grins like that?"

"It's a Cheshire-Cat," said the Duchess, "and that's why. Pig!"

She said the last word with such sudden violence that Alice quite jumped; but she saw in another moment that it was addressed to the baby, and not to her, so she took courage, and went on again:—

"I didn't know that Cheshire-Cats always grinned; in fact, I didn't know that cats *could* grin."

"They all can," said the Duchess; "and most of 'em do."

"I don't know of any that do," Alice said very politely, feeling quite pleased to have got into a conversation.

"You don't know much," said the Duchess; "and that's a fact."

Alice did not at all like the tone of this remark, and thought it would be as well to introduce some other subject of conversation. While she was trying to fix on one, the cook took the cauldron of soup off the fire, and at once set to work throwing everything within her reach at the Duchess and the baby—the fire-irons came first; then followed a shower of sauce-pans, plates, and dishes. The Duchess took no notice of them even when they hit her; and the baby was howling so much already, that it was quite impossible to say whether the blows hurt it or not.

"Oh, *please* mind what you're doing!" cried Alice, jumping up and down in an agony of terror. "Oh, there goes his *precious* nose!" as an unusually large sauce-pan flew close by it, and very nearly carried it off.

"If everybody minded their own business," the Duchess said, in a hoarse growl, "the world would go round a deal faster than it does."

"Which would *not* be an advantage," said Alice, who felt very glad to get an opportunity of showing off a little of her knowledge.

"Just think what work it would make with the day and night! You see the earth takes twenty-four hours to turn round on its axis——"

"Talking of axes," said the Duchess, "chop off her head!"

Alice glanced rather anxiously at the cook, to see if she meant to take the hint; but the cook was busily stirring the soup, and seemed not to be listening, so she went on again: "Twenty-four hours, I *think*; or is it twelve? I——"

"Oh, don't bother *me!*" said the Duchess; "I never could abide figures!" And with that she began nursing her child again, singing a sort of lullaby to it as she did so, and giving it a violent shake at the end of every line:——

"Speak roughly to your little boy,
And beat him when he sneezes:
He only does it to annoy,
Because he knows it teases."

CHORUS

(in which the cook and the baby joined).——

"Wow! wow! wow!"

While the Duchess sang the second verse of the song, she kept tossing the baby violently up and down, and the poor little thing howled so, that Alice could hardly hear the words:——

"I speak severely to my boy,
I beat him when he sneezes;
For he can thoroughly enjoy
The pepper when he pleases."

CHORUS

"Wow! wow! wow!"

"Here! You may nurse it a bit, if you like!" the Duchess said to Alice, flinging the baby at her as she spoke. "I must go and get ready to play croquet with the Queen," and she hurried out of the room. The cook threw a frying-pan after her as she went, but it just missed her.

Alice caught the baby with some difficulty, as it was a queer-shaped little creature, and held out its arms and legs in all directions, "just like a star-fish," thought Alice. The poor little thing was snorting like a steam-engine when she caught it, and kept doubling itself up and straightening itself out again, so that altogether, for the first minute or two, it was as much as she could do to hold it.

As soon as she had made out the proper way of nursing it (which was to twist it up into a sort of knot, and then keep tight hold of its right ear and left foot, so as to prevent its undoing itself), she carried it out into the open air. "If I don't take this child away with me," thought Alice, "they're sure to kill it in a day or two. Wouldn't it be murder to leave it behind?" She said the last words out loud, and the little thing grunted in reply (it had left off sneezing by this time). "Don't grunt," said Alice; "that's not at all a proper way of expressing yourself."

The baby grunted again, and Alice looked very anxiously into its face to see what was the matter with it. There could be no doubt that it had a *very* turn-up nose, much more like a snout than a real nose: also its eyes were getting extremely small for a baby: altogether Alice did not like the look of the thing at all. "But perhaps it was only sobbing," she thought, and looked into its eyes again, to see if there were any tears.

No, there were no tears. "If you're going to turn into a pig, my dear," said Alice, seriously, "I'll have nothing more to do with you. Mind now!" The poor little thing sobbed again (or grunted, it was impossible to say which), and they went on for some while in silence.

Alice was just beginning to think to herself, "Now, what am I to do with this creature, when I get it home?" when it grunted again, so violently, that she looked down into its face in some alarm. This time there could be *no* mistake about it: it was neither more nor less than a pig, and she felt that it would be quite absurd for her to carry it any further.

So she set the little creature down, and felt quite relieved to see it trot away quietly into the wood. "If it had grown up," she said to herself, "it would have made a dreadfully ugly child: but it makes rather a handsome pig, I think." And she began thinking over other children she knew, who might do very well as pigs, and was just saying to herself "if one only knew the right way to change them——" when she was a little startled by seeing the Cheshire-Cat sitting on a bough of a tree a few yards off.

The Cat only grinned when it saw Alice. It looked good-natured, she thought: still it had *very* long claws and a great many teeth, so she felt that it ought to be treated with respect.

"Cheshire-Puss," she began, rather timidly, as she did not at all know whether it would like the name: however, it only grinned a little wider. "Come, it's pleased so far," thought Alice, and she went on. "Would you tell me, please, which way I ought to go from here?"

"That depends a good deal on where you want to get to," said the Cat.

"I don't much care where——" said Alice.

"Then it doesn't matter which way you go," said the Cat.

"——so long as I get *somewhere*," Alice added as an explanation.

"Oh, you're sure to do that," said the Cat, "if you only walk long enough."

Alice felt that this could not be denied, so she tried another question. "What sort of people live about here?"

"In *that* direction," the Cat said, waving its right paw round, "lives a Hatter: and in *that* direction," waving the other paw, "lives a March Hare. Visit either you like: they're both mad."

"But I don't want to go among mad people," Alice remarked.

"Oh, you ca'n't help that," said the Cat: "we're all mad here. I'm mad. You're mad."

"How do you know I'm mad?" said Alice.

"You must be," said the Cat, "or you wouldn't have come here."

Alice didn't think that proved it at all: however, she went on: "And how do you know that you're mad?"

"To begin with," said the Cat, "a dog's not mad. You grant that?"

"I suppose so," said Alice.

"Well, then," the Cat went on, "you see a dog growls when it's angry, and wags its tail when it's pleased. Now *I* growl when I'm pleased, and wag my tail when I'm angry. Therefore I'm mad."

"*I* call it purring, not growling," said Alice.

"Call it what you like," said the Cat. "Do you play croquet with the Queen to-day?"

"I should like it very much," said Alice, "but I haven't been invited yet."

"You'll see me there," said the Cat, and vanished.

Alice was not much surprised at this, she was getting so well used to queer things happening. While she was still looking at the place where it had been, it suddenly appeared again.

"By-the-bye, what became of the baby?" said the Cat. "I'd nearly forgotten to ask."

"It turned into a pig," Alice answered very quietly, just as if the Cat had come back in a natural way.

"I thought it would," said the Cat, and vanished again.

Alice waited a little, half expecting to see it again, but it did not appear, and after a minute or two she walked on in the direction in which the March Hare was said to live. "I've seen hatters before," she said to herself, "the March Hare will be much the most interesting, and perhaps, as this is May, it wo'n't be raving mad— at least not so mad as it was in March." As she said this, she looked up, and there was the Cat again, sitting on a branch of a tree.

"Did you say 'pig,' or 'fig'?" said the Cat.

"I said 'pig'," replied Alice; "and I wish you wouldn't keep appearing and vanishing so suddenly: you make one quite giddy!"

"All right," said the Cat; and this time it vanished quite slowly, beginning with the end of the tail, and ending with the grin, which remained some time after the rest of it had gone.

"Well! I've often seen a cat without a grin," thought Alice; "but a grin without a cat! It's the most curious thing I ever saw in all my life!"

THE PLOT TO SAVE THE WORLD
michael brownstein

Not too long ago in the hills of our fatherland, on hill 311 to be
exact, there lived a young girl divided into three parts: one part
rock candy, one part fervent hope, and one part creative seclusion.

This girl spent the final years of her childhood perfecting a fool-
proof and at the same time fair system for the national lottery.
She also developed a cheaper way to stamp coins and was the first
person to reject microfilm storage of information using laser beams
in favor of simple reliance upon memory banks honed to maximum
flow in and minimum flow out. Through discoveries in the field of
biochemistry so brilliant as to seem obvious she translated the
metaphor of human-life-as-movie into actual biological fact, thereby opening the way to organ and gland transplant by means of the
relatively simple and easily learned techniques of film editing. Acting on a hunch, she was able in one short day to revolutionize the
scope of human sexual and creative energy through an elementary
"sidetrack" process, whereby the *time* any particular act consumed,
if thought of in terms of *space*, was reduced drastically, since most
of these acts involved very little movement—such as sitting down,
lying down, spreading out, and so on.

Although certainly not the first girl to visit France, she was perhaps the first to put into workable algebraic function the girlish realization that France "really is unique," that although this uniqueness was on the wane it could be preserved once changed into an immutable mathematical formula—and that what held true for France would also hold true for any nation or cultural bloc. So that, finally, each national identity could disappear in one sense (something which, she realized, was inevitable anyway) only to pop up again in another more permanent one, in a form obviously requiring no politicians, human blood sacrifice, or waste of time . . .

She astonished the world by her observations on trees as regulators of electricity, as possible media for electrical communications, and on the world-wide disasters which the clearing off of forests to make paper is likely to occasion. . . . Her solitary walks in the Black Forest and the Blue Ridge Mountains opened to her new and original views on the harmonies of creation.

During the one or two hours before her bedtime set aside for leisure she painted, composed and played electronic music, and revolutionized the field of night photography. . . . And two nights before her eleventh birthday she finally trapped and killed what had been her most elusive *bête noire*, namely sleep: not to avoid it, of course, but how could it be activated, how could sleep in its own way be made to stand up and contribute? Discarding the possibility of somehow "using" her body while it slept, she realized with sudden intuition as she woke up shouting that night from what had been only the third nightmare of her life that, through firm and patient training, two very striking things could be accomplished. One, the virtual elimination of subsidiary dream figures, and also non-human dream figures except for those coming under the heading of "landscape" or general atmosphere. Two, the selection and training of *principal* dream figures to the point where, as highly accomplished laboratory assistants, research scholars, typists, lathe operators, etc., they could be given increasingly complex problems and tasks related to those the girl herself was working on. . . . So that after only a few months' time she was able to wake up every morning several days ahead of herself, with solutions to problems she had only just formulated the night before.

She was in addition an excessively good-looking and of course widely read young lady, and, anticipating before she was twelve the loss of time and sour moods resulting from body repression, she initiated a fine relationship with a boy from one of the nearby hills, a publisher's son. Usually, when leaving to go home after sharing her love, he would take with him the manuscript for her next technical paper or book, also relaying any pressing messages to the outside world and generally acting as her go-between and all-purpose factotum.

To gain the necessary psychological perspective on the world in which she lived, she participated in or observed one orgy, one coup d'état, one manic depression, one sunny day, one rest home, one sheep slaughter, one anonymous phone call, one transvestite, one sales-pitch, one workers' commune, one sleeping village, one alpine meadow, one computer analyst, one wind tunnel, one savage domestic squabble, one happy family, one bigot and one small favor. . . .

Since her uncle, moreover, was President of the Fatherland, she luckily avoided that stubborn resistance to fundamental change—to new ideas—which has been the proverbial stumbling block and torment of so many highly original minds throughout human history. She merely had to formulate an idea to have it thoroughly and objectively tested and, more often than not, speedily adopted. Her unbearable fame spread far and wide, very fast, while at the same time she managed to keep it from spreading to her head in the form of exaggerated self-importance. Contrary to what was expected, the rate of her discoveries and their uncontested value and profundity sharply increased rather than leveling off or dropping, so that by the time she was fourteen innovations of the first order were being explained, tested, and put into practice at the rate of three a week. . . .

A persistent high-pitched hum could be heard in the valleys and meadows surrounding hill 311. That peculiar light and heat denoting exceptional psychic activity began to dominate the landscape, radiating out from the domed roofs of her compound like the gradual unfolding of some staggering cosmic theory. Neighbors who resisted falling under her influence for a short period of time talked of leaving the area and resettling elsewhere. They complained that their children were losing interest in toys and the mindless games of childhood and were spending more and more time alone in their rooms, or off wandering the hills at all hours of the day and night, filling notebook after notebook with "pointless gibberish" and organizing spontaneous talk fests, lasting hours, from which all adults were excluded. . . . A concerned mother would force her way into one of these sessions only to be greeted by a stony silence, followed by the restless scraping of tiny chairs. Eventually the children would leave, or sometimes one of them would produce a baseball or Monopoly set and they would begin to play, quietly looking over their shoulders at the mother until she felt she was intruding on nothing, as it were, and subsequently left, swiping at the tears as they formed on her cheeks with the back of a trembling hand.

But those neighbors who on the contrary didn't feel threatened by the power emanating from the top of the hill, never felt better. The wives found that perhaps for the first time since girlhood they were happily occupied, spending their afternoons hoeing earth and improvising the complicated flower gardens that began to appear throughout the neighborhood, spilling down the slopes before their homes. . . . Some of these women got carried away to the point of converting every square inch of their lawns to a succession of enormous words spelled out by various flowers that bloomed from early spring to late autumn. Words like FASCINATION, IN-SPIRATION, and LUCK, or phrases such as LOVE ME, I AM GOD, and TOUCH MY TRIGGER began appearing everywhere, composed of tulip beds, hyacinths and roses—of carnations, zin-nias, and sunflowers—running in large suffocating clumps from the front porch to the street below. The words were programmed to change as new flowers came into bloom. LOVE ME after a period of several weeks would become LOVE MY SHORTCOMINGS TOO, although for the most part these gardens were given over to huge single words—BEAUTY, for example, was a great favorite —spelled out in different colors as the summer progressed. . . . Soon every house within a radius of two or three miles of where the young girl lived was surrounded by these obsessive, charming patterns. The wives would finish a day of strenuous labor with their bodies hardened and their spirits ready for the humble chores of dinner and the delirious chores of love.

But they also had to learn the virtue of patience, because their husbands, upon returning home from work, found themselves re-tiring to their workrooms or tool sheds as soon as dinner was over. There, surrounded by a clutter of tools and technical manuals, these middle-aged men experienced a resurgence of the blinding enthu-siasm of early youth. Before the young girl's psychic energy af-fected them they had spent their evenings staring into television screens and darkly guzzling endless cans of beer. Now they sud-denly began planning additions to the house, working on a new patio or even teaching themselves a little mechanical engineering in order to implement the unprecedented rush of "bright ideas" they had for some new labor-saving contrivance. As time went on they found themselves working in electronics, microbiology or structural design. One man, for example, invented a new and much sleeker miniature hull for ocean-going yachts, allowing yachtsmen to use the space formerly taken up by a ship's hull to carry more supplies, servants, and young orphan girls with their rucksacks and diaries, happy for a free chance to see the world. Another, a bus driver by trade, found a way to combine television, phonograph, telephone and refrigerator into a single master appliance that pointed the way to a sort of transistorized domestic unit promising a revolution in the technology of everyday life.

Others, more ambitious, brought their new-found lucidity to bear upon problems of psychology and the bewildering gamut of human emotions. They began to tackle such lumbering enigmas as —what, precisely, is the nature of ambition? what, if any, is the relationship between an individual's facial structure and his capacity for mental concentration? why do "perfectly healthy" people the world over find themselves just sitting around? etc.

Meanwhile, on hill 311, the young girl's dizzying rate of activity continued non-stop. She knew the precise extent of her own mental and physical energy and was careful to stop work as soon as it was totally depleted. Those neighbors, however, who were especially advanced in their work found themselves irresistibly drawn to her side as if in a trance, to collaborate and to learn, and she couldn't refuse them. She knew they were an extension of her own vital energy. . . .

The hum from the hill grew louder as increasing numbers of these men spent more and more time on hill 311 with the girl, skipping supper and sometimes not even returning home at night. They would appear the next day at the breakfast table, haggard and shaking from exhaustion, but determined to drink some coffee and go off to their regular jobs. Their wives, by the way, thought all this was "just marvelous," and some of them spent the long evenings making sandwiches which they would take up the hill at one or two o'clock in the morning, only to find the girl and her followers collapsed around the work tables in her cavernous laboratory. . . .

Suddenly the hum became unbearably painful to hear, as it turned into the siren-like wail of what amounted to a small town, all of whose inhabitants were expending their last shred of mental energy, at work upon a single task. This in turn spread its magnetism further and further across the countryside, until people numbering in the tens of thousands began planting gardens and working in their tool sheds, only to abandon these projects at a certain point and migrate to hill 311. The girl's last report to the outside world came just before the sound became deafening and her hill was wracked and destroyed by a catastrophic series of earth-shaking tremors. She enthusiastically announced a plan, which she said was "at this moment being successfully implemented," to mobilize the fragmented mental energy of the countless individuals wandering the globe into one mighty, disciplined outburst of scientific achievement, with which the whole world could be instantaneously and completely transformed.

LOVE
yurii olesha

Shuvalov was waiting for Lola in the park. It was noon and it was hot. A lizard appeared on a rock. Shuvalov thought: on that stone the lizard can be spotted easily. "Mimicry," he thought. The thought of mimicry brought chameleon to his mind.

"Here we go." Shuvalov said. "That's all I needed, a chameleon." The lizard scuttled away.

Angry, Shuvalov got up from the seat and walked rapidly down the path. He felt offended, like rebelling against something. He stopped and in a quite loud voice said:

"To hell with it! Why should I be thinking about mimicry and chameleons? Thoughts like that are completely useless to me."

He came out from under the trees into a clearing and sat down on a tree stump. Insects were flying about. Stalks quivered. The architecture of the flight of birds, flies, ladybugs, was transparent, but still it was possible to discern some sort of dotted outline of arches, bridges, towers, terraces which, constantly expanding and contracting, formed the skyline of a city that kept distorting itself, elastic castles-in-the-air.

"I am being subjected to outside influences," Shuvalov thought.

"The field of my attention is being polluted. I am beginning to see things that don't exist."

Lola was late. His wait in the park was a long one. He walked up and down. He was compelled to become convinced of the existence of many species of insect. A bug was crawling up a stalk. He picked it up and put it on the palm of his hand. Suddenly its belly glittered. He became angry. "To hell with it, half an hour more and I'll be a naturalist."

Stalks, leaves, the trunks of trees—there was a variety of them; he saw that some blades of grass were jointed like bamboo; he was struck by the variety of colors in what is called turf; and the different colors in the soil itself came as a complete surprise to him.

"I don't want to be a naturalist," he begged. "I have no use for these haphazard observations."

And still there was no Lola in sight. He had already drawn a few statistical conclusions and produced some sort of classification of his data. He could affirm that in the park trees with wide trunks and leaves shaped like playing-card clubs prevailed. He could recognize different insects by their buzzes. Against his will, his mind was filled with things which didn't interest him at all.

And still no Lola. He was sad and angry. Instead of Lola, an unknown citizen wearing a black felt hat appeared. The citizen sat down on the green bench next to Shuvalov. The citizen sat drooping slightly forward, one white hand on each knee. He was young and quiet. Later it turned out that the young man suffered from color blindness. They got into a conversation.

"I envy you," the young man said. "They tell me that leaves are green. I've never seen green leaves. I am forced to eat blue pears."

"Blue is inedible," Shuvalov said. "A blue pear would make me vomit."

"I eat blue pears," the color-blind man said sadly.

Shuvalov started.

"Tell me," he said, "have you ever noticed that when there are birds flying around you, you have a city of imaginary lines?"

"Never noticed," the young man answered.

"So does that mean that your senses convey a correct picture of the world to you?"

"The whole world except for certain color details."

The color-blind man turned his pale face toward Shuvalov.

"You in love?" he asked.

"In love," Shuvalov answered honestly.

"You see, in my case, there is only a certain confusion of colors, but for the rest, everything is fine."

Saying this, the young man made a condescending gesture.

"Still, blue pears are no joke," Shuvalov snorted.

Lola appeared, still far away. Shuvalov jumped up. The color-blind man got up, raised his black hat, and started to walk away.

"Aren't you a violinist?" Shuvalov shouted after him.

"You're seeing things that don't exist," the young man answered.

Shuvalov shouted aggressively: "But you look like a violinist!"

The color-blind man continued to walk away. He said something that sounded to Shuvalov like:

"You're on a dangerous path."

Lola was approaching rapidly. Shuvalov got up and took a few steps. The branches with their club-shaped leaves were swaying. Shuvalov was standing in the middle of a walk. The trees were rustling. Lola was approaching, welcomed by this ovation from the foliage. The color-blind man, who was following a path which curved to the right, thought:

"Why, it's windy!"

And he looked up at the foliage. The foliage behaved as would any other foliage disturbed by the wind. The color-blind man saw swaying blue treetops. Shuvalov saw green treetops. But then he came to an unnatural conclusion: "The trees are greeting Lola with an ovation." The color-blind man was wrong, but Shuvalov was even more wrong.

"I am seeing things that don't exist," Shuvalov repeated.

Lola came up to him. In one hand she had a bag of apricots while she held out the other to him. The world suddenly changed.

"Why are you screwing up your face?" she asked.

"It seems as if I were wearing glasses."

Lola took an apricot out of the bag, pulled apart its tiny buttocks, extracted the stone, and threw it away. The stone fell into the grass. Frightened, he looked back. He looked back and saw a tree had appeared at the spot where the stone had fallen, a slender, bright little tree, an enchanted umbrella. Then Shuvalov told Lola:

"There's some kind of nonsense going on. I'm beginning to think in images. I'm no longer bound by laws. In five years, an apricot tree may grow in that spot. Very possible. That won't go against science. But now, against all natural laws, I have just seen the tree, five years early. Nonsense. I am becoming an idealist."

"It comes from love," she said, bleeding apricot juice profusely.

She was leaning against the pillows waiting for him. The bed was wedged into a corner of the room. The coronets on the wallpaper were gold and shiny. He came up to her and she put her arms around him. She was so young and so light that, scantily dressed in a skimpy nightdress, she seemed unbelievably naked. Their first embrace was a stormy one. The little medallion she had had since girlhood flew up off her chest and got caught in her hair like a canary. Shuvalov lowered his face over hers, which was sinking into the pillow like the face of one dying. The light was on.

"I'll turn it off," Lola said.

Shuvalov lay under the wall. The corner had advanced. Shuvalov was moving his finger over the pattern on the wallpaper. He realized that that part of the pattern on the wallpaper, that section of the wall under which he was falling asleep, had a double existence—the usual one, the daytime one, ordinary coronets with nothing remarkable about them, and another existence, a night-time one which only opened itself up to him five minutes before he dived into sleep. Suddenly, a part of the pattern came close enough to touch his eyeballs, was magnified, revealed previously unseen details, changed its appearance. On the threshold of sleep, close to childhood's sensations, he did not resist the transformation of familiar and lawful forms, especially as the transformation was touching: instead of the rings and spirals he discerned a she-goat and a chef in his white cap. . . .

"And that is a violin key," Lola said, understanding him.

"And the chameleon . . ." he said, already asleep.

He woke up early in the morning. Very early. He woke up, looked around him, and let out a shout. A blissful exclamation. That night, the transformation of the world that had started the day they met had been completed. He awoke on a new earth. The brilliance of the morning filled the room. He saw the window and, on the sill, pots of multicolored flowers. Lola was sleeping with her back turned to him. She was rolled up in a ball, her back rounded and the spine showing under the skin like a slender reed. A fishing rod, Shuvalov thought, a reed. On this new earth everything was touching and funny. Voices flew in at the open window. Some people outside were talking about the flowers on the window sill.

He got up and dressed, making an effort to remain on the earth. The earth had lost its gravity. He had not yet mastered the laws of this new universe and had therefore to be careful; he was afraid to cause an explosive effect through some little carelessness. It was even risky to think, to recognize the things around him. What if, during the night, he had been given the power to materialize his thought? He had reason to suspect it. Thus, buttons buttoned themselves. Thus, when he had to wet his brush to freshen his hair, he heard the sound of falling droplets. He turned his head. On the wall, under the sun's rays, hung Lola's dresses, iridescent as soap bubbles.

"Here I am," the tap's voice informed him.

Under the multicolored dresses, he found the sink and the tap and a piece of pink soap. Now Shuvalov was afraid to think of something fearful. "A tiger entered the room," he was about to think, but managed to distract himself. However, full of terror, he glanced at the door. The materialization had taken place, but inasmuch as the thought had not been fully formulated, its effect was reduced, only approximate: a wasp flew in at the window. It was striped and bloodthirsty.

"Lola! A tiger!" Shuvalov hollered.

Lola woke up. The wasp suspended itself over a plate. It was humming like a gyroscope. Lola jumped off the bed. The wasp flew toward her. Lola waved her arms. The wasp and her medallion circled around her. Shuvalov stopped the medallion with his hand. They ambushed the wasp. Lola covered the wasp with her crackling straw hat.

Shuvalov left. They took leave of each other standing in the draft, which in this world seemed to be very active and many-voiced. The draft opened the doors downstairs. It sang like a cleaning woman. It made an eddy in Lola's hair, picked up Lola's hat, released the wasp, and blew it into the salad. It was whistling. It picked up Lola's nightdress and stood it up.

They parted, and his happiness preventing him from feeling the steps, Shuvalov got downstairs and was outside. Further on, he did not feel the sidewalk, and then he discovered that it was no illusion, that he was actually floating in the air, flying.

"Flying on the wings of love," somebody said inside a window as he passed. He soared. His shirt turned into a crinoline. His upper lip throbbed. He was flying along snapping his fingers.

At two in the afternoon he went to the park. Exhausted by love and happiness he fell asleep on a green bench. He slept, his collarbones prominent under his open shirt.

A man wearing heavy blue glasses, a black hat, and a coat reminiscent of a cassock was slowly and ponderously walking up the path. His hands were joined under his behind and he kept raising and lowering his head.

He came to sit on the bench next to Shuvalov.

"I am Isaac Newton," he introduced himself, lifting his black hat slightly. Through his glasses he scrutinized his blue, photographic world.

"Hello," Shuvalov said.

The great physicist sat stiffly, on the alert, ready to jump up all in one movement. He was listening, his ears kept giving little jerks, the index finger of his left hand was pointing up as though he were demanding the attention of an invisible choir which was ready to burst into a hymn on a signal from that finger. All around, plant and beast became quiet. Shuvalov slipped behind the bench and hid there. Newton was listening to the silence of the elements. Far away, above the cupolas of leaves, a star was becoming discernible, and it became cooler.

"Listen, listen," Newton suddenly said. "Can you hear?"

Without turning his head, Newton caught Shuvalov by the tail of his shirt and pulled him out from his refuge.

They walked across the grass. The physicist's ample shoes stepped softly on the grass, leaving white footprints behind them. Ahead of them, often glancing back, ran a lizard. They went through a thicket, and the metal frame of the great man's glasses became adorned with fluff and ladybugs. In the clearing, Shuvalov recognized the sapling that had appeared yesterday.

"Apricots?" he asked.

"Of course not," Newton answered with irritation. "It's an apple tree."

The frame of the apple tree, square, light, and fragile, like the frame of a dirigible, showed through its scanty cover of leaves. Everything was still and quiet.

"Here," Newton said. He bent down and his voice came out like a bark. "Here!" He held out an apple. "What does this mean?"

It was easy to see that he was not in the habit of bending. When he had straightened up again, he pushed his shoulders back several times, to relax the old bamboo rod of his spine. The apple was resting on a support formed by three of his fingers.

"What does this mean?" he repeated. His snorting prevented his voice from sounding clear. "Wouldn't you care to explain why this apple has fallen?"

Shuvalov stared at the apple the way William Tell must have done.

"The law of gravity . . ." he muttered.

Then, after a pause, the physicist said:

"If I am not mistaken, you have been flying today, young man?"

He asked the question like an examining magistrate. His eyebrows shot high above his eyes.

A ladybug crawled from Newton's finger onto the apple. He followed it, his eyes squinting. The ladybug looked blindingly blue to him. He screwed up his nose. Then she took off from the very highest point of the apple, using a pair of wings which she took out of somewhere behind her back, like taking a handkerchief out from underneath the tails of a frock coat.

"You have been flying today, haven't you?"

Shuvalov said nothing.

"Pig," Isaac Newton said.

"Pig," Lola was standing over him. "Pig, you go to sleep while you wait for me."

She took the ladybug off his forehead, smiling at the realization that the insect had a metal belly.

"Hell," Shuvalov said, "I hate you. Once I used to know that that was a ladybug and nothing else about it. Well, I could perhaps make a few conjectures as to the origin of its name, whether it's religious or what. But now, since I have met you, something has happened to my eyes. I see blue pears and I see the resemblance between a toadstool and a ladybug."

She wanted to put her arms round his neck.

"Leave me alone!" he shouted. "I've had enough of it! I am ashamed of myself."

Shouting these words, he galloped away like a deer. Snorting, bounding along wildly, he ran, pushing himself off from his own shadow, his eyes squinting. He stopped, out of breath. Lola had vanished. He decided to forget everything. The lost universe had to be recovered.

"Good-by," he said, "we won't see one another again."

He sat on the slope of a hill from which he had a view over a wide space sown with summerhouses. He was sitting on the crest of a prism, his feet resting on a sloping plane. Under him, the umbrella of an ice-cream cart was turning. The whole outfit of the ice-cream man reminded him of a Negro village.

"I am living in paradise," the young Marxist said in a broken voice.

"Are you a Marxist?" Shuvalov heard a voice next to him.

It was the color-blind young man in the black hat. He was sitting next to Shuvalov.

"Yes," Shuvalov said.

"So you cannot live in paradise."

The color-blind man was playing with a twig. Shuvalov sighed.

"I cannot help it. The earth has become a paradise."

The young man was whistling softly. He scratched his ear with his twig.

"Do you know how far off I went today?" Shuvalov continued in a complaining, whining tone. "I flew today."

A skate was stuck on the sky. Not quite straight, like a postage stamp.

"Shall I demonstrate to you? Shall I fly up there?" Shuvalov pointed to the skate.

"No thanks, I don't wish to witness your degradation."

Shuvalov said, "Yes, it is terrible." He remained silent for a moment and repeated: "I know, it's terrible." Then he added suddenly: "I envy you."

"Do you really?"

"I give you my word. It is so wonderful to understand the world correctly and be confused only about a few details of color. You do not have to live in paradise. The world has not disappeared for you. Everything is in place. And me . . . Just think, I am completely healthy, I am a materialist . . . then, suddenly, before my eyes, occurs a criminal, antiscientific perversion of elements, of matter. . . ."

"Yes, it is terrible," the color-blind man said, "and it all comes from love."

"Listen to me!" With sudden heat, Shuvalov grabbed his neighbor by the arm. "I agree. Give me your cornea and take my love in exchange."

The young man began sliding down the slope.

"Forgive me, I'm in a hurry. Have a good time in your paradise."

It was difficult for him to move down the slope. He pressed his body close to the soil, losing his resemblance to a man, beginning to look like a man's reflection in water. Finally he reached the flat surface, straightened himself up, and walked off chirpily. Then he threw his twig up in the air, blew Shuvalov a kiss, and shouted:

"Give my best to Eve!"

Lola was still asleep. One hour after his meeting with the color-blind young man, he found her in the heart of the park. Since he was no naturalist, he could not determine what surrounded her, whether it was hazel, hawthorn, elder bushes, or wild roses. From every side, branches and bushes pressed in on him. He walked like a merchant with baskets on the upturned palms of his hands, baskets loaded with the light tangle of vegetation. He kept discarding these imaginary baskets; berries, petals, thorns, birds, and eggs were scattered around him.

Lola lay on her back, her pink dress open at the breast; he heard the crackling of membranes inside her nose swollen by sleep. He sat down next to her.

Then he put his head on her breast. His fingers felt the thin cotton, his head lay on her sweaty breast, he could see a pink nipple, with wrinkles as delicate as those of the skin on boiled milk. He heard a crackling, the sigh and breaking of dry branches.

The color-blind man stood behind the leaves of a bush. The bush was in his way.

"Look here," he said.

Shuvalov raised his head. One of his cheeks felt warm.

"Will you stop following me about like a dog?" he said.

"Listen, I am willing now. . . . Help yourself to my cornea and give me your love. . . ."

"Go and eat your blue pears," Shuvalov said.

THE LOCKER ROOM

w. s. merwin

This time no one told us anything. We do not even know where the battle was, on which our fates depended. But there is not a word of surprise as we find ourselves, at our age, being herded down those iron stairs to the pale-green foyer lit with naked bulbs. Bulletin boards. Frosted-glass windows and doors—one of the big windows open, revealing several men younger than we are, in white smocks, seated or standing at desks, among filing cabinets. We are kept waiting. There are no benches. We look around to see who we know. We see a face we recognize, and we smile little wincing smiles, but then wonder whether we should indicate that we know anyone there at all, and from then on we stand still, saying nothing, feeling our stomachs like dark ships slowly sinking. We are told to take off our shoes. Keep the socks on. We stand holding our shoes, watching how the others hold theirs, without meeting eyes. Yesterday this time, or even two hours ago, we were being deferred to in positions of relative eminence. Our modesty became us. Almost certainly it became us. We deprecated. And quite genuinely: aware that the esteem in which apparently we were held exceeded our deserts. Yes, but we did not then stand in our socks, with our shoes in our hands, waiting, on a cement floor that was not quite dry, smelling the shoes, the socks, the floor, something else, and beyond double frosted doors the unlit locker room. Some of us, clearly, had taken no exercise for years. Some were perspiring. Some seemed to be looking for things in their pockets. It's true that we'd been picked up without warning, and just as we were. Told we would need nothing else. Probably no one knew where we were. A clever-looking young man, growing bald already, hurried out from the room with the desks. His white smock billowed around him and he was carrying a clipboard from which sheets of paper struggled to detach themselves and fly away across pallid horizons, where they would settle quietly on vast plains, in the spring twilight, two by two. He opened the locker-room doors, switched on the yellow bulbs inside, and motioned us through, checking off each of our names as we passed him, and giving each of us a little string with a tag on it, bearing a locker number.

The strings were dirty.

"Don't put the tags in your mouths," he told us, though no one seemed tempted to do so. And we filed past, holding shoes in one hand, tag in the other, and began to drift and eddy up and down the rows of lockers, a slow yellow-lit tide backing up into an old harbor. Then the sound of the first tin locker doors. A few voices, laughing a little at having found them. Striking up new acquaintance, with an effort at jocularity, even at such a time, in such a place. And the smell of the lockers. The care with which hand after hand hesitantly sets about undoing its necktie. And there are no hangers for suits which have always had hangers. Years ago we did not have suits that were used to hangers. The ones we have come in with hang uncomfortably on the snub hooks, and at once dust seems to have begun to settle on them. Out of the corners of our eyes we see garters, and white calves, and white shirttails, and then shirts fluttering into the lockers like guilty things, but all we hear is an occasional creaking and snapping of joints, heavy breathing, wheezing, sniffing, a stifled moan. And the squeaking and banging of the locker doors. Pale sides of skin emerge to right and to left, bending, patting, sighing. Some of us must have had no exercise for years. Some of us plainly have had no exercise for years. Some of us obviously have revealed our birthday suits only to the bought bulbs of bathrooms, for years. The young man with the clipboard moves along the aisles, checking. He tells us to hang the tags on the locker doors when we are finished and then close the lockers and stand with our backs to them. There is a muttering. Some are saying prayers. The smell of us grows stronger than that of the old locker room, but when I look up at the ceiling I can imagine that we

THE LOCKER ROOM 255

are still as we once were, years ago, standing under those same yellow tiles, with no hair on our cold privates, shivering, and I cling to that image.

Almost all of the locker doors must have shut, and almost all of the abdomens must have turned slowly, the shoulders squaring a little, the eyes seeking out some spot on the locker across the aisle, when another clever-looking young man with a clipboard comes through the doors and confers with the first one. They speak together in low tones for a moment, comparing their papers. Then the first young man nods and straightens.

"As you were," he says. "Get dressed."

The sigh. The sound of bodies falling as one or two faint. The fumbling with the lockers. The underwear. Feeling tight. Feeling clammy. The shirt. Feeling dirty. And too small. The trousers. Feeling tight. And short and strange, and looking different in the light. Yes. They've grown old. Very old. As old as though we'd been standing there for years. Or as though they'd been hanging there since we were children. And the jackets. Much too small, too short in the arms. And old. With holes in some of the pockets. And in others nails. Clasp knives. Crumpled pieces of paper which we remember but about which we say nothing. The socks. Dirty, fished from among several dirty pairs. The shoes. Sneakers. Too small. The first young man with the clipboard is going among the aisles telling us to hurry. The wallets. Almost nothing in them but our names. The sound of somebody sniffing again. And the first young man with the clipboard and the billowing smock leading us rapidly down a green hall that echoes like an inner tube to the gymnasium, where samples of our blood, our urine, our hair are collected. And then the safety doors clanking open and the cold air of the recreation ground, where we are released—yes, released—one by one and allowed to walk away in silence, past the new windows.

THE MOUSE AND THE WOMAN
dylan thomas

1

In the eaves of the lunatic asylum were birds who whistled the coming in of spring. A madman, howling like a dog from the top room, could not disturb them, and their tunes did not stop when he thrust his hands through the bars of the window near their nests and clawed the sky. A fresh smell blew with the winds around the white building and its grounds. The asylum trees waved green hands over the wall to the world outside.

In the gardens the patients sat and looked up at the sun or upon the flowers or upon nothing, or walked sedately along the paths, hearing the gravel crunch beneath their feet with a hard, sensible sound. Children in print dresses might be expected to play, not noisily, upon the lawn. The building, too, had a sweet expression, as though it knew only the kind things of life and the polite emotions. In a middle room sat a child who had cut off his double thumb with a scissors.

A little way off the main path leading from house to gate, a girl, lifting her arms, beckoned to the birds. She enticed the sparrows with little movements of her fingers, but to no avail. It must be spring, she said. The sparrows sang exultantly, and then stopped.

The howling in the top room began again. The madman's face was pressed close to the bars of the window. Opening his mouth wide, he bayed up at the sun, listening to the inflections of his voice with a remorseless concentration. With his unseeing eyes fixed on the green garden, he heard the revolution of the years as they moved softly back. Now there was no garden. Under the sun the iron bars melted. Like a flower, a new room pulsed and opened.

2

Waking up when it was still dark, he turned the dream over and over on the tip of his brain until each little symbol became heavy with a separate meaning. But there were symbols he could not remember, they came and went so quickly among the rattle of leaves, the gestures of women's hands spelling on the sky, the falling of rain and the humming wind. He remembered the oval of her face and the colour of her eyes. He remembered the pitch of her voice, though not what she said. She moved again wearily up and down the same ruler of turf. What she said fell with the leaves, and spoke in the wind whose brother rattled the panes like an old man.

There had been seven women, in a mad play by a Greek, each with the same face, crowned by the same hoop of mad, black hair. One by one they trod the ruler of turf, then vanished. They turned the same face to him, intolerably weary with the same suffering.

The dream had changed. Where the women were was an avenue of trees. And the trees leant forward and interlaced their hands, turning into a black forest. He had seen himself, absurd in his nakedness, walk into the depths. Stepping on a dead twig, he was bitten.

Then there was her face again. There was nothing in his dream but her tired face. And the changes of the details of the dream and the celestial changes, the levers of the trees and the toothed twigs, these were the mechanisms of her delirium. It was not the sickness of sin that was upon her face. Rather it was the sickness of never having sinned and of never having done well.

He lit the candle on the little deal table by his bedside. Candle light threw the shadows of the room into confusion, and raised up the warped men of shadow out of the corners. For the first time he heard the clock. He had been deaf until then to everything except the wind outside the window and the clean winter sounds of the night-world. But now the steady tick tock tick sounded like the heart of someone hidden in his room. He could not hear the night birds now. The loud clock drowned their crying, or the wind was too cold for them and made commotion among their feathers. He remembered the dark hair of the woman in the trees and of the seven women treading the ruler of turf.

He could no longer listen to the speaking of reason. The pulse of a new heart beat at his side. Contentedly he let the dream dictate its rhythm. Often he would rise when the sun had dropped down, and, in the lunatic blackness under the stars, walk on the hill, feeling the wind finger his hair and at his nostrils. The rats and the rabbits on his towering hill came out in the dark, and the shadows consoled them for the night of the harsh sun. The dark woman, too, had risen out of darkness, pulling down the stars in their hundreds and showing him a mystery that hung and shone higher in the night of the sky than all the planets crowding beyond the curtains.

He fell to sleep again and woke in the sun. As he dressed, the dog scratched at the door. He let it in and felt its wet muzzle in his hand. The weather was hot for a midwinter day. The little wind there was could not relieve the sharpness of the heat. With the opening of the bedroom window, the uneven beams of the sun twisted his images into the hard lines of light.

He tried not to think of the woman as he ate. She had risen out of the depths of darkness. Now she was lost again. She is drowned, dead, dead. In the clean glittering of the kitchen, among the white boards, the oleographs of old women, the brass candlesticks, the plates on the shelves, and the sounds of kettle and clock, he was caught between believing in her and denying her. Now he insisted on the lines of her neck. The wilderness of her hair rose over the dark surface. He saw her flesh in the cut bread; her blood, still flowing through the channels of her mysterious body, in the spring water.

But another voice told him that she was dead. She was a woman in a mad story. He forced himself to hear the voice telling that she was dead. Dead, alive, drowned, raised up. The two voices shouted across his brain. He could not bear to think that the last spark in her had been put out. She is alive, alive, cried the two voices together.

As he tidied the sheets on his bed, he saw a block of paper, and sat down at the table with a pencil poised in his hand. A hawk flew over the hill. Seagulls, on spread, unmoving wings, cried past the window. A mother rat, in a hole in the hillside near the holes of rabbits, suckled its young as the sun climbed higher in the clouds.

He put the pencil down.

3

One winter morning, after the last crowing of the cock, in the walks of his garden, had died to nothing, she who for so long had dwelt with him appeared in all the wonder of her youth. She had cried to be set free, and to walk in his dreams no longer. Had she not been in the beginning, there would have been no beginning. She had moved in his belly when he was a boy, and stirred in his boy's loins. He at last gave birth to her who had been with him from the beginning. And with him dwelt a dog, a mouse, and a dark woman.

4

It is not a little thing, he thought, this writing that lies before me. It is the telling of a creation. It is the story of birth. Out of him had come another. A being had been born, not out of the womb, but out of the soul and the spinning head. He had come to the cottage on the hill that the being within him might ripen and be born away from the eyes of men. He understood what the wind that took up the woman's cry had cried in his last dream. Let me be born, it had cried. He had given a woman being. His flesh would be upon her, and the life that he had given her would make her walk, talk, and sing. And he knew, too, that it was upon the block of paper she was made absolute. There was an oracle in the lead of the pencil.

In the kitchen he cleaned up after his meal. When the last plate had been washed, he looked around the room. In the corner near the door was a hole no bigger than a half-crown. He found a tiny square of tin and nailed it over the hole, making sure that nothing could go in or come out. Then he donned his coat and walked out on to the hill and down towards the sea.

Broken water leapt up from the inrushing tide and fell into the crevices of the rocks, making innumerable pools. He climbed down to the half-circle of beach, and the clusters of shells did not break when his foot fell on them. Feeling his heart knock at his side, he turned to where the greater rocks climbed perilously up to the grass. There, at the foot, the oval of her face towards him, she stood and smiled. The spray brushed her naked body, and the creams of the sea ran unheeded over her feet. She lifted her hand. He crossed to her.

5

In the cool of the evening they walked in the garden behind the cottage. She had lost none of her beauty with the covering up of her nakedness. With slippers on her feet she stepped as gracefully as when her feet were bare. There was a dignity in the poise of her head, and her voice was clear as a bell. Walking by her side along the narrow path, he heard no discord in the crying together of the gulls. She pointed out bird and bush with her finger, illuminating a new loveliness in the wings and leaves, in the sour churning of water over pebbles, and a new life along the dead branches of the trees.

It is quiet here, she said as they stood looking out to sea and the dark coming over the land. Is it always as quiet?

Not when the storms come in with the tide, he said. Boys play behind the hill, lovers go down to the shore.

Late evening turned to night so suddenly that, where she stood, stood a shadow under the moon. He took its hand, and they ran together to the cottage.

It was lonely for you before I came, she said.

As a cinder hissed into the grate, he moved back in his chair, making a startled gesture with his hand.

How quickly you become frightened, she said, I am frightened of nothing.

But she thought over her words and spoke again, this time in a low voice.

One day I may have no limbs to walk with, no hands to touch with. No heart under my breast.

Look at the million stars, he said. They make some pattern on the sky. It is a pattern of letters spelling a word. One night I shall look up and read the word.

But she kissed him and calmed his fear.

6

The madman remembered the inflections of her voice, heard, again, her frock rustling, and saw the terrible curve of her breast. His own breathing thundered in his ears. The girl on the bench beckoned to the sparrows. Somewhere a child purred, stroking the black columns of a wooden horse that neighed and then lay down.

7

They slept together on the first night, side by side in the dark, their arms around one another. The shadows in the corner were trimmed and shapely in her presence, losing their old deformity. And the stars looked in upon them and shone in their eyes.

Tomorrow you must tell me what you dream, he said.

It will be what I have always dreamed, she said. Walking on a little length of grass, up and down, up and down, till my feet bleed. Seven images of me walking up and down.

It is what I dream. Seven is a number in magic.

Magic? she said.

A woman makes a wax man, puts a pin in its chest; and the man dies. Someone has a little devil, tells it what to do. A girl dies, you see her walk. A woman turns into a hill.

She let her head rest on his shoulder, and fell to sleep.

He kissed her mouth, and passed his hand through her hair.

She was asleep, but he did not sleep. Wide awake, he stared into darkness. Now he was drowned in terror, and the sucking waters closed over his skull.

I, I have a devil, he said.

She stirred at the noise of his voice, and then again her head was motionless and her body straight along the curves of the cool bed.

I have a devil, but I do not tell it what to do. It lifts my hand. I write. The words spring into life. She, then, is a woman of the devil.

She made a contented sound, nestled ever nearer to him. Her breath was warm on his neck, and her foot lay on his like a mouse. He saw that she was beautiful in her sleep. Her beauty could not have sprouted out of evil. God, whom he had searched for in his loneliness, had formed her for his mate as Eve for Adam out of Adam's rib.

He kissed her again, and saw her smile as she slept.

God at my side, he said.

He had not slept with Rachel and woken with Leah. There was the pallor of dawn on her cheeks. He touched them lightly with a finger-nail. She did not stir.

But there had been no woman in his dreams. Not even a thread of woman's hair had dangled from the sky. God had come down in a cloud and the cloud had changed to a snakes' nest. Foul hissing of snakes had suggested the sound of water, and he had been drowned. Down and down he had fallen, under green shiftings and the bubbles that fishes blew from their mouths, down and down on to the bony floors of the sea.

Then against a white curtain of people had moved and moved to no purpose but to speak mad things.

What did you find under the tree?

I found an airman.

No, no, under the other tree?

I found a bottle of foetus.

No, no, under the other tree?

I found a mouse-trap.

He had been invisible. There had been nothing but his voice. He had flown across back gardens, and his voice, caught in a tangle of wireless aerials, had bled as though it were a thing of substance. Men in deck-chairs were listening to the loud-speakers speaking:

What did you find under the tree?

I found a wax man.

No, no, under the other tree?

He could remember little else except the odds and ends of sentences, the movement of a turning shoulder, the sudden flight or drop of syllables. But slowly the whole meaning edged into his brain. He could translate every symbol of his dreams, and he lifted the pencil so that they might stand hard and clear upon the paper. But the words would not come. He thought he heard the scratching of velvet paws behind a panel. But when he sat still and listened close, there was no sound.

She opened her eyes.

What are you doing? she said.

He put down the paper, and kissed her before they rose to dress.

What did you dream last night? he asked her, when they had eaten.

Nothing. I slept, that is all. What did you dream?

Nothing, he said.

8

There was creation screaming in the steam of the kettle, in the light making mouths on the china and the floor she swept as a child sweeps the floor of a doll's house. There was nothing to see in her but the ebb and flood of creation, only the transcendent sweep of being and living in the careless fold of flesh from shoulder-bone to elbow. He could not tell, after the horror he had found in the translating symbols, why the sea should point to the fruitful and unfailing stars with the edge of each wave, and an image of fruition disturb the moon in its dead course.

She moulded his images that evening. She lent light, and the lamp was dim beside her who had the oil of life glistening in every pore of her hand.

And now in the garden they remembered how they had walked in the garden for the first time.

You were lonely before I came.

How quickly you become frightened.

She had lost none of her beauty with the covering up of her nakedness. Though he had slept at her side, he had been content to know the surface of her. Now he stripped her of her clothes and laid her on a bed of grass.

9

The mouse had waited for this consummation. Wrinkling its eyes, it crept stealthily along the tunnel, littered with scraps of half-eaten paper, behind the kitchen wall. Stealthily, on tiny, padded paws, it felt its way through darkness, its nails scraping on the wood. Stealthily, it worked its way between the walls, screamed at the blind light through the chinks, and filed through the square of tin. Moonlight dropped slowly into the space where the mouse, working its destruction, inched into light. The last barrier fell away. And on the clean stones of the kitchen floor the mouse stood still.

10

That night he told of the love in the garden of Eden.

A garden was planted eastward, and Adam lived in it. Eve was made for him, out of him, bone of his bones, flesh of his flesh. They were as naked as you upon the seashore, but Eve could not have been as beautiful. They ate with the devil, and saw that they were naked, and covered up their nakedness. In their good bodies they saw evil for the first time.

Then you saw evil in me, she said, when I was naked. I would as soon be naked as be clothed. Why did you cover up my nakedness?

It was not good to look upon, he said.

But it was beautiful. You yourself said that it was beautiful, she said.

It was not good to look upon.

You said the body of Eve was good. And yet you say I was not good to look upon. Why did you cover up my nakedness?

It was not good to look upon.

11

Welcome, said the devil to the madman. Cast your eyes upon me. I grow and grow. See how I multiply. See my sad, Grecian stare. And the longing to be born in my dark eyes. Oh, that was the best joke of all.

I am an asylum boy tearing the wings of birds. Remember the lions that were crucified. Who knows that it was not I who opened the door of the tomb for Christ to struggle out?

But the madman had heard that welcome time after time. Ever since the evening of the second day after their love in the garden, when he had told her that her nakedness was not good to look upon, he had heard the welcome ring out in the sliding rain, and seen the welcome words burnt into the sea. He had known at the ringing of the first syllable in his ears that nothing on the earth could save him, and that the mouse would come out.

But the mouse had come out already.

The madman cried down at the beckoning girl to whom, now, a host of birds edged closer on a bough.

12

Why did you cover up my nakedness?

It was not good to look upon.

Why, then, No, no, under the other tree?

It was not good, I found a wax cross.

As she had questioned him, not harshly, but with bewilderment, that he whom she loved should find her nakedness unclean, he heard the broken pieces of the old dirge break into her questioning.

Why, then, she said, No, no, under the other tree?

He heard himself reply, It was not good, I found a talking thorn.

Real things kept changing place with unreal, and, as a bird burst into song, he heard the springs rattle far back in its throat.

She left him with a smile that still poised over a question, and, crossing the strip of hill, vanished into the half-dark where the cottage stood like another woman. But she returned ten times, in ten different shapes. She breathed at his ear, passed the back of her hand over his dry mouth, and lit the lamp in the cottage room more than a mile away.

It grew darker as he stared at the stars. Wind cut through the new night. Very suddenly a bird screamed over the trees, and an owl, hungry for mice, hooted in the mile-away wood.

There was contradiction in heartbeat and green Sirius, an eye in the east. He put his hand to his eyes, hiding the star, and walked slowly towards the lamp burning far away in the cottage. And all the elements come together, of wind and sea and fire, of love and the passing of love, closed in a circle around him.

She was not sitting by the fire, as he had expected her to be, smiling upon the folds of her dress. He called her name at the foot of the stairs. He looked into the empty bedroom, and called her name in the garden. But she had gone, and all the mystery of her presence had left the cottage. And the shadows that he thought had departed when she had come crowded the corners, muttering in women's voices among themselves. He turned down the wick in the lamp. As he climbed upstairs, he heard the corner voices become louder and louder until the whole cottage reverberated with them, and the wind could not be heard.

13

With tears in his cheeks and with a hard pain in his heart, he fell to sleep, coming at last to where his father sat in an alcove carved in a cloud.

Father, he said, I have been walking over the world, looking for a thing worthy of love, but I drove it away and go now from place to place, moaning my hideousness, hearing my own voice in the voices of the corncrakes and the frogs, seeing my own face in the riddled faces of the beasts.

He held out his arms, waiting for words to fall from that old mouth hidden under a white beard frozen with tears. He implored the old man to speak.

Speak to me, your son. Remember how we read the classic books together on the terraces. Or on an Irish harp you would pluck tunes until the geese, like the seven geese of the Wandering Jew, rose squawking into the air. Father, speak to me, your only son, a prodigal out of the herbaceous spaces of small towns, out of the smells and sounds of the city, out of the thorny desert and the deep sea. You are a wise old man.

He implored the old man to speak, but, coming closer to him and staring into his face, he saw the stains of death upon mouth and eyes and a nest of mice in the tangle of the frozen beard.

It was weak to fly, but he flew. And it was a weakness of the blood to be invisible, but he was invisible. He reasoned and dreamed unreasonably at the same time, knowing his weakness and the lunacy of flying but having no strength to conquer it. He flew like a bird over the fields, but soon the bird's body vanished, and he was a flying voice. An open window beckoned him by the waving of its blinds, as a scarecrow beckons a wise bird by its ragged waving, and into the open window he flew, alighting on a bed near a sleeping girl.

Awake, girl, he said. I am your lover come in the night.

She awoke at his voice.

Who called me?

I called you.

Where are you?

I am upon the pillow by your head, speaking into your ear.

Who are you?

I am a voice.

Stop calling into my ear, then, and hop into my hand so that I may touch you and tickle you. Hop into my hand, voice.

He lay still and warm in her palm.

Where are you?

I am in your hand.

Which hand?

The hand on your breast, left hand. Do not make a fist or you will crush me. Can you not feel me warm in your hand? I am close to the roots of your fingers.

Talk to me.

I had a body, but was always a voice. As I truly am, I come to you in the night, a voice on your pillow.

I know what you are. You are the still, small voice I must not listen to. I have been told not to listen to that still, small voice that speaks in the night. It is wicked to listen. You must not come here again. You must go away.

But I am your lover.

I must not listen, said the girl, and suddenly clenched her hand.

14

He could go into the garden, regardless of rain, and bury his face in the wet earth. With his ears pressed close to the earth, he would hear the great heart, under soil and grass, strain before breaking. In dreams he would say to some figure, Lift me up. I am only ten pounds now. I am lighter. Six pounds. Two pounds. My spine shows through my breast. The secret of that alchemy that had turned a little revolution of the unsteady senses into a golden moment was lost as a key is lost in undergrowth. A secret was confused among the night, and the confusion of the last madness before the grave would come down like an animal on the brain.

He wrote upon the block of paper, not knowing what he wrote, and dreading the words that looked up at him at last and could not be forgotten.

15

And this is all there was to it: a woman had been born, not out of the womb, but out of the soul and the spinning head. And he who had borne her out of darkness loved his creation, and she loved him. But this is all there was to it: a miracle befell a man. He fell in love with it, but could not keep it, and the miracle passed. And with him dwelt a dog, a mouse, and a dark woman. The woman went away, and the dog died.

16

He buried the dog at the end of the garden. Rest in peace, he told the dead dog. But the grave was not deep enough and there were rats in the underhanging of the bank who bit through the sack shroud.

17

Upon town pavements, he saw the woman step loose, her breasts firm under a coat on which the single hairs from old men's heads lay white on black. Her life, he knew, was only a life of days. Her spring had passed with him. After the summer and the autumn, unhallowed time between full life and death, there would be winter corrugating charm. He who knew the subtleties of every reason, and sensed the four together in every symbol of the earth, would disturb the chronology of the seasons. Winter must not appear.

18

Consider now the old effigy of time, his long beard whitened by an Egyptian sun, his bare feet watered by the Sargasso sea. Watch me belabour the old fellow. I have stopped his heart. It split like a chamber pot. No, this is no rain falling. This is the wet out of the cracked heart.

Parhelion and sun shine in the same sky with the broken moon. Dizzy with the chasing of moon by sun, and by the twinkling of so many stars, I run upstairs to read again of the love of some man for a woman. I tumble down to see the half-crown hole in the kitchen wall stabbed open, and the prints of a mouse's pads on the floor.

Consider now the old effigies of the seasons. Break up the rhythm of the old figures' moving, the spring trot, summer canter, sad stride of autumn, and winter shuffle. Break, piece by piece, the continuous changing of motion into a spindle-shanked walking.

Consider the sun for whom I know no image but the old image of a shot eye, and the broken moon.

19

Gradually the chaos became less, and the things of the surrounding world were no longer wrought out of their own substance into the shapes of his thoughts. Some peace fell about him, and again the music of creation was to be heard trembling out of crystal water, out of the holy sweep of the sky down to the wet edge of the earth where a sea flowed over. Night came slowly, and the hill rose to the unrisen stars. He turned over the block of paper and upon the last page wrote in a clear hand:

20

The woman died.

21

There was dignity in such a murder. And the hero in him rose up in all his holiness and strength. It was just that he who had brought her forth from darkness should pack her away again. And it was just that she should die not knowing what hand out of the sky struck upon her and laid her low.

He walked down the hill, his steps slow as in procession, and his lips smiling at the dark sea. He climbed on to the shore, and, feeling his heart knock at his side, turned to where the greater rocks climbed perilously to the grass. There at the foot, her face towards him, she lay and smiled. Sea-water ran unheeded over her nakedness. He crossed to her, and touched her cold cheek with his nails.

22

Acquainted with the last grief, he stood at the open window of his room. And the night was an island in a sea of mystery and meaning. And the voice out of the night was a voice of acceptance. And the face of the moon was the face of humility.

He knew the last wonder before the grave and the mystery that bewilders and incorporates the heavens and the earth. He knew that he had failed before the eye of God and the eye of Sirius to hold his miracle. The woman had shown him that it was wonderful to live. And now, when at last he knew how wonderful, and how pleasant the blood in the trees, and how deep the well of the clouds, he must close his eyes and die. He opened his eyes, and looked up at the stars. There were a million stars spelling the same word. And the word of the stars was written clearly upon the sky.

23

Alone in the kitchen, among the broken chairs and china, stood the mouse that had come out of the hole. Its paws rested lightly upon the floor painted all over with the grotesque figures of birds and girls. Stealthily, it crept back into the hole. Stealthily, it worked its way between the walls. There was no sound in the kitchen but the sound of the mouse's nails scraping upon wood.

24

In the eaves of the lunatic asylum the birds still whistled, and the madman, pressed close to the bars of the window near their nests, bayed up at the sun.

Upon the bench some distance from the main path, the girl was beckoning to the birds, while on a square of lawn danced three old women, hand in hand, simpering in the wind, to the music of an Italian organ from the world outside.

Spring is come, said the warders.

A COUNTRY DOCTOR

franz kafka

I was in great perplexity; I had to start on an urgent journey; a seriously ill patient was waiting for me in a village ten miles off; a thick blizzard of snow filled all the wide spaces between him and me; I had a gig, a light gig with big wheels, exactly right for our country roads; muffled in furs, my bag of instruments in my hand, I was in the courtyard all ready for the journey; but there was no horse to be had, no horse. My own horse had died in the night, worn out by the fatigues of this icy winter; my servant girl was now running round the village trying to borrow a horse; but it was hopeless, I knew it, and I stood there forlornly, with the snow gathering more and more thickly upon me, more and more unable to move. In the gateway the girl appeared, alone, and waved the lantern; of course, who would lend a horse at this time for such a journey? I strode through the courtyard once more; I could see no way out; in my confused distress I kicked at the dilapidated door of the year-long uninhabited pigsty. It flew open and flapped to and fro on its hinges. A steam and smell as of horses came out from it. A dim stable lantern was swinging inside from a rope. A man, crouching on his hams in that low space, showed an open blue-eyed face. "Shall I yoke up?" he asked, crawling out on all fours. I did not know what to say and merely stooped down to see what else was in the sty. The servant girl standing beside me. "You never know what you're going to find in your own house," she said, and we both laughed. "Hey there, Brother, hey there, Sister!" called the groom, and two horses, enormous creatures with powerful flanks, one after the other, their legs tucked close to their bodies, each well-shaped head lowered like a camel's, by sheer strength of buttocking squeezed out through the door hole which they filled entirely. But at once they were standing up, their legs long and their bodies steaming thickly. "Give him a hand," I said, and the willing girl hurried to help the groom with the harnessing. Yet hardly was she beside him when the groom clipped hold of her and pushed his face against hers. She screamed and fled back to me; on her cheek stood out in red the marks of two rows of teeth. "You brute," I yelled in fury, "do you want a whipping?" but in the same moment reflected that the man was a stranger; that I did not know where he came from, and that of his own free will he was helping me out when everyone else had failed me. As if he knew my thoughts he took no offense at my threat but, still busied with the horses, only turned round once towards me. "Get in," he said then, and indeed: everything was ready. A magnificent pair of horses, I observed, such as I had never sat behind, and I climbed in happily. "But I'll drive, you don't know the way," I said. "Of course," said he, "I'm not coming with you anyway, I'm staying with Rose." "No," shrieked Rose, fleeing into the house with a justified presentiment that her fate was inescapable; I heard the door chain rattle as she put it up; I heard the key turn in the lock; I could see, moreover, how she put out the lights in the entrance hall and in further flight all through the rooms to keep herself from being discovered. "You're coming with me," I said to the groom, "or I won't go, urgent as my journey is. I'm not thinking of paying for it by handing the girl over to you." "Gee up!" he said; clapped his hands; the gig whirled off like a log in a freshet; I could just hear the door of my house splitting and bursting as the groom charged at it and then I was deafened and blinded by a storming rush that steadily buffeted all my senses. But this only for a moment, since, as if my patient's farmyard had opened out just before my courtyard gate, I was already there; the horses had come quietly to a standstill; the blizzard had stopped; moonlight all around; my patient's parents hurried out of the house, his sister behind them; I was almost lifted out of the gig; from their confused ejaculations I gathered not a word; in the sickroom the air was almost unbreathable; the neglected stove was smoking; I wanted to push open a window; but first I had to look at my patient. Gaunt, without any fever, not cold, not warm, with vacant eyes, without a shirt, the youngster heaved himself up from under the feather bedding, threw his arms around my neck, and whispered in my ear: "Doctor, let me die." I glanced round the room; no one had heard it; the parents were leaning forward in silence waiting for my verdict; the sister had set a chair for my handbag; I opened the bag and hunted among my instruments; the boy kept clutching at me from his bed to remind me of his entreaty; I picked up a pair of tweezers, examined them in the candlelight and laid them down again. "Yes," I thought blasphemously, "in cases like this the gods are helpful, send the missing horse, add to it a second because of the urgency, and to crown everything bestow even a groom—" And only now did I remember Rose again; what was I to do, how could I rescue her, how could I pull her away from under that groom at ten miles' distance, with a team of horses I couldn't control. These horses, now, they had somehow slipped the reins loose, pushed the window open from the outside, I did not know how; each of them had stuck a head in at a window and, quite unmoved by the startled cries of the family, stood eyeing the patient. "Better go back at once," I thought, as if the horses were summoning me to the return journey, yet I permitted the patient's sister, who fancied that I was dazed by the heat, to take my fur coat from me. A glass of rum was poured out for me, the old man clapped me on the shoulder, a familiarity justified by this offer of his treasure. I shook my head; in the narrow confines of the old man's thoughts I felt ill; that was my only reason for refusing the drink. The mother stood by the bedside and cajoled me towards it. I yielded, and, while one of the horses whinnied loudly to the ceiling, laid my head to the boy's breast, which shivered under my wet beard. I confirmed what I already knew; the boy was quite sound, something a little wrong with his circulation, saturated with coffee by his solicitous mother, but sound and best turned out of bed with one shove. I am no world reformer and so I let him lie. I was the district doctor and did my duty to the uttermost, to the point where it became almost too much. I was badly paid and yet generous and helpful to the poor. I had still to see that Rose was all right, and then the boy might have his way and I wanted to die too. What was I doing there in that endless winter! My horse was dead, and not a single person in the village would lend me another. I had to get my team out of the pigsty; if they hadn't chanced to be horses I should have had to travel with swine. That was how it was. And I nodded to the family. They knew nothing about it, and, had they known, would not have believed it. To write prescriptions is easy, but to come to an understanding with people is hard. Well, this should be the end of my visit, I had once more been called out needlessly, I was used to that, the whole district made my life a torment with my night bell, but that I should have to sacrifice Rose this time as well, the pretty girl who had lived in my house for years almost without my noticing her—that sacrifice was too much to ask, and I had somehow to get it reasoned out in my head with the help of what craft I could muster, in order not to let fly at this family, which with the best will in the world could not restore Rose to me. But as I shut my bag and put an arm out for my fur coat, the family meanwhile standing together, the father sniffing at the glass of rum in his hand, the mother, apparently disappointed in me—why, what do people expect?—biting her lips with tears in her eyes, the sister fluttering a blood-soaked towel, I was somehow ready to admit conditionally that the boy might be ill after all. I went towards him, he welcomed me smiling as if I were bringing him the most nourishing invalid broth—ah, now both horses were whinnying together; the noise, I suppose, was ordained by heaven to assist my examination of the patient—and this time I discovered that the boy was indeed ill. In his right side, near the hip, was an open wound as big as the palm of my hand. Rose-red, in many variations of shade, dark in the hollows, lighter at the edges, softly granulated, with irregular clots of blood, open as a surface mine to the daylight. That was how it looked from a distance. But on a closer inspection there was another complication. I could not help a low whistle of surprise. Worms, as thick and as long my little finger, themselves rose-red and blood-spotted as well, were wriggling from their fastness in the interior of the wound towards the light, with small white heads and many little legs. Poor boy, you were past helping. I had discovered your great wound; this blossom in your side was destroying you. The family was pleased; they saw me busying myself; the sister told the mother, the mother the father, the father told several guests who were coming in, through the moonlight at the open door, walking on tiptoe, keeping their balance with outstretched arms. "Will you save me?" whispered the boy with a sob, quite blinded by the life within his wound. That is what people are like in my district. Always expecting the impossible from the doctor. They have lost their ancient beliefs; the parson sits at home and unravels his vestments, one after another; but the doctor is supposed to be omnipotent with his merciful surgeon's hand. Well, as it pleases them; I have not thrust my services on them; if they misuse me for sacred ends, I let that happen to me too; what better do I want, old country doctor that I am, bereft of my servant girl! And so they came, the family and the village elders, and stripped my clothes off me; a school choir with the teacher at the head of it stood before the house and sang these words to an utterly simple tune:

Strip his clothes off, then he'll heal us,
If he doesn't, kill him dead!
Only a doctor, only a doctor.

Then my clothes were off and I looked at the people quietly, my fingers in my beard and my head cocked to one side. I was altogether composed and equal to the situation and remained so, although it was no help to me, since they now took me by the head and feet and carried me to the bed. They laid me down in it next to the wall, on the side of the wound. Then they all left the room; the door was shut; the singing stopped; clouds covered the moon; the bedding was warm around me; the horses' heads in the open windows wavered like shadows. "Do you know," said a voice in my ear, "I have very little confidence in you. Why, you were only blown in here, you didn't come on your own feet. Instead of helping me, you're cramping me on my death bed. What I'd like best is to scratch your eyes out." "Right," I said, "it is a shame. And yet I am a doctor. What am I to do? Believe me, it is not too easy for me either." "Am I supposed to be content with this apology? Oh, I must be, I can't help it. I always have to put up with things. A fine wound is all I brought into the world; that was my sole endowment." "My young friend," said I, "your mistake is: you have not a wide enough view. I have been in all the sickrooms, far and wide, and I tell you: your wound is not so bad. Done in a tight corner with two strokes of the ax. Many a one proffers his side and can hardly hear the ax in the forest, far less that it is coming nearer to him." "Is that really so, or are you deluding me in my fever?" "It is really so, take the word of an official doctor." And he took it and lay still. But now it was time for me to think of escaping. The horses were still standing faithfully in their places. My clothes, my fur coat, my bag were quickly collected; I didn't want to waste time dressing; if the horses raced home as they had come, I should only be springing, as it were, out of this bed into my own. Obediently a horse backed away from the window; I threw my bundle into the gig; the fur coat missed its mark and was caught on a hook only by the sleeve. Good enough. I swung myself on the horse. With the reins loosely trailing, one horse barely fastened to the other, the gig swaying behind, my fur coat last of all in the snow. "Geeup!" I said, but there was no galloping; slowly, like old men, we crawled through the snowy wastes; a long time echoed behind us the new but faulty song of the children:

O be joyful, all you patients,
The doctor's laid in bed beside you!

Never shall I reach home at this rate; my flourishing practice is done for; my successor is robbing me, but in vain, for he cannot take my place; in my house the disgusting groom is raging; Rose is his victim; I do not want to think about it any more. Naked, exposed to the frost of this most unhappy of ages, with an earthly vehicle, unearthly horses, old man that I am, I wander astray. My fur coat is hanging from the back of the gig, but I cannot reach it, and none of my limber pack of patients lifts a finger. Betrayed! Betrayed! A false alarm on the night bell once answered—it cannot be made good, not ever.

THE BUS THAT HAD NO SIGN
hilde abel

*"At dusk, too, Berlin experiences a mad rush on all its transit
lines. . . . None of the passengers knows where the bus goes, for
it carries no route sign, but they figure it will take them some distance
along the way they want to go."*—From an article in the New York
Times, January 30, 1944.

His feet slipped, stuck, and pulled out of the lava that had not quite
cooled in this city without volcanoes, mountains or tropical vegetation.

Painfully he toiled over the fallen linden columns of this triumphal way, painfully he hacked his path through last night's under-
brush of splintered branches, from which now, in March, buds had
begun to tip, tiny and hard as a child's unsprouted nipples. He
skirted a toilet bowl, white and hard and smoothly polished, that
they had used, once, to keep behind a door, in private. He climbed a
marble staircase, stepping over a toupee, an alarm clock that ticked,
a glove that had no hand in it, an exquisite antique fragment of
forehead out of which grew, like a flower, the Semitic-influenced
nose that terminated in a spiked mustache, stepping over a rat that
could only have caught it from the concussion, for it had let escape

not one drop of blood but lay quite still and peaceful and cozy on its side, like a snoozing pussy cat.

He was about to make his way down the other side of the marble staircase, when, just in time, he observed that the other side was the perpendicular, customarily cemented up against a wall.

He withdrew his foot from air to the pedestal of the top step. Well, well, he thought . . . Well, well, we have hurried time. In one single blow we have achieved the beautiful uselessness of antique junk, the patinaed mutilation of time's castration complex. From this vantage point, he observed that the futility ahead still preserved some aspect of an avenue, in much the same way as did a canal on Mars, or a defile through the stony mountains of the moon.

Who's to get the credit for this speed-up?

A cold stillness fell upon him and held frozen his tic, that jovial winking of his eye and that jolly lift of the left corner of his mouth, in a smile. Did *he* get the credit? Well, well . . . Delusions of grandeur. . . . Dementia praecox. . . . A simple, ordinary run-of-the-mill citizen, Mr. See-no-evil, Hear-no-evil, Speak-no-evil. . . .

Relief that he could not possibly have any connection with bringing about all this dusty antique grandeur, released his frozen tic, and up it started again, rhythmic as a heartbeat.

But already the dusk was marching and soon the evening sparrows would rise up out of that western sky, in which the sun—when there was sun in these cool, gray, Prussian winters—sank so quickly, leaving the field clear to the birds. . . . He came down the marble stairway, double time.

On either side of his Martian canal the dusk marched into edifices that rose above the mountain ranges of rubble and were without windows and even without walls, but preserved the fine, strong, twentieth-century skeleton of steel. The dusk, a lumpy and gray army of occupation, was quite satisfactorily bivouacked in place of the Portrait, the walls, floors, washbasins, desks, filing cabinets, wastebaskets, paper clips, and civil servants that had B.B. (Before Blockbusters) been enclosed there, cozily tucked out of sight behind bricks.

But, with it, dusk brought a new component—silence.

As he walked, his ears grew long as a donkey's with listening.

He had, at an earlier period of his life, listened with the same intensity, and in a scenery not unlike this, of lava, craters, trenches, and bits of anatomy, to the silent downward floating of the olive branch, gentle and noiseless as a feather wafted downward by a white dove in its flight. And what had he got for his troubles?

Merely, he had just about jumped out of his skin when, after the moment of silence, the noise had suddenly started up again—bawling commands: "Eyes right! . . . Eyes left! . . . Eyes left! . . . Eyes right!"; running feet; stones smacking steel helmets; and the reply, military and boogie-woogie—*bang* bang bang *bang* bang *bang*. So he had learned his lesson and now he did not trust silence any longer. (Soon the evening birds would wheel out of the western sky.) The noise had gone on for quite a time and then, without warning, silence had clapped like thunder.

The new silence had begun so innocently. He had simply been sitting in a café with a friend—having just stopped by at a Tabak Regie for one of those outspoken newspapers—well, there he was, just sitting and chatting with his friend over a nice cup of coffee and whipped cream, when some poorly dressed lads turned the street of this rather fashionable quarter and began building a bonfire on the corner. *"Excuse* me," his friend had said, rising and going over to the corner. Heinz had continued chatting with the waiter, a pleasant and intelligent fellow, who had been holding forth on Nudism or Vegetarianism or Socialism—Heinz couldn't remember any more—anyway, one of those panaceas for the betterment of mankind, and then he had heard a bawling voice that had quite interfered with their amiable exchange of opinion on Vegetarianism or Socialism or whatever, since neither he nor the waiter could hear each other. He had turned his head to see what all the fuss was, and there on the corner, that little comedian, whachamacall him, Charlie Chaplin, was making a speech in front of the bonfire, and on the edge of the crowd, he could just glimpse his friend, quite red with cheering. Since then there had been silence. The citizenry had been handed over to the board of stockholders, See-no-evil, Hear-no-evil, Speak-no-evil. But Heinz had learned that there was no such thing as nothing. Nature abhorred a vacuum. The absence of speech was the presence of the recoil of the aorta, the writhing ebb and flow of the lungs, the shuddering of the gray convolutions in the brain.

Boomps! Down he went in a great clatter of masonry, ashes, bricks and powdered stone. Up he came, white with dust, and sneezing, and clutching in his hand, the spar that he had grasped at in his drowning. An arm! Well, he thought, well, well, everything is all right again because any moment now he was bound to wake up.

The arm proved to be of a remarkable smoothness and hardness, not really lifelike as They had advertised. Turning it over, Heinz saw that where it had been attached to a man, there were a few rusty stains. Presumably, by one of those little ironies of existence, the man had been blown away and the arm left to continue its self-contained, intense, inanimate life. . . .

Now, what was the inner meaning of this dream? Here he was, privileged to wander through the dream life, the free association of the twentieth century—a toupee, a clock, a glove, a Hellenic fragment, an arm, a rat, a staircase that led nowhere—and he was quite lost as to the meaning of all this rich symbolism.

"Hände hoch!"

Up went his hands. Down went the arm, falling in a rigid embrace across his feet.

"Pillaging is *verboten!*"

"Excuse, *Herr Polizeimann* . . . I wished only to report an arm to the Missing Persons Bureau."

The policeman wrote down his name and address.

"In this case, you understand, there can be no reward. . . . It is a patriotic duty to assemble the members, so that on Judgment Day, each citizen will rise up whole and perfect, a tribute to the regime."

"Naturally, Your Honor . . . I hope the poor chap gets together all right. . . . So difficult to identify an arm. . . . So impersonal. . . . Especially this mass-production kind . . ."

"That's enough! Beat it!"

Heinz went on, thinking how easily he had put one over on established authority, since he had no interest in Judgment Day, but had only intended to use the lifelike pink arm as a staff in his mountain-climbing.

Now and then he stepped over those who had preferred to lie face down, clutching the oddest assortment, rather than relinquish these treasures. One, a hammer and sickle, pilfered probably—to what conceivable purpose?—from some exploded hardware shop; another, a tin cup and a black eye-patch, stolen, no doubt, with a view to a probable profession after The Victory.

He felt only contempt for these bundles of rags with their curious pilferings, when he thought of all the *really* prize possessions, the *really* ripe plums that he had let fall from *his* hands, without once thinking to fall with them. Well, like the outspoken newspaper—that day in the café!—that had a really first-class gossip column—who shopped where, and for what; who banked where, and why; who traveled to which renowned resort, and with whom and on what train. . . . And what had he done unlike these foolish wretches? Industriously spent hours in the café toilet, tearing up the outspoken newspaper into tiny fragments that would flush easily. . . .

He could not remember when, but at some point he must have turned off the triumphal way of fallen lindens. He reasoned that he must now be under an umbrella, from whose ribs the silk had been ripped away, so that the gray sky poured down through the naked spans, for there was absolutely no evidence to support the theory that the tipped meeting overhead of the marvelous twentieth-century steel structures ever had been opposite sides of a street.

Through the gray and Gothic arch of dusk, formed by the umbrella's foremost ribs, he made out a formidable-sized company gathering, and he noticed then, for the first time, and with great astonishment, that he was not alone, but that myriad silent gray shadows were streaming along beside him in the dusk.

It was the strange character of this time of nightly emanations that you always supposed you were alone, and then the scene slowly opened out, from a close-up to a mob-shot. Thus, in the shelter last night, when the final mischievous firecracker had gone off, each one of which, he had been certain, as it burst, was engraved with his name on its fuse, Heinz had made the discovery that there were others in the shelter with him, quite a few in fact, each one of whom had presumably been alone until their camera-eye had opened up to include Heinz in the background of their personal mob scenes. Thus were all destinies, nowadays, like pictures upon a screen, dissolving, fading out, pandissolving again.

Well now, what was up out there beyond the security and protection of the naked umbrella? He broke into a run, and beside him the silent shadows began to run too, but he kept pretty well ahead. Indeed, he kept so well ahead that suddenly everything seemed to change and all the silent, swarming feet were pursuing him. . . . He opened his mouth but no scream came.

Then, before him, he made out an oblong shape of transportation, whose surfaces, he could just see in the last dusk, were painted to represent rubble, a clock, an Hellenic fragment, an arm, a rat, a staircase that led nowhere.

The homeward-bound bus, camouflaged! And he had simply stumbled on it. What a bit of luck!

There were no longer any prearranged starting points, for so many starting points had been simply eliminated. This element of accident was indeed most propitious for the regime, which recognized the tactlessness in gathering a formidable mass on the same corner every evening, which might, in time, come to look forward to that routine assemblage, and out of this innocent waiting for the more-or-less homeward-bound bus, the mass might easily become the masses. Thus did the two ostensible enemies—the hawks in the air, the hound-dogs on the ground—work with one another, ironically enough.

Actually, no one—not even the driver—knew just where the bus was headed, for a series of unavoidable detours might land it possibly in the Wilhelmstrasse, or the Tiergarten, or the Alexanderplatz. For this reason, the busses carried no route signs; one hoped merely that they would take one some distance along the way one wanted to go. Hope springs eternal in the human breast. Cut off the breast and it's still just as likely to reappear in the anus.

The regime, at this home-going moment, ringed the masses with steel from all the fine vantage points of ruin and futility, for with scientific fervor, it could detect and diagnose the ailment—is it not possible to hope that things might just possibly be the least bit, not better of course, that is impossible, but different—long before the infected masses had become aware that there was a tiny lump, the size of a pinhead, just below the left nipple.

The bus was already full to bursting, yet the gray shadows were still swarming, like great gray rat-shapes into their trap, pouring through the windows, streaming up the steps, swinging onto the roof, and crowding upon the bumpers.

Heinz leaped into the midst of the silent turbulent stream. He punched, he bit, he scratched, he knocked heads together and heard them split. He lost his brief case, his derby was smashed, a front tooth was knocked out, his nose was bloody, but, "Hoop-la, *wir leben!*" he screamed in this drunken ecstasy of at last making himself felt, of murdering flesh not unlike his own, as soft and vulnerable.

His eye wandered a moment, seeking a really worthy opponent, and swept the regime that was posted on the commanding heights of ruin. The regime, with its machine guns, tear gas, carbines, howitzers, et cetera, was an opponent really worthy of his hands that were knotted and swollen with power, but before the thought had more than knocked at his mind, it was gone again. He saw that the entire mass had broken up into small and personal maelstroms, from which erupted whoops of savage joy, grunts of impassioned struggle, sweat, blood and tears—a fact on which the machine guns that ringed the scene, at alert, had counted in providing this divertissement, this going-to-Jerusalem bus, that had not enough place for all the would-be wayfarers.

All had forgotten the homeward-bound bus, and with what might be called typical Asiatic cunning, Heinz took this opportunity to chin himself up through the window into the bus.

As he crouched a moment in the window, he knew all of a sudden, that he did not want to get into this bus that carried no sign, whose itinerary was unknown, and whose destination. He could not go back, and he could not go forward. . . . Then the chill hand of the one who, he somehow knew, waited again at the end of the journey, released his red-frozen heart and pushed him. . . . He opened his mouth and an alien scream rent his brain. . . . It was not the floor on which he had landed but the swollen bunions of an old woman. . . . He waited for her cries to awaken him, but nothing happened—nothing changed. . . .

Well, well . . . In that case, it was necessary to go on with the journey.

The driver made the gear shifts. Being in his immediate vicinity, Heinz could glimpse a fragment of the fellow's face, tilted down at him, from the rear-view mirror. Whether or not he felt comfortable in being driven by this fragment, Heinz could not quite determine. He could see the end of the nose, bulbous and pugged; the thin, tight, secretive mouth; and the unamiable, stubborn line of the jaw, whose termination was cut off by the ending of the mirror. It was, in short, the face of a young proletarian, to whom the poets of the second Reich had written such paeans that the prophets of the third Reich had rattled chains.

Heinz wondered why a young fellow who seemed perfectly sound should have been shipped back from the Front to run a bus. It must be something that did not show. For instance, his eardrums might have been punctured by the concussion. (There was, of course, plenty of concussion on the Home Front too these days.) Or he might have been deafened. That old banality, "The deaf hear only what's not intended for them," took on new meaning. If one said, for example, "What a charming bus ride!" the driver would be sure not to hear. But if one said "The bus seems to be a little overcrowded," he would of course hear an innocent statement of fact—and possibly construe it as a criticism of the regime. A citizen who heard only what was not intended for him could indeed be very useful to established authority. On the other hand, he might carry over this quality to his relationship with the company that employed him, and being quite deaf to what "they" told him, might go off entirely on his own in an equal and opposite direction. In short, he was an uncertain quantity and might prove to be rather a mixed blessing to his bosses.

Heinz's philosophical ruminations were cut off abruptly by the sound of the bus starting.

With the roar of the motor, shrieks of despair rose from those outside who had not been able to find place, while within the bus a great huzzah rose from the passengers—"Hooray! Hooray! We're off!" Heinz joined his cheer with theirs, but before it passed his lips, a strange transformation occurred that he was powerless to prevent and out came his cheer as a little burp—"*Where?*" He was overcome by embarrassment, the embarrassment of being thrown in the clink. However, the noise of his anxiety and his stomach went unnoticed, such was the general conviviality of joy and enthusiasm and innocent merriment that swept the wayfarers, who, after the long night in the shelters without sleep or food or hope, and the equally long day in the offices without hope or food, were off now, no one knew where, but at last under way, on the move, on the march, on the make. "Hooray! Hooray! We're off!" Burp!—*"Where?"*

"The driver will thank the cheering section to shut up," the rough, tough proletarian voice said. "Let them try driving a bus through all this dust and ashes. Wherever this bus might be going, it's not there yet by a long shot."

Heinz found that what might have been an alarming and sinister manifestation of opinion by the driver, was rendered negligible by this curious, this offhand and detached way of referring to himself in the third person, which made him seem not actually to exist. Indeed, one often came to think of the proletariat in such terms. The driver of a bus was merely the motor. A waiter was merely a tray burgeoning with wiener schnitzel, and so on. And then, sometimes, something suddenly happened and there they stood before you, about to spring the trap of the guillotine in which your neck was stuck. However, at the moment, there could be no question of the guillotine, and Heinz, quite at ease now that his sudden seizure of burps had passed, surveyed his fellow-travelers with that customary contempt which one wayfarer reserves for another at the beginning of a journey—and is merely the product of fear or shyness —until alliances have been made and friendships formed.

The wayfarers were all either aged civil servants or females or returned heroes. One of the heroes, hanging from the same strap as Heinz, had a rather arresting face. What had once, from certain lingering evidence, been blond Aryan features had been transformed into the racial forms of a Chinese face, with perfectly flat contours, through the agency of something having passed over it— a tank perhaps. But since the hero's eyes had been cooked white as hard-boiled eggs (after they are peeled) his appearance could not have affected his self-love much one way or the other, for he could not perceive the expressions, as they glanced at him, of those for whom he had died. And that, after all, was the main thing and irrefutable proof of the existence of the mercy of God.

Far off, beyond hope of touch or contact or of any meeting, far away at the other end of the bus, Heinz perceived a wonderful face, the woman for whom one longs. And, as in dreams one is prevented from the consummation of one's longings, so now was he kept from her by the thousand sweating, swaying destinies that intervened. . . . He began to sense a certain melancholy charm in this unknown journey. It would be, he saw, not unlike one of those ocean voyages, over which hovers the constant presence of the unknown one, for whose sake one would throw oneself into the white, churning wake, yet to whom one never speaks, simply and tragically because each moves always within the respective cordons of those whose deck chairs are propinquant. But now and then the eyes may meet, and one would know that, to the last heartbeat, each would remember those glances and those unspoken vows. . . . So now, the eyes of the lovely, dark, mysterious one were on Heinz. . . . The woman for whom one longs. . . . A melancholy smile parted his well-chiseled lips, touched his eyes, still clear as a child's, and burning (in his youth women had simply made fools of themselves over him) and automatically his hand lifted to his smashed brown derby in a gesture—a salutation of abnegation and of dedication. . . .

The bus swayed and jolted him against the uncushioned fanny of one of those new, modern girls. . . . He returned from the far-off horizon, the unglimpsed shore of coconut and coral. . . . Ah well, ah well—that was all behind. You marry the right woman or the wrong, in the end it makes no difference, you grow portly and somehow everything seems to turn out more or less satisfactorily. No doubt the bus ride would too. Certainly it never pays to make a fuss. The driver wasn't going to make known his destination just to please Heinz.

"Wherever this bus might be going, it's not there yet by a long shot," Heinz merrily repeated the driver's words. "Well, well! Ha! Ha! Just as if you didn't know where you're taking us. Ha! Ha! That's pretty good!"

"Shut up!" the driver said surlily. "The driver never said that!"

"Well, I could have sworn that you—" Heinz mumbled, discomfited.

"Shut up! . . . Did the guy in the smashed brown derby ever hear the one about the Flying Dutchman and the Wandering Jew?"

"I have heard the one about the Flying Dutchman," Heinz said elliptically, sensing some danger in confessing a recollection of that other now-mythical creature, the Jew.

Seeking solace in the glance of the marvelous woman, Heinz all at once recognized her. The woman for whom one longs, his first-grade teacher, so many years ago. . . . That had been his one absolutely pure love—and then he suddenly remembered the drawing he had made of her and himself—but he remembered that he had torn it up before he had locked his desk in the schoolroom, yesterday.

He knew now, beyond a doubt, that he was in his old school bus, drawn by a fine spanking team of horses, and all at once he knew that he had left the drawing in his desk and he must get off, and run ahead and tear it up before the bus and the teacher and all the other children got into the school yard, but—my God! my God!—he couldn't get off. Had he torn it up or hadn't he? Had he or hadn't he? But of one thing he was sure—he was in terrible trouble and his pants were all of a sudden wet, and his cheeks began to turn green. Somehow or other, all his little schoolmates, not wishing to be spattered with his fear, made room for him, although the kiddies in this old school conveyance were wedged one upon another, just as on one of those box-car excursions to the land of Chopin and Paderewski. . . . All the little kiddies made room for him, until he was right beside the window, his nose flattened against the cold glass; and Heinz began telling himself, as he did every morning when he hadn't prepared his lessons, "This old bus isn't going to the old school; it's going to turn off just at the bottom of the hill and go on to the beer garden, and everything's going to turn out jolly."

But when he noticed the things outside the window he knew this was not the old school bus. *What bus was this?*

At some time they must have left the earth, but he could not remember when. An exclamation of surprise must have been torn from his lips.

"The guy in the brown derby," said the driver in response to Heinz's exclamation, "thinks we've gone clear off the track!"

"Is this really still the earth? . . . But I do not see," Heinz said, not unreasonably, "just what you go by."

The driver spat on the floor and then carefully rubbed the spittle out with his foot. "The guy in the smashed brown derby," he said surlily, "don't seem to be aware that some folks, including His Excellency the driver, have been looking out of windows—tenement windows, or whatever they called them in the old days, factory windows, prison windows—and seen the same, or worse, for five thousand years—Hell on earth!"

"Excuse me," Heinz said hastily. "Excuse me, but I don't think I quite caught your last remark."

And he stopped his ears with his fingers, Mr. Hear-no-evil. Hell on earth! Indeed! . . . Everyone knew they were everywhere these days, provoking and spying out, but to have one actually driving the homeward-bound bus! . . . Well! Well! . . .

He turned away, shuddering, from the young proletarian who had really found himself a fine spot for carrying on his particular department of culture. Why, how simple it was!—Any moment, he could just drive up to the nearest police station—Dear me, dear me, such things don't happen. . . .

Heinz peered out of the window again but it was impossible to ascertain whether any of this dusty havoc were a police station. As he looked, his anxiety vanished in an all-pervasive wonder. Who was the genius whose dream had so transformed the *gemütliche* earth that one simply could not recognize it? . . . Presumably, he wandered in someone else's dream, which was of itself a strange enough phenomenon. It just was not possible that all this free association of the sleep of the twentieth century could have been brewed up by his own brain. For he now recognized—now that he was middle-aged and settled in his little niche, now that the overwhelming orgasm of youth had long ago gushed forth—he recognized that he lacked entirely that vast, creative imagination, that scope and grandeur and boldness that could stem only from God or Michelangelo. Ergo, he wandered in someone else's dream or—and here the little hairs stood up stiff on the back of his neck —this was not a dream at all.

That was what was so horribly confusing. The very last circumstance that he could distinctly and coherently recall, before this grotesquerie, this dream, or whatever it was, had started, was his tearing off his filthy uniform and flinging himself down to sleep, a young discharged soldier, on his mother's bed. It was after that this whole confusing business had started—an abdication, a Republic, an afternoon in a café with his friend and the waiter, and the lads building a bonfire. Until now, years and scenes later, he found himself on a bus that had no sign. What was the significance of all this?

He could even distinctly recall the very last things he had done before he lay down on his mother's bed. . . . He had jumped from the steps of the troop-train before it had completely come to a stop. And he had jumped right down into all the noise that had somehow started up again, after the silence of the drifting white wings. He had trudged home, and those whom he knew had not greeted him but had looked away with white and weary faces. His mother had not been able to give him anything to eat when he had finally reached their little house, and he had thought he would just lie down and doze until the shops opened again.

No wonder that he was anxious to know whether all that followed had been a dream or not. For supposing he suddenly woke and must start all over again from that point—a young man with an honorable discharge, lying on a lumpy bed, hungry, penniless, and without a profession. Often during the night of the long dream, he had experienced unpleasant and distressing sensations, due probably to hunger and the fact that there was only one very thin blanket on the bed, against the cold. Yes, that no doubt accounted for some of the unpleasant and even gruesome aspects. Yet, despite all these discomforts, he could not say that he exactly looked forward to waking up (were this all a figment of someone's imagination), having had a preview, as it were, of the coming attraction.

Though actually, the unreeling of the reality of the years was sure to be quite different from all this Hollywood *kitsch* of blond heroes and dark villains. He remembered distinctly, in all that mangle of noise that he had stepped into, off the train, one cry, "Never again war!" that alone brought a certain balm to this odd situation and almost recompensed him for the fact that, any minute, the main feature might be due to come on again and he might have to wake up and be young again.

Heinz looked away from the window, from that stupendous creation of inanity and dust outside, and he found with a start, that the eyes of the returned hero were peering directly into his; whether with hostile or friendly intent was impossible to ascertain, since all expression had at one and the same time been plucked out of his eyes, together with sight and the iris.

For no apparent reason, the returned hero had, somehow, at some time also made his way from the aisle between the seats in the center of the throng, where he had been standing with Heinz, to the window, out of which he certainly could not see. Indeed, he could not see Heinz either. Naturally, Heinz began to wonder if he were being followed and why, and this induced in him quite a feeling of persecution.

Nevertheless, looking at that rather unusual face, Heinz could not help but speculate: out of what rancorous revenge motif had the dreamer transformed the returned hero into a non-Aryan Chinee, from a flaxen-haired, blue-eyed child in Saxony, gathering a bouquet of cornflowers for his mother?

In exalted fear-and-pity that quite banished his terror of the returned hero's persecution of him, Heinz grasped the arm of the poor chap to tell him, "Never mind! This can't go on much longer. Someone will scream us awake out of this genius' stupendous and colossal night-blooming life, and you'll simply vanish with your poor flat Chinee face and your white absent eyes."

Heinz was about to confide all this, but grasping the hero's arm, he felt it hard, smooth, and unyielding. He grasped the other arm. The same. My! My! . . . What about the legs? . . . Goodness gracious! Ersatz also! . . . Well! Well! . . . A twentieth century centaur, half man, half doll. The age of T.N.T. is not without its own mythology.

"Hey—move over! Give me a piece of the strap, too," a young, coarse voice shouted.

"Certainly," he said, glancing at her without interest.

But even as he glanced he felt some slight stiffening of interest. She was of his immediate little group, one of those new modern *Mädchen* with blond eyelashes who had been prone to Sunday parades, arm uplifted, head crowned in cornflowers, and round, thick legs, untapering from thigh to ankle, like a gingerbread man's, dangling out from a boy's white shorts. She had one of those faces that would look just fine served up on a Sunday table with an apple in its mouth. The stories that went around about such girls stiffened his interest.

But at that interesting moment an irresistible urge called his glance upward, and he saw, far off, the face of the woman for whom one longs. Shabby and unfashionable, the deep serenity, the calm, that entwined her like garlands of lilies, with the affected and outmoded coquetry of a past century.

Now sadness veiled her eyes, as they rested for an eternal moment on his. How far the separation! how wide!—and beside him, the modern girl-boy-pig, against whose legs his own legs rubbed. For a man must, of necessity, choose what is at hand, the sexual squirt being unable to surmount distance.

"Come on, big-hearted, move over!" The modern *Mädchen* closed her muscular hand over Heinz's strap.

"Give me the low-down on her," the returned hero said.

"My son-in-law was on the Eastern Front, too," Heinz said, pursuing his own line of thought.

"Give me the low-down on her eyes, hair, lips, knockers, hips. Describe them."

"She has the usual flaxen hair, blue eyes, lips, knockers—as you put it—hips, and blond eyelashes." Heinz paused a moment, then he went on, "It seems to me—" He broke off, wondering whether what he had been about to say was, after all, in the best of taste.

"It seems to you—" the returned hero said eagerly, and the expression of hope that blossomed upon his rather unusual face reminded Heinz of a buttercup that he had seen growing up through the snub nose of a skull on the Western Front, in *his* day, and which he had bent down and plucked out in much the same way that one wipes the nose of a baby who can't help itself. Or perhaps he hadn't plucked it out? Had he, perhaps, merely intended to return later, during the retreat, and come to the aid of his suffering comrade?

"It seems to me," Heinz said hastily, "that she has the usual fixtures and plumbing."

What he had really been about to say was, It seems to me that they could keep using you chaps on the Eastern Front. A plane isn't scrapped just because it loses a wing, is it? And since I understand that, beneath your undershirt, a series of straps over the real chest and back and real muscles thereof, and connected to the unreal upper arm, somehow manipulates the hook which substitutes for a hand, and communicates to it the motions of life, it seems to me that this same hook could be brought to again manipulate a rifle as well as a pork chop.

"I have the usual fixtures also," the returned hero said. "Unlike many of my comrades, I managed to bring them back with me, out of the Eastern Front. Concealing them on my person, so to speak. A first-class case of smuggling, so to speak."

There was a burst of cackles and giggles from the aged civil servants and females, and the young girls around, and the returned hero was immediately snapped up as the humorist of the crowd.

"A curious accident befell my son-in-law also," Heinz said. "He was separated rather severely from both his arms."

"It beats everything," the returned hero said, "how all the young fellows my age get into these accidents nowadays. A young fellow, nowadays, can't go for a little walk across a field without being run over by a tank, and if he takes a little *Kraft durch Freude* jaunt through the clouds, he's just as likely as not to come down in lumps of fertilizer on some little foreign farm." He shrugged. "They say when gunpowder first came in, guys were always blowing off fingers and noses too. I guess it's all just a matter of getting used to modern inventions."

His voice withered with lack of interest. He had, Heinz observed, the same curious apathy that had so strongly contributed to Heinz's own weariness that time just before he had flung himself down on his mother's bed and slept. . . . You butchered many muzhiks for the sake of aged civil servants, females, and boy-girls, such as are in this bus, and in turn you were butchered. The historic evaluation of these exchanges, which canceled each other out, was indeed difficult to arrive at, just as it had been difficult for Heinz in *his* day.

"Yes indeed," Heinz said tolerantly, "each generation has its own accidents."

Then the possibly critical significance of his own words struck him, and he began again, in an attempt to turn the conversation into new channels, "My son-in-law was, as you put it, just strolling across a field when—" No. . . . No. . . .That certainly wasn't any better. . . . And throwing to the winds all cautions of an inherent good taste and a certain innate refinement, he blurted out, "I mean I could not help but wonder on their wedding night. . . ." There— that was better. Everyone was interested in wedding nights. "My daughter was betrothed but did not actually *marry* the young man until his return *after* this unfortunate accident. . . . Almost as though—I mean it would almost seem like an unconscious act of expiation for a healthy young girl to—Some atonement-compulsion, or guilt. . . . Like continually washing the hands, or touching every other lamppost, or—Or don't you think so? . . . But of course you don't. . . . Of course not."

His tic was working in good time now. His eye gave that jolly wink and the corner of his mouth rose in that jolly smile.

"I am afraid," he said, "I am afraid I am expressing myself very badly, my dear young friend."

There was no answer. Two large tears formed themselves, crystalline-clear and perfect, in each of the two empty eyes and rolled like ribbons down the flat cheeks. All these young fellows with accidents weep rather freely, Heinz thought. . . . He could remember the evening when his then future son-in-law returned. . . . There had been a knock on the door. The spoons of cherry soup had remained frozen halfway to their lips. Then his daughter had risen from the table and moved toward the door, and in that moment his wife's eyes and his had crossed in a terrible burning intimacy, and their glance had unwound between them like a movie reel, the first placing of the girl at her mother's breast after birth, her first clumsy step, her first word, "Da-da," and all leading up to, and culminating in this, "What can she have informed about us? . . . What? . . . Informed about what?"

There had been one escape, the window, seven stories up.

But when his daughter had at last opened the door, the shadows of the hallway had parted like a curtain to reveal only the future son-in-law, who stood with his sleeves hanging stiffly at his sides as though empty. That was the curious thing, how empty they had seemed, though actually they had been well filled with ersatz. . . . The boy had simply stood there, not raising the sleeves to his betrothed, and slowly his eyes had filled with tears.

"Their bedroom is next to ours," Heinz went on, impelled into this intimacy with the returned hero, not through lack of delicacy, but rather because of it. Between them was that same tender brotherhood of apathy which can be observed in cows driven side by side in a farmer's cart to the stockyard, neither in its numbness touching the other by so much as a flick of the tail, yet both bound indissolubly by the invisible yoke of the looming butcher. . . . Heinz's Western Front—the hero's Eastern Front. Separated by twenty-odd years—or perhaps only a long dream. . . . The old comradeship remained. Yoked by the butcher.

"Their bedroom, as I say, is next to ours," Heinz went on, "and naturally I could not help but speculate what it was like, on one's wedding-night, to be embraced by bisque arms, and caressed by black-gloved hands. (My son-in-law always wore gloves at first.) Pajamas—and black gloves . . . Well! Well! . . . Piquant! Highly! . . ."

"Well, and what did she say the next morning?" the Rhine maiden, the girl-boy-pig, asked in her coarse voice, which was really quite exciting. "After all, maybe it was the first time for her—" She winked at the returned hero "—with gloves."

Unfortunately, her racy and provocative wink was lost on the white eyes of the hero, who was turned in utter fascination to Heinz, as a flower to the sun. "What did the bitch say the next morning?" he asked.

"I am not accustomed to hearing my daughter spoken of in such terms," Heinz said, and even to himself, he sounded a bit stuffy as he recalled the girls, cheering and blowing kisses and decking the erect bayonets with garlands of flowers that time when *he* had joined the parade. . . . His tic was driving his muscles very fast now, and the Rhine maiden returned his jolly wink.

"Come on now, you old pearl diver," she said. "No more giggling and winking and smut. Out with it! What did she have to say for herself the next morning?"

"The next morning," Heinz said, "she had gone off to the factory before either my wife or myself had awakened. She is patriotically employed in a factory whose products render ersatz arms necessary for the bridegrooms of enemy young girls."

"I am even more patriotic," said the Rhine maiden. "Where I work, we make a secret weapon to sterilize all enemy women. It's *verboten* to talk about. But I can tell you that we simply knock together something that kills all the enemy men."

"As for my son-in-law," Heinz went on, "he kept to his room for several days. We left his meals outside the door and my daughter was forced to sleep in the parlor. But after a few days, whatever false sense of shame or inadequacy discomfited him, vanished and he now mopes quite contentedly about the house in an old dressing gown of mine, of which we have had to lengthen the sleeves. . . . When my wife finally was able to enter the nuptial chamber and clean it up, she discovered smashed pink fragments under the bed. Somehow or other, my son-in-law had carelessly dropped one hand."

"That's our dress hand," the returned hero said. "They tell me it's real nice-looking but it's just for show. When a guy really has some work to do, he has to slip it off and put on the claw—or hook—instead. . . . I suppose your son-in-law just laid his hand on the bureau or somewhere and it got pushed off in the scuffle."

"I suppose so," Heinz said. "My son-in-law somehow never got around to replacing the dress hand, but with the claw—or hook—he's really very skillful, I must say. He can smoke a cigarette, fry a chop, and—and—perform—"

"And perform all his duties as a husband?" the rough, tough voice of the driver, to whom nothing was sacred, broke in. "How does she like the guy clawing her? Ha! Ha! Ha!"

Heinz did not like this at all. He could see reflected in the rearview mirror a fragment of the driver's face, the nose, the upper lip, a part of the jaw. The fragment of face wore the menacing stupidity of a pig, but beneath the piggy pinkness was the color of clay, sullen and lowering.

"So you have a hand for courting and a hook for work?" the Rhine maiden said to the hero.

"Not unlike other men," the hero said wittily.

This commonplace, this matter-of-fact exchange of pleasantries, brought Heinz back from the shadow of uneasiness. . . . He could not but applaud the wisdom of the regime, when it advised that one should treat all these young fellows who had undergone unfortunate accidents, exactly like anyone else, casually, cavalierly, and cheerfully. After all, a hand is a hand, whether of flesh or bisque.

Phidias and other sculptors throughout the centuries have molded hands of marble, bronze, gold—and does anyone shudder? Certainly not!

"Sure he has a hook," the driver said. "Even the cross is hooked these days. . . . And especially the double cross. Ha! Ha! Ha!"

No one joined in his mirth.

"Ha! Ha! Ha! We've all been decorated with the double cross."

The sweat poured down Heinz's back. He no longer was sure whether or not he had heard those incredible words. Who, alone, would dare to speak such words? Who laid the trap and the snare? In the silence, he heard his trapped heart beating against the bars of his ribs, and at last he heard his voice, shrill and glib, seeking to break this unendurable silence, saying to the hero the first thing that came into his head, "I, too, had an accident once. Twenty-six years ago."

O God, what had he said? Might it not sound to him who brought this bus through unknown journeyings, who said dreadful and provocative things, who was not what he seemed, and who seemed what he was not—might it not sound like some despairing criticism? . . . Of what? . . . Of whom? . . .

Now, even as Heinz watched, the blue lightbulb above the mirror joggled and the pig's snout seemed to lengthen out and become long and pointed. The whole face darkened as the pinkness receded beneath the clay color, and the short squat teeth became long fangs. Before Heinz's eyes the pig became a wolf.

"You too?" the returned hero said to Heinz; and a mask of indifference replaced the mask of private sorrow.

O God, Almighty God, Heinz prayed. . . . Now everything was changing. Now nothing was any longer as it had been only a moment before, jolly and commonplace. . . . Now again the wolf-face was changing into a squat snout, but beneath the bright pink hue, the darkness of the wolf still lingered. The swift, the keen, the fierce, the predatory, beneath the pink and stolid brutishness.

His eyes beat about the bus, seeking escape, seeking flight, and they came to rest upon the dark and wonderful face. She for whom one longs. . . . And the remote peace of some remote sorrow flowed into him like a vast slow benediction.

"You too?" the returned hero repeated, with a peevish and bitter indifference.

"Yes," Heinz said, tearing his eyes from the wonderful, far-off face, "a rather curious accident befell me once. I have a silver stomach."

"So what?" the Rhine maiden said. "At least, it's nothing that shows."

Yes, Heinz thought, the accident of the returned hero, twenty-six years after mine, shows. Thus do the times grow steadily worse! My God! What had he thought! He glanced around in hasty terror to see whether anyone, the maiden, the hero, the wolf-pig—all men are enemies, all—had heard his unuttered thoughts, seeking with a passionate conviction to repudiate them. In every moment of crisis, his accursed mind betrayed him, and he hated and feared it like a tooth that is almost dead but continues in the death throes to throb and torment, and that one cannot let alone but must continue to seek out with the tongue, and inflame. Was there perhaps some brain-dentist, who could pluck out the last little bit of mind that remained alive and aching? But vaster than all other fears, there loomed the ultimate fear of the dentist.

"I had a couple bad accidents too," the driver said, and as he spoke his mask changed from sullen anger to fierce bitterness. "One time in Paris in that goddam cemetery—what's its name—La—La—Lachaise, that's it. I was killed there against that wall—whachamacall it. . . . Blood and brains and guts splashed out against that wall . . . Mur . . . Mur des Fédérées, that's it. . . . Cockeyed foreign name. . . . Had another bad accident not long ago in Spain. . . . Got buried alive. . . . Never collected any accident insurance either. I've been putting in claims and fighting the companies every time I dig myself up. Now I'll have to file claim again one of these days. . . . New company's been underwriting me lately. Papers signed and stamped with the double cross. How many times does a guy have to be killed before he collects?"

In the terrible silence that had fallen upon the bus, his voice boomed out like thunder.

Heinz's tic began to pass across his face like a windshield wiper across the window of an automobile, cleaning his face, with each revolution, of the spasmodic twitch of nerve. Others in the bus had begun to take note of the sinister phenomenon, and already there was a split between the wayfarers. Those of the Right Wing maintained that this smile and wink were merely the jovial and friendly emanations from a kindly and pleasant nature, casting a rubicund glow over his words. Whereas, the Left Wing maintained that his words themselves were of no importance; it was rather this bitter jeer or sneer, pointing up the words and giving them an exactly opposite meaning, that was to be reckoned with, and that alone made his words so sinister, a provocation and a trap.

A low and ominous murmur swept the bus, and Heinz felt himself infected anew by this atmosphere of terror and suspicion, of which, all-unknowing, he was himself the Typhoid Mary. . . . He knew now that this dream would not swerve from its ultimate conclusion—the dread dark figure that waits at the inevitable destination, and as it slowly drops its veil to disclose the horror on which one cannot look, one wakes strangling, and terror lies in long, cold coils beside one through the night.

"Driver!" some of the passengers were shouting. "Driver, the next corner, please! Ludwigstrasse, please!"

"What makes them think the next corner is Ludwigstrasse?" the driver said to no one in particular. "Don't everything look alike these days—dusty?"

Peering out of the window, at these words, Heinz was able to realize for the first time that the earth was a planet, for it presented now an aspect similar to that which he had glimpsed once before, as a student, gazing through a telescope at the moon. But now he could no longer accept the theories of his professors. Now he had not the slightest doubt but that the moon also must be inhabited, for this that he saw now without life or hope or vegetation, but reduced to the barest markings—ashes, ridges, craters, canals, and dust—was the mark and the sign of the habitation of man.

"Driver! Driver! Stop!" the passengers shouted.

"What gives them the idea the next corner is Ludwigstrasse?" the driver said irascibly. "If any of those jerks think they know where they're heading, the driver wishes they'd tell him!"

Well Heinz knew that in every shadow drifted and mingled the dark angel, the agent of provocation. . . . Now, somehow, all the pilgrims had been gathered up and collected on this blind and stumbling conveyance, and they were being driven by One of Them— *Where?* Why? Why? . . . Heinz knew now that he must have done something terrible—he must have committed some unspeakable crime—but he could not remember what. O God! O God! He needed a lawyer, twenty-five lawyers, fifty lawyers. . . . Even a hundred lawyers could no longer help him. And he could not remember what was the crime of which he was guilty, he who had always seen no evil, heard no evil, and spoken no evil.

"Well, doesn't the guy in the smashed brown derby agree?" the driver said. "Nowadays all streets look alike—dusty?"

Now, in the rear-view mirror, Heinz could see only the small bloodstained eyes that might have been those of a pig or a wolf, but were cunning and without mercy.

"Well?" the driver said. "Well?"

"I don't know," Heinz stammered. "I don't know." The blood whistled through his ears. "No one ever asks my opinion any more." Why had the driver chosen him, from among them all? What was he after? "I don't really know. . . . I mean all streets do look alike these days, don't they?"

He felt that he had not made himself clear, and he must make himself clear or he would entangle himself deeper and deeper in whatever quicksand sucked him down, sinking deeper and deeper into a crime that he could not remember having committed.

He began again, speaking very slowly and distinctly, "Brick for brick, I mean. . . . Or rather, ashes to ashes and dust to dust. . . . I mean, the signs all being down. . . . All roads lead to—"

Heinz stopped, terror-stricken. Had he said too much? Had he said too little? Now, try again. Take it slowly. Make it clear and distinct.

"I mean actually I suppose this is what the city of tomorrow is moving toward. . . . I mean, that is, the process of standardization. . . . A leveling. . . . I mean, I am an architect and the trend of the city of tomorrow seems—"

"Change the record," the driver said surlily. "We heard you the first time." His eyes were of a deep, iron malevolence. "These jerks who are never sure of themselves! Well now, how do they like what they've dished up for themselves—Dust! In the eyes, in the nose, in the gullet. Phew! Might as well be buried alive!"

"Driver! Driver!" the voices shrilled in despair. "We've passed it! We've passed Ludwigstrasse!"

The bus drew to a violent halt.

There was a scream from the Rhine maiden. "That's not it! That's not Ludwigstrasse!"

"Take it or leave it!" the driver said.

"Listen," she jammered bitterly to the other passengers, "don't let him put that one over. When I passed Ludwigstrasse yesterday morning on the way to work—"

"It's Karlstrasse," fussed an aged civil servant who was too short to see out of the window. "Obviously, by the route the bus has been taking. Out of my way there, everyone!"

"Well," the Rhine maiden said with a final philosophic sob, "it's the same with *them*." She grimaced angrily at the returned hero. "You can't be sure with them either, the next time you see them, if it's the one you kissed good-by."

The bus waited quite a time while those whose destination was either Karlstrasse or Ludwigstrasse pushed their way out. There were others also who dwelt in the dust on or near these streets, but they were now so completely demoralized and unsure of themselves that they no longer knew whose judgment to trust—whether the driver's or the dissenting passengers' or their own.

Heinz looked out of the window again.

It was the Day of Judgment.

Here on this tombstone *arrondissement* of marble silence, the evening birds had, the previous night, let fall their droppings. Freed at last, the dead were disposed in various attitudes of the living, some lying in that same stiff livid way in which their breathing brothers flung themselves to escape the shrapnel; some sitting up and facing each other, out of their wooden shelters, with unseeing eyes, as the living did each evening in *their* shelters. Some, even, had been wounded. But here, unlike their more fleshy comrades, they were self-contained and gave forth no stinking pools of blood. Indeed, Heinz was struck, above all, by that self-contained quality which he had observed identically in the living when faced with disaster—that quality of aloofness and inner absorption and mystery that wrapped the living about like a shroud, while each communed with the death in himself.

As he looked out of the window, Heinz slowly began to feel fear, observing how it was the dead who had been freed, while the living were more securely imprisoned within the four walls of this bus as in some great mass grave.

The driver, as though moved by this same fear, stepped on the gas, leaving behind those who had mistakenly alighted and were pleading now for the bus to be opened to them again, hurling themselves against the adamant doors and windows, moaning and shrieking and wringing their hands.

Even the Rhine maiden was shaken. As the bus gathered speed, she said somberly, "What we should have done was to leave Berlin to the Jews, while we should have moved to Poland."

There were a number of scattered laughs—a typic nervous and hysterical reaction—and the maiden was immediately snapped up, with the returned hero, as the humorist of the crowd. Indeed, the wayfarers, with exquisite tact and perception, moved up around those destined two—pressing her flat hard breasts closer against his bisque arms, pressing her hard lumpy-muscled thighs closer against his bisque legs—giving tacit approval to the match. And why not? They were both at that age when love's young dream is most beguiling and the rosy clouds of dawning day deepen to ruby as the sun rises ever higher over the dew-drenched fields. Besides, she certainly wouldn't find anything better around at this historic moment in the destiny of her race. . . . Some returned heroes, indeed, had not even been able to smuggle the one really important thing out of the Eastern Front, but had sown the frozen steppes with a million little flaxen-haired boys and girls, with immeasurably great scientists, plumbers, poets, movie actresses, and leaders, first freezing and then slowly shriveling in the snows of the Eastern Front, to be glanced at a moment and then kicked aside by insensitive muzhiks.

Bo-ong! Cr-r-ack! "Keep your dirty hands to yourself," the Rhine maiden shouted.

"I assure you, my dear," Heinz said in the same fatherly tone that he used with his daughter. "You are mistaken. Quite mistaken."

From the corner of his eye, he glimpsed that far-off lovely face. Over it, now, spread a glance of utter melancholy. An impassable distance separated them, and manlike, he contented himself with lesser loves. He felt, with a pang, that she had misjudged him— she who offered the ultimate, the finite understanding. Yet, had she, after all? Wasn't there something about that girl-boy chippie who'd open her door to the insurance salesman's knock just as soon as not in her brassière and panties? Why was she making such a fuss now because she'd been pinched? Could it be possible that she liked to pick her pinchers herself?

"Who's talking to you, you dirty-minded civilian?" the Rhine maiden said. "It's him—" And she slapped the returned hero who, in answer, merely held out his hands. The fingers, encased in black gloves, were stiff as silver spoons.

The Rhine maiden bumptiously withdrew the black gloves.

"I merely ask you," the returned hero said, "to try to move these fingers."

The expression of hope and triumph—in having proved the point of his helplessness—blossoming on that rather unusual face, induced in Heinz a terrible sense of uneasiness, of something left undone. . . . And then there rose before him again the image of the buttercup that he had glimpsed once on the Western Front in *his* day, blossoming out of that no-longer-cartilaginous snub nose. . . . How it must tickle! It would make the poor chap sneeze! . . . But he had plucked the buttercup that time—or hadn't he? Had he—or hadn't he? . . . He could not endure this uncertainty. O God! Almighty God! . . . How? How did one begin the long journey back through time and through distance, first back from this bus to his mother's bed, on which he lay, a young soldier, hungry, weary, cold; and thence, marching backward through the white-faced town to the railroad station; and then back on the train, the wheels turning backward, backward through the landscape growing more and more desolate, until the train stops and he gets off and marches backward, backward, backward to the ultimate desolation, the final frosty revelation of the white skull on the blackened earth.

What a torment that buttercup must be to the poor chap! Heinz sneezed.

"And thus, you see, my dear child," he said to the Rhine maiden, "it is obviously impossible that our hero made the pinch. Now, return the gloves to him."

But she was already tucking them into her bosom. "I certainly could do with a pair of black gloves myself. And you can't find them anywhere for love or money. And baby, I mean *love!*"

A tear from each white eye ran in straight lines down the hero's straight subtly modeled Chinese face. . . . But he uttered no word of protest. . . . After all, had he not, in his time, lost, without protest, more than a pair of gloves? Heinz had never before considered really what an arm is—biceps, sinews, fat, gristle, veins, nerves, those marvelous telegraphs from the brain, and the red blood that pumps the whole. All that marvelous and intricate plumbing system that nature hands out so freely to each one at birth, whether prince or pauper.

"Then it's the driver," she said, "—That jerk with his dead pan." And indeed it was conceivable that the driver might have stretched his arm back and pinched the maiden's fanny, for the little crowd of Heinz, the hero, and the maiden were standing directly behind him, yet so deeply wedged into the crowd that it might indeed have been anyone.

"No," Heinz said hastily. "No! It could not possibly be the driver!" Almighty God, one does not accuse The Accuser. Almighty God, did only he of all the pilgrims realize just what the driver was?

"Why couldn't it be?" the driver snapped, and he turned his head to the window beside him, revealing as he did so his profile.

Heinz saw, with horror, that the right profile, which he now beheld, bore no resemblance to the fragment of face that he had earlier glimpsed in the mirror. Nor did it bear any resemblance, even, to the left profile which the mirror now reflected. Three different faces! Three disguises! Maybe a thousand! O God, how he put these masks on and off! The hand is quicker than the eye. Heinz's teeth began to chatter.

His glance falling wildly away from the varying disguises of the driver, Heinz observed that the returned hero still stood with his stiff bright-pink hands pushed out in front of him against the hard bosom of the Rhine maiden. Then, even as Heinz watched, he became a little white poodle with pink paws, clinging to the breast of his mistress. O God! O God! The hand is quicker than the eye. . . . In a twinkling instant, he was again a returned hero with quite lifelike hands.

Was the returned hero The Accuser, the magician? Maybe it was not the driver who had transformed the hero into a little poodle, but the hero himself who had performed this sleight of hand—to what purpose? Almighty God! If one could only know! Which was The Fearsome One? Which?

"Ooow!" the Rhine maiden screamed again.

"The hero's pinching," others in the bus were shouting, unaware of the fixed quality of the lifelike hands.

"Ssh! Ssh!" Heinz tried to soothe through chattering teeth. Was he the only one who realized. . . . Danger, danger. . . . He had committed some foul and heinous crime, but he could not remember what it was, and because of him, they were all followed, watched, hemmed in. He would die and they would all die for him. As Jesus had died for all, so would they all die for him.

"It's the one with the smashed derby, he who winks."

"It's the blind one, the hero."

Even those who were so far removed that they received only garbled accounts from those who were in the vicinity, had taken sides.

"Throw the blind one out!"

"Throw the smashed derby out . . . winking and smirking, the war profiteer!"

In the menace of the lynch spirit, a sense of solidarity swept the little group. They drew closer together and with a blinding flash, the suspicion was borne upon Heinz that the returned hero was also, perhaps, merely a fellow-victim, and not The Accuser.

"Shut up!" the Rhine maiden screamed. "Leave my pals be!"

"Shut up, you chippie!"

The mob's violence hung in the balance.

"The slut—throw her out, too!"

A voice screamed, "Ooow! Someone's letting go on me!" And in that moment the little group was saved.

Other shouts could be heard. "My ankle's wet! . . . My shoe's soaking! . . . Who's the dirty bastard who's baptizing—"

"Shut up!" the driver said to what was rapidly again becoming a mob, its menace turned against some unknown source. "Everybody shut up!"

In the abrupt fall of silence, the driver's voice could again be heard. "Their Excellencies ain't used to it yet, after only eleven years. Let them be peed on for five thousand years. Like the driver. It makes a man begin to think."

There was not the slightest mutter of an answer to this incendiary remark.

The driver, Heinz thought. . . . It was the driver, after all! The bus was being driven by One of Them, to what goal and what destination, no one could know.

He turned to the hero in that deep impulsive sympathy that sometimes springs up between victim and victim, when he noted that the profound, the utter sadness, that lingered like an aura about the returned hero since the filching of his gloves by the Rhine maiden, was slowly changing to an aura, a mask, of mistrust and horror as his empty eyes shrank from the unseen thieving faces about him. . . . Good God, Heinz thought, the way he puts the masks on and off! The hand is quicker than the eye! . . . They're working together, the hero and the driver—one to provoke, one to nab. . . . The blindness is only another mask, through which the last man peers.

How proficient he was in his devilish work! But would a real master advertise his trade? . . . Maybe the jig was up and it no longer mattered whether or not the spy was known in his disguises, the agent in his provocation. . . . That's what you get for just climbing on a bus without knowing where it's going, just because everyone else is climbing on. Who ever said this was the home-bound bus, anyway? Why did anyone need a home-bound bus? Were there any homes left? Why hadn't he thought of that before?

Now he knew. This was it. The last ride, the box-car excursion, the one-way jaunt, absolutely free, gratis, fare paid. Why? Why? What had he done? What had anyone done? I want to get out, he tried to scream. I want to get out.

Any moment the switch would be thrown in the electrically charged floor, and in one flash of lightning, they would all go black. . . . The maiden's flaxen hair would go black and frizzly as a nigger's. . . . And the hero's white-boiled eyes, black as lumps of coal, and popping. . . .

For days now, they had been going on and on in the sealed car, without food and without water and without air, and yet the body went on throwing off life, throwing off the precious stinking substances of life, sweat, urine, vomit, throwing off its poisons, the pus seeping from incendiary burns, washed with carbolic. Here and there those who had died on the journey stood wedged between the living and the windows could not be unsealed, nor the door. The horror and the abysmal anguish of the journey were sealed up in this car forever. . . . Why? Why? What had he done? What had anyone done? . . . The journey went on and on in darkness. . . . The grinding of the wheels on the railroad bed went on and on—and the nauseating sway of the car. . . . On and on and on until, next day or next week or next year, the car would draw up to the electrically charged barbed-wire gates behind which stretched the sandy desert of the regime's desolation, the cemetery in which forever after they would exist, the living and those who had died on the journey.

In a last anguish of farewell, he sought her, the woman for whom one longs. . . . Now it had come to him whose face that was —the wonderful, sad, mysterious face of his mother, who alone could salve the child's terror in the dark waking-and-sleeping night. He sought her. She was gone! In her place a black-clothed figure stood, from whose head fell a black veil over features that he could only dimly penetrate. Now she had assumed the veil of darkness, and it was not a disguise but merely the ultimate revelation. This, he knew at·last, was the dark figure that waited beyond the final desolation of the end of the journey and he would be enfolded for-ever in the serene blessed arms of death, the woman for whom one longs.

Then, between himself and his vision of the dark, veiled figure, the returned hero insinuated himself. The hero was disintegrating before Heinz's very eyes. Shreds of flesh fell off; in the no-longer-cartilaginous snub nose, a buttercup appeared. Now he had taken off his last disguise and Heinz saw that the white, blind eyes had truly been only a mask for these hollow sockets, the flat unfur-rowed face, only a disguise for this grinning bone. Heinz had not gone back to his old comrade. The comrade had returned to him from the trench.

Heinz's eyes measured the sealed window, beyond which was the free and dreadful, the dark and open night.

"What do you see there?" the maiden said. "O God, what are you looking for?"

He opened his lips but no scream came forth, only a little gasp, "It is clear tonight."

His eye winked, the corner of his mouth lifted in a smile.

Silence. The maiden did not answer. No one said anything.

Again the gasp drove itself through his lips, "It is clear tonight." Again the smile and the wink.

Again silence.

He could not recall his words.

"It is clear tonight" meant, "The birds will return tonight" meant, "I hope the birds will return tonight," meant "I hope the birds will return tonight and let their droppings fall on the regime," meant *"Do you not also hope—?"*

Provocateur!

He felt the still terror of the crowd, which was like the terror of an animal who stands suddenly frozen, sensing just before it in the brush, the cold, shining coils swaying and rising. Provocateur! He was afraid of their terror of him. He tried to whisper "Save me! Save me!" No sound came. Then suddenly it was they who were the snake, and in the black, glittering, beady eyes, was reflected his fear and his guilt. The head lifted to plunge into his breast the reflected poison of his guilt and fear.

Someone screamed.

And the dream changed. The bus gathered speed. All of a sudden it was driving down a long, straight street on which all the windows and side walls had been blown out, and only the façades of the buildings remained, an intact shell.

The bus, churning in its wake a great wind, rushed through the street. Heinz saw, in the hole of a doorway, a tiny spark, a pin point in the darkness, a cigarette left burning. Now, as the wind fanned from the rushing bus, a flame leaped up, spread, and in less than an instant each side of the street was a sheet and a wall of flame.

The night became day, a dreadful artificial day of neon intensity, and in the bus the faces of the passengers were picked out, bluewhite, as in a police line-up, and they were all criminals, all with records, all nabbed at last. From their black gaping mouths screams, protestations of innocence poured forth, but in the abysmal roaring of the flames He who counted the sparrow's fall could not hear the agonized screams of His children.

The bus blistered, cracked, and swelled. . . . Heinz felt the heat shrivel him, felt his flesh crisping black and dry, and puckering from his bones. Almighty God, it was he who had left the cigarette, the pin point of light, burning in the darkness of the doorway! His clothes were drenched with the water that the heat had pumped out from his body, he heard the sweat sizzling and spitting and bubbling as it basted his cracked, roasted skin. . . . O Thou, Thou, nailed to the wood. . . . My Father, my Father, why hast Thou abandoned me?

Ahead a metal sheet of flame with glittering sawlike edges stretched across the street. The bus did not stop. Heinz saw the sheet of flame coming nearer and nearer and still the bus did not stop; it would jump through the wall of fire. . . . There was a crash like breaking glass as the bus plunged into the flame.

Then it was night again, and cold. . . . Heinz looked down at his hands. They were not black. No one was black. . . . It was a fire that did not burn.

He looked for the dark, veiled figure. She was gone! She for whom one longs, she, the gentle, the serene, the anachronistic one, was burned out of the world by the bright licking tongues of horror. There, in her place, stood the returned hero; and now Heinz knew that the hero still had some final trick, some last card to play. Through the hollow sockets of the skull, which was his final mask, two black eyes burned, and out of the bony, snubbed nose, the buttercup shook and trembled in lazy, wavering grace, blown about by the concealed breath behind the last mask.

Now the final revelation waited . . . the unspeakable . . . the unimaginable. . . .

Above the driver, the mirror hung blank and ashen, reflecting nothing. There, ahead, its back to the passengers, sat a figure of nameless dread, whose face was turned away to the glass of the window, peering into the gray craters and rubble and mountains of ashes through which he steadily drove the bus onward.

Heinz knew now whose face that was, and that would be the final horror, the turning upon him, at last, of that unseen face ahead. He must wake. He must wake out of this dream that was his own before that face turned and made his guilt known to his victims. . . . But the scream stuck in his throat and he could not wake, he could not pull himself and his victims out of this abyss.

Like a haunted sleeper, the bus shuddered, moaned, and then with a great splitting shriek, a sleeper waking, came to a stop.

The driver jumped up, and in the instant that he turned and made his face known, Heinz's heart burst and inundated him.

He saw, for an instant, his own face staring into his and then it passed so quickly that he could no longer be sure, and in its stead was a young, ordinary face, without horror.

"Stay where you are!" the driver barked and he leaped over the heads of the crowd, young and lithe, and Heinz saw him outside the door of the bus, though he had not opened it and the glass was not smashed. Then he heard a click, like a lock springing, the very sound of entrapment, although the driver had used no key.

Heinz clenched his hands into two fists and smashed at the window. The glass did not break, but streams of blood poured down to his wrists. The self-inflicted blood would deflect the realization of his guilt from his victims. He felt in this ultimate moment a brotherhood with those who were trapped here with him. Was he not, finally, his own victim?

The bus had come to a stop in some gray futility. How could they return from this landscape to the smashed and smoking walls, on which still hung the carved and colored beer stein; against which still leaned the violin, burnished, silent and unbroken. Somewhere something still remained, and the bus had broken down. O Thou, Thou, nailed to the wood, wherefore the long journey through the dreadful night, through the blue-white dreadful day of fire. . . . Wherefore, wherefore, O Thou, in Thy infinite mercy and grace!

As he still peered out of the window, he heard the returned hero shout with a voice that came up muffled from deep behind the mask of grinning bone, "Traitor! He's signaling the birds! We shall all perish!"

Again, Heinz tried to smash the window.

The mob swept upon him.

"Traitor!"

"He's signaling!"

"Traitor! Traitor!"

"We shall all perish!"

"No! No!" Heinz screamed. "No! No! . . . The driver! . . . He's the traitor! . . . He's running away! . . . He's left us here alone! . . . He's abandoned us!"

With his last despairing glance at the landscape outside, he saw the driver dive into a lake of ashes, come up dripping with dust, swim vigorously away, leaving strong ripples.

He was caught into the maelstrom of the mob.

The despair of utter recklessness gripped his bowels and he knew that, at last, and in this final face of ruin, he must make the supreme effort to wake out of this horror and fear that could not be endured and that was his own dream. . . . As though in answer to his despair, the Almighty One sent him a blinding vision of the walls of flame through which his dreaming mind had driven the bus.

"Fire!" he shouted, diverting their madness from him and his guilt. "Fire! Fire! Fire!"

And instantly all became a raging, roaring, stampeding herd. They abandoned him, they deserted their mad rage; they fought, they trampled, they murdered each other. They beat against the windows and the sealed doors; they beat against the walls. Bodies fell, piled up. The Rhine maiden went down beside him, screaming and screaming. The emergency exit was choked with bodies piled one on top of another. Death came horribly—by strangulation, the bursting of the lungs, the tearing of the heart, the smashing and shipwreck of all the inner organs.

Heinz, still alive, tried to crawl through the solid, fallen flesh to the window, the sealed square of freedom, cut into the ashen, burnt-out world beyond. A hand groped over his face. Weakly, he tried to beat it off with his fists, could not. It clung, it clutched. It sealed up his nose and mouth. A shoe trampled his neck. Another stepped upon his ribs; he heard them crack. A body, writhing, fell across his, was quiet. Still, he existed. His blood burst in a last spurt from his ears, his mouth, his eyes, his fingertips, his toes. The last horror . . . the last . . . the ultimate. . . .

Still he existed, still one final spark of life remained, unextinguished. He waited to wake up. He waited for the last spark, burning in the black empty hole of his skull, to be fanned into a blaze of life by the wind that roared and churned in his ears. A hand in death agony—the returned hero's—clutched his throat, and as they struggled, Heinz wrested from the skull, at last, the flower of that long-vanished battlefield. The hand pressed and choked and suffocated and as it extinguished the final spark, as the great darkness punched out his mind and heart, the final bubble in his boiling brain—Here is the waking up. . . . Now wake up, Heinz, wake up . . . the last horror . . . the ultimate—burst, and left his brain a swollen green sponge floating in a pool of blood. . . . Clutching the triumphant flower in his hand, he no longer heard the evening birds that were overhead now dropping their load of filth.